Strangers in Our Hearts

BRI EBERHART

Content Warnings

Death (including on page and off and mentions of previous deaths regarding parent and sibling), fire/fire injury, hostages/kidnapping (off-page), grief, panic attacks/disorders, profanity, violence, warfare

Dear reader,

Olivia here. You might remember how I died on homecoming night—ugh, what a cliché—but we're not here to talk about me. I'm here to remind you of what these fools have been up to since I've been gone.

Since I'm no longer around to keep Gemma out of trouble, I'm glad she's found others to step in and help, even if that help includes a backstabbing bi—never mind.

Let me back up and fill you in.

G's powers went absolutely haywire after she lost me. I mean, can you blame her? Fearful of hurting anyone, she made the dumb mistake of running away by herself. It all worked out, though. I might have had to convince our foster sister Amber to follow her, but at least the little shit finally listened to me. I guess all it took was me being dead.

Gemma ran into Theo, the boy from her dreams. Thankfully, he wisely took her in, leading her back to their hideout, where he lived with three others—Zay, Nora, and Elise, the girl who's seriously lucky I'm dead.

Everything was more or less fine for a time. Gemma tried to get a handle on her powers, and Theo kept her secret, but that eventually led Nora to search for her own answers and she ended up burned—seriously. She was actually left with a scar. The burn left a perfect imprint of Gemma's hand on Nora's chest when she accidentally snuck up on her, and Gemma tried shoving her away to protect her. Talk about a plan backfiring.

Regardless, they were surviving.

G was outgrowing the role of shy little sister who needed saving. She was making strides in rescuing herself. Of course, the Authorities were now a looming threat, shocking my sister and me. We knew she was different, and I commend myself for knowing we needed to keep this fact from others, but not even I could have imagined there was an actual group out to kill people like her. It makes me sick to my stomach just thinking about it.

Anyway, again, not about me.

Enter Draven.

Can you believe our parents murdered him just to inject Gemma with his powers to see what would happen? How messed up! And why did they skip over me? I was sitting right there! Should I be offended by this? I'm not quite sure.

Still, what happened to him doesn't excuse him from trying to trap Gemma and me in the same dollhouse where our parents sequestered his ghostly form. Thankfully, even though he was able to get his hooks in me and keep me trapped in this in-between place for a time, I was strong enough to convince G to let me go. And once she did, she broke the connection between all three of us, sending me on my way.

Skipping ahead, the memories turn a little blurry, but Draven was sucked back into his dollhouse of a cell, Gemma burned down the woods with her powers, and the Authorities arrived, with Theo's sister leading the charge—I mean, grab the popcorn! With nowhere else to run, their little chaos crew banded together and headed back to Florida, where our foster parents graciously took them all in. Even the girl I can't wait to meet someday—seriously, I just want to talk.

That's about it, though. You're all up to speed now.

Yours truly, and I'm sure forever missed,

Olivia XX

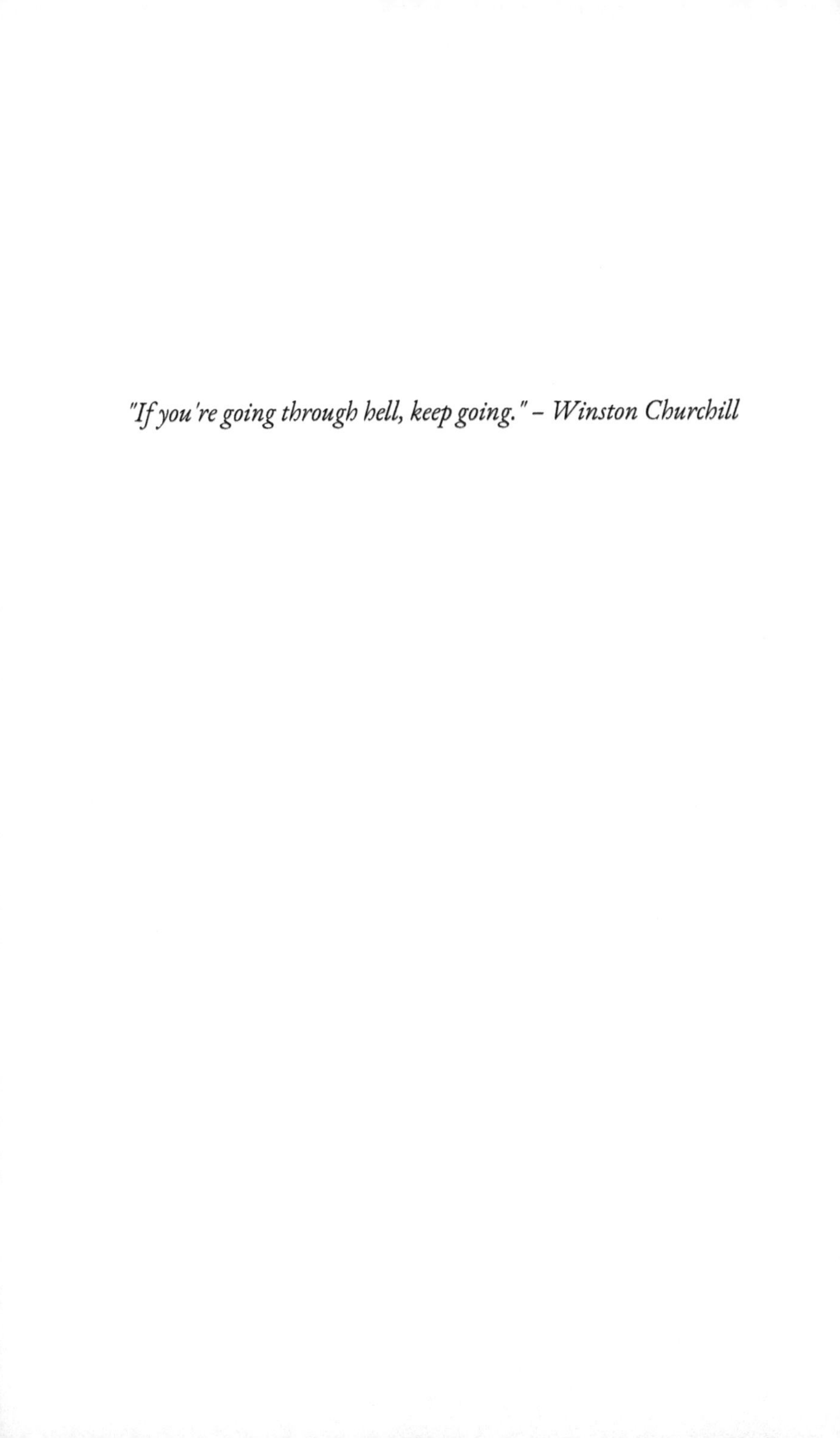

"If you're going through hell, keep going." – Winston Churchill

Chapter One

Caleb

THE INCESSANT BLARING OF sirens drowns out any previous thoughts of mutiny.

I proceed to the War Room, where an away team will no doubt be debriefing their latest mission—the alarms indicating their return. The alarms are supposed to be for intruders, but no one has figured out how to get the system to distinguish between friend and foe, so instead, they wake the whole base whenever anyone arrives. You'd think they'd turn them off until they have it sorted.

The War Room doors are already sealed shut, but I slip in through the back passage, keeping close to the wall so I don't interrupt the meeting, not that there's much to cut in on. No one can get a word in unless they want to scream at one another.

Tilly, the boss, sits in the middle of an oval-shaped table, with Jet, her right-hand man, sitting literally to her right. Leading the coalition and keeping point with the others nationwide gets you the big boy chairs, seated dead center in the room. Being one of the largest establishments, housing about fifty mutants certainly adds to their prestige as well.

Impressive? Sure, but it'd be more remarkable if they'd listen to me every once in a while.

The alarm finally cuts out, and my ears ring from the sudden silence. Tilly glances at the lot before her, reassuringly smiling at the clearly shaken group.

"Well?" she prompts.

Their team leader clears his throat. "We didn't get there in time."

My spine straightens the same moment Jet leans back in his chair, defeat marring his battered features, his leathery skin somehow managing to turn pale. He's only in his forties, but something about him looks beaten and weak. It's pathetic.

"Maybe our intel was bad," the woman starts, adjusting the tactical vest strapped to her torso. "We got to the location at precisely the same time we were told. It's not our fault—"

"No one is blaming you," Tilly speaks up, though her flat tone indicates she's disappointed in *someone*. "The Authorities could have easily gotten there sooner. Was he taken?"

"No." The team leader sniffs, shifting uneasily on his feet. "We brought his body back with us. It didn't seem right to leave him there."

"They must already have someone like him then." Tilly nods to herself as if she's keeping a running tab in her head of every ability the Authorities seem to be collecting. In this case, the dead mutant they brought back was able to manipulate the media.

The Authorities certainly have the media already under control, don't they?

Why take in someone as disgusting as us if there's no need? If they shoot him in the head, all they do is ensure we won't be able to combat them with a mutant of equal caliber.

I scoff to myself, failing to reign in my temper.

Tilly stands, effectively dismissing the crew, and does a double-take when she finally spots me in the corner. "Caleb," she says curtly.

My hands shake more with each step I take closer to the table. "Aunt Tilly," I begin, laying it on thick, hoping the pleading in my voice will wisen her. "When is this going to stop?"

Shadows gather around her like a protective shawl. "Don't start; it's been a long night."

I scrub a hand over my face, tipping my head back to focus on the dimming fluorescent light. Now that the "threat" has passed, the lights will continue to recede until morning, when they'll return to full strength. But for now, we must sit in the shadows as the others fall back to sleep, the air in here darkening even further with Tilly's mood.

"We're losing too many. We're too *slow* and always a step behind. What's the point of having powers if we're not using them to defend ourselves?"

"Son," Jet warns, his voice a low growl. He sits up in his chair, leaning his elbows on the table as Tilly starts piling papers together. "We've been over this."

I meet his stare, clenching my teeth together so hard my jaw hurts. I'm not his son, and thank god for that.

Most of the base calls Tilly "Aunt Tilly," but in my case, it's true, or at least by marriage. She married my Aunt Margot shortly before my parents decided having a family full of freaks was too much and left, leaving me on Tilly's doorstep when I was nine—a decade ago now.

Unfortunately, Margot must be working the night shift at the science lab. Otherwise, she'd have been here for the meeting, and it's usually much easier to persuade her to think my way.

It's never good when both leaders of Command agree we should play defense because then no one will listen to *me*. I've been lobbying for an offensive strike for months now. I can't sit around and listen to these meetings over and over—always a step behind, a second too late, too frail to fight.

It's all bullshit.

We shouldn't even exist, and yet, here we are. We've achieved the unknown. We could even rule the world if we wanted. Who would stop us if we weren't too busy hiding and actually took a stand?

I've seen a room plunged into freezing temperatures and moving objects controlled by thought. This whole infrastructure is hidden in the middle of the desert by a mutant-created illusion that keeps us concealed. And that's only scratching the surface of what we can do.

So, if not us, then who?

"If we keep going like this, we're all going to die." I grit my teeth, tempering down the anger before I explode.

Tilly sighs, rubbing the spot between her eyebrows, her golden-brown skin wrinkling as she frowns. "We're not strong enough to lead an attack right now, Caleb. I know you think you're invincible, but—"

I grunt, shaking my head before she can even finish the sentence, and turn my back on the room, slamming the door behind me.

What a useless Command.

They're too scared to do anything and too frightened of evolving, which is ironic, considering we've grown past the limitations of what it means to be human.

But I'm here to change that.

Mutants have been hiding in the dark for far too long.

It's time for us to make a stand.

Chapter Two

THEO
November

"ARE YOU SURE ABOUT this?" I gaze from the street, sizing up the abandoned house.

It's nothing like the Rib House, the dwelling that shielded us from *most* elements for nearly a year. It was the longest we had stayed anywhere. A rock settles in my stomach—it's not that I miss the place, but it offered more protection than here, even if its structure was a bit unstable.

This yellow house is in near-perfect condition, squeezed between two others on a quiet suburban street. The brownish grass is slightly higher than the lawns on either side since no one has tended it for a few weeks now, not since John, my dad, last left, locking the door behind him, never to come back home.

Amber cocks her head, angling it at the empty space next to her. Only, it's not really empty. Apparently, John is standing right there in ghost form.

She nods once before swinging her attention toward me. "I'm sure. And he says hurry up, or people will notice."

I clutch his keys until the metal bites into my palm, sweat beading at my temples. This is a smart plan. *His* plan. But I don't want to go through with it. I don't want to step into his home. Into a place where I could've lived if I had listened sooner. If I never ran away. If I had looked for Riley, instead of accepting she was dead even though there was no body.

If, if, if.

I really fucked this one up.

Amber brushes my arm. "Dude, breathe. You look like you're going to pass out." Worry creases her brows, but she rolls her eyes like she's trying to hide it.

She's been attempting to act older, more mature, or *something* since she returned to her foster parents. Judy and Dennis are stricter with her than us, for obvious reasons. She's their kid. We aren't. Amber's also the youngest at fourteen.

Still, she feels "left out," and I'm willing to guess that attempting to hide her worry is another way of appearing more grown.

"Not to rush you, but John said his neighbor to his left is nosy and is probably already onto us."

I face the neighbor's window, and sure enough, the curtains shift the tiniest bit, followed by the shadow of someone stepping to the side.

"Fine," I huff, scratching the back of my neck with one of the keys. "Let's get this over with."

The night the McIntyres took us in, I snuck out after everyone was asleep and stashed John's truck a few blocks away near an old junkyard. I didn't know how close or far the Authorities were—I still don't, for that matter. But every lurking vehicle or random salesperson at the door sends up giant red flags, a reminder that the Authorities can hide in plain sight, waiting for the perfect opportunity to strike. We're basically sitting ducks here. I didn't want the added clue of John's truck right outside their house to make it even easier to find us.

I drove in circles for an hour before I found a good enough hiding spot, and it took me double that to make it back since the area was too new to me. Gemma was waiting for me on the front steps when I finally returned. Relief and anger blended into one glare before she stormed inside, past an awake Judy and Dennis, and bolted up the stairs.

Judy gave me a small smile but drilled Dennis with a *look* that seemed to say, "What the hell did we just get ourselves into?"

Dennis briefly rested a hand on my shoulder and bid me goodnight.

I'd be lying if I said I haven't snuck out since, searching for any clues that they may be onto us—scoping out nearby abandoned buildings where they could be hiding and checking the windows of cars that seem suspicious. The only damning evidence I have is the pile of cigarette butts that have been accumulating near the gutter across the street since we arrived, but I never actually see anyone smoking them.

Our time here is running out; the itching in my muscles instructs me to move on, like always. Settling will get us captured or killed. But since I haven't convinced everyone else to pack up with me yet, I teleport out of the house at night, appearing several streets away, and walk—*and walk*—until I'm too tired to worry about much of anything. It's either this or finding a fight to lose myself in, which I'm sure Gemma wouldn't like.

Amber is already up the porch steps, even though I haven't moved from my spot on the sidewalk. She whistles to get my attention, waving her arms at the front door. Gradually, one foot moves in front of the other.

A week ago, John *arrived* and gave Amber this "sure-fire" plan. My stomach dips each time I think about it too long.

The plan: We return the truck to his home, leaving the keys inside it. Since he was a cop, someone *will* notice his disappearance, and eventually, they'll come looking for him. This way, it will seem like he disappeared into thin air.

The Authorities will, of course, know that isn't true since they're the ones who killed him. But either way, my dad is dead, and the local department will come looking. Little do they know they'll never see him again.

I've changed my mind. It's a stupid plan.

After I unlock it and give it a slight push, the door swings inward, but my feet remain rooted on the porch. Amber rushes inside, spinning in a circle, taking in the room as I watch from outside.

She stops when her eyes land on me and puts a hand on her hip. "Mrs. Rutherford can still see you from that angle."

I inhale the fresh air, holding it in my lungs before forcing myself over the threshold. Once the door closes behind me, I sag against it.

I used to keep this feeling of being dragged under somewhat controlled, this untethered part of me that would get lost in the flames, but knowing Riley is alive, I can't get a handle on it anymore. Any ability to ground myself is lost. It's like I'm constantly burning.

My chest rises faster and faster as the seconds tick by.

"What are we looking for?" Amber asks.

I scoff. *How the hell should I know?* But never mind. She speaks to the corner, having a conversation with someone who isn't me.

Amber dashes down the hallway without responding as I try to get my bearings.

This is fine. You're in your dad's house. And he's now dead. And his ghost is giving instructions to your girlfriend's foster sister to cover up his murder.

Yep. This is fine.

"Theo, in here!" Amber yells from down the hall.

The living room is attached to the kitchen in an open floor plan, and everything is bare. There are no photos or decorations, solely plain furniture. A single recliner sits in front of an old television, and next to the worn chair is a wooden tray with water rings stained into it.

The kitchen has the essentials—a fridge, stove, and microwave. There's even a toaster, but nothing else is on the counters, and there are no magnets on the refrigerator.

It's as if someone lived here but not. Like when you go to the hotel to stay for a weekend but don't bother unpacking your suitcase.

I make my way down the hallway, poking my head into the rooms as I go. There are two bedrooms, side by side, but one is empty. The other has a bed and a dresser.

The bathroom houses one toothbrush on the sink, next to a half-used bottle of mouthwash and a tube of toothpaste. I don't bother looking through the cabinets.

Finally, I find Amber in the room at the end, which must've been his office. It's the only space that's actually been used.

There's shit everywhere.

Piles of paper cover the two desks that have been pushed together to make an L-shape, and a CB radio is set up in the corner of it. A filing cabinet is beneath a corkboard filled with little *X*s over different spots on a U.S. map.

A lump lodges in my throat when I step closer—the marks cover most of the places I've been.

I brush a finger against the marker over Thornbrooke, Indiana, trailing the black ink to Illinois, Missouri, Arkansas... *X marks the spot.*

He *was* always looking for me, just a step behind. What separated us? Weeks? A day? A few hours? How close was he before I uprooted everyone and moved us to the next stop?

A part of me is smug, validated. I *knew* he was onto us. I had good reason to piss everyone off. But maybe if I'd known, if I had spoken to him sooner...

Those damn *ifs* again.

"John says everything he has on the Authorities is in the second drawer of the filing cabinet. Labeled *variants.*"

I tug open the drawer and pull out a binder as thick as a textbook, raising an eyebrow at Amber.

She shrugs.

"What are we supposed to do with this?" I flip to the middle, and a photo of a random face peers up at me. Records that must belong to the girl are underneath the picture that's clipped to the top of the stack. It's as bad as a police file—a life laid out in charges and suspicions. In bright red letters, it reads **SYMPHOKINESIS - MUSIC MANIPULATION**. I flip to the next page, and it's a photo of the same girl, but dead, her body splayed out on the ground, blood pooling beneath her. I suck in a breath and flip it shut before Amber can see.

"Real helpful," I grumble. "Thanks, John."

"He says there's more. Those are just cases he... he's found. John says there are others who are still alive." Amber squints up at the air where his ghost must be, seemingly taken aback by the words coming out of his mouth. She shakes her head as if trying to stay on task. "You can find them. There are maps of where they might be hiding. A list of allies we can trust."

"What if I don't want to find them?" I spit out.

Amber regards me with those big, blue eyes that become shinier the longer she doesn't blink, and my hand clenches around the binder.

"I'm sorry. I didn't mean to lash out at you."

Sometimes, I forget John isn't here in the room. I mean, he is, but he *isn't*. And I shouldn't shoot the messenger.

"You don't want to find others like us?" she whispers, the quietest she's been since we've been back in Florida.

"It's not—"

She pulls her hood up to shield her face on the way out of the room before I can finish.

I'm not sure if John stayed behind or followed the one person who could talk to him, but I mutter, "This is your fault, you know." I shove the binder back into the cabinet and follow her out of the room.

Amber keeps her back to me, her hand on the handle, preparing to whip open the front door a second prior to someone banging on it. She startles backward, letting out a small yelp.

I grab her shoulder, yanking her toward me to cover her mouth, when the knock sounds again. She twists to peer up at me, eyes blazing with trepidation, but nods when I let go of her mouth and raise a finger to my lips. The knock is softer this time, and we stand there frozen. It's probably just Mrs. Rutherford snooping. Or maybe the mail person hasn't caught onto the fact that the mailbox has been stuffed for weeks. Or perhaps...

The door handle jiggles.

I don't remember locking it on the way in, but thankfully, I did.

"I just want to talk," a muffled male voice calls from outside.

Nope, that's our cue. Amber stifles a groan as I wrap my arms around her and enter the void. We appear in an alley, and it takes me a moment to pinpoint where we are. My gaze lands on the blue dumpster with *Olive Grove* painted on the side in black; we're a block away from John's.

"Let's go." I push Amber forward.

"We're going to walk all the way home? It's going to take like an hour!" She tosses her head back, the gray hood of her jean jacket slipping as her blonde curls shake from the movement. "Can't you just"—she waves a hand around in the air—"whatever?"

"I don't have that kind of strength yet. For now, go." I push her again, but this time, she doesn't fight me on it.

After a couple of minutes of heading down different alleys that elongate our walk, Amber finally breaks the silence. It might be a record for her.

"Who was that, anyway?"

"I don't know. It's probably nothing." I kick a can laying on the ground, and it skitters across the rocks, landing near the tire of a black SUV I've seen before. While the parked car is a common model, the Nevada license plate is not. My breathing hitches, but I don't want to scare Amber.

"But I'd rather not leave a trail," I say, grabbing her arm and stepping into a different void. We emerge in the center of a football field outside an unfamiliar school.

"Oh yeah," Amber breathes. "Being in the wide open is a lot safer. Smart."

"Shut it." I glance down at her, my anxiety quieting some as she returns to her normal self, once again rolling her eyes at me. I must be already forgiven, and at least we're nowhere near the black SUV. "Do you know where we are?"

She spins, holding a hand up to block out the setting sun as she reads the sign on the building. "Toto, we're not in Kansas anymore."

"What do you mean?"

"We're not in Willow." She points at the school. "I've had dance recitals here before. We're a town over."

My jaw drops as I try to rationalize how we've teleported this far.

Dennis and I *have* been working on my ability lately, testing how far I can go in one leap and how many people I can take with me. He's not quite as concerned about packing everyone up as I am because, in reality, where would they go? They have a life here. But he still understands my concerns. So, we have an agreement: I'll get the crew out if any unwanted guests appear.

To work on this, Dennis scouts for discreet locations around town, marking them on a map and showing me where to go so I don't suddenly appear in someone's kitchen.

But it hasn't been anything like this. The only other time I've traveled this type of distance was when I took the crew one at a time to the empty field where the fair was held, but that was mostly panic induced. When I saw Riley—alive—something inside me broke.

Back then, I didn't even know I could teleport, let alone know where to go. We were surrounded by the Authorities, and my sister was breathing while holding a gun directly at us. We were cornered, and my brain, body, or whatever took over.

It was like I was on autopilot.

But now?

Does fear make me travel farther?

Amber sighs, pulling out her phone. "I'll call Dennis to come pick us up before we end up in Georgia."

DENNIS IS CONVINCED THAT traveling that far is a good thing. It means I'm getting stronger, and I have to admit he's right. I don't get the sensation of wanting to puke my brains out every time I teleport anymore, and I can traverse with more people. But the more I take with me, the less distance we cross. And I'll need to be able to take at least Nora, Zay, and Elise with me if CPS shows up to check on Gemma and Amber, so I'm not strong enough. *Yet.*

"We'll keep working on it." Dennis smiles as he gets out of the truck—entirely unaffected that he had to drive forty minutes round trip to pick up two stranded kids. "Amber, run inside and start your homework before dinner."

She stomps ahead, leaving the two of us in the driveway. Dennis gives me another grin before turning to follow her, but the tightening sensation in my chest forces me to stop him.

"Hey, Dennis?"

He glances over his shoulder at me, face sobering as he fully turns, his warm brown eyes filling with concern.

Should I tell him about what happened at John's? If they're really onto us, he has a right to know...

I stuff a hand in my front pocket, clenching my lighter tight, forcing words to pass through my lips. "Someone appeared at John's... that's why..."

Dennis lifts his chin, comprehension pulling his shoulders straight as he leans back against the hood of the truck. "Did they see you?"

"No, well, I don't know. It might not have been *them*. But a guy said he wanted to talk, and I'm not sure if he was watching Amber and me before we went inside."

Dennis's lips press together as he seems to think it over. It's not often that he isn't smiling about something, and serious Dennis makes me even more uneasy than I already am.

"Well, the good thing is you two weren't caught, and it was probably nothing, right? It's been weeks, and no one has shown themselves yet." He pushes off the truck, slapping a hand on my back and steering me toward the front steps. "What did Amber say?"

"Not much. She asked who it was, and I downplayed it to not upset her."

"Good. Let's keep this between us. It's no use scaring everyone if it just happened to be a concerned neighbor."

I fake a smile, bowing my head as he ushers me into the house. It's useless to argue the point. The crew, with their false sense of security, seems to be settling into their new roles here, and I'm left alone wandering the streets at night, waiting for the other shoe to drop.

I don't want to sound like the boy who cried wolf whenever something worries me.

The mouthwatering scent of lemon chicken drifts from the kitchen, and my stomach growls on cue. The one thing I've very much gotten used to is having a warm meal every night. Even more than that, we also get breakfast and lunch around here. And as Zay likes to remind me, "All the snacks in the world." He's going to eat them out of their house or at least force them to each get another job. Sighing, guilt churns its way through my gut at the thought of being a financial burden.

On the other hand, falling asleep every night with a full stomach is a feeling I haven't been acquainted with in over five years. And as much as I don't want to become complacent when we need to keep moving, there are brief moments like this—with laughter traveling from the dining room—when I'm sure as hell happy that Dennis and Judy took us in.

Chapter Three

Gemma

THERE'S A CHANCE I might've overstated how well I had my powers under control.

It's true I connected with them back in the graveyard once I severed the ties between Oli—my heart gives a painful tug—Draven and me. And I'm capable of making my hands glow whenever I want. But that's pretty much where the control ends.

Not to mention, my eyes are entirely violet now, which has to mean something, but I'm not sure what.

Sitting up, I check the clock on the nightstand, careful not to wake Nora. It's nearly one in the morning and Theo isn't back yet. Anger and dread build in my chest, and my hands shake—only a little, but enough for my fingers to curl together and my jaw to clench. *Great*, now there's broken glass some-where. He's probably out scoping the area again, and I know his intentions are good and that it's because he wants to keep everyone safe, but I wish he wouldn't go out *alone*.

I exhale, squeezing my eyes shut, then focus across the room on Elise. In the light shining in our window from the nearby streetlight, I can just make out her figure in what was once my bed, her light blonde hair sprawling free from underneath the covers pulled over her face.

I couldn't let Elise sleep in Olivia's bed, but there weren't many options besides the floor. Considering she handed me to Draven on a silver platter, I probably should have gone that route.

But no, I chose the lesser of two evils. She took my bed, and now Nora and I are in Oli's. I swear it still smells like her every once in a while, but then her rose perfume fades, and it seems like it's all in my head. Maybe too much time has passed, even though it doesn't seem like it has at all.

Nora hasn't forgiven Elise or forgotten that first heartbreak, which is, I guess, more harmful to her than me burning her because she begged to share a bed with me rather than be with Elise. Her choice was between us because Amber has a much smaller bed, and Zay and Theo split the remaining room.

It's a good thing Judy and Dennis are used to fostering kids. Though I'm pretty sure Judy is starting to lose her hair from stressing over an unexpected CPS visit. It would be hard to explain four extra kids. It's been two months since our last visit, but our case worker doesn't have the time to come as often as she should—a blessing. She's due to return soon, though. CPS can't go on pretending Amber and I don't exist forever.

The plan is for Theo to teleport the rest out if there are any unexpected knocks on the door. So, we try really, *really* hard to make it seem like only two kids are living here instead of six. Zay does his best, but even in the short time I've known him, he's sprouted up like the weeds he so fondly grows. I think he's even taller than Theo now. Between his stereotypical messy teenage self and his unbelievable eating habits, he lacks the most self-discipline out of all of us. We're working on it.

If our caseworker, Nancy Jacobs, arrives and sees his mess, she's going to suspect something is wrong. Maybe she won't automatically assume four more kids live here because that's a stretch, but she's seen this house before. She knows what Judy's version of clean looks like and how Amber and I follow it.

Sighing, I carefully get out of bed, the floor shockingly cold against my feet, as I tiptoe for the door. I pause, glancing over my shoulder at the two of them—Elise is snoring softly, and Nora is curled into herself under the covers.

Dennis probably knows Theo isn't home. He leaves the light over the kitchen sink on for him; he's a lot more understanding than I am when it comes to Theo searching for clues and risking himself like this. He can't keep going out there alone, exposing himself. What if he's right and the Authorities *are* watching us? If something happens—I cut my thoughts short when my chest starts to ache.

I can't lose him, too.

So yes, I'm still exploding light bulbs and resetting the microwave time without meaning to. Wilting plants as I walk by from accidentally siphoning from them. The one thing I have a hundred percent figured out is each heartbeat in this house. I will not, under absolutely no circumstance, tap into their life sources.

I *can't* lose control like that. It would end me, but more importantly, it would end *them*.

No one outwardly talks about it, though. I'm sure they all have thoughts, in addition to the suspicion dangling in the air that threatens to drown me. I can sense everyone's emotions as well as my own, and while I'm pretty good at blocking out one person at a time, it gets a lot harder when everyone feels the same thing.

But I haven't been able to say it out loud. How maybe I have absolutely no idea what I'm doing and that I've gotten in way over my head. Now, not only am I a danger to my foster family, the reason I ran away to begin with, but I've brought four other kids home with me who can also do weird things.

Everything is super.

When I get downstairs, I find that *surprise, surprise,* the sink light is out. I switch on the overhead light, grab the broom as quietly as possible, and creep closer to the shattered glass. After scooping it up, I use a kitchen towel to clean inside the sink. Once everything is cleared, I turn around and catch Dennis in the doorway watching me.

"Oh," I say as I startle. "Sorry if I woke you."

"You didn't." He gives me a knowing look as if my sneaking around is futile. I should come clean, but I don't. I might be upset with Theo for being out, but I don't want to blow his cover on the extremely small chance Dennis doesn't realize he isn't upstairs.

He uncrosses his arms and heads for the fridge, where he pulls out a carton of milk. "Want some?"

"No thanks." My gaze darts to the back door before quickly focusing back on him.

"Still not home yet, hm?"

Figures. There's no fooling Dennis.

I open my mouth to say something—*anything*—even to lie on Theo's behalf, but it's *Dennis.* He's always been able to see straight through me. If I didn't know any better, I'd assume he had powers, too.

"Don't be too hard on him." He chuckles to himself and grabs a glass from the cupboard. "Believe it or not, I was a teenage boy once. I might not have had *abilities*... but some things stay the same. I'm sure he's fine and just clearing his head."

My shoulders sag as I sit on one of the stools, forcing away the image of Dennis and me sitting here months ago, right after Oli's accident.

I run my fingers through my hair, scratching my scalp. "I don't know what to do."

"Let me talk to him." When I glance up, Dennis puffs out his chest and winks. "Man to man," he adds sarcastically.

I grin. "Thanks, Dennis."

"Go back to bed. I'll make sure he gets in all right."

My gut tells me not to leave, and I focus on the back door once more, but Dennis is right. There's nothing I can do, and I don't know how to fix Theo or convince him to stay inside. For a guy who loved hiding, he sure seems to like being outside now. My lips twist, and before I can get angry again at his self-sacrificing tendencies, I turn to go. From the corner of my eye, I spot Dennis pulling out another lightbulb from under the sink.

THE NEXT MORNING, I come downstairs to find Theo leaning against the back of a chair with a split lip and black eye.

"What happened?" I rush over to him, reaching for his face when he seems to have a hard time looking at me; his cheeks turn pink as shame rolls off him.

Zay and Nora immediately make themselves busy by reading comics and magazines while Elise files her nails.

"Did you—? Are you—" I can't form any complete sentences as my hand hovers over his skin, not wanting to touch and hurt him further. It couldn't have been the Authorities. They would have captured or killed him. So, what then? A fresh wave of guilt rolls off him and slams into my chest. The impact is worse than whatever blow dealt that mark on his face. I force myself to swallow and work through what emotions are mine and what are his.

"What happened?" I snap, dropping my hand to my side.

"It's fine. I'm fine. I'm sorry I worried you last night."

Crossing my arms across my chest, I do everything in my power not to lose it. "Did Dennis see you like this?"

His jaw twitches when he nods.

"*And?*"

"We talked. Everything is fine, though, I swear."

"Jesus, Theo." *If you say fine one more time.* "Did you just pick some random person to fight? What happened to lying low?"

Elise chimes in from the couch, "Oh, this should be good."

Nora jabs her in the side with an elbow as Zay whispers, "Are Mom and Dad breaking up?"

Theo shakes his head at Elise or Zay—I'm not sure which—but it's more or less directed at the entire couch.

"Yes, I was in a fight, but it's..."

My eyebrows raise as he stumbles over an explanation.

"He used to fight in illegal fighting rings," Elise supplies, smirking. "I guess he found one down here, too."

"I'm sorry?" I whip my head back to face Theo. "You *what?*"

"It's not as bad as it sounds. I sometimes fight for cash. To help... you know."

"No, I *don't.* What could you possibly need cash for?"

His shoulders tense as he pivots, resting his side against the chair so he no longer faces me.

We've had this conversation a few times already—maybe not about where he gets his money, per se, but more about why he thinks he needs it. We probably are at risk and most likely always will be, but right now, I'm merely trying to survive another day without my sister until I can graduate.

Anyway, he doesn't need money *right now*. I get why he needed it in the past, but we'll figure it out. Once I graduate, per Judy's rules, we can track down others and... and... *What comes next?* There has to be more like us. We can't be the only six in the world with powers. Well, seven, if you add Riley.

I stop any thoughts of the future in their tracks and turn to stand in front of Theo again; my resolve softens. His stunning gray eyes are wide with fear, and the bruise forming around one makes me want to reach up and kiss him. I glance at his split lip. *Or maybe not.*

"You have to stop doing this," I beg. "The sneaking out. The"—I throw a hand out to imply his face, stumbling over my words—"fighting. All of it. You're putting yourself at risk out there. It isn't like you to be so reckless."

Theo's gaze snaps to mine, his eyes narrowing, the gray turning into steel. "You really don't get it, do you?"

"Get *what*?"

"You spent what? A month with us?" He winces when his eyebrows lift but continues anyway. "You don't know what it's like—the hiding, the lack of food. You didn't even know the Authorities existed before we met. You don't know *me*."

The words might as well have been a physical blow. My throat closes, and I take a step back.

"Theo..." Zay exhales.

Even Elise is quiet for once.

Already, the anger is gone from Theo's eyes. "I didn't mean that."

I raise a hand, stopping him.

"It's not like I had it super easy before I met you." He should understand that. He came whenever I had a bad night and sat with me. But he didn't realize what I was really going through, either, did he? Because we didn't know each other.

Tears burn behind my eyes, but I blink them away. Car doors slam in the driveway, giving me an out when everyone turns to look at the front door. With Theo's pained expression turned the other way, I slip up the stairs and head for my bedroom.

"Gem—" he calls out, but I don't bother turning around.

I slam the door behind me, shaking out the purple surrounding my fingertips. My breaths come out harsh as the tingling spreads up my arms, and the tears finally slide down unbidden. We'd been strangers in each other's heads for *years*, but we'd never spoken until I was told to come find him, even though the message wasn't even *from* him. Then we got a few weeks together in person before Draven tried killing me.

After, we had maybe a week of normalcy before Theo started... being Theo.

Maybe he's right. Maybe I don't know him.

I wish Olivia were here. She was the boy expert, not me. She'd tell me what to do. How to handle my ribcage being torn in two. I lay down in bed, *her* bed, and let it all out—the worry of the unknown, the threat of the Authorities, missing Oli. Everything.

The more I think about her, the more I smell her rose perfume again, and the memory of her smell coming to life at a time of need is enough to drown me in sorrow.

The door opens with Elise huffing. "Stop being dramatic."

"Go away." I swipe the tears away, rolling onto my back to focus on the glow-in-the-dark stars stuck to the ceiling.

"Don't be so hard on Theo," she scolds. "He might be an idiot, but he isn't lying. He's been doing this for years. He gets in his head and needs to blow off steam… It probably wasn't even about the money—"

"It's not about the fighting," I snap. I mean, that's not great, either. But her words make my stomach sink even more. He's been having a hard time lately. Knowing his sister is alive, his dad died, the Authorities… I get that. But *fighting*? Rather than voice any of my thoughts out loud, I say, "It's the harsh reality that I'm absolutely, without a doubt, in love with a stranger."

Why am I even telling her all this? It's Elise Beck. She's just going to use this against me in some way.

Elise stomps over to me, slapping my legs until I move them to the side, and she sits on the edge of the bed. "First, gross. Second, you're not *strangers*. Again, with the dramatics. So, you two don't know everything about each other. Isn't that normal? If you met under different circumstances—"

"Well, we didn't," I interrupt her. "He's been up here this whole time." I point to my head and sit straight up, swinging my legs out from behind her so I can pace around the room.

"So, go learn about him now instead of running and hiding in here!"

I throw my arms up. "Why do you even care?"

Suddenly, we're yelling over each other about how clearly she hates me and her defending her actions with Draven because she wants her parents back until Judy is standing between us with a laundry basket.

"Girls!" She glances at the two of us. "What is going on?" When neither of us says anything, she sets the basket down on my—*Elise's*—bed. "Listen, Theo is a very handsome young man, but it's not worth…"

She trails off when Elise's face screws up in disgust. "Ew?"

"Hey!" I bluster. "You would be so lucky."

"Oh, so you're mad at me now because I *don't* want your boyfriend?"

I instinctively step toward her, heat flaming my cheeks, but why? She has a point. I'd rather her *not* be into Theo, but he's not gross! He's… My stomach dips, my face heating for different reasons now.

"Wait, so you two aren't fighting over a boy? Okay, what gives besides me failing the Bechdel test? I heard Theo's name and assumed…" Judy starts putting clothes in random drawers. "Anyway, what's with all the yelling?"

Again, neither of us answers her.

"Tell me," she demands, raising an eyebrow.

I take a deep breath, letting it all out in a rush. "Elise tried sacrificing me to some ghost so she could get revenge for her dead parents."

We told Judy and Dennis *mostly* everything that happened, but we—mainly *me*—left out some minor details, worried about how they'd react. Would they have let Elise in the house if they'd known the whole story sooner?

While I shouldn't have cared, a part of me didn't want to hold Elise's fate in my hands.

Elise now at least has the sense to look at anything but us. She picks a point on the wall and squints at it.

Judy's mouth drops open with a small "Oh." Then her shoulders straighten as she tucks a piece of strawberry blonde hair behind her ear. "Elise, sweetie, why don't you head downstairs and start working on lunch? We'll catch up in a minute."

Elise grunts in acknowledgment, closing the door behind her.

I sit next to the basket on the bed and start pulling on a piece of thread from my shirt. Judy sits beside me but doesn't say anything at first. She adjusts her position to pull my dead phone out of her back pocket and hands it to me.

I think she's trying to process everything she stumbled into—at least, that's what it feels like. However, instead of speaking her worries, she seems to latch onto her normal disappointed expression whenever I leave my phone uncharged as if she wants to ground herself with something familiar.

Finally, she turns to me, offering more of a grimace than anything reassuring. "I'm not going to pretend I know what it's like to be... you. Or any of you. Teenage girls were a lot different back in my day." She laughs at her own attempt at humor but stops when I don't join. "But do you think... maybe... this is too much?"

My brows furrow. "What do you mean?"

"I mean, maybe we can find other arrangements—no, I'm not saying we call anyone." The horror must have been clear on my face. "But I think we should figure out a different solution." She rubs small, smoothing circles on my back. "I know you think this is your responsibility, but you're just a kid. The weight of the world isn't on your shoulders, Gemma."

I shake my head. "It is, though. I'm the reason they're here, why the Authorities raided their house and Theo's dad..."

"John's death is not on your hands," she scolds with more force than ever before. "Don't you dare for a second feel guilty over that. He knew what he was doing and absolutely did the right thing by saving you." Her blue eyes are wet with unshed tears, her face turning red and blotchy like it always does when she gets upset. "Get that out of your head right this minute."

When she holds my gaze, I force a nod. "Okay," I whisper, my breath loosening the slightest bit. "If we could just find others like us, then maybe we can learn how to use our abilities. I could get my GED and start looking for them sooner."

"No. You're finishing high school. Get your diploma, and I will drive you to whatever secret headquarters you want me to after that. You're still a kid; enjoy it as long as you can." She grabs my head, planting a kiss on the top of it.

"If it's secret, how do you know where it is?" I tease, but we're both smiling now, and I'm glad Judy eavesdropped earlier. My chest is a bit lighter with the reminder that I'm not alone anymore.

"We'll figure it out," she promises. "But first, lunch. Oh, and Gemma?" She points at the phone on my lap. "Keep it charged, please."

Chapter Four

THEO

I'M AN IDIOT.

How could I be so stupid and tell Gemma she doesn't know me? The words just slipped out, and I would take another beating if it meant I could go back and choke them down.

Last night, I called the number on the business card I had for the sketchy guy back in Indiana. Everything suddenly became too much—the constant fear, my dad's ghost, the person knocking on the door at his house. I had to get it out of my system so I didn't explode. The guy seemed surprised to hear from me, but he put me in touch with someone from around here. The fight was at a gym across town this time. An easy five-hundred dollars if I tune out the pulse beating underneath my eye.

I do need to stop, though. I'm being reckless, and while the fight's physical effort ironically made breathing a little easier, the flash of hurt in Gemma's eyes wasn't worth it—or the fact that I was almost caught afterward.

Once the fight was over, a guy cornered me in the parking lot. I was close to teleporting out, unsure what would happen if someone witnessed me disappear into thin air, but I froze when he said he was a friend of John's. He also mentioned he was from Carson City, and my dad's earlier words about a buddy being out there rooted my feet in place.

He introduced himself as Jason Morris and said he was one of us and could help. He apologized for scaring us at John's the other day but said he'd been trying to talk to me because he hadn't heard from John in a while and knew he was on a mission to find me.

Jason seemed sincere enough, but I didn't want to make the mistake of believing him if he was lying, so I didn't offer any information on my dad's death, pretending like I had no idea who John Goodwin was. After playing dumb long enough, I took off down the street, and as soon as I rounded a corner, I teleported so he couldn't follow.

By the time I snuck back in, Dennis was waiting for me. He took one look at my face and grabbed an ice pack. My heart hammered against my ribs, waiting for him to lose it on me, but he didn't. The silent disappointment made it so much worse than if he had.

Nope, instead of yelling, he only said there was still good in the world; all I had to do was look for it. It didn't make much sense last night, not with my face busted open and my head throbbing, but I think his point was that I'm fucking it all up.

And now, Gemma hasn't even glanced at me all through lunch; my stomach sinks lower and lower until I can hardly eat anything.

I'm a disappointment across the board.

Judy supplies most of the conversation, asking how our studies are going.

Gemma and Amber have been back in school since they were already in the foster care system. But Dennis has taken it upon himself to homeschool the rest of us when he comes home from work. His primary focus is on Zay and Nora. I don't mind. Nevertheless, he fills my hands each week with books I *have* to read. Everyone has also been studying *differently*, focusing on our abilities.

Judy planted a garden in the basement, so Zay has been working on his elemental skills. He's getting better all the time, and now their cellar walls are covered with ivy, weaving together to bar the windows from prying eyes, which is also why we don't practice outside.

There's a meditation area set up in the corner for Nora. We don't know how to help since her visions tend to come and go. But maybe she can find a way to control them better while meditating so they don't control her. Neither Nora nor Gemma has shared the information Nora provided in the truck on the way here, the convenient fact she *erased* herself from her family's life, but I wasn't supposed to hear it. Even though Nora knew I wasn't asleep when the truth came out. If she can learn to control her visions, perhaps she can discover what happened with erasing herself from her family's memories, too.

I glance at Elise, who's aimlessly nodding along to Amber's rundown of who's being mean to who in her class. Elise takes another bite and offers a "mm" when Amber takes a small breath, and I fight back a smirk. I can basically see the words enter one ear and go out the other when Amber starts talking again.

Elise is Elise and pretty much always pissy that she can't do anything but read auras, and Amber continues to talk to dead people like John. It's tough to get used to. But the ghosts seem to present themselves to her rather than the other way around. Once they realize she's capable of speaking to the other side, they choose to show themselves. I guess it's better than being swarmed by ghosts all day.

And Gemma? I chance a quick look as I take a sip of water. She's amazing, as always.

Her powers—whatever they are—aren't as controlled as she'd like, but she's a long way away from when she burned down the woods outside the Rib House. Lights shatter here and there, like she needs an outlet, and her power zaps anything electrical to balance out. Zay has also mentioned that his plants are withering, but not because of him. So, she's still drawing energy from living things. But she's trying.

She wants to find others like us so we'll possibly find someone like *her*. Draven already taunted her by telling her they were different from the rest of us. So far, none of us have been able to help her control it. All our tricks seem inadequate compared to hers, like how none of us can break a man's arm with the touch of our fingers, and we don't have to drain the life out of anything to use our abilities.

Needless to say, I should probably stop upsetting her.

Ouch. My focus returns to the table when Nora kicks me and glances down at my nearly full plate with raised eyebrows. I take another bite, and the food gets stuck in my throat, scraping the edges as I choke it down.

"Dennis and I were thinking." Judy captures everyone's attention when she speaks up. "A family night might be in order to get you kids out of the house. Do you guys want to go to the drive-in tonight?"

Even though she betrayed our friendship, Elise and I make eye contact, our first instinct to hide overruling anything else. Old habits die hard, and I still look to her when making a judgment call. The rest of the crew perks up, grinning from ear to ear; everyone but

Gemma, that is. She stabs at her food, pushing it around the plate. It seems she also lost her appetite.

"Before you get in that head of yours,"—Dennis drills me with a look—"we worked it all out. The drive-in is the perfect activity. Outdoors, and we stick to our own vehicle. Interactions with others can be avoided."

My gaze flickers from Gemma back to Elise, and the latter gives a half-hearted shrug. "Could be fun?"

⁂

Gemma beats me to the porch after lunch. She's sitting on the front steps, twisting a fallen leaf between her fingers. She doesn't bother turning around to see who's joining her.

Her shoulders are hunched, her brown curly hair framing her face, and my heart hammers with regret. I would crawl on my hands and knees, begging her for forgiveness if it meant we could move past this.

"I'm sorry." My voice comes out hoarse.

She doesn't turn around, but the wind carries a faint, "Me too."

I sit on the top step beside her, gazing at the street. "I didn't mean it."

"You weren't wrong," she admits. Apprehension coils around my spine when I scan her face. "There's a lot we don't understand about each other."

"I lied. You know me better than anyone ever has, secrets included."

"You failing to keep a secret from me doesn't equate to me knowing you."

"I'm sorry," I say again, my voice on the edge of desperation. "I'll stop fighting and sneaking out. I'll stop being an ass, too."

Her mouth twists to one side as if deciding whether she wants to believe me; knowing her, she's probably reading my feelings right now. I don't mind. I want her to understand that I didn't mean to hurt her. Her eyes light with humor when she nods, most likely agreeing with me being an ass.

"I think you were just scared." She bumps her shoulder into mine. "I think you *are* scared."

I grip the edge of the stairs, scraping my shoe against a lower step to avoid her gaze. I glance around the street and stare at the trees, finally settling on her face. Her violet eyes study me. The cut on her face has been healed for a while now, but the faintest scar sits on her cheekbone, and all I want to do is lean in and kiss it.

"I'm not scared about us."

"No?" She cocks an eyebrow at me.

I pull her closer, my hand winding through her hair until her lips brush against mine. "No."

She melts beneath my touch, the ice between us thawing, and gives me one more kiss before leaning back slightly. "We do have to get to know each other, though, and properly date like real teenagers. Which means *talking*."

My hand crushes the leaf she's holding as my lips find hers again. "Sure. Let's talk." Her giggle lifts a weight off my shoulders. If I could carry it around in a bottle, I would.

"You're an idiot," she says, still smiling as her mouth presses against mine. Time passes, the flame between us igniting, and it's suddenly like we're in the woods again, getting soaked through with rain during our first kiss. I don't ever want to let her go. She pulls my shirt, tugging me closer, and I'm practically on top of her; we're going to fall down the stairs any second.

Stairs. House. *Right.*

Regrettably, I break for air and glance around. Sure enough, Amber is watching us from a window, pretending to gag. "Other people live here!" Her muffled voice travels through the glass.

I shake my head at her before she disappears behind the curtains. At least it's better than Judy or Dennis catching us.

Gemma is panting, a rosy blush staining her fair skin. She leans back against the porch railing. "Well, that's one way to get to know each other."

The back of my neck warms, and I let out a gentle laugh; my busted lip aches from her kiss. Then her shoulders straighten, and she tucks her legs up close to her chest, her face turning somber.

Great, we're about to *actually* talk.

"Have you seen her?" she whispers.

And it's gone. Our brief moment has passed, and I don't want to discuss this or talk about *her.* "I thought you were going to ask what my favorite color is or something."

"Fine. What's your favorite color?"

I grin. "Purple."

She rolls her eyes, nudging my leg with her foot. "Be serious."

"Oh, I'm always serious." She places her feet in my lap, and I curl my hand around her ankle, brushing the inner part with my thumb as she shivers. "What's yours?"

She puts a finger to her chin, tapping and humming like it's the hardest question in the world. "Maybe gray?"

"Not fair. You can't just steal my answer."

"Who said anything about stealing?" she asks with a sly grin. "Gray has always been my favorite; it's the color of storms. That it matches your eyes is just a coincidence."

"Uh huh, sure." I continue drawing shapes on her skin, right below where her leggings end.

We sit in silence for a minute while the wind kicks up. I close my eyes, listening to the porch swing creak and the tree branches shake. If only it could be like this all the time.

"Theo?" Gemma whispers.

"Hm?"

"I think you should try talking to her. It might help fix what's been broken."

I don't open my eyes and focus back on the wind, which is howling now. Its gusts bring swaths of smoke, filling my nostrils and smothering my lungs. I don't want to go to Riley's dreams. To see that she's alive. To know she murdered our dad and face that I left her behind that night. I thought she was dead. I thought. *I thought.* Heat licks my face, burning my fingertips. I clench my hands, but something moves beneath them.

"Theo!" Gemma's voice shakes me out of the memory. She's now kneeling, staring at me wide eyed. "Are you okay?" Her purple eyes are drowning in sadness. And I hate that it's directed at me.

"Yeah." My voice scrapes its way out, like I've actually been surrounded by smoke. "I'm fine."

WE'RE ALL SPRAWLED OUT on blankets and pillows in the bed of Dennis's pickup truck, Dennis and Judy opting for camping chairs on the ground.

Singing hotdogs and popcorn buckets with faces dance across the gigantic screen, which I find very unsettling. I catch myself scanning the other vehicles every so often, waiting to glimpse Jason's face among them, watching us. Maybe coming here was a bad idea. But the warmth seeping into me from Gemma, sitting by my side with our backs against the cab, quiets the anxiety building in my chest.

Nora, Zay, and Amber are all on their stomachs, closest to the tailgate, laughing at the animated food. Elise sits propped on the other side of the cab, mirroring my position, aimlessly eating Twizzler after Twizzler.

No matter how much I try to redirect my thoughts, they keep straying to the man from last night and whether or not he was telling the truth. Nora hasn't mentioned anyone to me lately, but when she states she has to run to the bathroom, I go with her to take the opportunity to make sure Jason isn't here stalking us.

"I'm a big girl, Theo. I know where to find the restroom," Nora states as we walk together, her auburn hair braided into pigtails despite her declaration about being grown.

I rotate the lighter in my hand, scanning the line of people waiting at the snack bar.

She side-eyes me before spinning in my direction, holding out a small hand to stop me in my place. "That's your worried face. What is it?"

"Have you seen anyone lately?"

Nora picks at her chapped lip, a clear sign that she *has* seen someone.

"Out with it."

"Yes, but they're not following us if that's what you're worried about."

"Is it a guy?"

Nora scrunches her nose. "A guy? No. I've been seeing the same girl over and over lately."

Oh. Well, that's a relief. Or is it just a different problem to handle?

"How do you know *she's* not following us?"

Nora's amber eyes bore into mine. "Because she's in a coma."

I squint back at her, trying to figure out what she means. "A coma? Are you sure?"

"Well, as much as I can be. Every time I have a vision of her, it's of her in a hospital bed, asleep, with all the machines beeping in the background. It never changes."

"Huh... that's weird. So, no guys then? Nobody that's my height, dark brown eyes with matching hair, tanned skin?"

"Why?" she drills.

Sighing, I confess and tell her about Jason and the incident at John's house and outside the gym. She listens with rapt attention but ultimately shakes her head.

"I haven't seen him at all, but I'll try to focus on him and see if that stirs anything."

With nothing else to do for the time being, Nora goes to the bathroom as I wait outside, scrutinizing every face that passes, wondering whether I'll meet him again.

<hr>

I FALL ASLEEP DURING the movie by accident, and with everything on my mind, I, even more by accident, end up in Riley's dream.

It has to be hers, and I immediately regret thinking about her earlier.

I'm back in our childhood house, everything is how it was when we were kids, long before the fire burned it down. It's quiet as I walk through the dark living room, heading for the lit kitchen.

The same yellow paint covers the walls, white dishes are stacked on the open shelving, and the black countertop reflects the overhead light. Even though the kitchen is empty, it takes everything in me to hold my ground and not run away.

"Hello?" I call out, unsure whether she'll be able to hear me. Gemma never could, but my powers have grown since then.

The light flickers when stomping comes from above—Riley's bedroom. I scan the ceiling, following her footsteps as they race from room to room. I swallow, almost cringing at how loud my gulp is.

I inch for the staircase at the other end of the house, contemplating whether I should go up there or wake myself up. How do I begin apologizing for the years I've abandoned her? Especially if no words escape my mouth, or if they do, but the words don't actually land, and my voice gets lost in the void. But I have to try. I owe her that much.

With as little noise as possible, I climb the stairs. The path of her destruction becomes visible as clothes, blankets, pillows, picture frames, anything she can get her hands on, it seems, is tossed into the upstairs hallway. Glass shatters against a door frame.

The old floorboards creak underneath me, and I freeze. So does Riley; the silence is deafening.

Her eyes find mine when she comes out of our parents' bedroom. We both stand as still as statues, taking one another in before her gaze focuses on me with deranged madness.

I open my mouth to explain, but flames ignite in her palms. She screams, throwing a fireball at me right as I startle awake, knocking Gemma to the side.

She twists to face me; eyes alert as she reads my eyes or my feelings, whichever one happens to be yelling louder. "What's wrong?"

My chest heaves as I try to slow my breathing so I don't disturb the others watching the movie. "I saw her," I rasp out.

Gemma cups my hand with both of hers, squeezing tightly. "And?"

"I don't think she forgives me."

I lay my head back against the truck's cab; my fist still balled between Gemma's hands. She doesn't offer any words of comfort as she snuggles closer into my side, reminding me she's there.

The dread of seeing Riley again ebbs away, the adrenaline of her fireball draining with it. It might be entirely irrational, but I need to try again. It wasn't Riley who killed our father. It might have been her gun, and she may hate me now, but whatever they did to her... Brainwashed? Stockholm syndrome? A person with the ability to influence minds controlling her? I have no idea, but there's no other choice.

I have to save my sister.

⸎⸎⸎⸎⸎ ⸎⸎⸎⸎⸎

THE FOLLOWING DAY, THERE'S a knock on the door. The news report on the television blares a boil-water advisory due to the risk of drinking contaminated water as we all freeze, looking at one another.

Judy and Dennis lock eyes. He slowly rubs his hands together as if contemplating his next move, then nods at me as he stands up to get the door. The news anchor in the background moves on to talk about radiation spikes throughout the country, but the heartbeat pulsing in my ears begins to drown her out.

The others rush to the basement; only Gemma and Amber are supposed to be here, so if things go south, I'll take the rest away. So, I linger, waiting to see if we need to move. My back is against the hallway wall where they can't spot me, but I can at least hear if they enter the house. If they do, we go. I shake my hands out, strain my hearing to listen past my raging heart, and bounce on the balls of my feet, ready to flee.

"Hi, Mr. and Mrs. McIntyre. I'm Officer Jason Morris." My brows furrow. Wait— "I'm looking for my partner, John Goodwin. He's been on a case but hasn't checked in in quite some time."

"Oh." Judy's voice is too high; she's going to blow it. "I'm sorry to hear that. Is there, uh, something we can help you with?"

"Well, the last time we spoke, he was looking for your daughter. Actually, I believe it was both of them. They ran away?"

Judy gives a shrill laugh. "When you put it like that, it sure does sound like bad parenting... Gemma ran away after—" She falters. "Then Amber, I guess, wanted to find her. So, John was helping us."

"But we haven't seen him since," Dennis adds.

"Your daughters are both home now?"

"No, they're out." Dennis has never sounded so sinister before. I search for the lighter in my pocket, squeezing it until my knuckles ache.

We should go. I need to get to the basement, but my body doesn't move. Maybe Jason was telling the truth if he's now here giving a similar speech to Judy and Dennis? I risk not heading downstairs to hear what else he says.

"But they did make it back safely? Did John bring them home?" Jason asks.

"Officer Goodwin was able to locate both girls, and they came home together. Haven't heard from him since." Dennis's voice leaves no room for argument.

"Right." There's a pause and a shifting of floorboards, but I can't risk turning around to look. "Here's my card. If you happen to hear from him, or if anything happens—anything at *all*—please let me know."

I lean my head back against the wall. He said he was John's friend, not his partner, but he did admit he was one of us. Maybe he said it to seem less threatening. But before, he only cornered me. If he's willing to come to the house... I squeeze my eyes shut, trying to think it through. Does coming here alone mean he's friend or foe? Can we trust him? I wish John would come back so Amber could ask him. Unfortunately, his arrival is unpredictable, so who knows when he'll return.

I don't move when the door closes, taking a few seconds to even my breathing, but I catch Judy hissing at Dennis, "We've just lied to the cops!"

"Calm down; it's going to be okay."

"That man is dead, and we just told the cops we haven't heard from him."

"We haven't," Dennis answers gruffly.

"This is only the beginning; they're going to come back."

I come out from my hiding spot, my head swimming with dread. They both stop talking instantly; Judy clutches her neck as she tries to smooth away the worry on her face. She offers a sympathetic smile, but I'm unable to return it.

I can't say for sure if Jason is one of *them* or not, but my gut is telling me he's safe. The Authorities would know John is dead. Why send someone searching if they know the truth? Or is that their ploy to get close to us? But John said his friend is from Carson City, so it has to be the same guy, right? I run a hand through my hair as I think of the plates from Nevada on the SUV that I keep seeing... maybe it's his car?

I stifle a groan as my head throbs with all the unanswered questions.

The one thing I know for sure is Judy isn't wrong; this is only the beginning.

Chapter Five

GEMMA

A CRAWL SPACE UNDER the basement shields Zay, Nora, and Elise. I shut the hatch as softly as possible, stacking plastic bins on top of it and closing the closet door behind me, further hiding them under the house.

I hope it's enough if anyone comes looking.

Wide eyed and ready to burst into tears, Amber waves me on to hurry up. *Not helpful.*

"Stay here," I order, but my voice comes out shaky, betraying me.

"No!" she pants, too afraid to actually yell at me. She tugs on my arm as I start up the basement stairs. Her terror knocks against my chest, begging to be let in. I grit my teeth, forcing it to roll off me instead.

"I have to go find Theo."

"He probably teleported out of here!"

"He wouldn't do that. Not without them." My heart thumps, fingertips threatening to spark. He would've come down here if there was a threat, so everything must be fine. I pry Amber's fingers off my arm before I accidentally hurt her, and her iron-like grip leaves red marks on my skin. "I'll be right back."

I contemplated shoving her through the hole in the floor with the others, but she's allowed to be here. Pushing her gently into the room, I close the door behind me.

As one last defense, I drag the wire cabinets in front of the door, wincing when the screeching bellows through the empty room. Dennis installed wheels on them to make them easier to move, and perfectly placed boxes of old, rusted tools are scattered on the shelves to make them look messy. A stranger would think it's junk and not worth inspecting.

The rest of the basement is filled with mundane stuff like our washer and dryer and boxes full of holiday decorations—all things you'd expect to find in a suburban home. Unlike the room I'm leaving behind, which is near rainforest level with Zay's recent increase in ability. That would be much harder to explain.

Once I hit the main floor, my stomach plummets. I probably shouldn't have locked Amber in there. If this *is* CPS and they find her with the wire cabinet blocking her exit, I'll have a lot more to explain than the plants.

I shake it off, focusing on the problem at hand. Muffled voices sound from the entryway, and I sneak over to the end of the hallway to eavesdrop.

"It's him," Theo's quiet voice drifts around the corner. "That's the guy who was at John's."

John's? Why didn't he tell me anyone showed up while he was there?

"Are you sure?" Dennis asks.

"Yeah, I met him after the fight. He said he was my dad's friend and is like us."

Judy's sharp inhale sends electricity down my spine. She's going to burst any second now.

"Why didn't you tell us?" Dennis sounds more confused than accusatory, but Judy's emotions are beating against me too hard to decipher exactly what's happening in his head.

Theo's hesitant voice is tough to make out, so I tiptoe even closer, biting my lip as I quell the guilt of listening like this. I shouldn't be spying, but it's only fair if they're keeping secrets that affect all of us.

"I figured there was no use scaring everyone if he was looking for just me. I lied to him and said I didn't know who John Goodwin was."

Dennis grunts, the noise oddly understanding.

I finally give up hiding and turn the corner, exasperated at being left out of whatever these two obviously spoke about before. Reading Judy's face, at least she seems as lost as I am. I stand beside her, glaring at the two before us.

I cross my arms, lessening my mood so I don't light up. "Either of you want to fill us in?"

Theo's jaw twitches, and his hand dips into his pocket. For his lighter, no doubt.

"John's partner is asking questions," Dennis begins, looking to Theo to add the rest.

He sighs, his free hand sliding through the light brown curls across his forehead. "He showed up at John's when Amber and I were there. Then he cornered me in the parking lot outside the gym the other night. He's different—like us—or so he says. But I'm not sure what he can do. My dad mentioned a friend to me before, and I think it's him. I just..."

"Don't trust him."

"Would you?" Theo asks me, his eyes widening. He's genuinely asking, and it cools the heat in my veins.

"I mean, maybe? It might be worth hearing him out." I glance at Judy.

She fidgets with her necklace, a business card clutched in her other hand. She scans Dennis's face, silently asking for his input.

"I don't think there's any reason to call him. But if he comes back, we'll invite him in and go from there. Sound all right to everyone?" The four of us glance at one another, no one else offering a better solution.

"I'll go let everyone out of the basement," I mumble but stop suddenly to face Dennis and Theo again. "But no more secrets," I demand. "I mean it this time."

NEARLY A WEEK HAS passed with no more incidents and no more appearances from Jason. We all breathe easier, assuming that at least one threat is behind us. We knew people would come sniffing around for John; now they have, and they've moved on.

Everything is fine. *It has to be*, I reassure myself.

Between Elise's ability to read auras and no one being able to keep their true feelings from me, we both agree that everyone is on a much calmer level. Even Theo's mood seems to be lighter, and he hasn't snuck out once. Plus, we've been talking more: his favorite snack is Hot Fries, his favorite beverage is Dr. Pepper, and his favorite band is The Strokes.

We haven't gone much deeper than our icebreaker questions, but I enjoy scratching the surface, asking each other needless daily inquiries to store the information away. It gives me butterflies whenever we steal a moment together like we're somehow beating the system—two not-so-normal teenagers who want very different things but are finding a way to make it work against all odds.

It feels rebellious.

Amber bursts into the kitchen, ripping the dish towel out of my hand.

"Hey!" I yell as she pushes me toward the stairs.

"Go put on better clothes."

I struggle out of her grasp, glancing down at my jeans and sweatshirt, nervously tucking a piece of hair behind my ear. "Why?" I frown. "I look fine. I'm only doing the dishes."

"Trust me. You want to look better." She pushes me again, forcing me up the stairs.

When we get to my room, I'm shocked to find Elise already there, tearing through my closet.

"Is this all you own?" Her voice is laced with disgust as if she wasn't recently living in a house that hardly had a roof. She throws another shirt onto my bed.

I snatch it, dangling it in the air to inspect the perfectly fine blouse. "Will someone tell me what's going on?"

"You're going on a date," Nora croons from the bedroom door, her hip leaned against the frame.

My stomach flips. *A date?*

"What do you mean?"

"A date, dummy. When two insufferable people seem to enjoy each other's company during a set activity, you've heard of them, right?" Elise mocks.

I make a face, fake laughing at Elise. "Yes, I've heard of them. I'm just confused about why *I'm* going on one."

"Why question a good thing?" Amber pipes in, shoving me into the chair at the shared vanity. She rips my hair tie out, letting my hair fall from the ponytail.

I wince. "Easy, there's a head attached."

"Sorry," she mumbles as she goes about fixing my curls. Nora finalizes the outfit as Elise spins my chair to work on my makeup.

My stomach continues to twist and turn in excitement, but there's also an underlying current of nerves.

Theo and I have never been on a real date before, but I don't need to tell them this because they already know—we've all been together since I met him in real life. So, instead, I ball my hands into fists and try to breathe through my nose.

I wish Olivia were here.

A swell of grief threatens to pull me under, and tears prick at my eyes. As the months pass, it doesn't seem to get any easier. The big moments—the big waves—still crush me. Like when I realize I'll never hear her laugh or listen to her sing her dumb drinking song again, but the smaller waves tend to be more deadly these days. They seem nonthreatening, but those little moments... Like how we'll never talk about boys again, or how she never got to meet Theo...

Elise's face softens for a moment, understanding pooling beneath the surface like she's reading my aura. "Close your eyes," she instructs.

If only Oli could see me now, going on an actual date with the boy from my dreams—*literally*. And I don't even have to hide who I am.

God, I miss her.

When I've been plucked, pampered, and all dolled up, the three of them inspect me like I'm a literal piece of work.

They wouldn't let any details slip on the date, and I nearly have to refrain from bouncing up and down as giddiness tangles in my chest.

Zay raps on the door, extending an arm. "I'm your escort, milady."

I smirk at him, giving the girls one last look. Amber gushes like *she's* the one going on the date. Nora beams; *did she see this coming?* Even Elise, with her arms crossed in front of her chest, gives me a stiff nod.

I link my elbow through Zay's, and he leads me through the house. Part of me expects him to guide me to the front door, but he heads in a different direction.

"Where are we going?" I inquire when he takes us into the kitchen.

Dennis is sitting at the counter with a mug in his hand, and Judy is pulling pizza rolls out of the oven.

"Oh, Gemma," she coos, dropping the pan on the stovetop. "You look wonderful."

"Uhm, thanks." I shift my weight as Dennis bobs his head in agreement. My cheeks heat from embarrassment as I try to avoid their eyes.

"Have fun!" Dennis calls out when Zay turns around and directs me to the back door.

A small gasp escapes me when the backyard comes into full view.

Chapter Six

Gemma

A FIRE PIT GLOWS in the center of the yard next to a blanket and picnic basket. A mound of pillows, the same ones from the drive-in, are propped next to the garden wall. Twinkle lights dangle from the tree branches, dotting the air with little beads of white.

Soft music drifts from the speaker on the back porch. I can't catch any of the lyrics, but the melody is sweet and fits the moment perfectly.

My eyes finally land on Theo, and I'm pretty sure I might melt right where I'm standing.

He's wearing Dennis's navy suit jacket, which is a bit too large for him, but he still made it his own style with a black shirt underneath. When he spots us, his face, lit by the reflection of the dancing flames, splits into an earth-shattering grin, and my nerves dissolve.

Zay bows, tipping an invisible hat, and dances back inside.

Theo and I lock eyes. My mouth drops open, but no words leave my tongue.

Taking a tentative step forward, my hands twist into my blue dress, the skirt ending just above my knees. Thankfully, Nora added a yellow cardigan, which combats the chill in the air.

He meets me halfway, grinning down at me. "You're beautiful."

"You're not too bad yourself," I finally muster. "What is all this?"

Theo spins around, holding out a hand to the blanket. "Our first date."

"First?"

"Hopefully, the first of many."

I follow him to the picnic basket, sitting down and smoothing my dress to cover my legs. The fire warms my back, but I angle my body so Theo can have the opposite side, furthest from the flames.

He pulls out two cans of soda and hands one to me. Clearing his throat, he quickly smiles before ducking his head in shame. "I'm sorry."

"For what?" I set the can aside, brows bunching.

"I should take you on a real date—"

The back door cracks open a foot, and Judy slides a plate of pizza rolls onto the deck before disappearing again.

Theo sighs as if that timely occurrence just made his point.

I sit up on my knees, capturing his face in my hands. "You have absolutely nothing to be sorry for. This is the sweetest thing anyone has ever done for me."

"You deserve so much more," he breathes.

I brush his lips lightly at first, then deepen the kiss. "This is all I need."

He breaks away, blinking as if deciding whether to believe me, before dashing to grab the pizza rolls. He brings the plate back over and sets it between us.

"Enjoy." His voice comes out quietly, like he's embarrassed he doesn't have more to offer.

I wish he were an empath right now so he could experience how lightheaded I am, understand how I could break down and cry tears of joy, and feel how madly in love I am.

Once we've finished eating, we talk for what feels like hours. We discuss music, movies, books, all things he knew before he ran away, and I try to catch him up as much as possible in one sitting. It's more complicated than I imagined. But we laugh until my sides ache and my face hurts from smiling.

"Dance with me?" he asks, and heat sweeps through my body.

I place my hand in his, and he pulls me up, drawing me into his arms as we sway to a song I've never heard before, but it's my new favorite song.

My cheek rests against his sternum, and I close my eyes, listening to the rhythm of his heart. I could live in this moment forever.

His chest rumbles when he whispers, "If you could relive one day, what would it be?"

I tip my head back to get a better look at him, and he watches me with such curiosity it's hard not to blurt out *the day I met you*. But my thoughts turn down a dark path, my heart constricting when I think of homecoming.

"I'd save Olivia."

His body tenses, and he doesn't speak for a long moment. He then squeezes my hand. "Sorry," he murmurs. "I should have worded that better. I think we'd both go for the obvious choice, so what day would you relive *outside* of that?"

I bite the inside of my cheek, going through the rolodex of memories that might be worth reliving, but nothing comes to mind. I exhale, giving up for now.

"You first," I say, nuzzling back into his chest.

He chuckles but continues to rub his thumb gently on my hand. "That's not fair."

"I'm thinking," I argue. "You've had more time to think about your answer."

Theo grunts, bringing a smile to my lips. I squeeze him tighter when he swallows a few times, uncertainty flowing out of him like he's gathering the courage to speak. Maybe he doesn't have a happy answer for this, either.

Finally, he says, "Not long before, uh, you know. Our parents took us to the fair." He pauses, his hand tightening on mine. "It probably doesn't sound like much, but the four of us doing anything was a rarity those days. My dad was always working the night shift, and my mom..." His voice trails off.

I wrap my arms around his neck, gazing up at him, silently urging him to continue.

"Well, anyway, there we were. Riley and I played games all day and ate disgusting fair food; it was great. I can still picture my parents following at a leisurely pace, holding hands as Riley and I bounced from one stall to another. I tried to act like I was too cool for my little sister most of the time, but that day was different. We were getting along. No sibling rivalry. No age difference. We were just having a blast."

His lips twitch, a slight grin flashing as his eyes go distant before he's fully transported back into the past. We stop swaying, and I hold my breath, waiting for him to continue.

"After the sun set, our mom decided it was time to get going, but we wanted to go on one more ride. Just one more. Riley begged and begged, so our parents finally relented. We chose the Ferris Wheel."

Theo's face pales a little in the firelight, and my heart skips a beat from his mixed emotions pouring out with this memory.

"We got stuck at the top," he says with a harsh laugh. "It was funny at first. I thought I could see the entire city up there. It turns out I couldn't, but the lights were mesmerizing. I'd never seen something so cool before. I felt like I was on top of the world.

"Well, five minutes turned into ten, and ten eventually turned into a half hour. By the hour mark, my parents were at it. I knew they'd argue sometimes. I would try to shield Riley from it, but they'd always fight in their bedroom, thinking the walls were soundproof or something; I don't know.

"Anyway, up there on the Ferris Wheel, my mom told my dad she wanted a divorce."

I blow out the air trapped in my chest.

"I'd never seen my dad so stricken before. I want to say he saw it coming, but I really don't think he did. At that moment, he seemed so... small. Suddenly, being on top of the world didn't seem as spectacular.

"Riley started crying, which made things even more awkward. I'm pretty sure both my dad and I wanted to crawl right out of that basket and risk the climb down. Of course, we had no choice but to stay, so we all sat silently. For another fifteen minutes."

"I'm so sorry," I breathe. "What happened after you got home?"

He shrugs. "Nothing. It was like the fight never happened. Then, a few months later, Riley burned down the place."

I gape, not knowing how to proceed. There's really no other way to ask what I'm about to, so I take a step back, clutching his hand in mine.

"Why would you want to relive that day?"

His eyes trail the fence, focusing on the twinkle lights before he lifts a shoulder. "I never would have gotten on the Ferris Wheel."

Chapter Seven

Ash sits on an unused tongue, crusted blood coating the inside of an arid mouth.

The tang of iron is long gone.

Lungs inflate but hardly move. On a shallow inhale, a rush of dirt clogs an airway, and wet earth loosens around a macerated body.

Gritty soil catches between hollow teeth, tastebuds receiving a sour lashing.

Somehow, it brings the memory of rain.

Chapter Eight

Gemma

"It's a pizza place," Amber deadpans. She stares at Theo so intently that I have to force myself not to laugh.

"Your point?" He raises an eyebrow, challenging her.

She rolls her eyes, throwing down the metaphorical gauntlet. "My point is I think you're losing it."

He sighs, leaning back in his chair at the dining room table. I know what he *wants* to say—all the evidence he has shows he's not actually imagining things, but he already kept information to himself so he wouldn't scare her. He has no argument if he doesn't want to reveal the full truth to her.

I can see the wheels spinning in his head to formulate a different rebuttal, but I chime in to break up their staring contest.

"Nothing happened at the drive-in, right? We can go pick up pizza this one time."

It's Judy's birthday today, and we're *trying* to thank her for everything she's done for us lately. Taking in four extra kids is no small feat. So, Zay, Theo, and I are on food duty. Elise and Nora—an unfortunate pairing on Nora's part—already went to get the cake, smartly sneaking out of the house without Theo noticing so they didn't get stuck going around and around like this.

And once she's done beating up Theo with her sass, Amber will beg Judy to run to the store to get her out of the house long enough for Dennis to decorate and for all of us to get back home with the food.

Judy is currently in the backyard reading, so we need to move *now* so Amber can enact her plan. We've already wasted too much time, and the pizza we called for will be ready soon.

"All I'm saying is, why can't we get the food delivered?" Theo purses his lips, but they quiver like he's fighting back a grin when Amber throws her arms up, exasperated.

"I think that'd ruin the surprise part," Zay says. He already has his shoes and jacket on, ready to go.

"I think Judy can live without the surprise," Theo argues.

"You don't have to come," I say innocently, shrugging as I stand. "Zay and I can handle pizza pickup by ourselves. It would be easier if we just teleported there, but"—I let out an exaggerated sigh—"I guess we'll just walk. Tacking on *all* that exposure time..."

"Right," Theo scoffs as he shakes his head in defeat. "Like I'd ever let you two go alone. It's bad enough that the others already escaped without me."

I give him a victorious smile, hugging him as he reluctantly gets out of his chair.

"Yeah, yeah. Let's get this over with," he says, even though he's smiling, too.

I CATCH THEO'S EYE from where he's sitting in the corner of the pizzeria with Zay and give him a coy smile. The corner of his mouth lifts when he provides a conspiratorial wink like he knows I'm thinking about our date. Zay's too busy folding the napkins into poor attempts at origami to notice our flirting.

Theo bites his lip, nearly healed from his fight, to refrain from laughing, and my knees weaken. After his confession last night, I was too absorbed in wanting to stitch up any of his open emotional wounds that I'd given him an official IOU for my backup answer on what day I'd like to relive. I distracted him as best I could, which led to a very long make-out session until Dennis broke us up, informing us our date was over.

I resist squirming, mainly from the memory of being humiliated when we were busted, but also from the feeling of Theo's soft lips against mine...

I hope she comes out with our pizza soon so I don't combust on the spot.

The twenty-minute wait at the pizza shop has put us even more behind schedule, but with Theo teleporting us back home, we should be there in no time.

And hopefully, the pizza holds up well in the void.

If not, then, well, I don't know what we'll tell them. We ordered light on the toppings, just in case.

Zay holds up his... swan? Successfully diverting Theo's attention and, unfortunately—or fortunately, depending on how you look at it—his gaze. Thankfully, the rest of the place is empty because I can only imagine how red my cheeks are when I catch myself twirling my hair, daydreaming again about last night. His hands on my hips, the tattoos covering old scars trailing up his arms...

I still can't believe he exists.

For so long, I thought he was a figment of my imagination.

But now he's here, and as irritating as he can be in person when we disagree on certain matters, or when he puts up such a stink on picking up pizza, of all the mundane things, he's still here with me.

Alive—real.

I'm never letting him go.

The cashier drops three large pizza boxes onto the counter, ripping me from my thoughts. The lady stabs the cash register with a stubby finger—her black nail polish chipped, nails bitten down into jagged edges. Her hands shake as she rings up the total, and she glances over her shoulder to the kitchen every few seconds, where the staff is currently yelling at each other.

She swipes her sweaty bangs out of her face, smudging her thick eyeliner in the process, giving her an even more disheveled look. Nerves crash against me, concern trickling into my bones, but I can't figure out why this woman is in so much despair.

A loud *crash*, like a pan falling in the kitchen, startles us both as we jump in unison.

I force a weak laugh as I hand over the cash Dennis gave me, hoping to leave this place—and her feelings—as soon as possible.

The lady disappears into the kitchen without so much as a "Have a nice day," practically throwing the change onto the counter. Theo and Zay come up behind me as I scowl, trying to collect all the money.

"Everything okay?" Theo asks.

I'm about to answer when Zay lifts a box, frowning. Theo follows suit and opens his. It's empty.

"What?" I snap, anger flaring. What kind of sick joke—

The windows in front of the shop explode, glass spraying the dining area. I drop to the ground, covering my head as bullets pierce through the air, lodging in the wall behind us. Zay's on his hands and knees, crawling behind the counter. Theo pushes him forward with one arm while the other is outstretched, reaching for me.

But we're too far away from one another.

"Go!" I yell at him, pleading for him to follow Zay.

My hands spark to life, fear vibrating through every inch of me. I back up further, stuffing myself between the counter and their pop machine as the onslaught continues. A stray bullet hits the soft drinks, and sticky, syrupy liquid flows to the ground.

I make myself as small as possible.

If I can get to the other side of the counter, I can follow them into the kitchen and, ideally, to a back door. I scan the air above me, unable to go up and over. I'd be in their direct line of fire.

Silence descends for a split second—not enough time to think the attack is over but long enough that it feels like everything is in slow motion. The glass littering the ground reflects the outside light, blinding me as I hold a hand up to shield my eyes.

This has to be the Authorities.

They aren't taking chances this time. They want us dead.

Theo's back slams into the counter as he covers his head when the firing begins again; a bullet hole appears inches above his hair.

"I'll catch up!" I scream. "Just go!"

If there's anyone strong enough to survive this, it's me. I might not be in complete control of my abilities, but I'm no longer a helpless little girl, either.

His haunted gaze searches my face, his concern worming into me as much as my own for him. Our eyes meet, the world standing still for a few bated breaths. My heart breaks as I read the alarm all over his face. I forced him to come here. He was right all along.

I nod to reassure him. "I'm right behind you," I breathe the promise.

Hopefully, it's one I can keep.

Theo's jaw twitches, eyelids fluttering when he ducks out of view. My hands are fully engulfed now, but no amount of purple flame will stop a bullet. I can at least slow them down, though.

I pull myself up off the ground, crouching, and prepare to run. I won't wait this time. They'll have to stop shooting eventually. They'll come to check inside, probably hoping they'll find our decimated bodies and collect us to do who knows what.

How are they going to explain this to everyone? A robbery gone wrong? Was the cashier in on it? Was she stalling, her shaky hands leading to our inevitable death? Did the screaming in the kitchen come from people defending us, or were they angry that they were caught up in all this?

And most importantly, will Judy and Dennis ever learn the truth?

If this goes wrong, Amber will lose another sister. My heart aches. Maybe I can come back as a ghost, too.

No. Stop.

We're going to make it out of this.

When the Authorities step inside, I'll be ready for them.

I count my breaths, stilling my mind.

I can control this.

When the moment finally comes, I shoot to my feet, keeping the sticky soda machine to my side, shielding me. Glass crunches as one, two, three, and now four people rush in. Their heartbeats drum in my ears, all fluttering over one another.

Only one remains steady and calm.

My fingers curl, but I aim for the lights above us instead of targeting them.

I surge all my pent-up energy into the electrical system, and the bulbs explode, sparks showering like snow as I make a break for it. I slide around the corner, ignoring the sting as glass bites into my arms, legs, and face.

Bursting into the kitchen, I pray there's actually a door back here and I didn't just trap myself further. But then I spot Theo heading back inside, coming back for *me*.

His eyes are wide and wild, but the slightest hint of relief shines through when he notices me.

Their raging heartbeats don't quiet, though. They're a second behind. I turn, throwing both arms out, releasing a scream as I focus on the rest of the electricity in the place. Anything I can possibly tap into and direct where to go.

The lightbulbs out front are already shattered, but a violent strike of electricity shakes through the pendant above the counter, detaching it from the ceiling. The live wire glides to the wet floor, and for a split second, it reminds me of a slow, slithering snake.

I almost shout out a warning, but the words don't pass my lips. They're caught in my throat as the horror sinks in. Our feet may be dry in here...

"Theo!" Zay cries from outside, his voice cutting out from the terror.

Theo spins on his heel, yelling at me to hurry.

I stumble backward, unable to tear my gaze away from the kitchen door and the fire beyond it, now spreading along the floor and engulfing the curtains. Part of me wants to give up right then and there. My legs shake, the reality seeping the strength out of my muscles.

Is it always going to be like this?

Our lives or theirs?

Incoherent shouts bellow from outside, slowly waking me out of my stupor; I turn my back on the fire, the smoke trailing behind me—*deal with the rest of the Authorities now and my warring emotions later.*

But those four pulses no longer follow.

The only heartbeat haunting me now is my own.

The sun bakes down on us, an utter contrast to the devastation in our midst. How can the sun shine so brightly when our lives are slipping through our fingers?

I cough, choking down fresh air. There's too much going on, and I need a moment to *think*, to process what's mine and what's not.

Zay's panic.

Theo's anger.

The Authorities give off a mix of disgust, hatred, and disdain.

It all blurs together, raging inside me, and my chest is ready to burst. I've already killed four. How many more before we're safe?

But I don't have time to think about that right now.

My ribs are going to splinter either from smoke inhalation or the panic punching its way through my sternum. If I don't release more of this energy soon, I don't know what kind of catastrophe I'll cause.

The parking lot out back is surrounded by nondescript cars pointing in every direction. They sent way more than last time, probably because we escaped.

They won't make that mistake again.

Zay's on his knees, hands behind his head, with a man dressed in all black standing behind him. A helmet shields most of his face, hiding his identity; only his eyes, two dark pits, remain uncovered. He has a gun aimed in Zay's general direction but focuses on getting the cuffs off his belt.

My heart climbs into my throat... They want to take Zay alive, and my mind seizes on Riley and what happened to her. *No.* This can't be happening.

Zay twists, and with the movement, an unnatural cloud of gravel swirls with him, blinding the stranger. While distracted, Theo tackles him to the ground, completely ignoring that there are at least twenty more officers around us. He punches him once, doing no lasting damage as he makes contact with the helmet, but it gives him enough time to reach over, grab Zay's shaking body, and disappear.

I exhale. They're out. They're safe. Theo did it.

But that doesn't help *me* right now.

The transformers surrounding the parking lot spark, exploding when the pressure in my chest snaps. There are so many pipelines *begging* to be siphoned. I can drain the life out of any of them. And I want to. I want to escape. I want—

But that would kill even more.

I can't...

I won't let them turn me into a monster.

Someone charges me from behind, shoving me to the ground. I grab their arm, twisting to take them down with me. Their bones shatter beneath my touch, and they scream out in pain. Another races at me from the front, and I hold out a lit hand, burning their face. They scramble backward, clutching their boiling skin, and the hand-shaped mark I left on Nora's chest shutters into view in my brain.

Two more come at me, and the onslaught continues.

I tune out their screams, the crunching of bones, the sizzling of skin. If I let it all in, I'll die. If they don't kill me, the guilt will. It's already trying to tear me in two.

It's my life or theirs.

It's my life or theirs.

It's my life or theirs.

I repeat the mantra so I don't give up. Keep fighting. Keep moving. Live another day. More and more officers barrel toward me, but now they form a half circle. They've finally learned they can't penetrate the purple glow that's fully engulfed me.

Guns are drawn, but no one shoots.

They want me alive, too. The realization fills my mind with horrific possibilities. Will they make me into someone like Riley?

I back against the wall, the brick biting through my shirt, but I hardly register the pain. I focus on their faces, my vision blurring the harder I try.

I can't keep this up; I need to draw more energy from somewhere...

I need...

My knees buckle, and the last thing I see is a man flipping over a car.

Chapter Nine

GEMMA

I startle awake, gasping for air, my throat parched. "Theo!"

"Who's Theo?" an unfamiliar voice asks.

I cringe, sitting up so quickly that my head spins.

"Easy now," he continues. His voice is smooth, like velvet.

I glance around, but no one is there. I don't even know where I am. Darkness drapes around me, as suffocating as a damp wool blanket. Various shapes sharpen around me: shelves lined with indiscernible objects.

My pulse buzzes as my hands spark to life again.

"That's a cool trick. I've honestly never seen anything like it before."

"Who are you?"

A head pops out from behind a shelf, lit by a flashlight that casts frightening shadows across hollow cheeks. "You blew out the whole town, by the way. It's a total power outage. I didn't think that kind of power was possible. I'm in awe, truly." A boy my age with light hair buzzed close to his head beams at me like he's proud of my accomplishment. "Caleb Mitchell." He nods toward someone I can't see who's further in the back of the room. "Asher Hicks."

"Who are you?" I repeat. "Where's Theo and Zay?"

"Don't worry; they're probably fine."

My heart jolts, my hands flaring. "Probably?"

Caleb tilts his head back, giving an overelaborate "Relaaax." Then he smirks, gesturing outside. "My friends have *probably* caught up to them by now."

Who are his friends? Who are any of these people? And where am I? The tingling in my fingertips ebbs away as I cradle my face, taking deep breaths to steady myself. Caleb doesn't give off any upsetting vibes; if anything, he seems indifferent to the entire ordeal, which is oddly calming. *How is he not affected by my glowing hands?*

What happened?

We were getting pizza, and then gunshots, and... I squeeze my eyes shut. It seemed like they were shooting to kill at first but then they tried capturing Zay and me. What was the plan? Plan A to kill, plan B to kidnap if we were weak enough?

It doesn't make any sense.

Would they have shot and killed Theo if they caught him?

My stomach lurches, saliva filling my mouth, and I almost throw up my breakfast.

I'm unable to do anything but focus on the floor and breathe through my nose, trying to gain the strength to leave and find the others.

"Are you with them?" I ask.

"Who?" Caleb busies himself with collecting things off shelves. "The Authorities?"

A deep laugh coughs out in the distance, and my spine straightens.

"That's a little insulting, but I suppose it's a fair question. No, we're not with them. We did save you, you know," Caleb says.

I frown as more puzzle pieces fit together. Everything is slightly fuzzy, but the picture becomes clearer with each passing second... Gunshots, electricity, fire...

Bones cracking. The burns.

Oh no...

A new guy, built like a tank, enters the room carrying a bin of who knows what. He's on the shorter side, squat, and has little to no neck. His hair is also cropped close to his head but much darker than Caleb's, and he has a dark beard.

His thick arms catch my attention, and the remaining memories surge back. "I-it's you," I sputter. "You flipped a car!"

Asher, or at least, who I presume is Asher, bows his head. He drops the container in front of Caleb as he inspects its contents.

There are so many questions I want to ask, but I need to find Theo and Zay and make sure they're okay. And to not think about what I did to those people... how easy it came.

They were trying to kill you.

I stand, shaking my head to clear the fog and brush the dirt off my trembling hands, which are otherwise unmarked from the fight. I finally see we're in the backroom of a store, although I'm unsure which one; I can't read any of the boxes to help narrow down where we are.

"Thanks for the save, but I have to go."

I spot the exit sign still glowing red, even in the blackout, but Caleb races over, blocking the way with his arm when I make it a few steps. "What's the rush?"

"I have to go find my friends." To make sure they're alive and explain to Judy and Dennis how... My thoughts abruptly change tracks, speeding out of control. What if I took someone's sister? Just like how Oli was taken from me. How am I going to tell Theo what I've done? For all I know, that could have been Riley in there.

I choke down the bile crawling back up my throat.

"Your friends will be brought here."

My eyes fill with tears. "But you said..."

Caleb furrows his brow, opening his mouth like he's going to address my reaction, but decides against it. Then he gives an exaggerated sigh. "Are you good?"

I bite my lip, not wanting to answer. But I'll probably never see him again, so who cares if he judges me? I need to voice what I've done and get it out in the open. The guilt already chews on my insides, and as much as I don't want to say it aloud, I need to. I need to process what I've done. Or at least try to. These powers... I'm a danger to everyone.

"I killed some of them," I whisper.

"The Authorities? Nah, I mean, you messed them up pretty good, but—"

"Not outside. Inside... before I got out."

"Oh," Caleb's mouth quirks upward. "That's fine."

"*Fine*?" I hiss. "I just killed those people without a second thought."

"Your life or theirs, baby."

I repress a shiver as he repeats the words I'd already used to try to console myself.

Does that make it right? Does the end justify the means?

I rub a hand across my forehead, suppressing the mounting pressure to get back on task. His bluntness only reinforces that I need to find the others and make sure they're safe.

"Trust me, we're good at what we do." He trails back to the discarded bin Asher brought him, changing topics like I didn't just admit a terrible sin. "My team will be able to spot your friends anywhere."

Team? My throat threatens to close, but I dash the tears away with the palms of my hands, reigning it in. "How many of you are there?"

"In general, or here in Willow?"

I struggle to swallow. I've wanted to find others like us all this time, and now they've found us. That can't be a coincidence, but I might as well start small.

"Here."

"Five. Well, six, but we didn't come with the one already here."

Jason? My mind drifts back to Theo explaining everything he knew about John's partner.

"I guess you make seven. Theo and Zay are mutants, too, no? I'm guessing they are, or the Authorities wouldn't have been so interested in you guys, so that'd be nine... Got any more friends?"

I sit on the edge of a desk, my mind in a tailspin. Six. There are six more of us. Wait—

"What do you mean by *mutants*?"

Caleb stops pulling items out and bends down so he's at eye level with me.

"Sweetheart, you know your hands glow, right? That's not exactly normal."

My lips press into a hard line. "Yeah, thanks. I got that. I didn't know there was a word..." I trail off, my mind still whirring with the idea that there are so many more of us. I had hoped there were, but with this new proof... it's hard to think straight. "How many... *mutants*... are there?"

"Oh, I'm not qualified to answer that." He resumes pulling items out, including pliers, batteries, and multiple first aid kits.

"Then why did you ask me?"

Caleb ponders while looking at the wall, then shrugs, tossing a bungee cord to the side. "Touché."

My eyes flicker around the dark room now that I'm finally calm enough to take in the area. It's hard to see much, but the faint glow from Caleb's—and now Asher's—flashlights light up a box with a graphic of a toilet. I blink before putting two and two together.

No wonder he has so many tools.

"Why are we in a hardware shop?"

"Because it was the nearest place that was closed, and we needed supplies."

"Supplies?"

"You sure do ask a lot of questions, don't you?" Caleb's apathy hasn't faltered, and thankfully, he's not annoyed by my questions, but he doesn't bother answering them either. He splits everything into piles like he's taking inventory as Asher, ever so silent, starts filling a backpack.

Even though I could have been stuck with two way more sinister people who meant to harm me, that doesn't mean I can idly sit by and watch them pack stolen items. More importantly, Theo and Zay could still be in danger and need me.

I make for the door again. "I really need to go. I can't just sit here and wait for your friends to show up."

"Wait!"

I pause, hand resting on the handle.

"You can come with us."

"Come with you?"

"Yeah." Caleb shrugs like it's no big deal. "There's plenty of space. All the mutants you can think of to pester with your questions."

I shake my head. It's unbelievable. All of this is happening so fast. It's exactly what I wanted, but I can't. Not now. Not without knowing where the others are or while I'm worrying about everyone's safety.

"I can't."

Caleb bites his lip, rocking back on his heels. He's not much taller than me—only by a handful of inches. I can take him, even though I shouldn't have to. He seems more eager than menacing.

Still, I can't take any chances if he blocks my way out.

I'm nearly face to face with him now; with Theo, I barely hit his shoulder.

Ugh. *Theo*. Please be okay.

My heart skips a beat, tears burning behind my eyes again.

"If we can find you, *they* can find you," Caleb interrupts my spiraling. He pulls out a card with *Bridlewood Motel* stamped on the front. "We're staying there until morning. If you change your mind, you know where to find me."

I grab the card, but Caleb doesn't let go. Not at first. We both stand there, holding onto opposite edges like idiots. I wrench it from his grasp, and as I push on the handle, the door whips open, the sunlight cascading inside. I stumble directly into a girl with dark, umber-brown skin and midnight-blue strands twisted into her dark braids. She steadies me as I apologize for bulldozing right into her.

She gives a soft, understanding smile as if she somehow knows what I've been through. *Who knows, maybe she does.*

"I believe I have who you're looking for." She steps to the side, holding the door open as Theo rounds it. His shoulders are rigid until he sees me, and I can feel the weight lifting from him.

I crush myself against him, unleashing the tears I've desperately tried to hold back. "Where's Zay?"

"I'm here," he calls, just a step behind Theo.

As hard as it is, I peel myself away and tackle Zay next. "Oh my god. I was so worried. I saw you two disappear, but then..." I trail off, squeezing him, before swinging back to Theo.

I collapse into his arms, and he kisses my head before seemingly remembering we're not alone. He eyes Caleb and Asher—the latter still lurking in the background, working on filling another backpack like he doesn't want to intrude on the reunion.

There's more of us than I could have ever imagined. But the worst part? It looks like Theo was right.

The Authorities do know where we are—and I've just openly killed four of them.

Chapter Ten

THEO

Eight of us are in a circle, the dark room lit by flashlights. Apparently, between Simone Jones's sonic hearing and Esha Chopra's ability to *see* powers, they were able to locate Zay and me within seconds of us teleporting a couple of streets over. I didn't want to risk going too far in hopes of jumping back to Gemma, but before I knew what was happening, I couldn't teleport at all.

That was thanks to Louis Zhang, the last of the trio who showed up to *rescue* us.

He's a shield and can block powers.

I certainly don't like *that*.

They said it was safer this way, that Gemma was fine, and they'd take me to her. We didn't really have a choice but to follow because of the magical-like barrier they had around us.

How far would I need to be away from Louis to regain my ability? Or would I have to knock him out completely? He's a few inches shorter than me and looks younger, too. He's undoubtedly smaller in build. So, it probably wouldn't be too hard.

I accidentally clench Gemma's hand even tighter, and she wiggles her fingers to remind me to ease up.

"How did you get out?" I ask Gemma after all the introductions, including ours, have been made.

She gives a quizzical glance at Caleb. "I don't even know. I..."

"Fainted?" he suggests.

Esha studies Gemma, frowning slightly like she's trying to figure out a puzzle, and my body automatically tenses. *What does she see?*

Gemma's mouth drops open, panic spasming across her face. "I don't know what happened," she eventually says, and it's hard not to hear the double meaning. She doesn't know how she was saved and doesn't know why she fainted.

She looks up at me, her eyes darting frantically between me and the rest of the group.

"We'll talk about it later," I whisper, edging closer to Zay.

I don't know how to test if Louis has his shield up, but if Esha can read Gemma, I'm going to guess he let his guard down.

We might be able to jump.

Would they follow us?

Zay's been silent this entire time, but considering he was just on the wrong end of a gun, I don't blame him. We need to get back to the house, regroup, and move... somewhere.

Hell, I don't even know.

Caleb sits on the corner of a desk, twirling a set of keys around his finger. "Asher here distracted the Authorities while I was able to get Gemma out."

"Thanks," Gemma mumbles, turning so she's closer to me.

Caleb straightens, fixing his jacket collar. "Like I was telling Gemma before, we can help you."

"With what?" I ask.

"You can come with us," he answers as if that's somehow magically helpful in itself.

"No, thanks."

"The Authorities aren't going to leave you alone."

"We've got it covered," I respond, even though I'm not sure we do. Nevertheless, this group showing up at the same time as the Authorities makes me question everything they're saying. "Zay"—I incline my head to the door—"let's go."

With a weak smile, he waves goodbye to everyone. We make it to the door unobstructed, and part of me is shocked they're letting us leave this easily.

Caleb's parting words hit home, though, because just before the door closes, I catch, "You know where to find us when that changes."

WHEN WE MAKE IT back to the house, Gemma breaks her hold and bolts for the open door.

"No!" I yank her back, but she slips through my fingers. Her hands are already lit up when she bursts inside. I yell at Zay to stay outside but second-guess it and drag him along. He's better with me than outside alone, I guess. Who knows where the Authorities could be after losing us a second time?

My body feels like dead weight when we cross the threshold.

The entire place has been destroyed.

Picture frames knocked off the mantel, an end table flipped over, and broken glass spans from here to the kitchen. It's like a tornado tore through the house. My breathing slows, and my vision doubles as I take in the destruction.

"Nora?" Zay cries out, running into the kitchen. He comes out with Dennis's wallet, tears filling his eyes.

"Zay." My voice comes out thick when it finally returns. *Think.* We had a plan for this, but it fails to come to me right away. My thoughts are too scrambled to remember anything we've planned for. He stares at me, panic creasing across every inch of his face as he waits for instructions. How vulnerable he looks reminds me of Amber at John's house not too long ago, right before Jason showed up here, and it jogs something loose. "Go check downstairs."

He dashes down the hallway as Gemma turns in a circle, her purple hands still lit.

I take deep breaths, crossing the room in an instant, holding her face in my hands. "Look at me."

Her violet eyes glow brighter and brighter. The television turns on, static blaring through the room, the blender screeches from the kitchen, and all the lights flicker.

She's losing control, and if I'm being honest, so am I.

"Gem, we'll find them. Okay? Just breathe."

If they were dead, there would be bodies. It'd look like a home invasion and not have this level of destruction—it would only appear as a tragic event. But there are no bodies. *Riley*—my hands burn, fingers going numb as invisible smoke fills my lungs.

I've learned. I know better now. If there's no body, there's a chance.

"Breathe," I say again, and I don't know if it's for Gemma or myself. "Breathe."

Breathe.

"I can't lose them," she croaks out.

"You won't." The world is off balance as if the rug has been pulled out from under me. Nora, Amber... *Elise*. Judy and Dennis are innocent in all this. They don't have powers. They just took us in—

They can't *all* be gone.

A shudder runs through me as we stare at one another, neither offering solace, but at least the appliances have all turned off.

"Theo!" Zay calls. "Downstairs!"

We break for the basement at the same time, and I'm glad Gemma is behind me because my legs almost give out, and I have to catch myself from falling when I spot Amber wrapped around Zay like a vine.

"Gemma!" she cries, releasing Zay to run to her.

"What happened?" Gemma's tears are flowing now, her hands no longer glowing.

Nora climbs out of the crawlspace, Elise shortly behind.

Breathing comes a little easier. They're alive. But that leaves...

"That is the last time you leave the three of us with no defensive powers by ourselves." Elise jabs me in the chest with a finger.

"Where's Judy and Dennis?" Gemma asks.

Elise focuses on her shaking hands, peeling skin from a fresh cut, and Nora picks at her lip, unable to make eye contact. Her lip is bleeding; she's been at it a while. My stomach is in a free fall, and I expect to hear the worst.

"They're gone," Amber whimpers. "The Authorities took them."

∗ ∗ ∗

WE'VE MADE IT UP from the basement, only to sit in stunned silence around the dining room table. I can tell from how everyone gazes at me every so often that they're waiting for me to decide what to do next. But I have no solution.

Before, we'd be on the road by now. We'd move on. Find a new place.

Simple.

But now?

We've never had to deal with someone being taken hostage. Judy and Dennis took the rest of us in when they didn't have to. And look at where that found them.

"We should go find Caleb and the others," Gemma states, rushing into the room with a backpack already on.

"No." I shake my head. "You can't be serious. For all we know, they're in on it."

"Why would they save us just to take Judy and Dennis?" she argues. "It doesn't make sense."

"Why were they here at the same time the Authorities were?"

"I don't know," she admits. "But we have to do something. I can't sit here. They're my *family*."

"I know." I reach out a hand, lying it on the table to bridge the distance. "I'm not saying we don't go after them. I'm saying we should be smart about it. Make a plan before we try to take down the people who very nearly killed us today."

She stares at my outstretched hand for a moment, and in that remarkably long second, I don't think she's going to take it.

But she finally relents, sighing, placing her hand in mine as she sits down. "I'm worried."

"We all are. But we'll figure it out. I think the first step is to leave here as soon as possible."

"Where will we go?" Elise asks.

"To John's," Amber states so matter-of-factly it's hard to believe she's only fourteen. "He has information there. A list of people who can help."

"Is he…?" Zay glances at me and then at the empty walls.

Amber shakes her head. "No, but he already showed us when we were at his house."

"So, we go to your dad's." Gemma's leg bounces like she might get up and run out ahead of us.

I run a finger along the scratches on the old wooden table. How many foster kids have sat here before eating breakfast? Laughing with Dennis? Being loved by Judy? It isn't fair.

None of this is fair.

"I vote yes," Zay says, even though we're not taking a stupid vote.

"I'm in," Elise agrees.

Nora chimes in with, "Me, too."

Amber quietly nods.

Determination bats away any uncertainty of moving forward; there's a time to run and a time to hide, and right now, I need to buck up and bring Judy and Dennis home.

"Okay," I agree. "The Authorities will probably be watching his place, too, so we need to be smart. Everyone go pack." When nearly everyone goes to stand, I add, "Amber, pack what you *need* to."

She's never had to run before. I resist the urge to throw something against the wall in frustration that she now has to.

Gemma holds out a hand to her. "Here, I'll help you. I'm already packed."

The stillness is unsettling. Soon, Nora and I are left alone, momentarily lost in the unnerving quiet. Before now, these walls have only heard laughter and the occasional bickering of children.

Nora breaks the silence first. "I'm so sorry."

I glance over at her, a wicked headache building in the middle of my forehead from exhaustion. "For what?"

"I should have seen them coming. I should have seen Judy and Dennis—"

"Hey." I turn my chair to face her, touching her shoulder. "This isn't your fault."

"Maybe I could have seen them, though, if this stupid girl wasn't always in my head! All I see is *her*."

"The one in the hospital bed?"

Nora nods, her eyes fixed on the table.

Nora's visions have been getting stronger lately, becoming more physical. Sometimes, she even collapses when they're over. But even though they seem more visceral to her, she still can't control what she sees. It's not her fault Judy and Dennis's future didn't come to her.

"We'll figure everything out, okay? We just need to decide on our next steps for now; one thing at a time."

She doesn't answer me but gets up to go pack as well, and I drop my head back against the chair, closing my eyes. I should move, too, but my body feels like it's filled with lead. I need another moment before we're back in that lifestyle—back to running all the time.

How did everything get so messed up so quickly?

I shouldn't be surprised. But things were calm for once. I thought—*hoped*—that after Jason stopped looking for John, we'd be in the clear, at least for a little while.

I don't know what to do now.

I don't know where to go next or how to get them back.

All I know is we can't stay here.

Caleb's voice haunts me: *You know where to find us when that changes.* Did he know this was coming? I don't know what his power is or Asher's. If they're anything like Nora, they could have seen it coming. *But why not warn us?*

I groan, scrubbing my hands over my face, my thoughts torn on who this new group could be. *They're like us*, I remind myself. Maybe Gemma's right; maybe we should go looking for them. But I also can't help feeling like adding *more* of a target on our back is the last thing we should be doing. It's hard enough hiding six kids with powers. Why add five more? Why not stand outside with signs, letting the Authorities know where we all are instead?

The argument in my head continues. Is there strength in numbers? Or are we better off hiding with fewer people to worry about?

And Esha's hungry eyes on Gemma; it's like she somehow knows she's different from the rest of us—the only one of us not born with their ability.

What does she see when she looks at her?

WELL, THE GOOD NEWS is I can take two people at a time to John's house without ending up in another town.

Dennis was right. I'm getting stronger. However, I won't be happy until I can transfer all six of us at once—especially now that so many new players are on the board.

Once everyone is at John's, we keep the lights off and stay away from the windows in case the Authorities are watching here, too.

Thankfully, blackout curtains already cover the windows, but Zay still turns the television around to face the wall, afraid the light could shine through somehow. He messes with the antennas until a news anchor appears and then sits against the wall with it on mute.

A boil-water advisory flashes in red, and the news ticker reading "DO NOT DRINK ANY TAP WATER" crawls across the bottom of the screen. The captions mention global warming, and how other natural disasters are causing more spikes in radiation throughout the country.

We haven't had much time to process anything, let alone the world falling apart around us. But right now, I'm more worried about what happened today.

I sigh as I sit on the ground next to him. "You all right?"

He bobs his head but doesn't elaborate.

"It's okay if you're not..."

His gaze cuts to mine, then he squints at the screen again, his shoulders bunching. I don't press him on it, but I don't leave him, either.

"For a second, I thought—" Zay says minutes later, not taking his eyes off the television. More silence stretches, but his shoulders finally relax. "Thanks for getting me out of there."

"Always."

I bump my arm into him, and his smile returns as he catches himself from falling over.

"We're going to get Judy and Dennis back, right?"

He's already had such a long day. I don't want to give him even more bad news, but I also don't want to lie to him. Settling on the amount of truth I can handle saying right now, I exhale and rest my head against the wall. "I sure hope so."

I don't realize I've fallen asleep until I open my eyes; I'm no longer at John's. I'm sitting against the living room wall in my childhood home. The stairs, still standing, are to my right. No scorch marks cover the walls.

It's as if the fire never happened at all.

I must be in Riley's dream again.

Shit.

I had no intention of revisiting so soon, let alone now. There's enough to worry about without my sister's hatred fueling the metaphorical fire.

Wake up.

I squeeze my eyes shut and spring them back open, but the room doesn't change. Out of nowhere, Riley's scream tears through the house, startling me to my feet.

"Riley?" I tear up the stairs, not caring that she tried killing me last time.

She's in her bedroom, the blankets twisting around her as she thrashes in bed. Riley lets out a low groan, her face scrunching in pain. Even at the doorway, I can feel the heat radiating from her body.

"Riley!" I rush over to shake her shoulders. "Wake up. It's just a bad dream!"

A bad dream within a dream—what a hellish nightmare.

The sheets begin to burn, and smoke rises around us. It's going to happen all over again. She's reliving the night of the fire.

"Ri!" I tap her face this time, still shaking her body to rouse her. "Wake up, damn it."

As if my voice truly calmed her, or simply by instinct, she eventually curls against me. Her trembling body settles, her hands losing the heat as I sit on the bed with her in my arms.

"Ri," I whisper. "Wake up."

My heart squeezes, threatening to turn to dust. I haven't hugged my sister in over five years, not since she was eleven and I was thirteen. She's not so little anymore... she's—

Riley's body goes rigid, and my shoulders tense. Our brief truce is over. She's awake now—well, in a sense—and must realize what's happening and who she's with. She lurches out of my grasp, and before I can get a word out, she slams her hands against my chest, pushing me so hard that I wake up back in John's house.

For a sliver of time, I'm calm—almost at peace.

Riley let me in, even if it was on some subconscious level. She might've been sleeping when it happened, but she responded to me as if I were still her older brother, who swore to always protect her.

I don't know how to get her to stop hating me long enough to listen so I can explain why I left her behind, but her frail body trembling in my arms solidifies the decision for me.

I have to keep trying.

Zay is no longer sitting next to me in front of the television. Instead, it's Gemma pouring over a large binder. The others are all sprawled out on the opposite side of the living room.

I stifle a groan and crack my neck. "Let me guess... Variants?"

Gemma flips the binder closed, nodding. "I didn't want to wake you. I figured we should rest while we can."

"Thanks," I mumble. "However, I wouldn't exactly consider it resting. I ended up in Riley's head again."

The truth is out before I can stop it, my inhibition drained from today's events, but Gemma whips her head to look at me, overly eager eyes widening.

"So, you saw her then? She's all right?"

"As well as she can be, considering." I run a hand through my hair, hoping to tame it as I stifle a yawn. "Why?"

"I—" She averts her gaze, focusing on her hands.

"What is it?" I place a hand over hers, and she recoils. "Gem..."

"I did something."

I wait for her to elaborate, my pulse pounding in my ears. There was something she didn't want to say in front of the others earlier, too. Is she finally going to tell me whatever it is?

"I—" She opens her mouth again, but nothing comes out.

Her pleading look pierces through me. The last time she was this wracked with guilt was when she accidentally burned Nora. *How can I reassure her that whatever she's done, it's okay?* Today wasn't normal; we were under attack and she shouldn't blame herself for anything that happened as a result.

"It's okay. You can tell me."

Across the room, Nora whips her head back, one hand gripping the side of the recliner, the other curling into a fist in her lap. The rest spring into action; Zay fetches a glass of water, and Elise stands behind the chair, holding Nora's shoulders back.

Gemma tosses the binder to the side, crossing the room in no time to grab Amber and pull her aside. Amber watches Nora with red-rimmed eyes, clutching Gemma's arm like she's holding on for dear life.

As for me, there's nothing left to do but kneel in front of Nora and wait, forcing the idea of whatever Gemma might have said out of my mind.

If Nora can locate Judy and Dennis, we'd have a lead, something to go on that will tell us what our next move should be. Amber hasn't seen John but hopes he'll return, too. I'm not sure how good ghosts are at tracking people, but he was a cop.

He has to know something.

Doesn't he?

Nora's eyelids flutter, her body twitching more violently than ever before. Elise holds her steady, and I grip Nora's hand on the recliner. Seconds turn into minutes; it's taking too long. If I could get into her head with her, I would, so she wouldn't have to do this alone. But I can't fall asleep that fast. She might already be out of it by the time I make it there.

Plus, I don't even know if her visions are considered a sleep state. Would I even be able to get in?

"Come on, Nora," I coax, hoping my voice will guide her back. My neck is slick with sweat as I remember the heat from Riley. I guided her back a short while ago, and now here I am again, trying to bring someone else back to themselves with only my voice.

It works, though. Or maybe it's just a lucky coincidence.

Nora gasps, her body jolting with the movement. Her wild gaze settles on mine, and it takes a moment before clarity dawns. Her shoulders relax when she notices it's me crushing her hand, not someone else.

Elise lets go of her shoulders, the threat of her falling forward over, and Zay stands next to me, holding the glass of water.

"It's her," Nora rasps.

"The hospital room?" I grab the cup from Zay.

He plops beside Nora on the arm of the chair so they sit side by side. Nora takes the cup and sips before bobbing her head.

"I still can't see anyone else. It's just this girl hooked to machines in a hospital bed. She hasn't been awake at all in my visions, and I haven't seen anyone else in the room. I caught a room number this time, though. It was on the whiteboard—number 940."

"Do you know which hospital?"

She shakes her head, taking another sip of water.

"I keep focusing on Judy and Dennis and end up there instead."

"Maybe they're in the same hospital?" Amber croaks out. "What if they're hurt? Oh god!" Her eyes turn misty, like she's remembering something awful. "What if they show up as ghosts?"

Gemma runs a calming hand over her hair. "Shh," she soothes, locking eyes with me. "That's not going to happen. We'll find them."

I sure hope she's right.

"Hey." I nudge Nora's leg, an idea slowly forming as we all sit in uneasy silence. "Do you mind if I jump into your dreams tonight? Maybe I can recreate your vision to see it for myself. If I know who to look for, perhaps I can get inside this mystery girl's mind."

"Do you think that would work?" Nora asks.

Doubt it. We've never even tried anything like this before. But instead of shutting down my own idea, I say, "We can at least try?"

Nora tugs at her lip, thinking it over, and eventually nods. "Yeah, let's do it."

I don't know if Nora's repeated vision relates to Judy and Dennis at all, and with our luck, it probably doesn't, especially since she showed up before they were even taken. But at least it's a start—if I'm successful, maybe the girl in the hospital can shed some light on whatever Nora is trying to see.

Chapter Eleven

GEMMA

"I CAN'T KEEP SITTING here, Theo." My voice cracks at the end, and I steel myself against the onslaught of emotions pulsating through me as I remind him of what I said earlier. My terror, mixed with guilt, Amber's panic, and even Theo's uncertainty, twist inside me like a tornado. "They're the only family I have."

I wince at my harsh words. I don't actually mean them. Most of my *family* is sitting in this near-empty living room with me, but we're all scared children, not knowing which way is up now that Judy and Dennis are missing—gone, just like Olivia.

"I know," he murmurs. "I'm not saying we won't go after them. But we need a plan first. We don't know where they went or if they're even still—" He stops short, his eyes growing wide.

"Alive?" I choke out, finishing the thought for him. I shake my head, refusing to believe it. "They have to be. I would know if..."

Would I, though? I sensed when Olivia's heart stopped beating, but I was near her when it happened.

Theo's right.

I don't know *anything.*

"I think we call it a night and figure out what to do in the morning," Theo states.

"Judy and Dennis could be anywhere by then!" *Or worse*, I think, but I keep that to myself, not wanting to scare Amber further. "The others are leaving in the morning, too. If we want their help, we need to go there now."

Theo's shoulders drop as he lets out a breath, propping himself against the wall near the kitchen, his arms crossed in front of him. His jaw works, and it's like I can see him running calculations in his head. "Do you really trust them?" he asks.

I hesitate a moment too long, and his eyes narrow as if that's all the answer he needs.

"I don't know," I finally admit. "I was trying to get a read on them, but it didn't seem like they wanted to harm us."

"You were wrong before." Elise raises an eyebrow at me from where she sits on the floor in the corner.

"Thanks for the reminder," I scoff.

She flicks a piece of hair over her shoulder, muttering, "You've been misled in the past."

"But they're like us," I plead, ignoring her point. "Caleb offered to take us somewhere that has even more mutants. That has to count for something, right? If anything, they know more about this than we do. Maybe they can help us find Judy and Dennis if they have connections, too."

Theo rubs a hand along his jaw, slowly shaking his head. "I don't know, Gem. I don't like it; something feels off about them, but I get where you're coming from." He glances around the room like he's imploring the others to chime in.

Amber crosses the small space to stand next to me. "I say we try."

"I'd feel better if I had a vision..." Nora chews on her lip, not giving a real answer.

Elise locks eyes with Theo, and I already know she's a lost cause. She's not going to cross Theo again, especially when she's already questioning my judgment.

Zay sits on the edge of the recliner, elbows braced on his knees and hands clasped. He hangs his head for a moment before lifting it, his eyes shimmering. "I'm sorry. I think we should sleep on it. After today..." He shifts uncomfortably, and my heart breaks for the amount of fear that's pulsing through him. "I want to find Judy and Dennis, too, but we all need a minute."

I suck in a breath, blinking away my own tears. "I'm sorry, Zay. I didn't think."

He *did* have a gun pointed in his face today, and I can feel how shaken he is over it if I sift through all the other cascading emotions pummeling me.

It feels like I'm giving up, but I don't know how to convince them.

Theo pushes off the wall, taking a few steps to stand in front of me, and grabs my hands. "Hey, we're not saying no, okay? Just not this second. We'll go through the rest of John's things in the morning and come up with a plan."

All I can do is nod.

TIME MOVES SLOWLY, AND each tick of the clock is a constant reminder that they're gone. The group outvoted me, but I can't keep sitting here doing nothing. The longer we wait, the further away they could be taken. Or maybe they haven't even left. They could be right under our noses, and we're sitting here for absolutely no reason when we could be saving them.

Zay, Nora, and Amber are all asleep in John's bed. Elise is passed out in the recliner in the living room, and Theo and I are in the spare bedroom on the carpet, him sleeping soundly beside me.

But I can't sleep.

The clock, never-ending and merciless, continues to taunt me. Each second, my chest cavity fills with pressure, like a balloon waiting to pop. Today's events whirl in my mind, suffocating me as they replay over and over.

I almost told Theo what happened back at the pizza place, but the words wouldn't come out. Is he going to think of me differently? He knows what I'm capable of, so he wouldn't be surprised, but the fact that it even happened...

Thank god it wasn't Riley, though.

I can breathe easier knowing I didn't accidentally kill his sister.

I've been assuaging my guilt by reminding myself it was my life or theirs. They shot first, and only after did I understand they were trying to take me alive. I still wouldn't have gone willingly, though. There can be fates worse than death—just look at Riley.

Who would they turn me into? Would they get inside my head and make me turn on those I love the most?

I'll do anything to never have the answer to that.

But it is my fault they have Judy and Dennis. I brought the Authorities right to their doorstep by coming back here, lugging four more kids with me. Who knows what's happening to them?

I can't close my eyes, or I picture the bullet holes in the wall of the pizzeria. Or Judy's face giving me a pained smile, trying to keep it all in for the sake of her children. Dennis's eyes crinkling in the corners when he gives a broad smile.

What if they've been killed?

The balloon in my chest pops, and I choke back a sob, careful not to wake Theo. He rolls over anyway, his back to me. I rest my hand between his shoulder blades, following his steady breathing. At least I didn't wake him.

His body is relaxed, and I'm confident he's not in Riley's head or the mystery girl's, which is a blessing because I know what I have to do, and he's not going to like it. At least if he's not knocked off balance from a visit with Riley or some complete stranger who's in a hospital somewhere, he'll have a clearer head when he wakes up to no one here with him.

I almost scoff out loud. Who am I kidding? Theo's going to freak.

An unbidden thought creeps up: *Am I strong enough to even do it?* But I have to drown it out because no one else can. My stomach churns with nerves, and I bite my lip to hold back from screaming. Fake it till you make it, I tell myself.

I'm doing what needs to be done.

I won't make the group do anything they don't want to, but I can't sit here and idly wait for some plan to magically form when it might be too late by the time we have one. I got them into this mess by bringing everyone home with me, and I'm going to get them out.

I sit up, stretching my arms out to loosen my shoulders. Staring at Theo's face, his slightly crooked nose, I trace his silhouette, committing every detail to memory.

I'm going to go find Caleb, and I'm going to get my foster parents back.

I'll make it back to Theo afterward to explain everything, even the lives I took, and apologize for keeping this dark secret from him, even when I was the one who said no more, to begin with.

I have to believe this isn't where we end.

A CHILL RUNS THROUGH me as I stand outside Bridlewood Motel, crushing the business card in my hand.

It would have helped if he had given me a room number.

The parking lot is nearly empty, and the moon casts a glow over the vicinity. The bushes outlining the lot rustle in the wind, and I glance over my shoulder so many times that my neck begins to ache.

I can't shake the feeling that I'm being watched.

Did someone follow me here? Did they see me leave John's? Do they know the others are there?

"Stop," I whisper to myself, feigning confidence. "Everything is fine."

I snuck out without waking anyone, going through the neighbor's yard until I reached the side street. No one out front would have seen me leave.

But now that I'm here... I don't know what to do.

I can't start throwing rocks at windows. I could try the front desk, but would they have checked in under their real names? Wouldn't they be hiding like we are? There are so many questions, and getting any answers seems impossible.

"Gemma?"

I startle, spinning around to find Simone behind me. She's wearing all-black clothing, blending into the shadows of the night.

"What are you doing out here?" I ask.

A sly smile stretches across her face. "I could ask you the same thing." But then she shrugs. "I heard you talking to yourself."

I unclench the card, offering it to her as my cheeks heat. I can't believe I forgot about her ability. "I need your help."

Simone's grin falls away, her mood cooling as if she expected something like this to happen. She closes her eyes briefly, tilting her head away, her sharp jaw angled. I don't know what she looks like when using her sonic hearing, but I imagine that's what I'm witnessing. I glance around at the parking lot, waiting for her cue about what happens next.

"Follow me," she instructs, her long lashes fluttering as her eyes open.

She leads us to room 141, pulling out a key card and swiping it before shoving the door open with her hip.

"We have company," she announces to the room like she's giving a heads-up in case anyone is indecent.

"Roberts, what a surprise." Caleb straightens in the computer chair, moving his feet from the desk to the floor. His flat tone doesn't make it seem like he's surprised at all.

Actually, none of them even feel surprised.

I glance around the room, and everyone is shockingly awake; my arrival must've been a foregone conclusion.

My eyes flash from one mutant to the other, finally settling on Caleb again, who's looking expectantly at me. The desk lamp gives his pale skin a yellowish glow but also highlights the brown in his eyes—a rich shade, reminding me of October. They're warm and inviting, and it makes breathing a little easier. There's nothing malicious in his gaze or his mood.

"Gemma said she needs our help." Simone leaves my side and sits on the edge of the bed next to Asher.

"The Authorities. They came for my family."

Caleb's lips thin as he twines his fingers together behind his head. "When?"

"It happened the same time we were attacked. They were gone before we made it home."

"So, they divided and conquered," Louis chimes in, not looking up from the game he's playing.

"I guess so," I mumble. "They took my foster parents."

"Alive?"

My chin wobbles; I *can't* cry in front of them. I need to come off as strong and put together so we can focus on finding Judy and Dennis. *Fake it till you make it*, I remind myself, with a gut-sinking feeling that I'm going to have to fake it for a while.

I clear my throat. "I'm hoping so. They were alive when they were kidnapped, according to my sister."

"A trap?" Simone asks Caleb.

"Maybe."

"To draw them out?" Esha suggests.

"Did they leave a note?" Caleb focuses on me again.

I shake my head. "Not that I saw, at least. They destroyed the place, so if they left something, it wasn't anywhere noticeable."

"Where are the others?"

"Somewhere safe. I came alone."

"Theo didn't want to join you?" Caleb's lopsided grin heats my blood, but I force myself to be nice so I don't lash out at him.

I need their help, after all.

"He didn't think it was a good idea," I stammer. "Can you help me or not?"

"Oh, I think we can help."

THE CHILLY MORNING AIR sends goosebumps rising along my arms. The dawn fills with palpable tension, electricity buzzing through the air as the sun slowly rises.

As we wait on the train platform, second thoughts race through my mind. Doubt and fear crawl into my brain, settling in. But I'm strong enough to do this. *I have to be.* Caleb can help us. He explained it all before I agreed to this asinine idea. Once the new group takes me back to their base, they can formulate a real plan. There, they have security cameras, inside men, and ways of finding out where Judy and Dennis are since he's sure the Authorities wouldn't have kept them close. It's too risky.

Caleb's base has things we have no access to on our own.

This is a smart plan. This might even be Theo's plan. He didn't want to rush in, and now I'm not. I'm getting the help we need. I wish he was here with me, though. But we'll be together again soon.

"Ready?" Caleb asks, sidling up next to me.

"Did you get the tickets?"

He gives me another uneven grin. I don't think he realizes it's not as charming as he seems to believe.

"Not exactly."

A train whistles off in the distance, racing closer to the station. Simone, Louis, and Esha all stand simultaneously, stretching their muscles.

"What do you mean *not exactly*?"

"Have you ever been a stowaway?"

"No," I snap at him—he failed to mention this part of the plan. "I can confidently say I've never been a stowaway."

"Well, today is your lucky day," Simone's silky voice drifts from my other side.

"How can all of us hide? Are you telling me that not one of us has a real ticket?"

"There are no tickets to buy."

Caleb laughs at the confused expression that must be plastered on my face. "Relax. It's a freight train."

"I don't know if that makes it better or worse."

"The conductor won't even know we're there. You just have to run and jump."

"Run and jump?"

The train barrels closer. It doesn't seem to be slowing down, but it has to, *right*? The whistle blows, and the crossing gates lower with their flashing lights.

Caleb peels the backpack off my arms, ignoring my protests, and slings it over one shoulder since he's carrying his own.

"Try to get in the same car as the rest of them, but I'll follow you in case you miss it. We wouldn't want you to be alone, not knowing when you need to duck and roll."

I shudder as the others get into position—no wonder they were all stretching beforehand. They all have packs as well, presumably the ones Asher was stuffing with supplies.

Caleb slaps me on my now empty back, letting out another chuckle. "You're going to do great."

"Please don't lose my bag." My voice cracks, and my throat closes around the words. Olivia's urn is in there, but I don't trust myself to be able to run and jump with it on.

Ever since the Authorities destroyed the house, I haven't let it out of my sight, in fear of them returning and me being forced to leave it behind.

We trace our original steps all the way back to the beginning of the platform, and I swallow my misery. Or at least try to.

The train is close enough now to vibrate my bones. My racing heart matches the beat of the engine, and I'm sure it's going to explode at any moment.

"Ready?" Esha smirks at me, folding herself in a runner's position, like she's about to start a race.

My teeth chatter, but there's no time to be afraid.

When the train whizzes by, I run as fast as I can, my shoes pounding the concrete as I study how the others jump—grabbing onto the bar and twisting themselves inside the car door. Louis and Asher jump in the first open door, and Esha and Simone in the second. That leaves one door open for me and Caleb.

I push myself harder.

I jump, clutching the bar, but flail since I don't have the upper body strength to pivot myself inside the car. Two hands haul me in, and I topple over Simone.

The two of us are tangled together on the train floor as Caleb swings his way in seconds before the platform ends.

"Whew," he breathes, sitting on the ground next to us and dropping both our bags. "You made me work for it there, Roberts."

"Sorry," I mumble as I peel myself off Simone, holding out a filthy hand to pull her up.

"It's cool." He brushes the dirt off his hands. "I never mind a little challenge."

My fingers skim my pants as I wipe them off, muttering, "I was apologizing to Simone. Not to the lunatic who just made me jump on a train."

"You didn't *have* to jump."

I huff, hugging my bag—more accurately, Oli's urn—to my chest. I turn my back to stand near the open door as my heart rate settles, thankful I made it onto the train. Not close enough to accidentally fall out, but close enough to see the world buzz by, the trees blurring into one prolonged, endless stretch of green.

"What happens now?"

"Next, we jump off at Etlente and pick up a vehicle to make the thirty-four-hour drive back to Nevada." Asher studies the watch on his wrist. This is the first time I've heard him speak, and his voice is deeper than I imagined. "We should be there in five hours."

I sit down, swallowing a groan as I keep my back against the wall and tuck my knees in, still cradling my backpack.

Esha catches me staring, and a dazzling smile reveals the bronze glow of her cheeks, her diamond nose ring twinkling in the light. Her long, straight black hair flows around her as she winks at me and then lies down, resting her head on her arm.

My gaze shifts to Louis sitting up next to her, his equally dark hair tied back at the nape of his neck. He's playing his game again, his long limbs stretched out and ankles crossed. There's a tinge of pink under his tawny skin as he glances up at me with dark eyes, but then he resumes his game, letting me off the hook as I focus my attention elsewhere.

As everyone else makes themselves comfortable for the long journey, Asher stands, rocking with the train's motion for a split second before he quickly crosses the car. At first, I think he's coming straight at me, and my heart leaps in warning, his T-shirt showing off his thick, tan arms, a glimpse of a dark tattoo on his inner forearm that I can't make out.

All I can picture is him flipping the Authority member's car and how he could probably kill me with one hand, but then he pivots for the door. He's able to get it closed, even with the high speed. He sits back down next to an already passed-out Caleb, which must be record timing on how quickly someone can fall asleep.

I can't help but focus on their unperturbed attitudes.

They're entirely unphased by jumping trains, and judging by the lack of urgency I feel in this car, being able to fall asleep on one isn't the most bizarre thing that they've ever done. This almost seems like a typical Sunday for them. Even their willingness to help gives credence to the idea that they do this often.

If I'm going to have any chance of finding Judy and Dennis, I need to fight through my fear, learn the ropes, and be more like them.

Fake it till you make it, I remind myself again.

Saving them means there's no more room for doubt.

Chapter Twelve

Theo

Something isn't right.

Dread pools in my stomach, and it takes everything in me to keep my insides from turning to stone. I dial Gemma's number again, but it goes straight to voicemail, so I hang up and toss the cheap phone Dennis gave me for emergencies onto the chair while staring at her note: *Went to Bridlewood Motel to find the others. I'm sorry for running off. If I'm not back by tonight, you know where to find me.*

That was yesterday, and I spent all day combing every inch of that rundown motel, plus the surrounding area, and found absolutely nothing to say where they could have gone. The worst part? I couldn't reach her in her dream, either. It has to be Louis. He must be shielding her, and the thought makes me want to murder someone.

Why are they keeping her from us? And does she know they are? She would have been expecting me, and her note even implied so.

My ribs feel like they're splintering from the inside out, and I regret ever falling asleep and letting her slip away. The worst part, it wasn't even worth it. I entered Nora's dream as planned, and the more she thought about her vision, the more it flitted into view in her dream. By the end, it was as if we were in the sterile hospital room, the machines steadily beeping as we stood next to the girl asleep in the bed. But nothing happened when I tried leaving Nora's dream to enter hers. The scene never changed.

"I can't believe she left," I mutter to Zay as he walks by again, wearing the tattered carpet down even further.

His corkscrew curls bounce with each step, unable to sit still for more than two seconds. The lack of plants in John's house offers him no room for an outlet or a distraction.

"Was he hotter than you?" Elise asks as she enters the room, licking peanut butter off a spoon. When I don't dignify her with a response, only drilling her with a look, she continues, "I'm just saying. That might explain it."

"I should have left you back in the field."

She stands toe to toe with me, clapping me on the shoulder. "But you didn't, and I *sincerely* thank you for that."

I close my eyes, pinching the bridge of my nose. "This isn't like her..."

Elise lets go of my shoulder, slapping her hand against her thigh with a dramatic grunt. "Gemma, right? The one who ran away after burning Nora?"

My eyelids flutter open, my chest aching even more. "That was different."

Elise has a point, even though I won't admit to that out loud. Gemma runs when she's scared of hurting more people, and there's something she's hesitant to tell me.

After the pizza place, she changed.

It was a lot, and I left her alone when I went for Zay. I hate that I had to make that choice, and even though she told me to go, I shouldn't have. I should have found a way to teleport them both at once. I should have been there for her.

What happened in those moments apart?

"Was it?" Elise tilts her head, interrupting my thoughts. "Seems to me she's fond of making dumb choices."

"Yeah, like you really wanted her to stay at the Rib House," Nora scoffs uncharacteristically.

I'm glad I'm not on the other end of Nora's anger. This is the longest I've ever seen Nora upset, and I don't know if she'll ever truly forgive Elise. I haven't.

"You tried exchanging her life for powers, did you not? I'm not sure you can judge anyone for making bad choices," Nora continues.

Elise crosses her arms, blinking rapidly before she glances away like she can't bear to look at Nora's aura.

What color is pissed off?

"This isn't helping anyone," Zay huffs, glancing at Amber, who's ignoring everyone as she holds her head in her hand and stares at the carpet. "We all need to stop bickering for a minute to figure out what to do next. Gemma left to go find Judy and Dennis, right? So, we start there. If we can figure out where she's going, we can meet her there and help."

"And how do we do that?" Amber asks from the recliner, breaking her silence. "It's not like she left a trail of notes for us."

"Did they say where they were going when they offered the invitation?" Elise asks.

I rub a hand over my face. "No. And I didn't think to ask, either."

"Super," she deadpans, going back to the kitchen with her spoon.

Nora sighs, heading for John's office. "I'll start searching through his files. Maybe it'll spark something."

I TRY TO ENTER Gemma's dreams, but nothing happens. We've been apart for two nights, and I've been unable to reach her. She must know I would've come for her by now. Does she think something is wrong? Does she think I'm mad at her for leaving?

A billion different scenarios twist around my head, and before I can plan what to do next, I'm in my childhood home.

I doubt Riley has a sympathetic ear to lend, but I'm slightly comforted by being here. Our last encounter didn't end well, but there was a brief moment when we were siblings again. And maybe, if I keep trying, we can fix what was shattered between us.

"Riley?" I call out, walking through the living room.

My steps slow when it dawns on me that her dreaming of this place so often is probably a bad sign. But it doesn't really matter, does it? I can alter it this time, like I did for Gemma.

I can level the playing field, find a neutral territory, and perhaps she'll lower her guard.

I go upstairs, find her trashing the place again, and raise my hands in surrender when fire wraps around her fingertips. I close my eyes, transporting us to a different dream world. We stand several feet apart on a beach when I coax my eyelids back open.

The waves crash against the shoreline, the sky darkening to a stormy gray, and the faint smell of rain hovers in the air.

We're on the cusp of a storm in more ways than one.

I flash Riley a nervous smile as the fire in her palm disappears. I watch her gaze at the ocean and blink up at the sky. Serenity smooths out the frown lines creasing her pale skin, and I will myself to take a step forward, closing the distance.

She watches me idly, which encourages me even more.

"Can you hear me?"

She narrows her eyes in response, but I can't tell if this means yes or if she only notices that my lips are moving.

"People can't always hear me when I enter their dreams..." I fumble through an explanation. "But I've been trying to work on that... so if you can hear me..."

"Can you hear *me*?" She tilts her head a fraction of an inch, her voice razor-sharp.

"Yes." I take another step forward, hope blooming in my chest. "I can."

"Then hear this," she growls at me. "Stay the hell out of my head!"

My eyes dart open; I'm back at John's. I place a hand over my racing heart and stay still until it calms, and the sweat on the back of my neck dries. It might be foolish of me to consider, but I think the change of scenery helped.

"Theo!" Nora barges into the room, flipping on the light, blinding me.

I squint, holding up a hand to block it out. "What?" I steel myself as I sit up, noting the excitement etched across her face. "Did you find her?"

"No." Nora grimaces. "Sorry. But I did glimpse Judy!"

"They're okay?" The pendulum swings from disappointment back to relief. Gemma is still missing, but if Judy and Dennis are alive...

"As far as I know, they're fine, relatively speaking." She sits down on the floor across from me. "I didn't catch a lot, so unfortunately,

I don't know where they are. But Judy was blindfolded and hand-cuffed to a metal table."

"And Dennis?"

She shakes her head. "I couldn't see him, but I heard him talking to Judy, reassuring her they were going to be okay."

A weight lifts from my shoulders. Dennis is still Dennis.

"Okay." I nod, formulating a plan. "This is good."

Just the reassurance that they're breathing gives me hope. This is all fixable. We'll figure out where they are and find Gemma along the way.

We've been in worse scenarios.

Haven't we?

We have the Authorities chasing us, my girlfriend is missing and being shielded by strangers I don't trust, Judy and Dennis are blind-folded and handcuffed by the enemy, John's partner is trailing me, and Riley, although back in my life, certainly doesn't want to be. I nod again, this time to myself, as Nora stares at me, waiting to be filled in.

"This is good," I repeat, although I feel less certain now, weighing the odds.

My thoughts halt, backtracking to Jason.

I lock eyes with Nora. "I think I have an idea."

Nora updates everyone else with what she's seen. Amber gives off mixed signals as if she doesn't seem to know if she wants to be elated or cry more, which is understandable since her parents are locked up somewhere. At least they're alive; I tell her to focus on that.

The idea of going back to their house to find the business card Jason left with Judy fills me with dread, but John mentioned allies. And hopefully, Jason is just that. He's been insistent enough, at least. I don't particularly want to ask for his help. I don't want to ask *any* adults for help, for that matter, but we need someone to lead the way, and he's the closest person to all this who could potentially lend a hand. And there's only one way to find out if he's truly John's partner.

And if he's not, I'll teleport out of there and come up with another idea.

Easy.

Everyone reluctantly agrees with the plan since we have no other options, wishing me luck as I step into the void.

I misjudge the distance and appear out of thin air in their front yard. The neighbor's dog starts barking at my sudden appearance, and I bolt to the front door, digging out my keys.

Shit, shit, *shit.*

I wrench open the door, slam it shut behind me and lock the deadbolt. If the Authorities *were* watching, they would no doubt have witnessed my fine entrance. I tear through the house, avoiding the destruction, scouring the place for his stupid card.

Was that a bang? I freeze. Silence hangs in the air, and I shake off the terror. I'm imagining things. The Authorities wouldn't knock.

Dennis's wallet is empty, and the card isn't stuck to the fridge. I even check their junk drawer. It's not here. I slam one of the open cupboards shut.

Think.

Where would Judy put it?

If Dennis's wallet is here, maybe Judy's purse is, too. I race to the front entrance, ripping jackets off the hooks until I unbury the bag. Dumping its contents right on the ground, I shuffle through everything until I unearth the flimsy card.

My heart pounds. Every second I'm in here, the higher the chance the Authorities will find me. Hands shaking, I dial the number.

Jason answers on the second ring.

"Jason? It's Theo. We need to meet."

I BRIEFLY RETURN TO John's to fill in the others so they don't think I also ran off, but all it does is end up in more arguing.

"I really don't think you should go alone," Zay states again, adamantly shaking his head.

"I can't risk taking any of you with me. If Jason can't be trusted, I need to be able to get out of there without worrying about anyone else. Plus, you're the only one with abilities who can protect everyone." I glance at the rest, who are all standing there, watching Zay and me argue for maybe the first time ever.

Zay tilts his head back, staring at the ceiling, but doesn't answer.

Elise made a fair point before about the rest of them being unable to defend themselves. They've all been somewhat trained for physical combat, but it isn't a match against someone with a gun.

"Go," Elise says. "We'll be fine." She grabs Zay's arm and tugs him closer.

Zay finally lowers his head to look me in the eye. "You better come back," he demands.

I give a nod before teleporting back to the pizzeria that's been closed since the shooting. At least I don't end up outside this time and step out of the void into the dark kitchen, confirming I'm alone and there isn't a trap waiting for me.

When I get to the front of the shop, I hold my breath and study the destruction in the dim lighting that peers in from between the wooden slabs over the front windows. The bullet holes remain embedded in the walls, and scorch marks travel along the floor, trailing to the curtains and up toward the ceiling. Glass crunches under my shoes as I drift over to the table Zay and I were sitting at. We would've been caught in the crossfire if we hadn't gotten up to meet Gemma at the counter.

None of this would matter if we hadn't moved.

We would have been dead.

I force myself to breathe, grab one of the chairs still standing that's not riddled with holes or burned to a crisp and sit to wait, my eyes following the pendant's cord, which now drapes from the ceiling and rests on the ground.

Everything about this is a huge gamble. But I have no other lead, no one else to turn to. So, whether I like it or not, I need to at least talk to Jason and see where this goes. *Plus, he was friends with John*; remember that.

Ten minutes later, the back door opens, and I straighten up. My fingers curl into a fist, and I get ready to leave if I need to.

"Hey." Jason bobs his head at me as he walks through the kitchen door with a flashlight. He stands behind the counter for a brief moment as he takes the place in, then whistles at the damage.

"I figured you've seen it already if you're a cop," I say, questioning his reaction.

"No, I only heard about what went down here."

He grabs a chair and pulls it over to the opposite side of the table, brushing off the glass, appearing completely unfazed by our surroundings.

"What's up?" he asks like we're old friends meeting for coffee.

I swallow, ignoring the feeling of my throat closing. "We need your help." When he doesn't say anything, I take a deep breath, forcing it all out. "I lied to you before. You were right about who I am. And John's"—I flex a hand again, focusing on the flashlight now sitting between us—"John's dead. He found me in Indiana and didn't make it out alive after the Authorities arrived."

He frowns, settling back in his chair, running a hand over his exhausted-looking face. "Shit. I'm sorry to hear that. He was a great guy."

I choose not to comment on John, instead focusing on the problem at hand. "And they found us again." I throw a hand out, pointing at the destroyed walls. "They've taken Judy and Dennis. And Gemma is gone."

Jason straightens as he sits back up, the wrinkles in his forehead deepening, highlighted by the light pointing up at the ceiling. "They caught Gemma?"

"No." I shake my head to drive the point home. "She went after, I don't know, some other people with abilities in hopes of finding her foster parents."

His brow furrows. "Do you know who the others are?"

"I met them once. Caleb, Si—"

Jason curses, getting out of his chair to pace.

"Why?" My pulse spikes. "Is she in danger? Do you know where they took her?"

He glances over his shoulder at me as if he momentarily forgot I was even here. "No, no. Sorry." His chest heaves. "Caleb shouldn't be here. He must've followed me. How many were with him?" When I start to answer, he cuts me off again. "Let me guess—four, right?"

I nod.

"Gemma will be fine with them. They aren't dangerous to other variants, but they do have a different way of thinking."

"What does that even mean?" My shoulders tense. "*Variants*? I saw a binder with the same name at John's house. But Gemma told me Caleb said we're *mutants*."

Before I fell asleep and she ran away with them, I think bitterly, overwhelmed all over again, but I brush the thought away to focus on Jason.

"Sorry." Jason smooths the back of his head with a hand, sitting down again. "Everyone tends to call them something different. At work, we call them variants; mutants tend to call themselves just that—mutants. Some others, like yourself, refer to them as people with abilities. All of them are technically correct."

"Do you know where they took her?" I ask again since he never answered the first time, my pulse pounding in my ears as I store his answer away to dissect later.

"If they're smart, they'd take her straight back to the base."

"And if they're not?"

Jason sighs. "Caleb is on a mission to free the mutants so we no longer have to live in hiding. So, with Gemma's power—yes, I know about it, John told me—who knows what he can do. But I'm assuming she went with them to find her folks, right? Caleb's smart. He'd fulfill his end of the bargain to gain her trust."

He spews all of this at me like I know any of these people, forcing me to glaze over the fact that John spilled secrets that weren't his to share. But my body goes rigid at the thought of them using Gemma like that—how Esha looked at her like she was a science experiment. I scoff. It all makes sense.

They're just more Dravens, more Elises.

"Can you take us to the base?"

"Of course." Jason bobs his head again. "Just a warning, though. It's a ways out."

"How far is it?"

Jason stands and pushes in his chair like he's on autopilot. "Nevada. It's a little less than two full days by car," he continues. "How many of you are there?"

"Five," I choke out, my mind seizing on the idea of Gemma traveling across most of the country with a bunch of strangers.

"Well, we better get to it then."

I FIND JASON IN John's office. His jaw ticks as he flips through page after page of the variant research.

I lean against the doorway, watching. He was my father's partner, but were they friends, too? There's so much I don't know about my dad—haven't wanted to know about him—since I left home. Was John a good man?

How do I ask something like that, though? Ask this random person to explain the intricacies of my dead father?

I sigh, biting my tongue. Jason looks up at the noise, closing the binder.

"You're..." he starts, but then loudly exhales. "You're not going to like what I have to say next."

When I arch an eyebrow at him, he glances around the room.

"I know your history. John told me all about what happened to you and Riley. I'm sorry about your sister."

I grunt, not answering since John never had the chance to tell his partner that she's alive.

"But..." Jason continues.

"But?"

"We're going to have to torch this place."

My heart leaps into my throat, my vision darkening.

"We can't take all this with us, and there's too much here. The Authorities are no doubt going to raid the place; I'm surprised they haven't already."

My fingers find the lighter in my pocket, and I cling to reality before the invisible smoke drags me under.

Why does everything in my life always lead to fire?

"I don't work in the same department as John, so I'm not sure if the locals here are going to accept my version of things when I tell them he's dead with no proof. His truck is here, though. We can make it look like the house fire was an accident."

"You want to pretend he died in the fire?" I ask incredulously. My blood heats, my face tingling from the unexpected emotion. He deserved better than this.

But this would be closure, right?

Is that why he's hanging around—because there hasn't been any?

We—no, *I*—left his body in the woods. I didn't go back for him. And who knows if the Authorities took him. His corpse could be rotting in the graveyard, for all I know.

It's possible no one would ever know he's dead.

But a fire? That'd be on the news.

That'd let people know that John Goodwin lost his life.

I wonder how poetic my mother would think it is, if she's even alive, that she lost both her daughter and ex-husband to flames. I shake my head, wanting to bash all the thoughts out of it. What's the point of trying to salvage anything? It's already gone—*he's* gone.

Let it burn.

"Do whatever you have to do." I stalk off, leaving it all behind.

I hide in the shadows beneath a tree, letting the darkness cover me as another home is engulfed in flames.

The hood beneath my leather jacket is up, shielding my face as it aches from how hard I grind my teeth. My eyes burn from the memories and from losing a piece of my dad all over again. There's a heaviness in my chest that's dragging me under, and I just want it to stop for one fucking second.

I want my dad back. I want to apologize. I want Riley to forgive me. I want Gemma within reach.

I want too much, and knowing I'll never get some of it hurts.

The flames now swallow the roof, blazing toward the sky, and the billowing smoke blocks out the twinkling stars. Wood pops, fracturing from the heat, and it breaks something inside me, too.

I press a palm hard against my eye, refusing to let the tears spill. I will not cry for the life I can never have.

It's too late now.

Jason appears next to me, his face covered in soot. I have no idea what he did to make it go up that quickly, but he wasn't kidding around. There won't be anything left to find.

"It's time to go, kid."

I don't say anything as I turn my back on the house, following him to the black SUV with Nevada plates, where the others have been waiting.

I take the wheel when Jason can no longer keep his eyes open; we're on a straight enough path that it'll be impossible for me to get lost for the time being.

Once he's out cold, snoring in the passenger seat, I catch Nora in the rearview mirror, pulling out the binder full of variants from her backpack.

When she meets my eye in the reflection, she shrugs.

It's the first time I crack a smile in what seems like an eternity.

When it's my turn to sleep, and I uselessly call Gemma for the millionth time, I focus on breaking down Louis's shield, in case that's who's blocking me out. I have to get to Gem and know she's okay. What if the Authorities caught up to them, too? I feel like I'm losing my mind.

Darkness shrouds me in the dream, and I continue walking without any direction.

Gemma, Gemma, Gemma. I focus all my thoughts on her, picturing her violet eyes, her soft lips, a brown curl escaping from her ponytail.

Pieces of her flash around me, whipping around in a frenzy, mixing within the shadows in my mind.

I stop walking, close my eyes, and deepen the connection.

The woods and the wildflowers where we used to meet.

Please, Gem. Speak to me.

I risk opening one eye. The images of her are gone, but the darkness fades into a lighter gray. I continue walking.

Our first kiss, the first time you showed me your power, the glow of your hands.

Think. Think. Think.

"Meet me here," I whisper out loud.

"Theo?" her voice calls, breaking open the dam within me.

I give a shuddering breath. I can't see her, but she's here. Somewhere.

"Gem? Where are you?"

"Theo? Are you here?"

"It's me." I spin in circles, frantically searching the void, unsure where to look. "Tell me where you are."

"I'm with the others... we're heading to Nevada, I think. Theo, why can't I see you?"

"I'm right here," I shout, but not because I'm angry with her. I'm furious at myself for not getting to her.

"Theo?" she asks again, but her voice is fading, the connection already disappearing.

"No, wait. I'm coming! I'm right behind you," I echo the phrase she told me in the pizza shop, praying that the message reaches her.

The curtain falls, the darkness settling back in.

When I wake, I squint at the raindrops racing across the windshield. One drop falls shortly behind the other, always a step behind.

Will it ever catch up?

Chapter Thirteen

Gemma

I wake with a jolt. I don't know where I am until my arm bumps into Esha's, and my entire body stiffens. Her golden-brown eyes squint at me like she's trying to figure out what I am. I have an overwhelming urge to tell her, *Trust me, I've been there.*

I'm in the backseat of a van Asher borrowed from the Etlente base. The base we're going to is bigger than that one, but they didn't tell me its location. Instead, Asher showed up an hour after we'd been sitting in a McDonald's parking lot, watching two people randomly scream at each other in the drive-thru line.

I'd hoped we could find answers closer to home, but Caleb said they didn't have the resources Nevada did. However, they apparently have spare cars to lend out. So, our journey continues.

It took two nights for Theo to make contact, but something was wrong. I could hear him, which is newer for us, his ability slowly growing stronger, but his voice was so distorted like he couldn't appear fully—even though he always could before, so why couldn't he do it now? Is my own brain playing tricks on me, and it was only a dream? *Or is something wrong?*

There's no way he wouldn't try to make contact. The first night? Fine. He's upset. Rightfully so. But two nights? Worry worms in my gut, threatening to consume me from the inside out.

I left them behind with the Authorities prowling around.

What if they've all been captured? Or some of them are even dead?

My fingers, wrapped around the useless brick in my hand, threaten to spark up right here in the car. I stuff them under my thighs before anyone can notice. Judy has told me to keep my phone charged countless times, but I never use it. What was the point of keeping it charged?

This, I realize. This was the point.

Esha turns her head and smiles at me. Next to her is Louis, and Simone, who stretches her long legs out, sits alone on the shorter bench in the middle. They are all the picture of calm, but me? It feels like my heart is going to burst through my chest.

My breathing hitches, and I remind myself that Theo—if that was him—told me he was on his way to Nevada. They have to be fine because he's following me. But the speck of doubt grows larger, trying to convince me that my brain made it all up because how does he know where I'll end up? I told him Nevada, but nothing specific since I don't even know. Was it all fake? Or did Nora see something? The tingling in my fingers spreads to my elbows, forcing me to ball my hands into fists. The radio in the car abruptly turns off.

"I have to go back," I blurt out.

Caleb—mid-conversation with Asher, who's driving—stops talking to turn around and look at me. "What?"

"I have to go back. I'm sorry. I made a mistake."

"It's a little late to go back, Roberts."

"Theo, he—" I stop. I've never shared his ability to astral project before, and I'm not going to start now. I pull my hands out from under my legs and cross my arms over my chest, curling in on myself. "Something is wrong. I need to go back."

Caleb drops his head, sighing like I'm an insufferable child. "We're a few hours from the base. When we get there, we can figure something out."

"*Please.*"

The anxiety buildup is over; I'm now officially two seconds away from having a full-blown meltdown, whether rational or not. The uncertainty of not knowing where or how my family is doing is a fissure in my bravado. I don't know why I assumed they'd just be safe and sit tightly until I returned with Judy and Dennis in tow. God, I'm an idiot, and I feel extra stupid for thinking I was strong enough to do this alone.

I'm not as strong as I once believed.

I feel like I'm suffocating, and I need to get *out*. I pull at the seatbelt so it's not crushing my chest as I try and fail to take deep breaths. "I need air." Their pulses drum steadily in my ear, gaining force the longer I try to keep my power at bay. "Please let me out!" I almost scream this time, and Caleb says something to Asher, but I can't hear any of it over the throbbing in my head.

Esha reaches for my seatbelt, unbuckling it as my hands shake. I launch myself out of the seat and then the van when Asher screeches to a halt on the side of a highway.

I pace in the ditch, the weeds up to my knees as I swallow air.

"Roberts, this is a really bad place to park."

"I just need a minute," I heave out.

Music blares from the radio, rapidly switching from one station to the next.

"Gemma..." Caleb slowly approaches me as if I'm a wild animal. "I'm going to need you to calm down."

I scoff—as if it's that easy.

"We're going to find your family, all right? I promise. Once we get to the base, we'll enlist everyone we need to. But I'm worried you're about to destroy our mode of transportation, so... if you want to get there, I'm gonna need you to, you know... stop."

I place my hands on my hips, my chest rising with each gasp, then shake my head, my fears warring with rationality.

He's right. I can't blow my one chance at saving Judy and Dennis. And if my brain *isn't* playing tricks on me, Theo said he's also on his way to Nevada. I don't know why his voice sounded so distant or how he knows where I am, but for the sake of everyone, I need to think logically and keep it together until our paths cross again.

I've already come this far. *I can do this.* I blow out a shaky breath. *I really hope I can do this.*

When we return to the van, Caleb climbs in behind me and follows me to the now-empty backseat. Esha moves to the passenger seat, and Simone makes room for Louis. None of them look at me, but they don't seem afraid either. More like they're trying to give me as much privacy as they can in very small quarters.

The anxiety bleeds out of me, leaving only exhaustion in its place. My brain has quieted, reassuring itself over and over that Theo and the rest of them are fine and will catch up in no time.

My mind isn't deceiving itself. He's fine, and he's on his way. I have to believe that or my remaining courage will shrivel up and die.

We ride in silence for what seems like an eternity before Caleb jolts me out of my stupor.

"I wasn't completely honest with you."

My brows furrow when I turn my head to question him. The news can't be *that* bad, considering he witnessed my freak out and still chose to get back in a car with me.

"Remember when I said I'm not qualified to answer how many mutants there are?"

I nod, worrying my lip. He's not entirely exuding nervousness; there's also a mix of excitement in there. But what he says next steals my breath away.

"There's more of us than you can possibly imagine."

"How many?"

"That I'm aware of? Five hundred, easy. And we're finding new mutants every day."

I put a hand to my forehead, blinking rapidly as I try to process this. *Five hundred?* I was shocked to learn there were even six more, let alone hundreds!

"I know," he says with a bemused expression.

"And you know all of them?"

"Personally? No. Those at the base I'm taking you to, yes, but there are about fifty of us there. We're the biggest base of them all, but we're scattered all over the country, like the base in Etlente—hiding in plain sight.

"My aunt Tilly runs the base I'm taking you to. So, she keeps tabs on all the others, swapping information on new mutants so we can find them before the Authorities do and give them the option to live with us. Safety in numbers and all that. I figured I'd give you a warning though before you see for yourself so you're not"—he glances at my hands—"overwhelmed."

"Is that why you guys were in Willow? Were you looking for us?"

"Yes and no."

When I frown, Caleb shrugs before offering up some sort of explanation.

"I knew Jason was tracking someone but didn't know who. So, we followed him. He doesn't know; we didn't exactly get permission for this mission, but we wanted to get off the base. We were trying to figure out who he was tracking before we came across.... well... you." He smirks. "Good thing, too. We showed up at the pizzeria right before you dropped."

My brain floods with images: the electrocution, the fire, and being backed against the wall before everything went dark. How easy it was to kill all those people... Shame burns through me, and I have to force the thoughts away before I freak out again.

"Jason *was* looking for us. Well... Theo," I finally admit.

"Oh?"

I sigh, shifting in my seat to look straight ahead again.

"Come on, I've told you my secret. You can tell me yours," he prods.

"It's not really a secret, just not my story to tell."

"What's the harm then?"

I glance at him, then tug on my fingerless gloves. "It's just a touchy subject. Theo, his dad..." My voice trails off, but after a long exhale, I continue. "John was Jason's partner. Jason's a cop, right?"

Caleb nods.

"Yeah, so I guess they were partners, and Jason tracked Theo down to ask him about John's whereabouts."

"Well, does he know where he is?"

I meet his eye, taking a deep breath before shaking my head. "No one does."

Something about Caleb's manner yanks at my instincts to lie. I'm not entirely sure why, especially since nothing about him or his feelings raises any red flags, but I have the vague sense he's not telling me the truth or at least all of it. I have no intention of spilling Theo's secrets anyway, but I can't risk repeating previous mistakes of trusting those who shouldn't be trusted. I need to proceed with caution.

"So, what's your ability, anyway?" I ask, switching topics.

"Hm?" Caleb says, his attention locked on the empty desert surrounding us.

"Simone's got her sonic hearing; Asher has super strength... what's the trick up your sleeve?"

"Oh." Caleb waves a hand. "Nothing."

"Nothing, as in... you don't have one?" My scalp itches, heat creeping up my neck. Is this offensive to ask? Maybe I should have kept my mouth shut.

He grins at me. "I'm not completely useless. I'm just not as cool as you guys." Before I can respond, he sits forward in his seat, throwing his arms around the headrest in front of him. "Hey, Hicks? Pull over for a minute. I need to take a piss."

Caleb climbs out of the van, heading off to the brush, keeping his back to us. He's not gone long, but he returns to the front this time, kicking Esha to the back with me.

Even with Caleb's warning, I'm not prepared.

We hit a stretch of wasteland, the pavement transitioning to sand, and then we keep driving with only Asher's headlights leading the way. I haven't seen another vehicle in ages.

It's nearing midnight when Asher finally stops and turns around in his seat. I can feel his stare more than I can see it. I peer out at the desert, the billions of stars lighting up the sky, and the full moon illuminates how vastly empty the land is.

"I don't get it," I finally say.

"Come on now," Caleb groans. "She doesn't need to be formally introduced."

"Rules are rules." Asher puts the van in park. "Out."

Louis slides open the van door, signaling to get out. "Have fun!"

I glance at Caleb, and he nods, motioning me to follow as he gets out of the passenger seat. "I'll come with." He's about to close the door behind him when he adds, "Since the rest of you are dicks."

Asher pulls away, running over his own tire tracks from where we came from.

I pull my backpack straps as I fight to take a breath. "Now what?"

"Now we wait."

"For?" I shiver from the cold already bleeding into my bones.

"Oh, someone will find us."

"Soon, I hope?"

"They might make us sweat, especially once they realize it's me out here, but they'll cave."

My thoughts drift back to him not having permission to go on his mission and how, if they're going to punish him for it, I'm now involved.

"You should have stayed with the others then," I grumble.

"I didn't think you'd want to do this part alone." He picks up a heavy rock, chucking it into the air, but it shockingly *clinks* off thin air and ricochets to the side.

When I whip my head at him, mouth dropping open in surprise, he raises his hands in surrender. "Just remember to stay calm."

Before I can question what he means, sirens blare from... who knows where? It surrounds me but comes from nothing at the same time. I cover my ears, attempting to block out the terrible noise, but it doesn't cease.

"What's happening?" I yell.

But Caleb doesn't seem to hear me. His arms are raised above his head, and he looks up into something I can't see.

I move closer to him, shoving his arm.

"Anytime now, Aunt Tilly!" he yells up into the sky.

Ten people in black ski masks materialize around us in a circle, and my hands light up on instinct—*so much for staying calm*. Everyone is armed; I can't believe I fell for it again! *How stupid am I?*

Caleb and his squad led me straight to the Authorities.

Anger licks my veins, and the glow turns to fire, destroying my gloves. I might not have trees surrounding me this time, but I *will* make something burn.

"Easy!" Caleb shouts, running to stand between me and the soldiers. He keeps his back to me and focuses on them. "She gets it."

The siren abruptly cuts out, and they all lower their weapons.

"Trust me, she's a bad person to test this out on. She will eat all of you alive."

"Is that so?" a woman's voice asks, and the group separates to let her through.

She walks straight to me, hands in her pockets, chin held high. She radiates authority, even though she's wearing a tactical vest and cargo pants, blending right in with the others. Her dark hair is chopped short and frames her narrow face.

The most shocking part about her, though, is the shadows that trail her.

I instinctively take a step back when she comes closer, but Caleb doesn't even flinch.

The shadows spread around us, blocking everyone else out; the three of us remain in the eye of the storm.

I spin around, watching the darkness swarm.

The flames in my hand flare, but I keep them close to my sides, one eye on the woman and the other on her ability.

"Caleb." Her voice is steel, her eyes as black as the fierce shadows around her. "Were you permitted to leave the base?"

"No, ma'am." His response is honest, considering what he already told me, but the cockiness in his words takes me aback.

Her shadows gutter.

I personally wouldn't want to be on the wrong side of this lady, but judging by the way the two stare each other down and the way the rest parted for her, I'm going to guess this is Aunt Tilly.

The flames snuff out, and the glow from my hands dims once I put it together; she's more of a threat to him than me right now. And now I'm stuck in an awkward family reunion.

Great.

As if noticing I'm finally there, she turns her sharp gaze on me, and I stand up a little straighter, raising my chin in sync with hers. I won't let her intimidate me, even if she is terrifying. *Be brave*, I tell myself.

"Have you come here for sanctuary?" Her eyes dart to my hands.

"I... uh... maybe? I really came here to ask you for help..." My voice breaks on the last word, forcing me to clear my throat. "... ma'am," I add awkwardly at the end.

She purses her lips, letting her shadows fall away. Once they do, we're back in the empty desert; all the other guards are gone.

"Tilly Gray." She holds out a hand. "You might hear some people refer to me as Aunt Tilly."

My mouth drops open, all manners wiped from my mind. "Ti-Tilly Gray? As in…"

Tilly looses a breath. "The president's daughter, yes, the one and only." Her combat boots dig into the sand as she spins and walks away.

Caleb gestures for me to go first. "Did I forget to mention that?" he muses when I walk by and shoot him a dirty look.

Tilly stops, stretching an arm out to stop us. "Henry, now."

Nothing happens—not at first. But then I stumble backward when a building suddenly appears directly before me. If I'd taken a few more steps, I would have walked straight into a wall.

I back up more, craning my neck to take in the entire structure. Tripping over myself, I fall backward, landing hard on the ground. But I don't bother moving. I stare up at the four-level hotel that was definitely not there a second ago, with a large sign over the door reading "Silver Sand Hotel."

The main floor is comprised of gray granite stones, but the upper floors transition to reddish-brown brick, like they were a late addition to the original establishment. The second and third floors have balconies jutting out from the side of the building, a black fire escape connecting them all. On top is a flat roof with a white cornice extending over the edge. To the side, another building sits, shorter and wider and made of metal. It looks like a garage of sorts and appears to have been built recently as if it was an afterthought. It's completely modernized compared to the vintage state of the hotel.

I can't take my eyes off the structure.

"How…" I start, but the words die on my lips.

"Henry," Caleb grunts, heading in the front door. Tilly must've gone inside while my mind was being blown. "Illusionist," he says like it explains everything. Caleb cranes his neck, holding the door open with one hand. "Are you coming or what?"

I scramble to my feet, heading after him into the building that shouldn't exist. We enter a thin but wide lobby that heads in two directions. The building's center is recessed to form two wings on each side, creating a U shape.

Straight ahead, there's a reception desk, and another door leads back outside. The area looks unused, with inch-thick dust covering every available surface and antique-looking keys dangling from their hooks behind the desk. The chair is weathered, with stuffing protruding out of the leather.

Mahogany paneling covers the walls, and three iron pillars break up the space between the wings. Large chandeliers hang from the beamed ceiling between them. Wall sconces surround the perimeter, and the lights dim the longer I stand here.

I raise an eyebrow at Caleb, and he seems to read my thoughts. "We try to conserve energy when we can." He motions for someone, and the rest of his group enters from who knows where. Maybe they managed to park the van in the garage without us noticing because of the illusion.

I ignore them, turning to explore more.

Next to the front door is an elevator with an old indoor telephone booth set up next to it. On the other side of the door is a public bathroom.

To the left, rounding the corner to where the wing begins, is a lounge covered in leather benches. Everything in this place screams the early 1900s, and for the most part, it looks like it hasn't been touched since. However, to the right side, at the beginning of the other wing, there's an unexpected contemporary-looking metal door with the word "infirmary" stamped onto it.

When I turn, I find Caleb standing nearby, his hands behind his back, quietly watching me as if he had paused to give me time to take it all in.

"Want a tour?" he asks. "We'll meet up with Aunt Tilly later to let her know about... your situation. She's finding you a room right now."

"Oh, that's okay..." I start, but my words trail off.

I doubt anyone can help me *right now* since it's the middle of the night. It would be nice to actually sleep in a bed for once and hopefully meet up with Theo. But the thought of sleeping in this hotel with so many people I don't know...

Caleb walks away before I finish arguing with myself.

I catch up to him as he opens the door to the largest dining hall I've ever laid eyes on, situated next to the lounge. I do a double take and notice two more doors at the end of the hallway, but only one is labeled: stairs. I focus back on the room before me, stepping inside as the lights dim even more.

Through the remaining light, I can make out the gold leaf ceiling. The room is packed full of empty tables of varying sizes.

"How many people did you say this base holds again?"

"Fifty. But there are eighty rooms here, forty each on the second and third floors. Most have their own bathrooms, but some have to share. I guess that's a future problem for those flocking here."

I nod like it all makes sense, even though my brain is spinning out of control. Theo is never going to believe it. We might actually be able to stay here. Somewhere to call home once we get Judy and Dennis back.

"Jet and Tilly have suites on the first floor. The fourth floor and basement were redone to, er... meet our needs." Caleb flashes a grin.

"We can explore all that later. Hungry? There's a kitchen through there." He points to the door at the end of the hall.

"Jet?" I ask as I follow him into the kitchen.

Caleb doesn't answer me at first as he rummages through some of the shelves.

There's another exit to the back right, which must be the unmarked doorway from the hallway. This room has also been remodeled, with stainless steel everywhere, pots and pans hanging from a rack set up in the middle above an island, and huge gas stoves lined against the wall.

"He's like Tilly's right-hand man. Pretty much runs the base with her," he finally answers as he tosses me an apple. "The annoying bast—"

Someone clears their throat, and I spin around to find another unfamiliar face.

"Jet?" I ask again but whisper this time, unsure if the person standing before us would run the base, considering he can't be much older than us.

"No," Caleb mutters, setting his apple back into the fruit bowl. "Worse." Louder, Caleb flips a switch, giving an award-winning smile. "Henry! Did you miss me when I was gone?"

I hesitate to drop my own apple back in, but it's probably bad manners if I start eating when no one else is. My stomach grumbles in annoyance, but I follow Caleb and the one he called Henry out of the room.

Caleb prattles at the newcomer, who doesn't bother responding to anything, and leads us to the opposite wing. We pass the infirmary on our way. This wing has another set of stairs at the end, but this side has three unmarked doors, all on the right side.

"Jet and Tilly's quarters." Caleb points to two of the doors, leaving the one in the middle unspoken for.

The other guy knocks on it twice, and Tilly's muffled voice instructs us to come in.

"War Room," Caleb mouths at me just before we enter.

War Room?

Exhaustion begins to tunnel through me, weighing heavy on my limbs, and I suppress a yawn. Four more new faces sit at the oval table, two on each side of Tilly. They all study me with interest, and it suddenly feels like I'm applying for an important position.

What if I'm not mutant enough to stay here? Since I'm not even like them, will they sniff me out and realize I'm a fraud?

The worry of making another grave mistake makes me doubt myself. I have nowhere to go if they kick me out, and Theo is already—*hopefully*—on his way here. What will happen if he shows up and I'm gone? And even if I'm allowed to stay, what if they don't bother helping me find Judy and Dennis?

Panic flickers to life, but I take a deep, steadying breath. None of their body language or emotions seem like they aren't at least interested in hearing me out first.

You're just tired, I remind myself.

"So," Tilly prompts, leaning back in her seat. "Tell us a little about yourself."

I clench my hands together, rubbing my thumbs along my fingers to ground myself and keep the tingling at bay, debating on just how much to tell her.

Chapter Fourteen

Rain. *Rain.* Why is that word familiar?

The taste—water dripping into an open mouth, gaping wide, unquenchable thirst. A shiver, broken teeth chattering, grinding together. *Crack.* An edged tooth splits the skin, blood pooling on a dry tongue.

A swallow gets stuck, immovable; there's not enough liquid to free the muscle. Rain, if only there were more rain, then the misery would end.

Chapter Fifteen

GEMMA

"How long have they been gone?" Tilly leans forward with interest.

"Four days."

Tilly glances at the slightly balding man beside her, who I've learned is Jet. "What do you think?"

He shrugs noncommittally, his tired blue eyes narrowing. "We can have Griffin take a look and see if he can find anything."

"Griffin?" I inquire.

"For the sake of simplicity, let's just say Mr. Kirby can easily intercept any video camera. If it's attached to the internet, he can find it."

"How?"

"Above your pay grade, sweetheart," Caleb interjects.

I scowl at him. "Who am I going to tell? Clearly, I know everyone here is not normal."

Tilly smirks. "You have a point, but so does Caleb. The less everyone knows, the better. It helps keep us safer."

When my brows furrow, she elaborates. "Sometimes the Authorities don't kill people."

"They take them," I whisper, putting two and two together. Riley, I imagine, isn't the same little sister Theo lost, considering she killed her own father and wants us dead, too. But I didn't allow myself to think of what went into changing her.

I feared ending up like her, not entertaining the route the Authorities took to make her that way.

"Oh god," I mutter.

The woman to Tilly's left, Gwen Haynes, with angry acne blemishing her chin, adds, "We could use any additional allies right about now."

Everything about her looks messily put together, like she doesn't want to be here, but she gives me a reassuring smile, and the empathy wafting off her puts me at ease—*almost*. The situation is dire, so it isn't possible to totally calm my thoughts.

Tilly folds her hands together, resting her chin on them as she focuses on the table in front of her, more than likely devising a plan.

Caleb taps my arm, inclining his head toward the door. "They're going to argue about this for a while. Might as well catch some sleep while we wait for the verdict."

Mostly against my will, I give in, and my feet drag themselves one after the other, following Caleb out of the War Room. Before the door closes, I glance over my shoulder to see the four of them in discussion. The last person, Holt Tucker, didn't bother chiming in. His cold demeanor makes me sort of glad he kept his mouth shut because I'm pretty sure he'd vote against helping. As of now, my family and I are no one to him, and they seem to have enough to worry about. Why take on another case? At least, that's the vibe radiating off him as he sits in his chair, staring at the table.

They don't know me or my foster parents. And I'm asking them to risk everything.

I'd probably want to discuss it, too.

Ironically, it's probably going to come down to a vote. My heart gives a painful tug. *Theo.* Unfortunately, I don't think I'm going to get a say in this one.

I just hope they vote in my favor.

Caleb leads me to room 209, unlocks the door, and swings it open. Everything is in varying shades of brown. The walls appear to have a reddish hue, matching the mahogany walls downstairs, but the glass lamps are so dim that I can't fully tell.

The carpet seems to be dark brown, and tan drapes cover the windows—sadly, I have no balcony. I frown. Maybe you have to earn one. From the little I've seen of this place, it does seem to have its own ecosystem.

I walk over to the small wooden dresser perched next to an even smaller table containing a warped mirror and idly run my finger over it, creating a line through the dust. A door is cracked open to the side, and through the slit, I glimpse the ends of a clawfoot bathtub.

I give a little sigh of relief. At least I don't have to share a bathroom with anyone.

Lastly, two twin mattresses, both with brass headboards, take up the rest of the small room. There are no sheets, blankets, or pillows. I stand there, staring at one of the empty mattresses as everything slowly sinks in, and I feel the overwhelming urge to cry again.

Another crack in the armor threatens to pull me under. I'm here; I actually made it, but I have to wait for what happens next. I feel so close, yet still so far. And I'm so tired. My emotions are even more haywire.

"Ah, we'll fix that." Caleb breaks the silence and points to the empty bed I'm gaping at. "Simone, can you grab Gemma some bedding?"

I scan the room; there's no one here but us. "Um..." Oh, right. Her sonic hearing. Never mind. "So." I sit on the edge of one bed as Caleb takes the other.

His hands are in his front pockets, and he hitches his shoulders to his ears. "So."

"How is this all possible, or is that also above my pay grade?"

"Depends on what you want to know."

"Heat? Water? The electricity? The fact the building is even here? I know Henry cloaks it somehow, but—" My thoughts boomerang, a fact circling back around, derailing my sentence. "Your aunt is the freaking president's daughter!"

"So, you want to know everything," he deadpans, slumping his shoulders down. "Yes, Aunt Tilly is related to that piece of shit. But they haven't spoken in... oh... I don't know. Ever since shadows started leaking out of her, and he tried killing her?

"Previously, daddy of the year formed the Authorities to try to hunt others like her, unaware that his own daughter was a mutant. Eventually, his award-winning thinking to rid the world of us landed him in the White House. Of course, no layperson really *knows* this. But money leads to power, and he made all the right moves to end up sitting pretty. For the rest of your question, it's mostly generators, but everyone has their part to play. You'll learn."

My mind reels. *He tried killing his own daughter? How could someone...* my thoughts trail off when tears prick my eyes. My parents tried sacrificing me to see what happened when it came to Draven's power. I guess I shouldn't be that surprised.

Tilly and I might be cut from the same cloth.

I clear my throat, smothering the emotions so they don't spew out. "When will I learn more?"

Caleb shrugs again. "When Aunt Tilly decides whether it's worth saving your family."

I open my mouth but shut it again when he continues.

"That's why you came here, isn't it? If they don't agree to help, what are you going to do?"

"Find another way," I say.

"Exactly." He stands, taking his hands out of his pockets and smoothing the front of his shirt. "If you're not going to stay here, it's not worth sharing our secrets."

"Caleb—"

But he's already gone, closing the door behind him.

Tilly's words from earlier come to mind: *The less everyone knows, the better. It helps keep us safer.* So maybe you have to prove yourself first. Once you agree to stay, they'll tell you more about the place. But if they decide not to find Judy and Dennis, then I'll need to leave and figure out a new way.

I fling myself back on the bed, groaning. *Don't let the negativity sink in. You can control your thoughts. Mind over matter.*

My fingertips tingle anyway, the tips of my ears going numb. *They'll help you. They have to.* I clench my hand. *Theo has to be on his way. You didn't imagine hearing him. It was just a bad connection, and he'll be here soon. You can explain everything then.*

This is the first time I've been alone since the incident at the pizzeria, and now that no one is here to witness it, the last of my bravery chips away.

You've killed people.

My breathing comes in gasps.

It was your life or theirs.

That doesn't make it okay. I took their lives.

Focus. Don't lose hope.

I might not have been mutant-born, but no one has to know I'm manmade. Caleb even said it himself that he's never seen anything like me before and didn't think this kind of power was possible. My thoughts shift tracks, and Draven's taunts of us being different from everyone come back to haunt me. I shake off a shudder as tears stream down my cheeks.

Mutant or not, someone here has to be able to help me figure out my powers so it never happens again. I can learn to control it. If I can defend myself by only incapacitating the person, then it doesn't have to mean another lost life.

I settle on a plan as I take a few deep, steadying breaths, curling into myself: *Ask for help, but keep your past to yourself. You might be picked apart otherwise, just like how your parents killed Draven.*

The last thing that haunts me behind closed eyes is Esha's hungry gaze and her grinning at me like I'm her next meal.

SUN STREAMS THROUGH THE partially closed drapes, and I rock upward in the stiff bed, momentarily lost as I take in the brown surrounding me.

I haven't slept that hard since before the incident, yet Theo still didn't show.

My stomach plummets, and I force myself out of bed. I don't know what time it is, but surely, they've had to have made a decision by now.

On the opposite bed sit clean sheets, a blanket, a pillow, and a fresh set of towels.

Simone must have been here after I fell asleep. While my immediate response is alarm over her coming in without me noticing, I'm somehow more comforted by the idea of being welcomed.

Maybe this will all work out.

I'm not sure where to go or what to do, so I make my way toward the first floor, the idea of Tilly deciding by now driving me downstairs. I opt to take the stairs, reluctant to run into anyone else in the elevator. Caleb mentioned fifty people live here, and I certainly didn't meet them all last night.

Do they run this place like its own city? Do people have different shifts in various areas to keep the base running? What about children? Do they have a school here? I already glimpsed the infirmary. But how do they get supplies? Even if they're self-sufficient, surely, they can't grow or make *everything*.

By the time I leave the stairwell, my mind is spinning with questions, and I nearly bump into someone who's heading up.

"Oh, sorry," I say, but the person doesn't even glance back.

I breathe a sigh of relief. I'm glad I'm not newsworthy enough to be stared at. Maybe not everyone here knows each other, and I'm not immediately seen as the newcomer.

"Roberts," Caleb calls from the end of the hallway. "You're with me today."

I do a double take at the now-empty staircase, straighten my shoulders, and take off after Caleb. When I catch up, he's about to enter the dining hall, and my steps falter. It's a lot busier than it was last night. Nearly half the tables are full, but no one looks at me. Caleb waves me over to the buffet line and hands me a warm plate when I reach him.

"I don't have any money," I blurt.

It's not entirely a lie. I have some, but I'm saving it in case I need to leave here.

"Shocking. Here, I thought you were just too cheap to chip in for gas money."

My cheeks warm, and I focus on the scrambled eggs in front of me.

Caleb groans. "I'm kidding! You don't have to pay."

I scoop some onto my plate, my hand freezing when he adds, "Well…"

"Caleb."

"You're working with me today, so I guess you pay in that sense."

I finish scooping them onto the plate. That's easy enough.

"Have they made a decision yet?" I ask, holding my breath as we move down the food line, praying they have and said yes.

"Not yet. You'll be the first to know."

My stomach is in knots, but it gurgles since I haven't had a real meal since before Judy and Dennis were taken.

If I'm going to save them, I'll need my strength.

There's time to feel guilt later. Right now, I need to focus on rescuing them and finding a way to *actually* contact Theo. When I finally got my phone charged, his went straight to voicemail. Typical.

Everything else needs to be—*has* to be—locked up in a box in my mind and shoved into the corner. I can worry about unpacking it all later.

Caleb leads me to an empty table, and I sit across from him, scanning the room. Simone, Esha, and Louis sit in the corner.

"You're not going to eat with your friends?" I muse.

Caleb sits back, flabbergasted. "Are we not friends?"

I roll my eyes. "You know what I meant."

"I'm sick of them. You're much more interesting."

"Hm..." I pick up my orange juice, taking a sip as I process his response, eventually changing tactics. "Are you able to get a hold of Jason?"

"Probably. Why?"

"He already knows where the others are. He can tell Theo I'm okay and where to find me."

On the slim chance that I am losing it and only dreamt of Theo, this can at least be a backup plan. While everything in me wishes that I didn't imagine it and that Theo is currently on his way here, I'll feel better knowing Jason can pass the message along if needed.

"Uh huh." Caleb stabs at a piece of watermelon with his fork, seemingly distracted. "Yeah, I'll reach out."

"Thanks..." I respond, but he still studies his fruit. "So... what do you do?"

He glances up at me. "Huh?"

"For work. What are we doing today?"

"No spoilers."

I huff, sitting back in my chair, and push around what's left on my plate. I should eat more, but the pit in my stomach makes it impossible.

When we finish, I follow Caleb into the kitchen, and he throws a pair of gloves at me. We stand shoulder to shoulder in silence, washing all the dirty plates from breakfast. Someone else has dismantled the buffet, and its pieces are stacked behind us to be washed.

The silence is unbearable. It leaves too much room for doubt, guilt, frustration, and other negative emotions to run through my veins, threatening to light me up. But not Caleb; he's as cool as a cucumber, standing next to me as the smell of lemon dish soap surrounds us.

I turn, leaning my hip against the sink. "What's the deal?"

He raises an eyebrow but continues washing.

"There's no way this is your normal job."

"Are you too good to wash dishes, Roberts?"

"No." I turn back to face the sink. "This makes sense for me because I'm new. I'm confused as to why *you're* here."

"I didn't want you to be lonely."

"See!" I spin again. "That's it! That's exactly what I'm talking about! What's the deal? Am I not allowed to be alone? Are you watching me? Protecting me? What is it?" I demand.

"Do you doubt I hang out with you because of your charming personality?"

I heave a frustrated sigh, ignore him, and return to the dishes. If he needs to watch me, as if I'm some flight risk or some threat to their establishment, then fine. I'll play my role, do the dishes, and hope they say yes to helping me—anything it takes to bring Judy and Dennis home.

⁂

AFTER CLEANING UP AFTER breakfast, lunch, and dinner, and scrubbing all the public bathrooms, and doing countless loads of laundry, I collapse in my bed, utterly drained. I ran around so much today, throwing myself into the work as much as possible, that I didn't allow myself to think.

Caleb said he couldn't get ahold of Jason, and there's no word from Tilly, so all I can do is wait.

The pile of linens Simone left sits on the bed, and I force myself to get up and shower, leaving most of my contents, including Olivia's urn, still packed away in my backpack. If I need a quick escape, which is laughable since I'll no doubt die alone in the desert if I try to leave here alone, I'll at least be ready to go.

With my curls dripping wet, I make the bed, and an overwhelming urge to scream threatens to devour me. The box I packed away in my mind isn't as secure as I thought, but if I let it all out now, I'm not sure when it will stop. I need to keep the brave face on for a while longer.

I swallow my emotions, ignoring my trembling lip and shuddering breaths, when a sharp knock raps on the door.

"Come in," I squeak. My eyelids flutter as I blink away the tears, trying to compose myself. I swipe at my face, willing the emotion to smooth itself away.

Tilly pops her head in. "Hey, got a moment?"

I nod, afraid my voice will betray me. I motion for her to sit on the other bed.

"Listen…" she begins. Concern crinkles her eyes, and her soft tone puts me on edge. The carefully built dam is ready to break. If she tells me no *now*, then no amount of boxes will be able to contain my anguish.

She tugs on her vest jacket, situating herself, and crosses her ankles. "We came to a vote."

I bite my lip, holding my breath.

"We want to help," she says, holding up a hand as I visibly deflate, my breath leaving in one long exhale. "But… it's going to take a while."

"A while?"

"Griffin was able to locate your foster parents. They're at a detention center, but the Authorities are smart. They're bouncing them from place to place, so who knows where they'll be tomorrow."

"Then how do we save them?"

She puts her hands on either side of her, pressing into the mattress so she can lean forward. "Let me handle those details, and I'll fill you in when I can. But I promise, we're going to do everything possible to help."

"I can't just sit here and wait around. If it's about privacy concerns, I'll sign whatever you want. Please. Just let me help. There must be something I can do!"

"It's probably you that they want, Gemma." The sympathy in her eyes is in total contrast to her harsh voice. "Your folks aren't mutants. For all we know, there's no real reason for them to even take them, let alone keep them alive."

"Well, let me go then! I can take them. If they're up for an exchange—"

"You can't take them."

"You don't know how powerful I am!" I rise from the bed, anger getting the best of me. "It's not fair for them to be held captive if it's me they want. I can go alone so none of the others get hurt."

Tilly shakes her head. "It's not that simple. They're not setting a trap. If they were, they would have left behind a location for you, with instructions on where to go. But they *didn't*. If they're moving them around, it's because they *don't want to be found*—not yet, at least. We're going to continue monitoring the situation—"

When I open my mouth, she holds up her hand again.

"We're going to *monitor* the situation," she repeats. "And when the timing is right, and we're a step ahead and know where they'll be next, we'll go in."

"But—"

"There is no but," she argues, the sharpness in her voice returning. "Good grief, you're as bad as Caleb," she mumbles under her breath.

Then she takes a deep breath. "You're welcome to stay here, but there are rules to follow. Number one being following orders."

I sit on the edge of the bed, the inability to do anything weighing on me as tears blur my vision.

"I'm sorry," she says. "But if we do this, we *will* do it right."

Seconds later, the door closes behind her, and the fight leaves me. The unceasing guilt rips at my seams, and I lie down, letting the fear pull me under.

I JERK AWAKE TO sirens blaring through the base.

My hands are already glowing purple, my body sensing a threat before the alarms did.

I whip off the covers, stumbling around in the low light until I can put on my shoes and jacket. Fumbling for the doorknob, I'm finally out in the hall, rushing by the few people already out there.

Someone shouts, "Freakin' Griffin!" as they return to their room and slam the door shut.

I rush down the stairs, passing a few others who shout over the noise, querying whether this is a real alarm or not.

One pair sounds like they're actually placing a bet.

My steps slow as I reach the first-floor landing. No one else seems to be in a hurry, and I start to question my reaction. Maybe Griffin *is* to blame. He does mess with electronics.

But the lights flash red in rhythm to the wailing alarm.

Better safe than sorry.

I meet Simone outside the War Room, but she stares at her shoes as others bustle by. Maybe she's listening to see what caused the alarm?

"What's going on?"

"We have company."

Her response sends a chill up my spine. "Do you know who?"

"Not yet."

"What do we do?" I ask, but this time, she ignores me. Her eyes narrow a little as she focuses on the ground.

I glance both ways down the hall, shifting my weight from foot to foot. My fingertips tingle, but I don't allow them to glow again—not yet, not until I know there's a real danger. The fewer people who witness my hands, the better.

Caleb whips open the door to the War Room. "Roberts," he greets me as if this is a totally normal occurrence. But who am I kidding? It probably is for them. "You should get back to bed. This doesn't concern you."

"Is the base under attack?"

He shakes his head.

"Are you sure?"

"Positive."

I point above. "What's with all this then?"

"Griffin is working out some kinks to the alarm system. Off to bed, you go!" He turns me by my shoulders, gently pushing me in the direction of the stairs, but not before Simone's stare cuts to Caleb's profile, and her eyebrows raise just a fraction. Her doubt pulsating against me convinces me to turn around and head straight for the lobby, ignoring Caleb's protests.

My legs turn to jelly and almost give out when I round the corner.

There, in all his handsome glory, stands a very disheveled Theo. His hands are on his hips, a muscle in his jaw working as he focuses on Tilly speaking to some older man. From just behind their group, I catch a head of blonde curls.

"Theo!" I shout over the alarms, breaking into a run. He glances up, his mouth dropping slightly as I crash into him. "Oh my god, you're here!"

Amber punches me in the arm before squeezing me. "Don't ever do that again!"

"I'm sorry!" I let go of her, giving Nora and Zay a quick hug as well. "I wasn't thinking. I just needed to do *something* and didn't want to put you all at risk."

Elise and I don't exchange any pleasantries, but she gives me a curt nod. It's almost like she's admitting she's glad to see I'm still alive. *Almost.*

Anger radiates off Theo, but the undercurrent of relief is evident, too, and I try not to squirm beneath his intense gaze.

"Is that...?" I use my chin to indicate the guy talking to Tilly.

"Jason? Yeah." Theo runs a hand through his hair as he breathes a sigh. Dark bags hang under his eyes as if he hasn't been sleeping. Is that why he hasn't come to see me? "I had to ask for help."

"I'm sorry," I say again, wincing. Theo asking an adult for help would be at the absolute bottom of things he wants to do.

"Are they going to help rescue Judy and Dennis?"

I nod. "They're not rushing, which is infuriating, knowing Judy and Dennis are being subjected to who knows what, but at least they said they'll help."

"I guess it all worked out then." The chill in his voice drops the room's temperature.

"Theo..." I reach for his hand, but he pulls away just as Tilly turns around to face the group. The sirens abruptly cut off, and the lights return to normal. My stomach sinks to my toes. Theo is justifiably mad, but I'd hoped we'd reconnect before we started arguing.

"So, Jason has filled me in on the situation. You're all welcome to stay here, but as I explained to Gemma"—her gaze snaps to mine—"we have rules." After a bated breath, she glances away. "We're going to test your abilities and assign you to a work program, and the younger of you will begin classes. You'll also all be properly trained to fight. There are enough rooms, but we'd like you to pair off to save space for any more potential newcomers.

"Now, don't worry. We're not going to give up on trying to find Judy and Dennis, but until we have a plan in place, you're expected to act like you're one of us. Once we have the situation under control and the rescue mission happens, it'll be up to you whether or not you decide to stay and be a part of the fight.

"We don't force anyone to be here. But if you're here, you earn your way. We have a system, and it works. Any questions?"

"I'd be willing to work more if those three could focus on their studies only." Theo nods toward Nora, Zay, and Amber.

Tilly smiles. "That's sweet of you, but everyone pulls their own weight around here. We do take into consideration the workload provided, and their jobs will apply to their abilities, so essentially, their work is a part of class."

"They're just kids," he argues.

Jason crosses his arms. "Not anymore. Unfortunately for all of us, we don't have the luxury to coddle the young when it's mutants versus the Authorities."

Theo's shoulders tense at first, like he wants to fight the idea, but then they sag in defeat, and he doesn't comment any further.

"Now that that's all settled, Caleb will show you to your rooms."

I glance behind me, and he's right there. His hands are behind his back, his feet shoulder-width apart, and he looks like he's playing the role of a good little soldier.

Why did he want me to go back upstairs? Did he know Theo was here? Seeing Theo and the rest of them standing in the lobby, I was so overwhelmed that I didn't even think to question Caleb's motives. *What was his intention?* I glance away, uneasiness blooming in my chest. I push it to the back of my mind for now and focus on the rest of the group.

Tilly smiles at everyone again, and it's open and warm like she's genuinely happy to add six more members to the base. "Get some rest. We start tomorrow."

Chapter Sixteen

Theo

THE PENT-UP ENERGY AND frustration bleed out of me the longer I'm next to Gemma. I'm sure she can read me like a book and knows my anger about her leaving is waning.

But I don't want to admit that to her yet. More or less, I'm relieved that she's alive, but her running off—*again*—isn't all right.

We're supposed to be a team; she has the freedom to do whatever the hell she wants, but she should know by now that I'll always back her play. I shouldn't be left behind if I want to take a moment to think it through so we can plan accordingly.

I bite back a sigh as Caleb leads us to the second floor and assigns us a line of doors. Gemma is already in 209, so he gives everyone else 211 and 213. He leaves, mumbling something about blankets, and the rest of us stand in the hallway, staring at one another.

Gemma's gaze seers into the side of my face, willing me to look at her, but I hold my ground. *Don't give in yet.* I can still be upset about her leaving all of us behind, even if my body feels differently and just wants to hold her.

Amber bursts out laughing, shattering the tension. "Judy would *so* kill you," she tells Gemma before opening the door to 211 and giggling her way inside. "I needed that," she says as her voice trails off into the room. Nora shakes her head and follows behind Amber.

With sudden clarity, I stifle a groan. Gemma was staring at me because of the room assignments, not because she was trying to get my attention to hash it out.

I'm an idiot.

Elise bites her lip, grinning like she's holding back whatever sarcastic retort she was about to make, and pushes her way past Gemma into her room. Gemma spins and follows her in, closing the door quickly, leaving just Zay and me in the hallway.

He slaps me on the shoulder. "Tough break."

I don't bother hiding my groan this time as I follow him into the remaining room.

THE NEXT MORNING, ALL six of us take a tour of the base. Gemma and I walk side by side, and the ice I was trying to form between us has thawed. Any fleeting thoughts of being upset with her are long gone, and I want nothing more than to make up now that we're both in the same vicinity again.

We step out of the elevator and start our tour in the basement, the one piece of the hotel that isn't part of the U-shape. Where the outdoor courtyard would be above us, there's an indoor greenhouse. Lettuce, tomatoes, peppers, radishes, beets, potatoes, carrots, and various herbs grow in separate rows. Grow lamps hang above the soil, some brighter than others, with a sprinkler system zigzagging through the lights.

Around the greenhouse, the floor is painted like a track and goes from staircase to staircase on each side of the hotel. There's also a restroom, a drained pool that has cracks running through its foundation, and a training mat where Jet, one of the leaders of the base, informs us people fight and use their abilities against each other, which doesn't seem very smart. There's also a target practice section for knives and guns, a full-on gym complete with weights, punching bags, and where one-on-one training is held, and then next to that, a classroom where Nora, Zay, and Amber will be keeping up with their studies.

Lastly, there's a utility room filled with so many different systems that it's hard to keep track of them. Inside, there's an air supply system that helps remove carbon dioxide, a water supply system that also helps keep it clean, and some recyclable and trash systems they have set up to reuse any organic material while also getting rid of the unusable junk.

"I'm sorry," I interrupt Jet as he rambles through his explanation of technical systems and how they keep the base warm during the cold desert nights. "How do you power all this? Where's the energy coming from?"

"We can manipulate air and other gasses, along with metals, water, heat, soil, and electricity. We don't like to depend on mutant powers because if anything were to happen to them, our carefully built structure would fail. But those who can help lend their abilities to the fickle systems we do have in place to keep it running smoothly. The more mutants willing to help the cause, the more stable our operation becomes."

I frown. It's hard to feel comforted by the fact that this could all come crashing down in an instant, but what other choice do they have?

"You'll probably notice the copper," he continues as if the interruption never happened. "Copper is key when blocking radio frequencies, which is one of the main reasons we built a camp to begin with."

He looks over the six of us. The others are wide-eyed and have questions written all over their faces, which I'm sure mirror my own.

"... But we'll get into all that at a later date..." Jet clears his throat, glancing at his clipboard. It's almost ridiculous how formal this is, like we're getting a college campus tour.

"That's about it for the basement. You already glimpsed most of the first floor when you arrived, but that's where you'll eat your meals and get help from the medics if you need it. Upstairs also has a lounge if you feel like hanging out. And you'll find a chicken coop outside in the courtyard."

"There's chickens here?" Zay exclaims.

Jet nods. "We have some manufactured grass out there, so there's a bit of fake greenery out in the desert. You won't be fooled by it, but it gets the job done. Tilly and I both have quarters on the first floor as well, so if you need anything, stop by her place first." He cracks a grin at his own joke, but no one laughs.

We all funnel into the elevator as he tells us how floors two and three are the same—full of bedrooms. Then we spill out onto the fourth and last floor, which is divided into four giant rooms. To the far right is a science lab; next to it is a computer lab and library, and to the left of the elevator is the security room.

It's full of monitors, with people perched in computer chairs examining each screen. Hardly any of the feeds are of the base, though. It's mainly filming different locations, and I don't recognize anyone on the screens.

A guy about Jason's age with a blond crew cut, dressed all in tactical gear, steps up to a monitor, laying a hand on the screen. He closes his eyes; nothing happens. I take a step closer to see what he's doing, but Jet steers me away.

"We'll let Griffin do his thing," Jet mutters as he leads us back out into the hallway.

He points to the last door on the left. "That's storage. We stock up on whatever we can. A few of us go on missions every so often to gather supplies we can't grow ourselves. It's risky, and there's a chance we'll get busted. But it's the one thing we can do, so we have to try."

I'm nodding along before I even realize what I'm doing, understanding what it means to live this way. The only difference is we worked on a much smaller operation.

"If you need anything, ask first; someone else will check storage for you. Don't touch anything unless you're assigned a job requiring you to go in there. We need to keep our numbers straight so we know where we stand. Got it?"

Everyone bobs their heads, mouths shut. I'm still trying to process the extent of this hidden base, and I imagine the others are, too.

"Right," Jet says. "Well, let's head back downstairs to get breakfast, and then I'm going to pass you along to Gwen, who will start testing your powers and assigning you to a field."

⚜

"Nora?" A boy with wild red curls and green eyes, pronounced by his thick, round glasses, drops the breakfast tray he's holding.

His fair skin, peppered with freckles, reddens as he takes a step toward us. *How the hell does he know Nora?* I step in front of her, blocking her before he can get any closer.

He sputters, "N-Nora, it's me, Henry!"

"Henry?" Nora whispers. When I glance behind me, she's frozen, her face having lost all color. She looks like she's about to pass out. "It can't be," she says, but it's so quiet that I almost miss it.

Zay and Gemma give each other questioning looks.

"Nora!" Henry says again, racing forward, but I stick an arm out, breaking his pace as his shoulder collides with my arm.

"Who are you?" I ask, immediately defensive.

"Henry?" Nora asks again, this time louder. "Is that really you?"

Henry ignores me as if I'm not holding him back. His scrawny figure makes no progress as he squirms against my hand, but he stands on his tiptoes, trying to peer over my shoulder.

Suddenly, Nora is barreling past me, shoving me to the side.

"Henry!" she screams as they collide into each other.

What the hell?

Tears stream down Nora's cheeks, and now I'm really confused. She pulls away from him, holding him at arm's length, her face breaking into a rare smile. Then she pulls him in and declares, "Henry" all over again.

"Who the hell is Henry?" I finally ask. Gemma shrugs, and Zay's brows furrow as he studies their reunion.

"Sorry!" Nora breaks into laughter, covering her mouth with her hands. "Sorry, everyone, this is Henry. Henry, this is everyone."

"We kind of figured," Gemma says, her mouth twisting as if to refrain from smiling. "How do you two know each other?"

Nora glances at me, then back to the kid standing next to her. "Henry is my cousin." She smiles again, throwing her hands in the air. "I just! I never! Oh my god!"

"Cousin? I thought you…"

She told us she erased herself from her family's lives… Did she forget someone?

"I did!" She bobs her head, answering my unspoken thoughts. "I don't know how this is happening!" She whips around to focus back on Henry. "You remember me?" she asks him as tears shine in her eyes again, and there's a deafening crack in my heart. Not because she found a family member. For that, I'm thankful. But it's clear how much being forgotten has hurt her all this time.

"Holy sh—" Zay begins, but I shove him toward the table we were all about to sit at.

I point at the empty seats. "Henry, why don't you join us?"

There's extra room at our table anyway since Elise has decided to eat with Caleb. My gaze involuntarily shifts to those two, locked in a conversation across the dining hall, and it takes everything in me not to scoff out loud.

If there's a douchebag around, Elise will find him.

"Yes! Please. Oh my god." Nora pulls out a chair, thankfully dragging me out of my thoughts. "How did you—When did you—"

Henry sits at the end of the table so the two of them are next to each other, and Gemma sits across from Zay. All three of us are glued to their conversation. *What does this mean? Will others remember her, too?*

"I don't know," Henry says. "I just… remembered. Not at first. You've been gone… what? Three years now?" His gaze flickers to the top of the hand imprint burned into her chest.

"Something like that," she murmurs, pulling her shirt up to block most of the scar.

Henry focuses on her face again, not bothering to question her mark, but from the corner of my eye, I catch Gemma slouching a little in her seat.

"It was last year. Before I ended up here, actually. Do you remember that Furby we used to scare your sisters with?"

Nora nods, her eyes shining with tears as she tries to smile.

"Well, I was packing up my things because I was heading out to this base and couldn't take it all with me. I came across it hidden in the closet, and it sort of... unlocked something in me.

"At first, I was staring at this creature, trying to figure out why I had it, and then all of a sudden, I just... remembered you. It's so hard to explain, but it was like the memories snapped back into place. I had no idea *how* you left or why you were suddenly back, but then I realized that it'd been *years* since I last saw you, and I knew it had to do with something..."

"Magical?" she asks.

"Exactly."

"Has anyone else...?"

Henry shakes his head this time, the dimple in his chin becoming more pronounced. "No, I'm sorry. I tried talking about you, but your parents thought I was a lunatic. They kept demanding, *How could I forget my own child?* It was clearly upsetting them the more I pushed, and then I left to come here..." He trails off before grabbing her arm. "I'm so sorry, Nor. If I had any clue I'd run into you again, I would have tried harder. But I didn't know what to make of it. You were just... gone."

I rub my temples, trying to wrap my head around how Henry even remembered her in the first place. *Is it because he's a mutant? Does Nora's ability wear off after a certain amount of time?*

She pats his hand, giving a sad smile. "It's okay, H. Really. I'm glad I have you back, at least."

Gemma sets down her fork and takes a small sip of her drink before clearing her throat. "Nora, do you remember what you did to *erase* yourself? You said you wished really hard, right?"

She picks at her lip. "I knew I had to leave, and I didn't want them to be sad, so I wished they'd forget about me. When it worked, I figured between that and my visions, I had some sort of control over the past and the future."

"Did you do anything special, though? Did you think about your memories with them or hide your belongings?"

"I did get rid of most of my things. I threw my clothes in with my sisters and removed myself from family photos, figuring it'd be hard to explain why I was in them. But that's about it. I didn't know if it'd *actually* work. So, at worst, I'd be a runaway. That would've killed my mother, though. So, I guess I'm glad it worked for some..." She sits back in her chair, blinking at the table a few times, clearly remembering that night.

I'd like to provide her with some words of comfort, but absolutely nothing comes to mind.

"Although..." Nora says, sitting up. "I put that Furby in your closet that night." Her eyes grow wide. "When I was getting rid of my things, I wanted you to have it, so I hid it in your room. So maybe I somehow left that piece behind by accident? Maybe I can't actually *erase* minds?"

"You lock memories away instead?" Henry offers. "Let me talk to Margot about it. She's the head of the science lab and knows the most about abilities around here. She'd probably be able to help figure out what you can do."

Nora's eyes brim with tears again as she lets out a shuddering breath. "I'm so glad to see you."

Henry beams right back at her. "You have no idea. I've been so homesick lately. This feels like a miracle."

"Wait!" Nora blurts. "You're here! Why? Are you different, too?"

A sly grin slides across his face, and an apple appears on the table before Nora. She startles, and when she reaches for it, her hand brushes right through the air.

"Ahhh," Gemma exclaims. "So, you're *that* Henry."

Zay finally speaks up. "I'm happy for you two, but I am *so* lost."

Everyone laughs at this, but poor Zay frowns, still looking confused. That makes two of us, but I can't get over what this means for Nora.

"I shield the place," Henry says. "I create illusions, so the reason no one can see the base is because I cloaked it."

"You can make anyone see what you want to?" I ask.

"I haven't found anyone it doesn't work on yet—besides Louis, but that's because of his shield."

Ugh. Louis.

"So, you're pretty important around here," Gemma states.

"Important enough that I'm not allowed to leave the base." He sighs. "I get it, though. They haven't found any other illusionists yet, so until they do, I'm their mask. Before I arrived, you could see the motel as plain as day.

"We'd still be in the middle of nowhere, of course, but if the Authorities flew overhead, we'd stick out like a sore thumb."

"Is anyone else in our family different?" Nora asks.

"I don't think so." Henry's shoulders droop. "We're the only two mutants in the bloodline, it seems. But let me go talk to Margot so we can see what your ability really is."

He gives Nora one more parting hug, promising to return soon, and dashes for the door, disappearing into the hallway.

My brain is truly melting after this morning's events and from trying to keep up with how the base is run and how everything about it works. And how are there so many mutants in the world? Let alone on other bases?

On top of that, Nora can apparently alter memories.

It's impossible to grasp all of it.

I find myself on the motel's roof, breathing in the sandy, dry air, concentrating on getting my lungs to work.

So much has changed recently. How did I go from hiding the four of us, always running from my father and the Authorities, to standing on the roof of a mutant base with dozens and dozens of people below me, keeping this entire operation running with their abilities?

I pull out a cigarette, light it, and focus on the flame seconds before the silence shatters.

"I'm so sorry, Theo," Gemma utters before the door to the roof closes.

This is the first moment we've had alone since we've been reunited, and the devastated look on her face pulls at my heartstrings, guilt racking me for not letting her off the hook immediately and stupidly trying to hold out on being angry last night.

Gemma wanted to find others, and we sure found them.

I stub the cigarette out on the wall, sliding it back into the case. "Why? You were right," I say, throwing my arms out, indicating the entire building.

"No." She shakes her head. "Please, don't say anything. Just let me get this out."

She walks to the edge of the roof and stares out into the desert. I swallow a few times, working up the courage to stand beside her. Four floors up isn't as high as the Ferris Wheel, but high is still high.

"I have to tell you something," she whispers. "I tried to that night before I ran off. I was scared, though." She rubs her upper arms, brushing off the cold that isn't there. The sun hasn't begun to set yet, and the desert heat lingers.

"What is it?"

"I did something." Her gaze flickers to mine, and then she squints at the horizon again. "Something terrible. I've been trying to convince myself that I didn't have a choice, that it comes with the territory, but I'm afraid I'm oversimplifying it to spare myself the repercussions and that I should own up to it and deal with the consequences. The guilt is..."

When she stops speaking for a long time, I urge her to continue. "Tell me."

"I killed someone," she says automatically like she was waiting for me to ask.

When I sharply inhale, she corrects herself. "*Someones.*"

"How?" My brows furrow. "When?"

"The pizza place." She faces me, her bottom lip wobbling and tears glistening in her perfect violet eyes. "You ran out to get to Zay, and I could still feel them chasing us. We were going to get cornered, and I..."

Her body shudders, and I grab her, pulling her into me.

"I don't know who I killed. It could have been someone's sister. It could have been Riley!"

"Shh," I try to soothe, but her body racks with sobs. "You saved us," I remind her. "You did what you had to do to get us out of there."

"You were able to escape without killing anyone," she cries into my shirt. "I electrocuted all of them! I felt their heartbeats stop."

"Oh, Gem." I hug her tighter. "Nothing I'm going to say will make this better for you. You just have to ride it out and let the emotions run where they will." I step back from her, cradling her face in my hands. "They were going to capture or kill us, and you did what you had to do."

She nods, tears streaming down her pale cheeks. I brush them away with my thumbs. "You're so brave. And so amazing. And I'm sorry I didn't agree to find the others right away. You shouldn't have had to deal with this on your own."

"It's okay," she says as she sniffles. "I shouldn't have left like that and should've been honest with you upfront. I know we said no more secrets. I was just so worried about what you'd think of me."

"I love you," I remind her. "No matter what you do, you won't shake me off that easily."

"Promise?" she asks.

"I promise."

She wraps her arms around me, and we stay entangled as the minutes pass. The honey smell is gone from her hair, replaced by a new floral scent, which must be what she showered with here. I don't mind the change, because either way, it means we're together, and I will do everything in my power not to get separated again.

That reminds me... she must have noticed how Esha looks at her, especially since they just shared a car together for so long. Gemma's power must look different, and we don't need anyone learning how she was created by Draven and not by a mutation. If anything Draven said about how people viewed him was true, we better not risk it.

"While you're here…" I lean closer so my lips touch her ear, and she stiffens. "Don't talk about the woods."

She leans away, her brows knitted.

I put a finger to my lips and tap my ear to indicate Simone and her sonic hearing. Her mouth drops open to form an O-shape, understanding filling her gaze.

"I think what we do *alone* should be kept secret."

My heart pounds, hoping Gemma is following my train of thought. Gemma filled me in on how Draven was murdered—in a sense—by her parents so they could steal his power. And now that she has some of it, she needs to keep her ability in control so she doesn't fly off the charts. If they discover how powerful she is, they'd maybe want to study her in their lab here. I don't trust these people enough yet to know if they'd truly help or pick her apart.

At the end of the day, it's better to be safe than sorry.

"I see…" Gemma says. "I wouldn't want to make anyone jealous of what I have…" She gives me a coy grin and a small kiss, and relief floods me.

We're back on the same page, and I can finally breathe again.

Chapter Seventeen

Gemma

WE CIRCLE THE TRAINING mat in the basement, all staring at one another. No one seems to want to volunteer, and the anxiety in the room about who will go first is palpable.

Gwen leads the group, advising us that we will start by displaying our powers, but we might move into more physical activities depending on how the day goes. She already showed off her telekinetic ability by removing all the chairs from the area and closing the door to the greenhouse with her thoughts. She isn't much bigger than I am, proving that power isn't linked to size. Her blonde hair, reminding me of straw, is tied back in a bun, and she wears a form-fitting olive-green tank top, revealing tan arms, and has black leggings on in case we move on to hand-to-hand combat like she first mentioned.

Holt towers next to her, running a large hand through his mousy brown shag haircut, pushing it out of his hazel eyes. His lips press together as he studies us all as if we're a bunch of actual schoolchildren about to fail a test. He's dressed more formally than Gwen, with pants and a sweater, but that's because he's not sparring today if we make it that far.

That falls to Griffin Kirby, who—I'm sorry, Theo—looks like a god with olive skin, blond hair, and sky-blue eyes. He's not as tall as Theo, but his tight clothing reveals a sculpted body like he works out five times a day. He has an easy smile like he's always about to crack a joke, so the exact opposite of Holt's expression.

I nudge Elise in the ribs, then point at my face. "I think you're drooling."

"Shut up," she hisses, reaching for her mouth anyway.

Amber breaks the tension, taking a large step forward so she's in the middle of the mat. She clutches her hands together behind her back and proudly lifts her chin to the three in Command.

"I'm Amber Blake, fourteen years old, and I can't demonstrate my power right now since no dead people are around." She goes through the list we were instructed to provide so Esha's hungry gaze can view what our powers look like as she categorizes them all.

"I can communicate with the dead, and before you ask, any dead. Or at least any ghost who chooses to seek me out. Theo has been showing me some combat moves, but I'm not that good."

She takes a step back, falling into the circle.

"Welcome, Amber." Gwen bows her head. "Next?"

Amber shoves Zay forward, and he stumbles as his foot catches the mat. He turns to glare at her, but she only smiles and gives him a thumbs up.

"I'm Zay Lewis, fifteen. Does anyone have a plant on hand?"

Esha stands and retrieves a potted tomato plant from the greenhouse.

"And a stick?"

Esha looks like she's about to roll her eyes, but she backtracks the few steps to the greenhouse anyway to grab a pole near the door. She hands it to Zay before returning to her seat in the corner.

Without breaking a sweat, Zay influences the plant to grow, tomatoes blooming off the stem as if they've been ready to eat for days. The vine climbs up the pole and stands almost as tall as he is.

"I have control over the other elements, too."

"Even fire?" Holt asks, crossing his arms.

Theo stiffens next to me at the suggestion.

"I can't create it, but I can control it."

Holt nods, and Zay takes a step back into place when no other questions are raised but then lurches forward. "Oh, and I don't really fight either." He flashes a nervous smile and steps back again.

"Nora Sanders. I'm turning seventeen next month. I have visions of the future, and, well…" She looks at Theo, and he gives her an encouraging head dip. "I thought I could alter the past, but it turns out I can't. I don't know what I can do, but my cousin Henry is going to ask whoever Margot is, I guess."

"Why did you think you could alter the past?" Gwen asks.

"Because until a year ago, Henry couldn't remember who I was. I thought I erased myself from my family's minds."

"Awkward," Esha says, not looking up from her notebook.

"But they remember you now?"

"Just him, as far as I know," Nora's voice quiets, and I don't know if the sadness filling me is mine or hers.

"I see. I guess we'll let Margot figure all that out." Gwen smiles. "Thank you."

Nora pulls on her lip, turning away.

Elise goes next, then Theo. Elise mutters through her ordeal, forever upset that she can't do more than read auras. Theo blinks in and out but accidentally goes a tad too far and ends up tripping the wire for the alarm when he lands outside the base.

Griffin's good nature doesn't fail as he dashes off to shut down the electrical system in the utility room. The entire time, he shouts, "Sorry! Sorry!"

When the blaring stops and the lights have returned to normal, I take center stage on the mat.

More people have now funneled to the basement to watch the spectacle. Caleb and Simone stand over near Esha's chair, and Louis and Asher hang out in the far back, their gaze settling on me like a weighted blanket. The rest are all nameless faces.

If there's ever a time to be in complete control of my power, it's now.

I don't need to hide who I am anymore, but I also can't give them full burning-down-the-woods wattage.

Esha already seems to suspect something is up with me, especially now as her back straightens and she gives me her undivided attention, setting down the notebook she's been pouring over this entire time.

But even with needing to limit myself, it feels good not to hide entirely—being able to claim this part of me.

I might not have been born with it, but it's still *mine*.

For now, both hands light up, purple orbs I can balance in my palms. If I gave it any more energy, they'd turn into flames, but I don't want to risk that.

The light ebbs from my fingertips, flaring slightly when everyone's heartbeats become too overwhelming. The panic heightens at having all eyes on me. I don't want to drain energy from any of these people accidentally, so I focus on blocking out their pulses.

Theo pulls a hand from his pocket, motioning it toward the floor. It's like he's in my head again, his voice telling me: *Easy. Breathe.*

I suck in the air, steadying the current in my palms before curling my fingers and extinguishing the orbs completely.

"Don't be shy, Roberts," Caleb says.

"I'm not," I say, shifting uneasily.

He makes his way over to the mat with a shit-eating grin. Spinning so he stands in front of me and faces the crowd, he drawls, "I saw her take out like ten Authority members herself. It was incredible. Never seen anything like it." That last sentence haunts me again, a reminder of what he said before, another indicator that I'm the odd one out and not mutant-born.

The audience lets out a collective gasp. I instinctively take a step backward, colliding into Theo's chest since he's already there to meet me. He grabs my arms, but neither of us moves back any further, waiting to see where Caleb is going with this. My hands don't spark back up with Theo's warmth bleeding into me, but I clench them into fists at my sides anyway.

"She snapped bones with hardly a touch, she burned the shit out of people with her hands, and she did something with the electricity and blew out all the transformers in town. The entire place went dark."

"Caleb," I warn.

He twists to look at me. "You're a badass, Roberts; don't hide it."

"I'm not," I argue. "But that was an extenuating circumstance. I'm not like that... all the time."

"Command should still know, though, so we can help you always perform at that level."

"I don't *want* to be like that."

"With a gift like yours—"

"Stop!" My fingertips light up, and I don't hide them this time.

Before, I could show how easily the power comes to me. But *this*. This is the problem. When emotions get the best of me, I lose any semblance of control.

Caleb *knows* I killed four people. He was the first person I ever admitted it to. So why is he pushing me like this? *Is he doing it on purpose?*

We circle one another on the mat, and Theo steps back, falling into line. I guess the physical part of the testing is beginning.

"Bring it, Roberts." Caleb smirks.

He's going to mess everything up. I can't accidentally hurt any of them. It'd risk everything. Would they still find Judy and Dennis if I'm a risk to everyone here?

I quirk an eyebrow and play it cool, even though my heart rages inside my chest. "As you said, I'm dangerous."

"I'm not afraid of you," he states, stalking me like *I'm* the prey. "You should be."

He gives me a cocky grin, coaxing me closer with a hand. "Prove it."

When I don't strike, he lunges for me. I squeal, scurrying out of the way as he lunges a second time. He just misses me, but his arm came close enough that I need to *stop* glowing. I can't outrun him forever.

I wring my hands, bouncing on my toes as I spin away one more time, breathing deeply until the tingling in my hands fades.

A second later, Caleb catches an arm, yanking me backward. I twist to face him, grab my fist with my free hand, and bend my elbow, effectively breaking his hold.

"Not bad." His chest heaves as he tries to catch his breath.

I shrug. "Theo taught me one or two self-defense moves."

"You need to learn to fight back. Not just self-defense."

"Maybe next time." I turn away, biting back my annoyance that he's put me on display in front of everyone.

He grabs my ponytail from behind, and instincts take over.

I step so we're side by side, hooking my elbow over his arm that's clutching my hair. Then I spin so I'm in front of him, breaking his hold and hooking a leg behind his. Using the momentum, I push him backward, tripping him, but Theo's training isn't as smooth in real-time, and Caleb brings me down with him, rolling on top of me so I'm trapped underneath.

He hovers over me, pinning my hands over my head, but it only lasts a second.

I swing my arms to my sides like I'm making a snow angel, which launches him forward. His hands slam on the mat above my head. I move my body up, circling my arms around one of his, block his leg with my foot, and roll. His elbow bends with the force, and gravity is on my side as I land on top of him and scramble away.

All this happens in the blink of an eye; I can't believe Theo's tricks worked.

I just took down a grown man with nothing but my own strength, powers excluded. A huge smile breaks across my face, and those watching clap. Caleb should quit while he's ahead, but of course, he doesn't.

He makes one more effort to bring me down, and this time, Theo's teachings don't kick in... my powers do. My fingers flare, and I rip my hand away from his, but his skin grazes mine anyway.

Caleb sucks in a breath, clutching his burned hand to his chest.

Gwen runs up, grabbing his arm to inspect the damage.

"I'm—" Tears fill my eyes as Caleb stares at me, his jaw twitching from his clenched teeth. "You idiot," I lash out. "I tried to tell you!"

Gwen glances up at me, her close-set jade green eyes narrowing as if Caleb didn't start all this. "That's enough. We're done for the day."

But then Asher is right there on the other side of the mat, his unbelievable strength making him nearly indestructible. I don't know if I'd even hurt him, but I certainly don't want to find out.

"Hicks," Gwen warns. "We're done."

His russet eyes flash to hers, his lips quirking, the smile sending pins and needles through my extremities. I'm no longer worried about hurting him; I don't want to see what *he* can do to *me*. He stalks closer, and I nearly trip over myself while backing away.

I throw a panicked look over my shoulder to Theo, but Louis has a hand on his shoulder, holding him back—literally—he's blocking him from jumping or getting to us.

Great.

I can't run anywhere else, so I throw my arms over my head, ducking and rolling to get away from his swing that will probably take my head off.

He catches the hood on my sweater, yanking me backward, and I can't breathe for a second. The clothing twists around my throat, and I scramble backward to keep from losing air completely.

Asher drops me on the ground, arm poised to strike; this is it.

This is how I die.

Purple exudes from my hands, and at the last possible second, I manage to catch his arm mid-swing. My hand closes around his fist, and the shock on his face must reflect my own. I twist away from him, his arm going one way and me the other, and his knees buckle, following the movement so I don't break anything.

When I'm standing, and he's effectively on the ground, I let go—stepping away with a myriad of emotions running through me. Disgust that he just tried to kill me, and shock—in addition to elation—that I have the strength to take him on.

"That's not possible." He wiggles his arm, running a hand over his forearm as if checking for any lasting injuries.

"Are we done here?" I ask.

"Not quite." Griffin takes Asher's place, but he wears a smile full of humor.

He's not menacing at all and doesn't seem like he wants to hurt me like Asher did. Instead, he looks curious about what I'm capable of.

I squint at him, and his hands spark up with white electricity. Almost like mine before they turn into flames.

We might be on an equal playing field.

He holds out his hand, his fingers sizzling and popping. "Humor me."

"This could be very bad," I warn.

"Oh, I know." He grins again.

I tentatively hold out a hand, my purple to his white. His fingers close around mine, and a shock runs through my entire body, my toes tingling from it.

"Not bad," he murmurs. "That all you got?"

I purse my lips, wondering how much power I can channel into my fingers without killing the plant Zay had worked on. I pump a little more into our connection, and Griffin hisses.

"There we go." He tries to laugh through clenched teeth.

"Had enough?"

"No," he whispers.

I can feel him trying to beat me, but his electricity doesn't hold a candle to mine. I feel lighter like I'm channeling his power and making it my own.

I smile. This... this feels nice.

And for once, with Griffin's power feeding me, I don't have to worry about anyone's heartbeat.

Griffin inhales again, eyes screwing shut as he bares his teeth. "Wait," he gasps.

I tilt my head, studying him. Why won't they ever learn? I can beat them. *All* of them. I'm not even showing an ounce of what's inside me, and—

My thoughts sail back to how powerful I felt in the woods when I was draining Theo during his horrible test, how nice it felt to be this powerful, but thankfully, I remember the costs that came with it.

"Oh my god." I break the connection, and when I do, all the lights in the room rupture.

Griffin staggers backward, not saying anything as he bends in half, dragging in air.

"Griffin." I move closer to him, but Theo is there, pulling me away. "I'm so sorry."

Griffin holds up a hand as if acknowledging me. "My own fault."

I have no idea where Caleb and Asher ran off to, but Gwen is now standing alone, and I don't have to bother reading her mood. Her face tells me everything.

And she is *not* happy.

"We. Are. Done. Here." She pronounces each word, reminding us she's said it more than once. But it's not my fault. I didn't challenge anyone.

They challenged *me*.

Everyone funnels from the room, muttering as they go, avoiding my eyes as they keep their heads down.

They're scared of me.

I not only injured one of their own, I ended up hurting three of them.

AFTER GWEN EFFECTIVELY CALMED down, she assigned job duties. I'm on watch.

Goody.

Now that they know I can hold my own against even Griffin's electricity, I'll have shifts watching the hotel perimeter in case anyone can see through the illusion. They've assured us there hasn't been an attack on this base, but it's still weird to think of being one of the people who surrounded Caleb and me when I first got here.

Theo will be physically training people. He tried reminding Command that he had no ground to stand on, but Jason spilled the beans about how he "liked to fight," and they wanted him to show the others. He somewhat trained our group and showed me those self-defense moves, so it shouldn't be too difficult for him.

Plus, he looks *really* good when working out, but that's a fringe benefit.

Amber will assist the nurse after her studies. Her ability to talk to ghosts won't really help with the process, but since they were at a loss on where to put her, she asked to be assigned there.

Nora will also be balancing studies and working with the security team. They're hoping to help her hone her visions so she can see more clearly. If they can get any intel on the Authorities' next move, they'll be able to beat them instead of always falling behind.

There's a section of the base Jet failed to show us, but that was apparently due to the dangers of it being a work in progress. Zay will work there with the other elemental mutants and help dig out tunnels. They want a cave system that goes further beneath the ground for additional protection from the Authorities.

And lastly, Elise. I tried not to laugh at her assignment, but it was too good. She's our newest cook!

When she rolled her eyes, muttering, "Go figure, I'm useless," I almost lost it. Her aura reading ability isn't of any use to Command members here, but she probably could've asked for an assignment like Amber did. But nope, she accepted the job, made a snarky quip, and swallowed the rest of what she was feeling.

It might even be considered growth for her.

It all feels too odd... We're finding a place here on this base, surrounded by others just like us, even if I have to keep part of my strength secret, but it doesn't feel like home, and I don't think it ever will. At least, not until Judy and Dennis are here with us.

Maybe then...

As always, my heart gives a painful tug when I think of finding a home without Olivia. The grief wave rolls in, and the tide is more turbulent today. But I think she'd be happy for me. Every day I'm on my own is another day I'm becoming stronger and finding a place where I belong.

If only a little.

Chapter Eighteen

THEO

A WEEK PASSES BEFORE we're invited to our first brief meeting—more specifically, Gemma and me. I suspect Jason did this since I don't see any reason why they'd allow us to be here, but I won't complain. I'd rather be in the know than not.

Age-wise, the rest of our group is too young to join us. Elise could've been here, but considering she's not bringing much to the table defensively, Jason didn't see why she needed to join. I surprised myself by arguing on her behalf, but Elise told me to drop it, that it wasn't worth fighting for.

It's my first time entering the War Room. Gemma squeezes my hand as we enter, taking seats near the end of the oval table, furthest away from where Tilly stands. She's talking to Jet in hushed tones as the others file in. I've slowly been learning names as I go, but Command is pretty small since there seems to be a limited number of adults around. Six in total lead the base, with Gwen, Holt, and Jason being the three other mutants besides Tilly and Jet. But the last, Ivan Mack, is normal—not a lick of power in him.

His pallid face, splattered with freckles, is closed off as he assesses everyone entering the room. His heavy-lidded green eyes narrow, like he's giving everyone a death glare, even though he seems to be a relatively nice guy, at least from the short time I've known him.

Most of the remaining adults don't have abilities; they're here because their family members are. Maybe things would have ended differently if John and I had found this place sooner. The irony is that John would have eventually learned of it because of Jason. Or maybe he already knew, but I was too busy running to listen.

Tilly excuses herself from the conversation and beelines to Gemma and me. Gemma sits up straighter, holding her head high. We've been trying to gather any news we can about Judy and Dennis, but Griffin informed us that not much has changed.

Physically speaking, they seem fine. But they've been gone for nearly two weeks now, and Griffin has commented on how, for the most part, they're separated from one another and are both hardly eating. But he's only been watching for the past week. Who knows what happened beforehand or what's happening in their heads?

I've tried locating them in their dreams to let them know we're okay and trying to get them, that they just need to hold on a little longer. But it's the same as it was with Gemma; I can't get through.

I drop the pen I've been clutching.

Why didn't I realize sooner?

"They have a shield," I reveal before Tilly can speak.

Her brows furrow. "Who?"

"The Authorities. Or, well, I don't know, maybe not all of them, but the ones guarding Judy and Dennis."

Jet walks up now, scowling. "How do you know?"

"Because I can't get into their dreams, the same way I couldn't get into Gemma's." The glint in Caleb's eye makes my blood pound as he leans against the wall, watching us. I get out of my chair to stand face-to-face with Jet. "I know my ability. If there weren't a blockage, I'd be able to reach them."

"There must be some sort of mistake," Gwen says.

"I couldn't reach Gemma because Louis is a shield."

Louis's head snaps up, his eyes growing large at the accusation. "I swear I didn't block her dreams," he states.

A muscle works in Caleb's jaw, but he deflates, back to being at ease.

"Mutants aren't allowed to use their abilities on other mutants," Gwen adds. "Louis wouldn't have shielded Gemma."

"Because I didn't!" Louis proclaims again.

Of course, he'd deny it. He'd be an idiot to announce to the entire Command that he broke the rules. But Gemma frowns, her gaze flittering to me with doubt shrouded in her eyes like she believes him.

He can't be telling the truth, though... he can't be.

"He already used it on me once," I counter. "When they found us in Florida."

They all side-eye each other like they don't want to believe me.

"Someone is blocking them, wherever they are. And whether Louis blocked me from Gemma's head, I can't say for sure. I don't have any proof, but I'm telling you, someone did. This is no different. And he already blocked me once, so why not again?"

"No, he's right," Gemma adds, standing next to me. It's us against the entire room. "Theo was in my head for five years before we even met in real life. He can astral project anywhere. True, Judy and Dennis have to be sleeping for him to enter, but surely, they have to have somewhat of the same sleep schedule as us? Especially since Griffin confirmed we're in the same time zone."

"You can get in *anyone's* head?" Jason asks, leaning forward in his chair.

I give a stiff nod.

It's strange to talk about all this. I've held it close to my chest all these years, not even letting my closest friends discover it, but I have to now; there's no other choice.

"As long as we're both asleep."

Jason sits back, rubbing a hand along the stubble on his jaw. He doesn't add any more to the conversation and stares off into the distance.

"There's probably a reasonable explanation for why Louis used his shield then. Louis?" Tilly inquires.

But Louis doesn't answer her, rather, Caleb speaks up, "We were under attack by the Authorities and needed to control the situation."

"Control the situation," I scoff. "You and your friends made it so we had no choice but to come with you if we wanted to see Gemma."

Caleb slides his hands into his pockets, shaking his head like I'm the impossible one. "We handled the situation as we saw fit because we didn't know who you were."

"And who gives you the authority to do that?" I snarl. "We didn't agree to be a part of your organization back then. You should have left us alone."

Caleb steps closer, eyes narrowing up at me. "I can promise you, you wouldn't be sitting in a cell next to your precious parents if the Authorities captured you. Or do you want your friends to end up like your father?"

I lunge at him, and the entire room moves with me. Chairs scrape against the floor as shouts try to outdo one another. Gemma startles backward, gasping as Jason and Jet both grab onto me and pull me away while Holt pushes Caleb out of the room.

"Enough," Tilly demands. Her voice isn't loud, but it cuts through the commotion.

"You had no right to tell him." I glare at Jason. "This is none of their fucking business."

Before they can reprimand me, I shove away from the two men hanging on to me and leave the room.

It's not until I'm alone in the stairwell that I realize Gemma didn't follow.

Nearly an hour later, she finds me on the roof. I'm still annoyed enough that standing this close to the edge doesn't phase me. Part of me wants to shove Caleb right off. Knowing my luck, though, he'd be able to fly.

What *is* his ability anyway? We've learned most of the others, but he hasn't shared his. I chew on the inside of my cheek, my thoughts torn in two. I can't exactly blame him for not revealing his secrets; I did the same thing, did I not? Plus, we're hiding Gemma's, for the most part. But I don't trust him. My gut wars with itself. Is he hiding his secret to protect himself or to protect his plan, however nefarious it may be?

Gemma comes up from behind me, wrapping her arms around my waist, and tucks her face into my back. "You okay?"

I grunt.

"Sorry I didn't follow you. I wanted to hear what Tilly would say about Judy and Dennis... and then stayed for the meeting to glean all the information I could for us."

I don't respond. I'm not angry she didn't follow me out, but I don't necessarily want to talk, either.

We stand like that for a few heartbeats before she whispers, "Talk to me?"

"About what?"

"Oh, I don't know..." She lets go to stand next to me. Her back faces the desert as she leans against the railing and taps her chin. "Would you rather spend a year living in an RV or on a sailboat?"

"What?" I bark out a laugh.

She narrows her eyes at me. "Answer the question, Mr. Goodwin."

"An RV, I guess?" I scratch my head. "I've never been on a boat, and it'd suck to get on one for the first time and find out I get seasick."

"I'll allow it." She spins around, dropping her elbows on the rail as she scans the horizon. "Caleb is a jerk," she announces. "Don't let him get to you."

I sigh. "I know."

"What he said about your dad..." She shakes her head. "I keep trying to give him the benefit of the doubt, and I don't know why."

"Elise seems to like him." They've spent nearly this entire week together. When she's not in the kitchen, she's hanging out with him and his crew. Good riddance, I guess.

Gemma snorts. "Yeah, real shocking."

"What'd they say about Judy and Dennis?"

"Jason is going undercover. If he can find out the next stop, Tilly will send a party in."

I bob my head, scuffing my shoe against the concrete roof.

"I asked to go."

My chest immediately constricts, but it's not my place to tell her she can't or that it's too dangerous. "If you're going, I'm going."

"I knew you would say that, so I volunteered you, too. But… Command said no to both of us," she huffs. "We have to be here at least three months and be halfway decent at physical combat to be assigned out. And I can't fight with anyone lest I burn them like I did Caleb, so I'm not going anywhere anytime soon."

"You haven't tried fighting me yet." A grin tugs at my lips.

So far, Caleb, Asher, and Griffin have all failed. Griffin walked away with the least damage since he could combat her electricity. Physically, Asher was fine, but Gemma's damage was more mental because he thought himself indestructible.

"No." She shakes her head. "No way. You guys are all off limits."

I sidestep right behind her, leaning my weight so she's slightly trapped between me and the railing. "You're assuming I won't win? Pretty haughty of you, Ms. Roberts." I throw her last name back at her.

She drops her head, giggling, and the sound is peaceful. For a brief moment, it's like our lives aren't in total fucking disarray.

The wind kicks up, blowing her curls in my face, so I move them to the side. My finger brushes her neck, and she shivers. I'm about to lean in when the roof door slams open.

"You guys need to hear this," Simone says, ignoring the position she catches Gemma and me in. Gemma's sweet face blushes as she follows Simone back inside, and I'm too confused as to why Simone is grabbing us to think about the moment we just lost.

"What's going on?" I ask as we trail her down the flights of steps.

"We just got word that the Authorities are developing a new testing system."

The moment isn't just lost; the memory is completely shredded as panic wraps itself around my rib cage and squeezes.

I don't know what they're testing for, but I can guess, and the way Simone's deep brown eyes widen when she glances back at us shakes me to the core. I haven't known her for long, but so far, she's been the most unflappable person I've ever met. It seems as if nothing gets to her.

If she's scared, none of us are going to like it.

Most of Command is right where I left them when I stormed out earlier. Only Jason is gone. Unfortunately, Holt must've brought Caleb back to the War Room, but I know how to behave. Now's not the time to argue. Esha stands next to him, her arms crossed, and a new woman is leaning against the wall, emulating Esha's position. Simone sits with us at the table as we take our previous seats.

When the newer lady spots us, her eyes widen behind thick, black frames, and she pushes herself off the wall, her windblown chestnut curls bouncing as she races over to us. She juts out a hand and talks a mile a minute before we can react.

"Margot Mitchell." She grabs my hand in both of hers, shaking it more vigorously than she needs to. "It's so nice to meet you. Sorry I've been delayed, but wow, do I have questions for you guys." She drops my hand, turning to Gemma to shake hers. "Henry told me about Nora; I'd love to meet her sometime to figure out what's going on."

"Uh, sure," I say, not knowing how else to respond.

Her hooded, blue-green eyes cut to mine, and her smile is so wide that it's a little off-putting. How can one person be so chipper, especially given how dire things are as we await even worse news?

As if reading my mind, she apologizes. "I know. I can be overzealous sometimes. I run the lab upstairs, and I think I can help your friend. Whatever we can do to help each other out, right?" She beams at Gemma this time, and it's slightly less frightening than before.

Gemma's mouth quirks upward. "Right."

"Well, anyway, it was nice meeting you two. I better get back over there. Bring Nora around, yeah?"

She zips back to her spot near the wall before I can respond. The room finally quiets, everyone taking their seats or finding a spot along the wall, and the meeting—for better or worse—begins.

"To catch you both up to speed, long story short, a flaw in our DNA causes our mutations. Our blood type isn't like other peoples', but it causes our unique abilities," Jet says.

When Gemma and I do nothing but sit in stunned silence, trying to process the information, he continues, "Well, it turns out it also leaves a marker in your blood."

"So, a simple blood test could tell if you're a mutant?" Gemma asks.

"Ah." Margot launches into another fast-talking speech. "There lies the problem. Before, it wasn't detectable. It's not as simple as running a blood test to check for, say, tumor markers or anything already established. But now..."

She paces the room with her hands behind her back like she's giving a lecture, slowing down her words so we can all keep up, but she ends up rambling to herself anyway.

"I don't understand what enzymes or chemicals they're using to detect a reaction... or maybe it's looking for abnormal cells... But what abnormality would they look for? Surely, if it's that noticeable, we'd have been detected beforehand. So, it must be an enzyme test..." She trails off as the magnets from the whiteboard pull cleanly away by themselves and start floating around her.

The papers they held all float to the ground. No one bats an eye like they're used to Margot's ability.

"Margot." Tilly snaps her fingers.

Margot lifts her head as if returning to the moment, and adjusts her glasses. The magnets return to their rightful spots. "Right. Sorry. Anyway, certain blood tests have markers that can test for any sort of condition."

"And apparently, now that includes mutants," Caleb says dryly.

"So, what happens next?" I ask.

"We need to figure out our own way of finding mutants before they do. As of this moment, their device is in the beta phase, so they aren't actively using it. Yet. So, we need to beat them before they do. There could be people out there who don't even realize they're different, their power not yet manifesting," Jet says.

"Imagine their surprise when they roll it out. Most of society doesn't even know we exist, let alone finding out you're different then suddenly being hauled off to who knows where?" Holt shakes his head in disgust.

"How are they able to do this?" Gemma asks.

Tilly rubs at her temples and closes her eyes. "Jason said the government will announce they're testing for radiation poisoning. If anyone tests positive, they must immediately be removed from their surroundings for treatment."

My heart skips a beat. All those boil-water advisories on the news... they've been planning this for a while.

"And their families won't wonder why they never see them again?" Gemma's shoulders tighten; I can't even begin to imagine what she's feeling right now as the temperature in the room plummets—literally, thanks to Holt. "It doesn't make sense. Are they going to lie and say they succumbed to radiation poisoning?" she asks.

"Who knows what lies they're spewing." Ivan angrily runs a hand through his tousled reddish-brown hair, making it stand out at all angles. "No one thinks to question anything because no one realizes there's anything they can do about it. It's all blamed on natural disasters, so no one examines the real problem."

"It's genius," Caleb says.

"It's sadistic," Gemma spits back at him, shoving her hands underneath her thighs, probably to hide their glow.

Caleb flippantly lifts a shoulder. "Sadistic, but genius."

"Margot's team is working on a contraption," Tilly says, ignoring them both. "And it seems they're onto something already, so if they can get it up and running, there's a chance we can find them first. We can at least give them an option. Take them to a base if they want to join the cause and be protected or tell them to get the hell out of Dodge, so they're not tested and captured."

"There's so many of them compared to us, though," Simone finally chips in, leveling any hope the plan might've instilled.

"There's more you should know," Tilly says.

I didn't think it was possible, but my stomach sinks even further. "More than mutant blood tests?"

"So, basically"—Holt glances between Gemma and me when the silence stretches a moment too long—"the government is using radio frequency waves to brainwash civilians into fighting each other."

Gemma freezes next to me, but no one else seems fazed. Memories of robbing Hilda's float to the surface, and how strange it was that the two seemed to get into a fight with each other and then trash the place as they stole beer and cigarettes. Was that the result of these radio waves?

"Real nice, Holt." Gwen rolls her eyes. "Tactful."

He holds out his hands, palms up. "How else would you put it?"

"You've got to be kidding me," I finally say.

"Trust me. I wish I were."

"How are they getting away with it?" Gemma asks.

Caleb scoffs. "Who exactly is going to stop them?"

"Um, I don't know. Us? The people? How are they okay with this?" Gemma shoots back, pulling her hands out from underneath her to signal all around.

"They don't know that it's happening. It's little changes at first, but essentially, they remove all inhibitions, so when people are angry, they act on it. It keeps the little people fighting while those in charge continue to see profits and stay in power.

"Everyone is fighting the wrong person. The middle class is mad at the poor; the poor are mad at the middle class. They're mad within their own classes. But no one is looking up." Holt points to the ceiling. "It's so much easier to punch down, and the government is speeding it along with their radio frequencies."

I scratch the back of my neck, fidgeting in my chair, and Gemma leans forward, hiding her face in her hands.

"How do we stop it?" I breathe.

"From what we've gathered, the mutation in our genes protects us from the radio waves' influence. That's why they want to destroy us. We're the only thing risking their version of Eden where everyone else runs themselves into the ground.

"There should be enough copper in this building to block out the radio frequencies so those without powers here are safe. Plus, Griffin was able to manipulate the radios we *do* have here, so we can still be privy to news reports without sacrificing the safety of those without abilities. But we're still working on some other ideas to help"—Jet glances at Ivan—"the others.

"Ivan has offered to help test Margot and her team's newest invention to see if it will help protect those without abilities when they're outside the base walls, but even if it does work, we don't have the resources to help everyone."

"How do we know if someone's been affected?" Gemma asks.

Margot chimes in, "We have a test for that."

"Oh?"

"It's a serum that we inject, inducing a dream sequence. If the person can wake themselves up, they're still in control of their faculties."

"And if not?"

"For some, it's a slow descent into madness until they don't wake up at all."

"But not everyone?" I ask.

Tilly explains, "It also seems to factor in genetics, just like with us, but for nonmutants, it mainly focuses on their audio sensitivity. Some will be more affected than others by being more susceptible to the radio frequency. So, you'll have some in comas, some brainwashed into believing whatever the hell the government wants, and to those who remain completely awake, it'll just appear like the world is going to hell."

"Which it is," Ivan adds bluntly.

Tilly side-eyes him but doesn't argue his point. He's not wrong. She looks at Gemma and me again.

"If the government can control even a fraction of the population and keep the rest distracted by disasters, no one will bother looking up at them. Lambs led to the slaughter; the rich and powerful stay rich and powerful, and the rest, well, to hell with us. We'll just be mindless drones who won't fight against the system."

I refrain from breaking something as the implication sinks in further and further. The rest of the meeting flies by as Margot mostly talks to herself about enzymes. I end up tuning her out as my brain tries to work out all the information it's been overloaded with lately.

This place is so bizarre. It's its own sort of Utopia, where those with abilities can live in peace. But then there's the harsh reminder that we're staying at what's essentially a military base, and we're on the precipice of war.

Between government mind control and the Authorities hunting down mutants with a blood test, the world is balancing at the edge of a cliff.

And I'm afraid we're all going to fall.

GEMMA, ZAY, AND I are on the back patio, trying to regain some pretense of normalcy after the meeting. We're standing in the fake grass, next to an artificial tree—thank you, Henry—when Simone comes out with a few children. All three must be younger than ten, and I'm somehow surprised that Amber isn't the youngest one here.

The kids must be on a completely different schedule than the rest of us. Considering we're all in the same hotel, it would seem like we've crossed paths with everyone by now, but I notice new faces occasionally, realizing we're all still somehow worlds apart.

But the most startling revelation is the giant hawk that swoops down from the sky, completely penetrating the illusion surrounding us and landing on the littlest girl's shoulder. The hawk is half her size; she can't be older than five and buckles under its weight for a moment before straightening herself back out.

Her fawn skin seems to glow as she catches me staring. She bursts into a giggling fit, hiding her face behind two small hands. Then she whispers to the bird, which tilts its head at me.

"That would be Ruby Wolf." Simone grins at the little girl. It's the first time I've seen her show any sort of happiness, and then she diverts her attention to the two polar opposites standing beside her. "And these are the twins, Gelid and Singe Stone."

Zay's eyes grow large as he takes a step forward. "Fire and ice? That's so cool!"

He approaches the boy who looks no older than ten. His hair is so blond it appears white, and it matches his eyelashes and eyebrows. Even his lips are an unnaturally pale color. If I'm being honest, he looks like a walking corpse who had the color drained out of him. The one vibrant thing on him are his bright, aquamarine eyes. He stands next to his sister, who has fiery red hair, and her eyes have the same tint, with almost unnaturally blood-red lips and pink cheeks. The boy is smiling; she is not. In fact, she rolls her eyes, clearly not impressed.

I cross my arms and stand next to the fake tree as Zay takes another step closer to them.

Zay holds out his wrist, Spiderman style, to the boy. "Can you like"—Zay makes a *thwip thwip* noise, motioning a fake web shooting out of his wrist—"but with ice?"

The siblings look at each other, and now the sister smiles. It's not malicious, but she's definitely not up to any good. The boy closes his eyes for a moment.

"Can you like"—Zay makes a *thwip thwip* noise again—"but with ice?"

Wait, what?

"Can you like," Zay starts again, and I drop my arms, lurching forward at the same time as Gemma. At least I'm not the only one freaked out.

What the hell is going on?

"Zay—" I start but don't finish because he suddenly steps back, rocking his head back and forth. "Well, that's a bummer."

"What was that?" I ask, my chest tightening.

Gemma touches Zay's shoulder, turning him as she examines his face.

Zay seemingly glitched right in front of us. There's no other way to explain whatever the hell we just witnessed, but Zay seems unaffected, like it never happened at all.

The two kids laugh uncontrollably as they bend over, clutching their stomachs. Zay frowns, as lost as we are.

Simone chuckles, too, *tsking* the two younger kids. "They're messing with you. Just playing a prank, that's all." She points to the girl. "*That* is Gelid. I know. Their parents were cruel while naming them. You'd think the one who appears frozen would be named after the ice and vice versa."

The boy stops laughing and holds out a hand to Zay. "I'm Singe."

Zay accepts the handshake, flashing a confused smile. He has no idea what just happened. But he's not alone because I don't either.

"They can reverse and fast forward time in a very limited window. Their names are because... well." She motions a hand over them.

"Zay's okay, though, right?" Gemma asks.

Simone snickers. "Yes, he's fine. Gelid sped up his timeline, so he's back in sync with us."

Zay's mouth drops open. "I'm *what?*"

"What's the last thing you remember?" I ask him.

His forehead wrinkles as his eyebrows bunch together. "I asked if he could shoot ice out of his wrist, and he said no. And then they broke out laughing."

The twins high-five each other and run off into the "yard," with Ruby following behind, yelling at them to wait up. Her short legs carry her as fast as they can.

"Maybe we just stay away from those two..." I whisper to Zay.

Simone obviously hears me and shakes her head disapprovingly.

"Those two know the rules by now. They won't use their powers on you again. Plus, they can't just rewind and fast-forward *anything*. They only have a few seconds until an event is locked into place, and they can no longer affect the timeline. But Command wants them to know how to control and use their abilities anyway because we don't know if their power will expand as they age."

"That's reassuring," I scoff.

"What else can you do?" Simone asks rhetorically.

Ruby runs closer to us again, turning her brown doe-eyes on me as she gives a little wave, and the hawk takes off, darting back into the sky. She runs away, arms outstretched, following the twins around the yard, her dark, wavy hair flowing behind her in the wind.

"What's her deal?" I ask Simone, jerking my chin toward the little girl.

She sighs. "We have no idea what happened to her family. Griffin tried finding them, but nothing came up since we never learned her real last name. Holt found her during a mission two years ago, and she called herself Ruby. And he found her in a wolf den, so..."

"Ruby Wolf," I whisper.

"Why haven't we seen them around before?"

"All three of them are orphans and live with our nurses who volunteered to care for them," Simone says. "They stay in class, which basically doubles as a daycare when their caregivers are working, and then they all alternate based on the schedule. Others pitch in when they can, so the entire base is kind of raising them." Simone shrugs as if any of what she's saying is okay.

I stuff my hands in my pockets, fishing for my lighter as I watch Ruby chase the other two. The pressure in my chest feels like it might burst the cavity completely. Those poor kids—not necessarily *alone* in the world, but still missing their parents. I inhale a sharp breath to keep the invisible smoke at bay.

"Ruby can talk to animals," Simone continues. "I'm not sure if she can do it with all of them, considering there's only so many animals that find her out here. But if she survived living in a wolf's den, then my guess is her channel works with anything."

"How does it work?" Gemma asks.

"I'm not sure. Telepathy, maybe? Not sure how she speaks to or understands them in her head, but animals are drawn to her and tend to be at her beck and call, so there's some sort of connection there."

"That's pretty sweet," Zay chimes in.

The kids are playing tag now, and Ruby runs up to me, stopping to brush the hair out of her face.

"What's up, Rubik's Cube?" I squint down at the little girl, ignoring the pain in my chest over her having no parents. I grin just for her so I don't look as sad as I feel.

She giggles. "That's not my name!"

"It's not?" I open my mouth, feigning shock.

"It's Ruby!" Her round cheeks bunch under her eyes when she smiles.

"Ohh"—I throw my head back as if understanding her now—"Ruby Roo, okay."

"Ruby!" she screams but continues to laugh. Then she reaches out, tapping my leg, her touch as light as a feather. "Tag!" Ruby runs away.

"Oh, man." A glowing smile spans Gemma's face. "I think someone likes you."

I step toward her, eyes narrowing, as she takes a playful step back, suspicion gleaming in her violet eyes.

"Don't you dare," she starts but squeals as I lunge for her, and she chases Ruby into the yard.

Even Zay and Simone join in on the game, and the impending war is briefly forgotten—for a few wonderful moments, we're just a group of kids playing tag in the yard.

Chapter Nineteen

GEMMA
December

THE SCIENCE LAB DOOR is closed when I arrive. I lift a shaking hand, hesitant to knock.

Margot wants to do right by us.

Her work with Nora alone has been unbelievable, helping her channel her visions using meditation so they aren't as violent, enabling her to come out of them quicker and with fewer physical effects. It's pretty hit or miss, but we can all tell she's improving. They've also started using the variant binder from John's house to try to track any mutants listed in there who might still be alive. Even though it hasn't worked, Nora is adamant about continuing to try.

Plus, Margot has been creating theories to retrieve memories if Nora potentially locks any more away. They haven't been tested yet, but it's a step in the right direction.

I can trust Margot.

I knock once, holding my breath.

"Come in," she calls.

I inhale, shake out my hands, and open the door.

"Gemma," she says as she smiles. "Was I expecting you?"

"No, sorry. Do you want me to come back later?"

"No, no! It's fine." She waves me in. "What can I do for you?"

I twist my fingers together, taking another uncertain step. I don't really know where to begin. This could all blow up in my face, and the chance that someone else could learn about me would be even higher.

Noticing my hesitation, she holds up a hand to stop me before I even begin. She reaches for a phone behind her desk and makes a call. "Can you come up to the lab real quick?" Pause. "Uh huh." Another pause. "Okay, thanks." She drops the phone back onto the receiver.

We stand there staring at one another, but since she doesn't start talking, neither do I.

I glance at the walls of her lab, papers strung up everywhere, but I'm too far away to make out what they say. The silence swells, and I'm beginning to regret my decision. But then Griffin appears from behind me, giving me a nod before he walks the perimeter of the room.

"All clear," he finally says.

"What...?" I shift uneasily.

Griffin excuses himself, shutting the door behind him, a lock clicking into place. It's a subtle sound, but it might as well have been an explosion in my head. My heart hiccups with fear. *How could she already know? Why did she lock me in?*

"You're free to talk now." Margot smiles again, the earlier tension wiped from her face.

"Uh..."

Her smile turns into an outright laugh. "Sorry about that. I didn't want you to say anything before Griffin checked for any bugs. This room is soundproof. Not even Simone can eavesdrop. That's why I've been working with Nora in here. Her talent is rare, and the fewer people who know, the better. But whenever I sense someone wants to talk"—she gives me a questioning glance—"privately, I ask him to come to check for any listening devices. He gives the room a rundown at least weekly anyway, but we can never be too safe."

"And you trust him?"

A pinch of guilt appears since I have no reason not to trust Griffin. He's been nothing but kind to me since I arrived, even trying to help me with my electrical ability, but the words are out before I can stop them.

"I do. I take precautions, but Griffin is one of the few I trust implicitly."

"Who don't you trust?"

She shakes her head. "It's not that I *don't* trust anyone here. We're a good group. It's just..." She walks over to me, leaning against one of the lab tables. "If someone shows you who they truly are, believe them."

If someone shows you who they truly are, believe them... I repeat the phrase in my head until it sticks, and then tell her everything.

How my parents murdered Draven and injected me with his powers, and here I am, years after meeting Theo in my dreams. I don't gloss over the details of how I injured Caleb and could have broken Asher's arm if I tried any harder and that I could have drained Griffin's power if I hadn't broken our connection.

The truth pours out of me. The dam breaks, and there's no stopping the flow.

It feels almost as good as when Theo learned the truth about me, knowing I no longer had to hold onto this secret alone. But with

Margot, it's different. Not that I'm not any less relieved, but she's someone who can maybe help me figure it out.

Margot sits in silence, never once interrupting me. She takes it all in while jotting down notes in the notebook she always has on her. That part is a little more concerning since someone could find it, but she goes to great lengths to keep this place bug-free, so maybe she writes in code or something.

"And I'm scared," I finally say to finish my spiel. I drag in a large breath, and Margot stands, crossing her lab to fetch me a glass of water.

"You're scared you're going to hurt someone? Or that you'll pass out again if you don't draw in enough power?"

"Both, but that's not what I'm talking about."

She frowns and hands me the glass. I take a small sip and set it down, watching a drop of water slide down the outside and land on the metal table.

"If I'm not a mutant... What if the radio waves can get to me?"

"Oh."

"I know this place is protected and whatnot, but—"

"It's a legitimate fear." Margot pulls open different drawers, grabs various items, and tosses them all on her desk. "I think I can help. But it's going to take me a few days."

My chest swells with hope. "Really?"

"Have you ever worked with crystals?"

I shake my head. "I've only ever siphoned from living things."

"You can draw energy from certain crystals, too. If I can get the stones right, you shouldn't have to draw from anything living ever again. And it'll protect you from the radio frequencies as well. You'd just have to keep the stones charged."

"How?"

"I'll let you know when I finalize them." She gets down on her hands and knees, pulling open the last drawer and heaving a wooden box out of it. "Give me a couple of days. I'll have something ready for you then. In the meantime, don't leave the base."

As if I could.

"There's one more thing," I say. When Margot pauses her riffling, I continue, "I'd like to take the test."

"Oh," she says again, somewhat shocked.

"Is that okay?"

She wipes her hands on her pants. "Of course, I'm just surprised. You've been here long enough that I don't think you're a sleeper cell or anything." She gives me a good-natured smile, but I don't return it.

"I want to know for sure. It's been weighing on me since the meeting last week. Out of everyone in our group, I wasn't born a mutant, and while I might not seem affected, I'd like to confirm that I'm in full control."

Margot sighs, her understanding blending with my determination. "Come back tonight; I'll have it ready for you."

"One last thing—please don't tell anyone. Especially not Theo."

CALEB CATCHES ME LEAVING Margot's lab. My cheeks warm as if I've been busted, and I kick myself for not being able to maintain any sense of composure.

"What's up?" he asks.

"Oh, nothing. I was hanging out in Margot's lab, seeing how the blood test is developing."

"And?" He follows me into the elevator.

My mouth dries. I don't know how to answer since I didn't bother asking her. "It's going," I finally say, refraining from shaking my head at my stupidity.

We descend two floors in silence; then he stops the elevator, the contraption jolting as I grab onto the railing.

"What are you doing?"

I'm surprised this old elevator even works and that he'd risk messing with it. I reach for the button to start it again, but he stops my hand.

"Are you mad at me or something?" he says.

"Or something. Why are you trapping me in here?"

"I want to talk."

"We can do that somewhere that isn't this death box."

"Not if I don't want your shadow appearing."

I roll my eyes. He's talking about Theo, of course.

"Why do you always get on his case?" My anger flares, and I have to keep myself in check, or this really will be a death box. "He's done nothing to you, and you throw something like losing his dad in his face. What's wrong with you?"

"I can tell you're getting mad." He holds up placating hands. "Really. I can see it written all over you. I'm sorry for upsetting your boyfriend. But we need to talk about something more important than him, and I think I know you well enough by now to know you'll agree with me."

I cross my arms, hardly accepting his apology. "We've known each other for less than a month, and for most of that, you've been nothing but annoying."

"I don't agree with how Tilly runs the place," he deadpans.

What? I press my fingers against my forehead, briefly closing my eyes to absorb the shock. He could have said dragons are real, and I would be less surprised than I am right now. He rubs the back of his neck like he's suddenly shy, and I'm so confused that I don't know what else to do but follow through.

"Why not?"

"Because." He pants, pacing in the small box. "I don't think we should be hiding in fear. We're stronger than any human with unaffected genes out there... Why does it make sense for us to be the odd ones out? We should be the ones running things around here."

I'm sure doubt flickers across my face since, for a split second, I'm unable to contain the nervousness fluttering through me, which is heightened by his excitement. World domination wasn't on my bingo card of Caleb's different facades.

"And I don't want to tell you this in front of your *boyfriend* because Theo is a rule follower. People like him are a dime a dozen. He'd fall right in line with Tilly's other good little soldiers. But you're different, Gemma. I can sense it. You can make a difference."

Good little soldier... isn't that what I thought of Caleb only a couple of weeks ago? How one could wear such different masks has my brain waterlogged. He knows the role he's meant to play, and boy, does he play it well.

I roll my head to ease the tension molding my muscles into stone. He doesn't know Theo at all. He might be playing a role here, but he's spent most of his time running and hiding. I can't imagine a world where Theo would willingly become a soldier... *Can I?*

"This is lunacy. Isn't there a happy medium? Where we can simply coexist with those without powers?"

My thoughts drift to the radio waves and the government's already well-known indifference to coexisting with us. But I refuse to believe everyone has that mentality. There have to be more people like Judy and Dennis out there.

The world would have already burned to the ground if not.

Caleb scoffs, bracing his hands against the back of his head. "Maybe in some fake futuristic paradise. But we need to come out of hiding first if we ever want a chance at living among them."

His earlier statement rings in my head, reminding me of what he really wants: *We should be the ones running things around here.*

"Does it have to be all or nothing? Exist without ruling? That seems so... evil."

Caleb barks out a laugh. "It's not evil if you're just trying to live, Roberts. We're humans, just like them... we've just adapted to our surroundings. When the world eventually burns someday, we'll be the ones left standing."

"I guess so..."

"Don't you want to live without fear?"

"Of course, but I don't even know what that looks like. Or how we'd achieve that."

"First, we need to defeat the Authorities."

I'm lightheaded as the words sink in. "All of them?"

"At least the ones who are in control." He shrugs. "Cut the head off the snake, and the entire organization might shrivel up."

"Who's the head?"

"President Gray."

I spin, throwing my hands in the air, wishing I could escape him, but the elevator still hasn't moved. "You can't be serious!"

He turns me so we're face to face. He plasters on a pleading expression rather than his usual haughtiness, like he wants me to understand his plight. Another mask. Another version of him. "He's in charge of them. He has to go."

"You can't just kill the president... that's—that's—"

"Wishful thinking? Hopeful? An amazing plan?"

"Blasphemy!" I shout. "Absolutely insane! A terrible idea!"

"Why?" he asks. "Give me one good reason why this isn't doable."

I open my mouth, but nothing comes out.

"Is it because there's not enough of us? Fixable. Can't get through his security? We have Asher and Louis. Won't know where he's going to be? Simone can help with that."

I take a step back but meet the corner. I slam on the button to continue going to the first floor.

"And with you?" He takes a step closer so I'm effectively trapped. My shoulders raise to my ears when he whispers, "We'd be unstoppable."

"Not like this." I shake my head. I hit the button three more times for good measure. "There has to be a different way."

He exhales, close enough that my hair shifts from his breath. "You'll see, Roberts. Stick with me for a while, and you'll understand why we're sick of hiding."

My lips turn into a sneer, my stomach dropping when the elevator shifts into motion. "Now you sound like Elise," I mutter.

Elise. No wonder she spends so much time with Caleb and his crew. If they all agree with this plan, it's right up Elise's revenge alley.

Margot's words, and how fitting she chose to tell me today of all days, rise to the surface. *If someone shows you who they truly are, believe them.*

I exhale when the elevator doors finally slide open, but Caleb changes facades again, switching from mutiny to his usual role.

"Worry not. Once we have word, I'll be off to save the day and bring your parents home in one piece. Then you'll owe me." He winks.

"Caleb, please take this seriously." I worry my lip, the anxiety roiling in my stomach. Talking with him is like being on the

Tilt-A-Whirl. I can't find my way to true north. "If something happens to them…" I don't want him blackmailing me *or* jeopardizing the mission.

"Something already did happen to them," he points out.

"I don't want anything *worse* to happen. Or for them to die in the crossfire of you seeking your vengeance."

"Who, me? I would never." He puts a hand on his chest like he's affronted.

When I only stare at him, he rolls his eyes. "Relax, Roberts. I'm one of the best foot soldiers they have. I'll have them out of there in no time, and before you know it, you'll all be a happy little family again."

"Promise?"

He holds out a pinky finger. "I promise." I don't move to take his finger, so he drops it, sliding back into his arrogant role. "And then you'll have a decision to make," he whispers as he passes by, pulling out his phone and leaving me alone in front of the elevator doors.

❧ ❦

CALEB'S WORDS HAUNT ME the rest of the day. I can't wait to fall asleep tonight to tell Theo everything. I'm too nervous to speak it out loud because of who might overhear. Plus, I have to get through this test first. If I'm eventually not in charge of my faculties, we'll have way more problems than Caleb's scheme to kill the president.

Part of me wants to run back upstairs and stay in the private lab to escape it all, but Margot is his *aunt*. There's no way I can tell her this. She'd never believe me over Caleb, and there would be no chance of me getting any crystals or taking this test to ensure that I stay awake.

When Elise comes to our bedroom, it feels like my head will explode, and if I don't do something now, I'll lose it. But how much does she know? Is she in on his plan already? And if she is, does she think killing the president is a good idea?

I try to broach the subject without revealing too much. "You and Caleb seem to be getting pretty close."

Elise pauses making her bed, her shoulders going rigid. "I guess so."

Her attention returns to her task, and I study her. Every once in a while, like now, it catches me off guard how much she reminds me of Olivia. Of course, Olivia was a lot nicer to me. But those two would have raised hell together. A painful stab to my heart has me glancing away from the girl who could never be my sister but who makes me long for her all the same. I turn my back and catch her gaze in the mirror.

Elise's sharp emerald eyes narrow. "What?"

"Nothing."

"Say it," she huffs.

"It's nothing. I just want to make sure you're being careful."

"With?" Her pink skin darkens, and if her flush doesn't give it away, the guilt pouring out of her does.

"I think you know."

"I don't plan on trading your life to Caleb anytime soon, if that's what you mean."

"I'm not worried about me." *For once.* "I know your ideas align pretty well, but he seems to be on team world domination, and I think you should—"

"I should what?" she snaps.

I bite my tongue, choosing my words carefully so we don't start fighting. I settle on, "Watch your back."

Judging by her reaction, it's safe to assume she's at least aware of Caleb's ideas, but embarrassment with a hint of jealousy seeps from her pores, and I'm taken back to the night in the attic with Draven.

"Elise," I groan. "Come on. Don't be like that."

She storms out of our room, whatever retort she wanted to say kept behind closed lips, and she doesn't bother returning.

I text Zay, asking him to come to my room, and seconds later, there's a knock on my door. I whip it open while his fist is still hanging in the air and smile at him, but he frowns at me.

"What?" he says. "What's that look for?"

"I'm smiling."

"You're grimacing."

I exhale, rolling my eyes. "We need to go to Margot's lab, and I'm hoping you'll escort me." I link my elbow with his, pulling him along before he can ask any questions.

"Uh, okay, weirdo."

Racing up the stairs, I don't give him any time to get words out until I'm quite literally shoving him through her lab door.

"Hey, hey, hey," he argues. "Watch the merchandise."

When I let go, Griffin salutes, letting himself out and locking the door behind him. Good, that means Margot had him sweep the room twice today, taking this as seriously as I knew she would.

"What the hell is going on?" Zay points at the door. "Why did Griffin just lock us in?" Then he points at the dentist-looking chair Margot rolled in from somewhere. "And what the hell is that?"

I try to provide the most reassuring smile I can this time. "I have to take a minor test. And I didn't want to do it alone."

"We have to take a test?" Zay blanches.

"No." I wave my hands. "Just me. But I need you to stay here." After he stares at me dubiously, I explain everything we learned at the meeting last week and how I might be under their influence. "This test will tell us for sure."

"And Theo isn't here because...?" he asks.

"He can't know about this unless something is wrong. Then you can tell him everything."

He sighs. "I don't know... it seems like he should be here. This is more his thing." He hesitates before adding, "Not to mention I don't feel right about keeping secrets from him..."

"Zay, please," I beg. "Theo would panic and try to get in my head or something, and he could mess the whole test up if he helps me. I need to wake myself up to know that I'm good. If Theo barges into my dream, how will I know what's real?" I know I've won when his lips press into a hard line. I squeeze his hand. "Thank you."

He grunts. "Let's get this over with."

After Margot explains the procedure, which is simpler than I thought, she's just going to inject a serum into me to induce a sleep simulation; I'll fall asleep and will have to wake myself up. If I do, I'm safe. If I don't, then... The tip of my nose tingles, and I blink away the avalanche of terrible thoughts about how it could already be too late for me.

"Hey." Zay holds out a hand, sitting in a lab chair next to the makeshift bed. "You're going to be fine."

I slide my grip into his and bob my head in agreement, even though this suddenly feels like a really stupid plan. I inhale through my nose, exhaling out a shaky breath. No signs indicate that I won't wake up on my own. This is just a precaution so I can ease my worried mind. Still, facing the needle is a bit unnerving. I just need to get this over with so I know for sure.

"If I don't wake up, tell—"

"If you don't wake up, Theo will be there before you know it."

Margot steps closer, needle in hand. "You ready?" But before I can answer her, she pierces my neck, sending me under.

I squeeze my eyes shut, blocking out the harsh sunlight streaming through the window, burying my head under the comforter when Olivia hums, "Lloyd, I'm Ready to Be Heartbroken."

"Give it a rest," I finally say after she repeats the song.

She rips the blanket off me. "Well, good morning, sunshine."

I groan, replacing the blanket with a pillow. It's too bright out. Too early. Why is she even awake?

"Up and at 'em," she demands, wrestling the pillow away from me.

I sit up, angrily brushing my hair out of my face. "What is your deal? How are you so chipper right now?"

She spins around, holding her homecoming dress against her body, twirling in circles, the rose-red material billowing in the air. "Love is in the air, my dear sister. Come, come."

When I stare at her, her shoulders drop, and she tosses the dress on her bed. "Jeez, you try to be happy one time." She knocks my legs aside, sitting on the edge of my bed. But then she's back to smiling. "I think Scott finally likes me."

"Good for you." I drop my head back down on my bed. "What's this have to do with me?"

"Because we're meeting him at the park in an hour."

"We're?"

"You didn't think I'd let you sit home all by yourself and sulk in your loneliness, did you?"

"You have before," I muttered. "Please don't make me go." I could do so many other things today, like finishing the book I've been reading out on the front porch swing with a cup of tea. "Please, don't make me go," I repeat.

"Too late. I'm sending Amber in if you're not ready in thirty minutes."

I groan as she leaves our bedroom. Olivia doesn't usually need me to supervise her dates—in fact, it's normally quite the opposite.

Thirty minutes later on the dot, I head downstairs, showered and dressed.

I make a beeline straight for the kitchen to help Dennis with breakfast, but it's empty when I walk in. Huh. I head for the dining room, but there's no one there either. That's weird... we've all had breakfast together since Olivia and I arrived.

"Olivia?" I yell out, but the house is empty.

That witch! Makes me get out of bed and ditches me!

I stomp back up the stairs, flinging open the bedroom door, but freeze when Olivia spins in the room with her homecoming dress held tight against her. She doesn't hum this time, but her dancing to the eerie silence is creepy.

"Well," I sigh. "I'm ready to go."

"Well, good morning, sunshine," she says.

I frown. "Uh, right... Are you ready or not?"

She takes my hands, letting the dress fall to the ground as she spins me.

"What is wrong with you today?"

"Love is—"

I hold up a hand, stumbling to a halt as I stop her. "In the air, got it. But why are you repeating yourself?"

Olivia's body goes rigid, mouth open as if she is about to respond, but nothing comes out.

My mouth dries as I step forward, clutching her shoulders. "Olivia?" When she doesn't do anything, I shake her. "You're starting to freak me out. Stop."

Nothing happens.

I drop my arms to my sides, worry thrumming through me as my hands begin to shake. This isn't right; something must be wrong. I back up across the room, my eyes never straying from her still body.

Her gaze suddenly snaps to mine. "Wake up."

"What?" I shuffle a little closer, but fear roots me in place and keeps me away from her. "What's wrong?"

Dennis, Judy, and Amber materialize beside me. I spin away from them all, falling to the ground as they hover above me. At the same time, all their slack faces yell at me to wake up.

A tear slides down my cheek as Zay's face swims into my sight. His brows are furrowed as he studies me. I blink a few times, letting the room settle around me.

"Are you okay?" he asks.

"I saw her," I croak out. "Olivia."

Margot comes into view as Zay helps me sit up, sadness filling his chestnut-brown eyes. She looks the opposite—thrilled, even.

"Am I...?"

"Awake? Yes, you're fine, Gemma." She grins.

"Well, that's good because Theo would have killed me," Zay states. "What was it like?"

I shake my head, a headache brewing in my temples. "It was so bizarre. I didn't even know I was dreaming," I recount.

Margot nods along. "Every dream is different. We can never tell people what to expect because the possibilities are endless. You were under for two minutes, though, even if it seemed a lot longer. You have nothing to worry about." She pats me on the shoulder, heading back to her desk.

Zay helps me out of the chair, holding me steady as a wave of vertigo crashes over me. Bile climbs up my throat, and I choke it down so I don't puke on him.

"That'll fade." Margot glances up from her paperwork. "It's the side effects of the serum. Go sleep it off; you'll feel fine in the morning."

We both thank her, but just as we're about to leave, Zay stops me before we walk out of the soundproof room. "Do I still have to hide this from Theo?" The concern in his eyes is so innocent it almost makes me laugh.

"No." I shake my head, patting him on the arm. "I'll tell him tonight. Don't worry."

A smile melts the concern off his face, and as he escorts me back to the room, the nausea continues to build, and I have to blink back tears. But I don't think it's from the serum.

Would that dream be an alternate reality if Olivia had survived?

Chapter Twenty

Theo

THE NEXT BRIEFING IS a cacophony of media reports, radio stations, and mutants yelling over one another.

We might as well throw Griffin's alarm in for good measure.

Simone finds me in the back of the room, leaning against the wall, studying the mayhem.

"How on earth are you not dying right now?" I ask as she approaches, not bothering to take my eyes off the scene before me.

"You get used to the noise."

"Even at your level of hearing?"

She doesn't answer this, but considering there isn't blood coming out of her ears, she must've adapted over time.

The War Room apparently has a hidden compartment. The last time I was in here, it only had the oval table with some chairs around it, but now the side wall is open, and seven television monitors hang off the newly revealed wall.

All seven screens play a different news station. Most of the reporters talk over each other, but the captions are all on:

Seven dead in shooting.
Wildfire strikes the West.
Stampede injures dozens at local concert.
Riot at mall.
Blizzard hammers the East Coast.
... A desperate plea for money...
Will anyone challenge President Gray's ruling?

The radio stations aren't much better. They relay different information about other parts of the country succumbing to violence, climate change, contaminated water, or famine—the loudest channel describing an incident on a public bus, an altercation between two passengers over a single seat.

It makes me sick to my stomach.

Especially now, knowing the violence is induced by mind control and how ordinary folk don't have a clue that it's not *all* their fault they're angry. It might not be the *only* reason they're enraged, but it's certainly not helping anyone's temper.

Speaking of temper, I have to control mine as Caleb sits in the middle of the chaos with his hands behind his head, appearing utterly unaffected by the turmoil around us. All it does is make me want to punch his smug face. Especially after what Gemma told me last night. He watches it all unfold with pleasure lit in his eyes like he set the blaze himself.

"What's his deal?" I ask Simone, gaze fixed on the clown, wondering how much she'll tell me. Simone doesn't seem as close to the group as I first imagined when they showed up in Florida. At the base, the other four stalk together like they're a herd of some kind, Simone coming and going when she pleases.

I'm not sure if that's a good or a bad thing.

She picks at her nails, focusing on them rather than the rest of the room. "He wants change, and the further we descend into madness, the quicker it'll happen."

"And you agree with him?"

When she doesn't answer, I turn my head to look at her, but she doesn't meet my eye, unbudging and plainly unwilling to respond.

I lose track of time as they eventually cut out some of the noise, and everyone sits at the table to discuss options. Most of Command argues over one another about where to strike next as we wait for Jason to return with more news on Judy and Dennis.

I wish Gemma were here, too, but she couldn't stomach the thought of hearing any more news of what's happening, not without knowing how her powers would react.

The shock that rolled through the room after Jet delivered Jason's information made Gemma's fingertips flare. The Authorities plan to start testing for mutant blood in smaller cities and sampling all its citizens, eventually building their way up to more prominent places. After stuffing her hands under her thighs, her shoulders connected with her ears until the meeting was over, and she darted from the room.

I found her bent over, clutching her knees as she tried to suck down air.

Now I come to these meetings alone.

One radio blares how the radiation poisoning is causing panic, and I get further lost in my thoughts about the upcoming rescue.

If we can save Judy and Dennis, will we all stay here? Will they want to go back to Florida? They won't be safe out there unless we somehow stumble upon a crap ton of copper. Question after question beats at me until Simone nudges my arm.

"Sorry, what?"

"Jason sent word," Tilly repeats herself, her gaze piercing my own.

I sit up straighter.

"This is the best chance we'll have. They're sending them to Devil's Gate, about four hours from us. They're supposed to land tomorrow, but we've been too late on other missions, so we're sending our group in tonight.

"Holt, you take point. Gwen, you're second. Jason is already out there. Caleb, Louis, and Asher, I want you on for this one. Simone, it's your call if you want to join."

Simone bows her head.

I raise my hand.

"No, Theo."

"But—"

"You're too close to the situation. We couldn't risk sending you in even if you were ready for a field assignment."

"I could get them in and out without anyone realizing."

"Unless there's a shield like you already insinuated. Unless traps are set up. Unless they're waiting for you to show." Caleb lists reason after reason, ticking them off on his fingers.

I grind my teeth together but keep my mouth shut.

Simone follows me out of the room once we've been excused and slides a piece of paper into my hand. I glance down, reading: "Roof. 8:00." By the time I look back up, she's already gone.

⚜ ⚜

GEMMA AND I ARE tucked away in the back corner of the dining hall, waiting for the others to arrive. Zay, Nora, and Amber have all settled into their classes and training, meeting new friends, or, in

Nora's case, catching up with her cousin, but we make it a point to eat together.

And now that Caleb is gone, I'm guessing Elise will join us for once, which she hasn't done since we first arrived. Whether that's because she's fallen for Caleb's schemes or because this is the first time since everything happened in the graveyard that she's been able to get space away from us, as much as we wanted space from her, I don't know.

Those first few weeks in the house were tense, but the base gives everyone a chance to spread out and breathe on their own a little bit. Why Gemma still feels the need to bunk with her, though, is over my head. I don't think I'll ever understand their relationship.

"Want to join?" I ask Gemma after showing her Simone's note.

She hands it back to me, shaking her head. "I told Amber I'd meet her in the library to help her study for a little bit."

"Study what?" Zay asks as he sets a dinner tray on the table beside me. "I think I'm flunking math."

Gemma drills him with a look. "Biology, but I better see you there now, too."

"You're going to help Zay with math homework?" I raise an eyebrow, refraining from laughing at the idea. "You hate math."

Gemma playfully shoves me, but Nora saves her from replying, stating she'll join to help Zay as she and Amber also plop down at the table, Amber stifling a yawn.

"How are you holding up?" I ask her. "Is the infirmary work too much?"

"No." She shakes her head. "I like working with the medical staff there more than my normal studies. If I'm going to drop something, I'm dropping school."

"No, you aren't," Gemma scolds. "Judy will have a conniption."

"Judy's not here." Amber stabs a piece of pear with her fork.

"She will be soon. Command is sending a rescue team tonight."

Amber glances up from her tray, dropping her fork, which stands straight out from the fruit. "Are you serious?"

When Gemma nods, Amber covers her face and breaks down. She pulls the hood up around her head and sinks lower into the chair after Nora tries to console her. A few other people glance our way, more filing in with the dinner rush, but no one says anything.

"They have a whole team going, the best they have," Gemma lies. The squad they're sending could very well be their best, but we have no way of knowing that. Gemma is only trying to appease Amber, and my hands clench when I realize she's probably trying to convince herself, too.

"It's going to be all right." Zay hands her his napkin. "They'll bring them back."

Amber sniffles, wiping her nose with it.

We spend the rest of the meal in silence as if talking about it too much will jinx the rescue. All we can do is sit and wait, and now I understand Gemma's study session; she's finding a way to keep herself distracted.

Simone beats me to the roof.

I came ten minutes early, hoping to pick a spot that wasn't near the edge, but she stands in the center, arms crossed, tapping her foot like I'm late.

"So... what's up?" I ask when the door closes behind me.

She tilts her head, listening for something. I strain to hear it myself but don't catch anything until I move closer to the edge. Voices drift up from below, and I swallow hard before glancing down.

It's two people on the watch team. I can't make out what they're saying, but I'm sure Simone can.

Then, all of a sudden, it's silent.

I can *see* the two are still talking, but not even their hushed voices float toward me.

"What the hell?"

Simone rolls her eyes. "I can manipulate sound. That doesn't just mean sonic hearing."

"So, no one can hear us right now?"

"No."

"Are you... here to kill me or something?"

Her dark eyes blaze, even with the lack of light. "Why would I kill you?"

"It was a joke... sort of." I peer down at the ground again and walk closer to the wall. "So, what's with the noise barrier?"

"I couldn't do or say anything with them here."

"Because Louis uses his shield on you, too?"

Her brows furrow in confusion. "Louis? No. It's Caleb I'm worried about."

"I thought you two were thick as thieves."

"We are. Or were. We used to be, I guess." She uncrosses her arms, rubbing her hands together like she's blocking out the cold. "He's... I don't know. I'm concerned about the path he's heading down. I don't think he's dangerous to us or anything, but I know he wants change, and I'm a little worried about what he's willing to do to get it. And he wants your girlfriend there to help him."

"I know. He's already asked her."

"She can't agree." She steps closer to me until we're nearly eye to eye. "She has to say no."

"She already did."

"No. She didn't. Not in those exact words."

Fear closes around me, and I replay our conversation. Gemma was adamantly against his plan.

"She would never agree."

"It's not about his plan," she hisses. She steps away, pinching the bridge of her nose. It's like I'm watching her internal struggle; the more she loses, the more outwardly it shows. Her shoulders slump like she's given up. "Caleb can—"

The door opens, and we both jump. The sound barrier doesn't create a *real* barrier, and I lock eyes with Gemma, relief coursing through me that it's not Caleb. Simone was *so* close to revealing something about him.

"Hi." Gemma takes a few steps closer. "Sorry for interrupting. We took a break, so I figured I'd sneak away from the study group for a minute."

"We were just talking. About Caleb." I stare at Simone, hoping she'll continue, but the moment is gone.

She straightens her shoulders, flashing a brief smile. "I was just heading back down." She walks past Gemma, but then she stops. "Gemma?"

"Yeah?"

"Don't give Caleb what he wants." She slips through the door before we can question her, leaving Gemma and me alone.

Worry lodges deep within me about what she wanted to say about Caleb, but Gemma drags her feet, coming to stand in front of me. "Sorry I ruined the moment."

I kiss her, showing her she doesn't need to be. She laughs, closing her arms around my neck.

"What are we going to do?"

I sigh. "I have no idea. Run away together? Hop on a train and never look back?"

"Hm," she breathes, closing her eyes. "Let's wait until Judy and Dennis get back first. Then we can hit the road."

She's kidding; she has to be. But there's a small part of me that hopes she isn't.

Chapter Twenty-One

Gemma

THEY'VE BEEN GONE TOO long. My leg bounces as I chew on a thumbnail, itching to run out the doors and find them myself.

Theo reaches out a hand to still my leg without looking at me, his stare glued to the front doors. He gives my knee a light, reassuring squeeze when I stop fidgeting. But within seconds, I'm back to bouncing.

The six of us sit in the lobby, waiting for *anyone* to walk in the door.

Amber is on the other side of me as the three of us take up the couch; Zay, Nora, and Elise take different chairs.

Most of the base went to bed hours ago. The ones still working drift by occasionally, directing their attention away from us. Their sympathy screams louder than their pity and hope as they walk by. No one wants to watch the group of orphans crowd around one another, waiting to hear about the adults who took them in and loved them as their own.

"Anything?" Theo asks for the millionth time.

Nora shakes her head. "Only hospital girl."

He sighs.

A hush falls over everyone, and it's so eerily quiet we'd be able to hear a pin drop, even if we didn't have Simone's sonic hearing. Another hour passes, and Amber falls asleep on the couch beside me, curled up under Theo's leather jacket.

Zay and Nora look ready to drop, too, right when the sirens blare, and we all jump out of our skins.

It's the glorious sound we've been waiting for, but my lungs cinch tighter, not letting any air in. Who will walk in the door? What if they were too late? What if the radio waves got to them and they're no longer Judy and Dennis? They've been gone for three weeks. Who knows what happened to them in that time?

I shove the thoughts away, racing to the door just as Caleb and Asher carry in a screaming Holt. His legs drag behind him as they hold his upper body. The medical team meets them in the hallway, taking over and pushing them out of the way. Caleb's hands are covered in blood, along with Asher's clothes.

"What happened?" I grab Caleb's shirt, pulling him to face me. Dirt and mud cover his face as well. I rake my eyes over him but don't see any physical injuries.

"We were attacked." Caleb wrenches out of my grasp. For once, no biting remark or humor dices his words.

"Are they...?"

Caleb's mouth clenches shut as he looks over my head at the door behind me. I spin around to find Jason and Gwen. Both are just as dirty and exhausted-looking. And even though Jason's expression fills me with dread, he motions behind him with his head.

A lump lodges in my throat when I peer past him, and Judy's strawberry-blonde hair springs into view. "Judy!" I cry.

Now awake after all the commotion, Amber bolts past me, flinging herself into Judy's arms. She openly sobs, and it takes everything in me not to cry with her.

Dennis is a step behind, his dark brown skin also covered in grime and blood. A new scar, about two inches long, runs from his forehead to his temple, but it's already healed, like the injury that caused it must've happened weeks ago when they were first taken.

His weary gaze finds mine, and his lack of a smile pushes me over the edge. "Oh, Dennis," I whisper. His beard has grown even more since he's been away, and his shoulders droop as if they're carrying the weight of the world.

The haunted gleam in his eye shakes me out of my stupor, and I race up to him, throwing my arms around his middle. I expect to smell his familiar woodsy scent of cedar and varnish, but it's not there. He's been away for too long, and now he reeks like blood, sweat, and smoke.

At first, I'm afraid he doesn't remember who I am and that we really have lost him to the Authorities, but then his arms wrap around me, and for a brief moment in time, old Dennis is back. We stand like that for a while before I reluctantly back away, turning to find Judy crying over Amber. She turns to me next, pulling me into a hug as Amber switches gears to tackle Dennis.

The four of us are all a weepy mess, and my heart swells when they start hugging the others, too. Even Theo's eyes glint with unshed tears.

"Are you okay?" Judy kneels, touching Amber's curls and wiping tears off her cheeks.

Amber nods. "We're okay."

"I think more importantly... Are you guys okay?" Theo asks after he and Dennis are finished hugging.

Dennis looks away, and Judy does her sad smile while her hands hover over Amber, like she wants to make sure she's truly all in one piece. However, the smile is more stilted than usual, and the nervous energy they both exude makes my head pound with worry all over again about the Authorities and their mind-controlling abilities.

"We're okay," Judy echoes Amber.

Jason reappears, rolling his sleeves up and exposing a bit of clean skin. "I think we should get you two cleaned up, get some food, and sleep before the shock wears off, all right?"

Dennis nods, following Jason's lead. My stomach twists when he doesn't even glance back at us, but Judy is still Judy—unable to hide her emotions and worry. Tears glisten in her eyes when she glances at me, and then she focuses on Dennis's back.

"He'll be fine. They were a little harder on him than me, and they kept us separated most of the time, so he wasn't sure if I was okay. He needs some time."

I swallow, grinding my teeth together as I blink away the dread.

It's a messed-up world when I hope that he's acting like this because they tortured him and not that his mind is already gone.

THE NEXT MORNING, WE'RE allowed to accompany Judy and Dennis to the science lab, where Margot will administer the test to determine whether they're still "awake."

The base's protective surroundings, filled with copper wire and now water from the partial underground layers, will help keep the Authorities out of their heads, but we need to know if it's too late.

Thankfully, both passed and woke themselves up, Dennis taking slightly longer than Judy. Tilly informs us if we waited any longer, they might've had their hooks in him. It's going to take a while for him to mentally recover from what he endured, but as for the radio waves, he should be okay now that he's here.

None of this is a science, though, and they recommend we stay at the base for as long as possible. If Dennis is subjected to any more radio waves, whether it be a day or three months from now, they don't know what will happen.

So, the choice is made for us.

We're not returning to Florida anytime soon.

Once the tests are over, Judy and Dennis are guided to the War Room to go over what happened to them while they were gone. Dennis kicks us out for this part, and the idea of him not wanting us to know what they did to him makes me want to throw up. My thoughts flash back to the four Authority members I did happen to kill, and suddenly, I don't feel so guilty anymore.

I shouldn't feel this way. An eye for an eye makes the whole world blind, and two lefts don't make a right and all that, but to turn the sweetest man in the universe into a shell of a human who can barely smile makes me want to burn their entire facility down. Anger heats my veins, forcing me to step outside so I don't accidentally burn *this* place down.

Caleb finds me on the outdoor patio, feeding the chickens. All traces of last night are gone as he gives me a cocky smile.

"I promised I'd bring them home, didn't I?"

"Thank you. Is Holt going to be okay?"

I was so consumed with my own worries that I didn't spare any second thoughts for the man who came in screaming until we were all back in our rooms.

"I don't know."

"That's it?"

"What else do you want me to say?"

"What happened to him? Is he severely injured? He seemed pretty inj—"

Caleb slams the chicken coop door shut, making me jump. "He's an idiot. A fool. I told him to wait until my signal, and he went charging in any way."

"Your signal? Wasn't he the leader?"

"I'm the one with the bloody hearing," Caleb shouts. "He should probably listen to *me*."

I frown. "You have..." Simone's sonic hearing. Louis's shield that he *swore* he didn't use on me to block Theo out of my dreams. His comment on my mood. "Oh my god!"

Caleb freezes just a moment too long. His jaw twitches as if he's berating himself.

"You can duplicate powers, can't you?"

His face remains stoic, but his anxiety leaks out of him.

"I can't believe I didn't put it together before!" I think back to the car ride when I first asked him. What did he say? *I'm not* completely *useless.* I scoff, shaking my head. "I should have known. Always being so elusive with what you could do, and it's because you can do everything!"

"Not everything," he finally whispers.

"How does it work?"

The silence stretches so long that I don't think he'll answer. Then he finally relents, plopping down on the bench. I sit next to him, closing the corn bag I was feeding the chickens from.

"I need permission."

"Permission to use someone's power?"

"Permission to take it. Once it's mine, I'll always have it."

"But the person doesn't lose it?"

"No. You got it right. I duplicate it. I'm like an echo of some-one's power."

"So, I'm going to guess you can shield, you have super strength, and you can see powers as well?"

Caleb shakes his head. "Esha never gave me permission."

"Why not?"

"Would you?"

"Would I what?"

"Give me permission to use your power?" He leans closer, his face full of earnestness.

"Oh, I..."

No, there's no way. I don't even know if I can *give* this power away since it's not mine to begin with. But Caleb being able to do what I do? He really would kill the president. He'd be a danger to everyone.

I would *never* give him permission.

"Exactly," he says.

I know why *I* don't want to give him an ability, but Esha? They're close, and what would be the reason for keeping it from him? But at the same time, she doesn't really owe him anything. It's her ability, after all; she can do what she wants with it.

"I can't *force* anyone to give me their ability. Free will, and all that."

"Don't sound so bummed," I mumble.

"There's more Eshas in the world than not. So, while what I can do is cool, it's not the end all be all. I could do so much more if only people would let me."

"Maybe it's good that you have boundaries. Otherwise, you might do something stupid." I stare at him, making my case, and he scoffs.

"Holt..." he starts, changing subjects. "He has no use of his legs. If he makes it, he's going to be paralyzed. But that's a pretty big if..."

"Oh god, Caleb. I'm so sorry."

Holt rarely addressed us and probably didn't even like our group if I think back to his usual clipped answers, but he's a good soldier, respected, and well-loved by those who do know him. I've gathered that much during my time here.

"I heard them setting up the C-4, but he didn't want to listen. I tried shielding him from the blast, but I got there too late."

"It's not your fault."

Caleb frowns a little, rubbing his hands across his jeans. "I know. It's his."

I refrain from rolling my eyes. "Well, make sure you go tell him that before he dies."

"I'm only speaking the truth."

"Maybe you should learn some tact?"

"I am who I am. Take it or leave it."

My lips twist in disgust as I stand up to leave him in his pit of despair. He's allowed to hurt, but he should at least be mindful of his fallen comrade. When I get to the doorway, he loudly sighs.

"Wait, Roberts—"

"What?" I snap.

"I'm sorry. I'm not very good at all this."

"Emotions? Acting like a real human?"

Now, he's the one to roll his eyes. "At having friends. The others are all good and well and whatnot, but we've all come to a sort of understanding."

"And what is that?"

"We all want the same thing." He lifts a shoulder. "And I know that you don't. It doesn't seem to matter; I feel the need to be around you." When my cheeks warm, he adds, "Oh, calm down. I know you're with Theo. I didn't mean it like that."

"Good. Theo would honestly kick your ass."

Caleb smirks. "I'd like to see him try." But then he exhales. "You keep me on the straight and narrow. You're like an annoying conscience I can't get out of my head."

"Color me surprised you actually consider other people's feelings. Maybe you should go apologize to Holt."

"I didn't do anything that I need to apologize for."

"I'm willing to bet any amount of money you called him an idiot at least once on the four-hour drive back here. The poor guy is fighting for his life, and it's like I can hear you telling him *I told you so*."

Caleb sits silently for a few heartbeats as if replaying the events in his head. He gets up and brushes past me to head inside, but instead of heading to the infirmary, he veers to the right and shuts himself inside the telephone booth. I watch through the slightly tinted window as he pulls out his phone, scowling down at it before bringing it up to his ear. His shoulders hitch as he argues with someone on the other end.

My brows knit as the interaction continues, trying to figure out who he could possibly be speaking to. Maybe someone from another base? Caleb's shoulders lower when he hangs up, and he scrubs his hands over his face for a split second and exits the booth.

I turn away, hiding behind the wall so I don't get busted. When I'm sure he's passed, I peek around the corner, peering back through the doorway. Caleb lets himself into the locked infirmary, entering a code we're not privy to.

Crossing my arms, I study the now empty lobby, mulling over Caleb's silent phone call. Sighing, I whisper a silent prayer for Holt.

I'm not the praying type, and I'm not even sure if there's anyone to pray to, but I send out a wish for him to pull through, anyway.

The day drags in intense foreboding. Judy and Dennis spend most of it with Command, learning the ropes just like we did when we arrived. They're adults and have no abilities, so they won't need to undergo the vigorous training we did. They'll remain at the base and help however they can. Considering their careers, I already know where they'll end up—Judy in the infirmary and Dennis returning to teaching.

If he can return to teaching... Dennis's empty gaze haunts me when I close my eyes, and I refrain from shuddering. He has to be okay. He has to get past this.

Dennis needs to be Dennis again. I can't take knowing the Authorities erased his kindness and hardened him into someone he's not.

I won't accept it.

Later that evening, Tilly announces to everyone in the dining hall that Holt didn't make it. Gwen tried stabilizing him on the way back to the base, but he'd lost too much blood, and there was nothing they could do but try to make him as comfortable as possible.

"Can't people go to the hospital?" Judy asks.

Tilly shakes her head. "It's complicated. Some of us, Holt included, are on the Authority's watch list. They'd know where he is if we took him somewhere, and it wouldn't have mattered if they did help him. The Authorities would never have let him leave."

Judy's hands ball into fists; I can feel her struggle against her mixed emotions.

"Can't you hack the system?" Theo asks Griffin.

Griffin's jaw works as he fights through the grief drowning him. "I've tried. They have a team of people who re-implement the data

I wipe as soon as it's gone, so they can get pinged immediately if a name shows up somewhere nationwide. And they have paper charts on all of us that I can't access."

I think of John's variant binder and how the Authorities probably have a room full of old-fashioned physical records complete with mutant names as they try to collect more with their new testing device.

With no further questions, Tilly lifts a glass to the room. "For mutants like us, death is an honor. May we go quickly into the light and find what awaits us next. Here's to you, Holt. You'll be missed."

Everyone in the room raises their glasses, giving Holt a final salute.

Dinner turns into a wake, with the other Command members doing shots the longer the night goes on. Mostly everyone from our group has gone to bed, with only Judy remaining to watch us like a hawk. Eventually, even she succumbs to tiredness and leaves Theo and me alone.

This was the first time I'd seen anyone drink alcohol here, but they even gave beer to the rest of us, which Theo gladly accepted. I have no interest in having one; the memory of alcohol turns to ash on my tongue. The last time I had any was the night I lost Olivia.

Everyone goes silent when Gwen openly starts weeping at the table, having one shot too many. Her normal bravado fades away, replaced by a heartbroken girl who lost someone dear to her. My heart aches.

The longer the night goes on, the harder it is to remain there. It reminds me too much of Olivia's wake, and the emotions warring in my chest give me a headache. I excuse myself and head back to my room, leaving Theo with the few who are still drinking.

Margot catches up to me in the hallway, holding a necklace and a sheet of paper listing the five crystals and their abilities. Underneath the descriptions, her looping handwriting instructs: "Burn after reading."

"Hope it helps," she says before disappearing back into the dining hall.

We probably would have chatted about it more under different circumstances, but with all they've been through today, I don't blame her. I'm thankful she even did this much for me. I stuff the necklace and note into my pocket and head for my room, which is blissfully empty since Elise is spending another night with Caleb.

I sit on my bed and spread the piece of paper out in front of me. Holding the necklace up to the light, I study the five marble-shaped crystals surrounded in gold and linked together in a row.

The first is a teal-ish green, the next a clear yellow, the middle a dark blue and green swirled together, then a peach, and lastly, a sky blue. I twist them in their little holders, feeling their smoothness, and glance down at the paper to read about each of them.

Green aventurine: To block computer, television, and other electronic equipment emanations. To keep you safe from their wicked and cruel games.

Citrine: To enhance personal power. Draw strength from yourself and this charm so you no longer have to draw from others.

Chrysocolla: To calm, cleanse, and re-energize. It's to keep you level-headed so you can control your emotions and they won't control you.

Sunstone: To shield against negativity and encourage optimism. It will help increase your vitality and energy so you don't lose your strength.

Amazonite: For inspiration to speak your truth with clarity and confidence, no longer having to hide in the shadows.

Find a reason to pull an all-nighter on every full moon. Take a watch position, so you have an excuse. Recharge your necklace once a month in the moonlight and once a month in the sunlight.

Never take it off.

This will protect you.

-M

I put the necklace on, the crystals cold against my neck, a sudden rush of relief flowing through me. It's not the crystals acting that quickly, but the peace of mind that comes with them. If Margot is right, I won't have to draw from anyone ever again.

I slip into Theo's room and creep past a sleeping Zay to quietly dig into Theo's dresser for his spare lighter. Zay lays flat on his stomach, long limbs stretching beneath the twisted covers, his arms and feet dangling off the twin bed. I don't want to risk waking him with the smell of smoke, so I slip back into the hallway, shutting the door firmly before exhaling.

Turning the shower on in my room, I light the note on fire before dropping it into the sink. I run water over it until it disappears down the drain, waving the smoke away as it mingles with the steam.

When I leave the shower, my thoughts drift back to Theo, wondering if he's still drinking downstairs. The crystals sit heavy against my throat as I spin Theo's lighter around in my hand, holding it in front of my face while I lie in bed.

Caleb's words haunt me about Theo being a good little soldier. I have to admit, it's odd how well he fits into his role here, but it's also a reprieve from having to worry about him sneaking out every night to fight. Maybe he just needed the structure—a sense of purpose. Now, he gets to protect others without having to run. It's like he has the best of both worlds. But there's a sadness there, and it's infuriating to be unable to pick him apart and see what's causing the pain.

Is it losing John? Riley?

Is it the state of the world and how it's impossible to be happy when there's so much at stake?

He went from a kid hiding from his father to training mutants so they can fight against the government that's responsible for brainwashing civilians—no wonder he's all tied up in knots.

I roll over, tucking the lighter under my chin, hoping he'll go to bed soon. Maybe if he stays present in my thoughts, he'll find me in his dreams tonight.

Chapter Twenty-Two

Goosebumps run along cracked skin that's dried out and withered. The sensation is like a tidal wave crashing against the shore—sharp and painful.

Rotten flesh coats nostrils, and more words return. Rain, mud, worms—*worms*, that's it. Worms dance along fingers, weaving their way through pockets of wounds that should not be there. They burrow into the skin, finding a home next to the maggots feasting on it.

Fire rolls through veins, heating every inch, surely burning the creatures alive. The flames will rid them all, and the skin can heal once more... if it's even skin at all.

Chapter Twenty-Three

THEO

My head buzzes as I wander the base, a beer clutched in my hand.

I'm not *drunk*, but I've had enough that it takes the edge off a bit. We're stuck in this place for who knows how long. Dennis can't leave, and if he can't leave, then Gemma can't leave, and I can't leave without her.

I'm thinking *can't* too much.

I shake my head, stifling a laugh in the empty training room. I glance around. I don't even remember coming down here.

What I *really* mean is that I *won't* leave without Gemma. And I don't think she wants to go anywhere. This is what she was looking for, wasn't it? She wanted to find others like us and bring the fight to the Authorities, and here we are. Smack dab in the middle of the impending war.

I sit against the wall of mirrors, peeling off the beer bottle label. Focused on the task, I don't realize someone has entered the room until Jason clears his throat.

"Sorry about Holt," I say.

Jason nods, loosening his tie. He drapes his jacket on the back of the chair, and a strong burst of sandalwood surrounds us when he sits beside me. Freshly showered with his everyday cop attire, I put the pieces together.

"You're heading out again."

"I am."

I stare at the beer in my hands, my brain too muddled to figure out why this bothers me.

"I'm going to be gone for a bit this time... I can't really get into it, but I'll be back."

"Have a good trip." I wince when the words come out sounding hollow. I don't really care that he's leaving. Do I?

Jason shifts, about to stand up.

"Wait—"

He pauses, turning to look at me.

"What was John like?" When he doesn't say anything, only letting out a breath, I try to elaborate. "I mean, I know what he was like when I was a kid. But after. I've painted this picture in my head where—" I cut myself off. Why am I telling him all this? It doesn't even matter.

"Where he was the bad guy?" Jason inquires.

I swallow. The silence swells like a balloon, and I'm ready to pop with it.

"I was so sure he had Riley killed. I ran from him and kept running. Then he finally caught me. But he didn't turn us in; he offered to help and brought us food. And then—" My voice cracks, and I hate myself for it. "Everything is so screwed up. Riley is *alive*. She's out there right now." I point to the wall as if she's standing on the other side, even though she could be a million miles away. "Then

John took a bullet for Gemma, and I... I don't know which way is up anymore.

"Riley hates me. John's dead. I'm here of all places, but it's too late. It's too late to fix any of it, so what's the fucking point?"

And now I'm crying. I shouldn't have drank that last beer. I've had too much, which is embarrassing with Jason sitting here. Somewhere in the back of my mind, I realize this is the first time I've shed any tears since it all happened.

When the moment passes and my breathing turns to hiccups, Jason takes the beer out of my hand and sets it aside.

"John was one of the best officers I've ever had the pleasure of working with. We were in different departments, but our paths crossed since we were both looking for variants. Since I'm a tracker, I signed up for this special group of the police department, hoping it'd give me an in. I've been working undercover for the base now for, shit, close to a decade.

"I got in because of an old mentor of mine, Gerald Gibson." Jason pauses, smiling. "Anyway, that's a different story. Years later, John started looking for *you*."

A shudder runs through me. I tilt my head back against the mirror, closing my tired eyes. The buzzing in my head turns to drilling.

"He loved you, you know. He never stopped. And he was so damn proud of you."

"Me? Why?"

"John was so impressed that you outran him each and every time. Man, did it piss him off, though." Jason chuckles, and so do I.

"Always being one step behind drove him mad, but how he spoke about you and your ability to stay off the radar and how you kept yourself *alive*... That was the most important thing to him. He was fine chasing you to the ends of the Earth if that meant you were still alive to do the running."

I refuse to open my eyes, feeling the tears gathering behind my closed lids. I squeeze them shut even harder to keep them trapped.

"I can't speak to ghosts like your friend can," Jason says. "But what I do know about John? That's all he wanted—for you to stay alive. And you don't have to run anymore."

My throat feels like it's closing, and it takes everything in me not to lose it again.

"I can't guarantee your safety. This life..." He exhales. "It's not what I'd wish on anyone, let alone kids. But we're your best shot, all right? No more running. No more hiding. Train, learn how to use your ability, and fight back. That's all any of us can do anymore. Fight when we can."

I nod. My chest feels a little lighter, and my image of my dad alters. I can do this for him. I can do it for Gemma. I couldn't bring myself to leave her anyway, but hearing an actual invitation to stay around a little longer and see where this path may lead makes breathing easier. There's always time down the road for things to change. But for now, I can stay.

Jason does get up this time, patting me on the shoulder when he does. When I hear him grab his jacket, the chair scraping slightly on the ground, I finally open my eyes.

"Jason?"

"Yeah?" He turns, fixing his coat collar.

"I'll see you when you get back."

He smiles and heads for the door.

Exhaustion pounds like a jackhammer against my temples as I head to my room. The buzz has officially worn off, and my eyes hurt so badly that I can't wait to pass out. The dead weight pulls me under as soon as my head touches the pillow, and for once, I dream of nothing.

✦✦✦ ❧❧❧

JET MANIPULATES THE METAL around us, creating different obstacles for me to get through, throwing up a random wall here and there as I continue to teleport in and out as we attempt to limit the distance I travel. More than once, I've appeared a second before a sheet of metal has, and I run straight into it. After a half hour of this, I lie on the ground, panting.

"Again," Jet instructs.

My body aches, and I let out a small groan.

"It might help to envision something," Louis offers as he stands next to Zay.

I didn't even notice he was watching or that Zay had come in from the greenhouse to witness my spectacular failure. I've been too busy getting my ass kicked by Jet's metal.

"Like what?" I cough out, slowly sitting up.

"For my shield, I like to picture bricks."

"Bricks?" Zay asks.

One side of Louis's mouth quirks upward. "If I need to protect someone, I throw up a wall of bricks around them. Of course, you can't see that, but I can."

"What would I envision, though, to teleport? I already picture the spot I want to be in. It just doesn't happen."

"You work from fear," Zay says. "Remember when we were surrounded? You were able to get us all to the same place then."

"So, I just need to picture you all dying every time? Super."

"Not exactly..." Jet says, the wheels clearly spinning in his head. "But Zay brings up a good point—your basic need is to survive. It could very well have to do with your blood pressure. Adrenaline makes your heart pump faster, raising your blood pressure, and then it's as if you're acting out of basic instinct. When you overthink it, you can't hit your target."

"Easy." Zay laughs. "Just stop thinking."

I grunt, dragging myself up off the ground. This time, I attempt to clear my mind. *It's like when I fight*, I tell myself. I need to let muscle memory take over. My body knows what to do, so I need to trust it.

I teleport right into Jet's wall.

"Again," Jet says.

After multiple attempts and when none of their suggestions work, Jet brings me into the stairwell. We climb up the first three floors, him leading the way, even though the limp in his right leg is more pronounced by the second floor. I keep my mouth shut and follow until sweat slides down my back, and my muscles coil the closer we get to the top. This crazy bastard is going to push me off the roof, isn't he?

Instead of heading to the roof, though, Jet turns around and shoves me backward. My heart free falls quicker than my body, and I'm at the bottom of the stairwell when I open my eyes. Alive. Fine. Shockingly, not in a heap of broken bones.

"What the hell was that?"

Jet laughs hysterically from above, leaning over the railing. "How do you feel?"

"Pissed off!"

He laughs harder, clapping his hands like I finally broke the cycle. "What was your last thought before you appeared at the bottom?"

I rack my brain, trying to think. I pretty much blacked out at that last second. I didn't have much time to think of anything except... "I wished I was in the basement again." *If there were no stairs to fall down, I wouldn't have to worry about breaking my neck.*

Jet smiles, limping his way back down the stairs. "Again."

Once training is over and I'm thoroughly beaten up, I ask Jet a question that's been swarming in my head for weeks, if not actual years. "Why are we different?"

Jet stops wiping down the equipment.

"I got the DNA flaw and all that, but why? What's the point?"

"Margot can explain much better than I can, but in simpler terms... Humans had to adapt to survive, and we're the result. The world is dying. You can pick any reason: war, disease, famine, global warming. The choice is yours. If our species didn't adapt, we would eventually cease to exist."

"So, we'll be the ones left standing when it's all over?"

He sighs. "It appears so. And there's going to be more of us soon. Our numbers are growing by the day. Most are kids, even younger than you, but we have a few adults, too. I think someone named Draven was the earliest case. He's the first ever recorded mutant, at least."

My entire body jolts. "Draven?"

Jet dips his chin as we make our way to the elevator. "The Authorities did all sorts of studies on him. Experimented. Tried figuring out how he ticks. Then his records stop. We never figured out what happened to him, but man, reading those reports... I don't know how anyone could survive what they did to him."

Fuck. Fuck. *Fuck.*

Of course Draven would be the first-ever recorded mutant because why not?

I smooth my face of any shock or alarm and file the information away to ask Jason when he returns. Maybe the Authorities have more records he can obtain. If we can learn more about Draven, we can learn more about Gemma.

"And you?" I ask as we exit into the lobby.

Jet stops walking. "What about me?"

"How long have you known you were a mutant?"

He wistfully smiles at me. "Another time, maybe." Then he limps toward his quarters, leaving me standing in the lobby, questioning my DNA and why, out of all the people in the world, I'm one of the chosen ones.

❧❧❧ ❧❧❧

TILLY DARKENS MARGOT'S LAB, shrouding herself and Nora in her shadows.

The last thing I see is Nora's eyelids fluttering closed as a metronome ticks steadily. *Tick... tick... tick.* The blackness swallows them whole.

Margot suggested they test hypnosis on Nora to see if that would help her experience a vision. She's been improving while studying here, but if they can get her to a point where she can control the visions completely, then they'll no longer control her.

I pace back and forth, my hands on my head, as I wait... and wait.

Tilly's shadows don't budge.

Even though there's no danger, witnessing a swell of blackness in the middle of a lit room is a little unnerving.

But I want to be here in case the hypnosis doesn't work. Nora's violent visions leave her scattered, momentarily lost, and I can't leave her to come back to Tilly and her shadows. Simone appears next to me. For someone with sonic hearing, she can sure as hell get around without making any noise.

"How's it going?" she asks.

I don't answer her as I side-eye the current cocoon of black.

"I heard you the other night."

I continue to pace, not bothering to answer. I had a complete meltdown in front of Jason, and it's no surprise that Simone overheard it. But that doesn't mean I want to talk about it.

"So, you're staying then," she continues.

"I don't really have a choice."

"When Dennis is better, I mean. You're going to stay after that?"

I flick my gaze over to hers. "Why? Would your friend rather we left?"

She grunts but doesn't indulge me with an answer. Something is going on with those two, but I can't figure out what, and she never talks about it.

"Are you good?" I ask her.

"Why wouldn't I be?"

I give up the charade of dancing around the subject since she always seems to appear but never says more than two words. "You don't have to hang out with that prick if you don't want to." Gemma has already informed me of his talents, and even if we weren't in a soundproof room, I don't care that he could have heard me.

She grins, and as Tilly's shadows start to unravel, Simone leaves without another word. Is she spying for him? Does she not want to be near him? I can't figure it out. I can't figure *her* out. But without the ability to read her mind, I don't know what her game is.

And it's infuriating.

I concentrate back on Nora now that I can see her again, but her body is frozen as if she's still in a trance.

I try shoving Simone to the back of my mind, but the opposite happens, and I latch onto all of them in their little group. Louis is the only other one who's halfway decent, even though his ability to block powers keeps me on my guard whenever he's around.

I can't fucking stand Caleb. Asher doesn't speak but is always near Caleb like he's his personal bodyguard. Considering he can flip cars, I'm not surprised he'd take on that kind of role, even if Caleb can do the same thing himself. And Esha. She's as silent as Simone but is always watching. *Always.*

It's creepy.

Simone isn't that bad, though. If she's not double-crossing me and feeding Caleb intel, that is, but I don't think she is, especially after our discussion on the roof. I think she's on our side and wants nothing to do with him, even if she doesn't say so out loud.

Our trust in the others at the base is growing, but we continue to keep some things quiet, like the source of Gemma's power. Thankfully, I can jump into Gemma's dreams whenever I want so we can talk openly about her next steps.

Her training isn't going nearly as well, and I feel for her. How badly she hoped someone here was more like her so she could figure herself out. Griffin helps, but his power is limited compared to Gemma's, so she has to refrain from hurting him. So, she ends up withdrawing even more, keeping to herself in the library and escaping into the fictional world of books. She's shoving her frustrations so deep that I'm worried she'll explode.

She opened up about killing those people, but she's still beating herself up over it, and I don't know how to help. Gemma needs to process the emotions because they'll come out one way or another. And when they do, we're all going to be fucked.

Nora gasps, breaking out of her vision and yanking me from my thoughts.

Her eyes dart around the room when Tilly tries speaking to her. I race forward, dropping to my knees.

"I'm here."

She focuses on me, her shoulders slumping. "I saw her again."

"Who?" Tilly asks.

"Some girl in a hospital." I shake my head, answering for Nora as her breathing slows. "We can't figure it out, but she's been seeing her since we were back in Florida."

"You don't know who it is?"

Nora tugs at her lip. "Sometimes I have visions about people like us... those who are different. I can see them coming. But this girl isn't going anywhere. She's just in a coma." Nora shrugs, appearing at a loss for what any of it means.

"I don't know anyone who's been injured." Tilly sits on her haunches. "Good work, though. At least you had a vision. Tomorrow, we'll have you lock up someone else's memory to see if they can get it back. It's time to test what you and Margot have been working on."

When Nora's mouth drops open, Tilly winks and launches herself to her feet, strolling away like we're not about to potentially ruin someone's life.

As it turns out, we're not locking up any crucial memories. But the idea of messing with anyone's brain sets me on edge.

Margot is leading this experiment as we sit in her lab. Griffin came in and cleared the place from prying eyes, so no one outside of our group should know about this. I feel like I'm risking a lot by asking Simone to be involved, but my gut tells me to trust her. And more importantly, we needed someone who didn't know much about Nora's ability. Otherwise, the experiment might fail.

"Are you sure you want to do this?" I ask for the hundredth time. Simone rolls her eyes at me, so I hand her the apple.

She takes it from me without hesitation, holding it in her outstretched hand, and turns to lock eyes Nora.

Nora's eyes squint in concentration as she follows Margot's instructions and *wishes* Simone would forget who handed her the apple.

"Who gave you the apple?"

"Theo," she says.

Nora's shoulders slump in defeat.

"It's okay," Margot says. "It's your first time trying. It's bound to take some time. Let's try again."

An hour later, Simone blinks when Nora asks who gave her the apple.

"I... I don't know?" She frowns, eyebrows furrowing as she sets the apple on the table, then grimaces like it's been poisoned.

Zay leaps up. "It worked!"

"What worked?"

"Okay, okay." Margot laughs. "Only step one has worked. Now Simone needs to try to remember."

"Remember what?" she asks.

I cover my mouth with a hand, trying not to laugh.

"Seriously!" She spins in her chair to look at everyone. "Remember what?"

"Remember who handed you the apple this time." Nora's lips twist to one side as she glances at Margot. "Do I need to tell her what I left behind? Or is the point for them to find it themselves?"

"Ideally, they should find it themselves, as Henry did. He didn't need prompting, so neither should they, but it might be something we need to work on for longer."

"Left what behind?" Simone hisses this time, the frustration evident on her face as she glares at all of us.

"Sorry," Nora says flatly. Then she starts tugging on her lip anxiously.

"You were handed an apple, and then..." I urge, guiding Simone along. I can't *give* her the answer, but hopefully, she can at least get there herself with some coaxing.

"I don't know," she growls.

"Think about the apple." I point at it. "Who gave it to you?"

"Rearranging the order of your question isn't helpful." Simone shoves away from the table, stomping out the door.

"Okay, so maybe I didn't leave a strong enough hint," Nora finally says, and I burst out laughing.

"At least it's not serious. What did you leave behind as a clue?" I ask.

She lifts a shoulder, cocking her head. "You."

Margot starts taking notes, her head bobbing. "Maybe that's it. With Henry, it was an actual memory you instilled in him. He remembered the Furby, so he remembered playing with you.

"Memories are attached to all sorts of stimuli. So, connecting your action to a specific sense might help them recall it more easily. The Furby was a visual Henry could see, and it brought back memories of you.

"If it's something as small as giving Simone an apple, maybe if you attach a phrase to it, the audio will trigger her memory. For future use, you can associate smells with it as well. Or maybe even texture. If they feel a certain item, it could help spark it."

"Okay, who wants to bring Simone back?" Zay asks. "Because she scares me."

I chuckle, offering to go myself. I enter the hallway and call Simone's name, not bothering to hunt her down.

Shortly after, she comes marching back into the lab. "I heard you," she grumbles.

And we try the test again.

Chapter Twenty-Four

Gemma
March

I'M RUNNING LATE WHEN the dining hall explodes.

I drop to the lobby floor, covering my head. A high-pitched squeal rings in my ears, but I can still make out faint screams echoing through the hotel. Smoke billows from the room, and it takes me a minute before I can pull myself up and scan the area. My thoughts are scattered, and nothing makes sense. And—my heart stops.

Where is everyone? I was meeting Theo for breakfast, and oh my god. *Where is everyone?* We're under attack. The Authorities found us.

I spin in circles, my hands lighting up. The purple glows brighter in the darkening room, and I carefully step around the debris, wishing my hearing would return fully.

"Theo?" I yell, but it sounds like I'm underwater, and I can't tell how loud my voice really is. He might not even be able to hear me.

Red lights flash in the corner; Griffin's alarm must be going off, but the siren itself is weak, hardly penetrating through the rest of the noise.

I check behind me, ensuring no one is coming through the front of the lobby, before darting closer to the dining hall to see if anyone is trapped inside. I'm lightheaded, and I don't know if it's my racing heart, or the explosion, or—I squeeze my eyes shut, then open them widely, attempting to blink away the black spots and smoke.

The heat from the flames stops me in my tracks, and I back up a step, shielding my face.

"Hello?"

My voice sounds less submerged, and the ringing lessens to a trill, but it's still there. No one answers, at least that I'm aware of.

I shield my eyes, leaning around the flames for a better view, but I see only destruction. If anyone's inside, it's definitely too late.

Theo would have teleported everyone out.

I repeat this to myself to stay above the crushing waves of terror. My heart threatens to stop beating, but I need to survive this so I can find them.

Turning my back on the flames, I lick my dry lips and duck below the smoke. I shouldn't go up if the building is on fire, but I can't trap myself in the basement either. The Authorities might be outside, so where do I go?

My hands tremble, and it takes everything in me not to sit down and give up. But the smoke burns my lungs, and I start to choke. If I give up now, I'll die. I run to the bathroom, kicking the door open. I need to find the others. *Anyone.*

It's like I'm having an out-of-body experience, watching myself go through the motions rather than living them. Everyone can't be gone—they can't be.

How did the Authorities find us?

The bathroom didn't receive much shock from the explosion, but a crack runs through the wall, and some of the tiles are disheveled. My dry throat tries to gulp the thinning air before this place is engulfed in flames, too.

"Anyone in here?" I cry out again, my voice cracking.

A stall door whips open.

"Gemma!" Amber runs toward me.

"We have to move. The dining hall is on fire, and the whole place will end up in flames soon. Do you know where everyone else went?"

She shakes her head.

Gunshots ring out from the lobby, and Amber and I both freeze. We stare at one another, my teeth chattering out of my skull. But as I look down at Amber, something cements in me.

It's up to me to get us out of here, and I won't fail her.

"Wait here," I instruct her, and for once in her life, she doesn't argue with me.

I crack open the bathroom door and peer out into the lobby. I don't see anyone at first through the billowing smoke that's spreading across the ceiling, fading into a lighter mist the closer it reaches the ground.

But then I spot Elise firing at someone at the front of the building. My heart leaps for a brief moment. If she's alive, maybe the others escaped, too. Another explosion jolts the building, and I duck, waiting for the ceiling to come crashing down, but it stays put.

I turn back to Amber. "I think the Authorities are here. Elise seems to be keeping some of them at bay, but I'm not sure where the rest are. You need to stay in here until we neutralize the threat."

"No," Amber whines. "This will all go faster if—"

"*Please.*"

"But—"

"Amber," I cut her off. "The fire is spreading with every second, and we need to get out of this building. But you shouldn't leave until we have a path."

She huffs, turns away, and closes the stall door behind her.

I grip the bathroom door handle, taking a deep breath, the last I'll get for a while unless I want it to be riddled with smoke. "Here goes nothing," I mutter, slipping out of the bathroom and creeping along the wall behind the lounge's couches.

Elise shoots a few more rounds, and I slip further to the side until I spot two Authority members dressed in all black, using the front door as a shield. If I can get behind them, I can drain them enough to knock them out, but if I go out into the courtyard, I risk running into more of them.

I lie on my stomach, peering from underneath the couch. They step further into the entrance, and I close my eyes, focusing on the electrical system. If I can at least short-circuit it, it might distract them enough for Elise to finish the job.

I open all my senses, homing in on the current and blocking out the rest of my surroundings. Even the ringing in my ears dies down. The smoke dissipates; the two things that exist right now are me and the electricity. Once I have a solid mental grasp on the wiring I need, I open my eyes, curl my fingers, and explode the circuits within it.

White sparks shower down on the two in the entryway, and they duck for cover. Elise rushes in, shooting off two, three, four more rounds.

Bang, bang, bang, bang.

When the shooting stops, I jump up. Elise is already reloading her gun.

She turns her back on them, raising her chin. "Nice job."

I meet her in front of the open doors, the fresh air giving a slight reprieve from the smoke filling the ceiling. We need to move faster.

"Where's everyone else?" I ask.

"I left Theo and Zay outside to come find you guys."

My chest tightens. How many are they facing if two have already made it inside? And where is everyone else? Caleb, Tilly, Jet. They can't all have been eating breakfast at the same time.

I swallow the panic.

Keep moving. If you stop, you'll die.

"Amber's in the bathroom," I tell her.

"Where's Nora?"

My chest deflates. "I have no idea."

"I'll start checking rooms." She cocks her gun. "I'll come back for Amber before we need to get out."

"I'll swap places with Zay to see if he can come in here and control the fire in the meantime."

"Deal."

We turn away from each other at the same time. It's extremely off-putting to be in sync with Elise, of all people, but having a plan makes me feel better. If I stop for too long or think too hard, I'll break.

Theo is alive and outside, and he needs my help.

I focus on that to keep myself moving and bolt for the courtyard doors, ignoring the blaze, the echoing gunshots, and the distant screaming.

Don't stop. Do not stop.

But the scene before me stops me in my tracks.

Just beyond where the fake yard ends, there are countless tan jeeps, built with machine guns, aimed at the hotel, and there's even a tank, which must be what they used to explode the dining hall.

What stops my breathing, though, is the massive tornado of sand whipping through the area. I don't know where Zay is, but this is no doubt his work, so he must be here somewhere.

The Authorities hide behind their vehicles, and Theo teleports from man to man and uses one of Margot's team's inventions, like a stun gun on steroids, leaving the men unconscious.

A mixture of emotions spins inside me, as fierce as the sand blowing through the air. I'm filled with pride at how much these two have grown since I met them, but at the same time, it shouldn't have to be like this.

We shouldn't be at war.

There's a sharp, stinging sensation in the side of my upper arm. I suck in a breath through clenched teeth and duck behind the chicken coop, my breathing coming quick and shallow. The pain radiates down my arm, and the burning sensation sets in. Warm blood trickles, and though my breathing comes in gasps and my hands ignite into purple flames, I will myself not to panic. I need to stay in control.

Move or die.

My arm has only been grazed by a bullet; I can keep going.

Move or die.

Move.

When the purple flames dissipate, returning to a tingling glow, I duck and run. I aim for the vehicle closest to me. My good hand closes around the back of a man's neck, and I siphon *just* enough energy to make him drop. He's unconscious before he hits the ground.

Theo and I end up meeting at the same jeep.

His eyes are wild with alarm. "Are you okay? You're bleeding."

"I'm fine." There's no point in telling him right now since there's nothing we can do about it until everyone is safe. "Can you get

Zay inside? The fire has to be contained, and Amber is hiding in the bathroom until we can get a clear path out. Elise is looking for Nora."

His jaw tenses as he peers around the mayhem. "You can't stay alone out here."

"We don't have time to argue." I grab onto him, forcing him to look at me. "Amber needs help. She's trapped in there."

He blinks at me, nearly frozen, and for a heartbreaking moment, we're back in the pizzeria. The world is slowing down as we once again need to make difficult choices.

"I'll hold them off. Get Zay inside, and then you can join me."

Theo grabs me, pulling me in for an ill-timed kiss, and before I can grasp what's happening and let myself truly melt into him, he disappears beneath my fingertips. Seconds later, the wind storm stops, and everything comes to a crashing halt.

Right... I should have thought this one through.

I shake out my good hand, my legs bouncing, and ignore the flare of pain from jostling my arm. I sprint to the next vehicle just as the Authorities start coming out from under cover.

Time passes, and thankfully, my necklace holds strong. I'm weakening from physical exhaustion, but at least I don't feel the threat of passing out. Theo has rejoined the fight, and the two of us go on and on and on.

We don't have any way of communicating, so I can only hope that Zay puts out the fire and that Elise finds Nora. So, for now, I continue to duck, run, cover, and fight.

Until a single shot rings out, and the world stops turning.

Theo—mid-jump—crumples to the ground.

Chapter Twenty-Five

THEO

I WAKE UP IN my childhood bed.

I stare at the off-white ceiling and try to remember what I was dreaming about, but nothing comes. Only darkness remains, like an empty void. I can't shake the feeling that I need to remember something. Did Nora erase my mind?

What the hell was I doing? And why am I at home?

I get out of bed and study the room; it's no different than before the fire. A guitar sits poised in the corner next to my closet, a shelf of books on the other side. My dirty baseball jersey is draped over the computer chair.

But this isn't right... I shouldn't be here.

I reach for the lighter in my pocket, but it's gone. *Am I in Riley's dream?* Why would I be here, though? My head throbs the harder I try to think. When I enter the hallway, voices drift from downstairs, and my insides harden into stone.

Mom.

I slowly shuffle down the stairs, listening to her hoarse chuckle from the kitchen. I haven't heard my mother's laugh in years.

Black spots darken my vision, and the hallway closes in on me the nearer I get. My pulse pounds in my ears, and I stumble forward. But I lose all vision when my dad crosses the room and wraps my mom in a hug, kissing her.

I reach out to the wall, holding myself upward.

This can't be real.

It's dark, but I screw my eyes shut anyway.

Wake up. Wake up. Wake up.

Nothing happens. Nothing changes.

My vision slowly returns when I open my eyes, and they're still here—laughing together. I can't breathe. This doesn't make any sense.

Where is Riley?

"Theo," my dad says. Straightening, he lets go of my mom and turns to approach me. His gray eyes, matching mine, squint in disbelief. "You shouldn't be here."

"Where am I?" My voice is thick, and I'm barely holding onto my sanity. And what the fuck is even happening?

I will for the dream to change, but my feet remain rooted to the floor.

I can't wake up, and I can't alter my surroundings, and why can't I remember?

"It's too soon," he says. "This isn't right."

"Dad," I croak. "Tell me what's happening."

My mom steps up to join my dad, her hand slipping into his. Her lips press into a straight line, her vacant green eyes reminding me so much of Riley's.

"Mom?" I ask.

I want to hate her so bad. She started all of this. If she had never asked for a divorce on the Ferris wheel, my entire life would have turned out differently. Riley would be here, and my dad would be alive.

But she's my mom.

I take a step backward. Riley isn't here, but John is. And I can't wake up, and I can't change the channel and...

"No," I whisper.

The house trembles, the cupboards opening and slamming shut, glasses shaking off the shelves and smashing on the counters, pieces flying across the floor. My parents are shrouded in night, and they're pulled further and further away from me.

Explosions and gunfire, and *no*—

Memories flood back; I was fighting *them*.

I grab my head, the pressure intensifying. It hurts so bad. I drop to my knees, the world still shaking.

"Theo!" Amber screams.

What?

"Theo! Hurry!"

I fight the blazing heat tearing through my skull and stumble down the disappearing hallway, the house crumbling away. I'm back in the void, but there's no beginning or end, and I can't teleport anywhere.

"Amber!" I yell. "Where are you?"

"Theo, hurry! I can't keep it open much longer!"

I sprint toward her voice, each footstep sending a spike through my temple. I run and run and run.

An invisible force grabs my arm, yanking me sideways. A hand is in mine now, squeezing, but I can't see anything.

"Amber?"

My heart is going to explode. Or my head. Both are ready to burst.

"I've got you," she says.

I shield my eyes from a blinding light, hacking up a lung as I try to catch my breath. My head pounds, but I'm no longer in my house.

"Oh my god," Gemma sobs.

I blink a few times, squinting as my eyes adjust to the lights. I study the gold-leaf ceiling of the lobby. There's no evidence of an attack, like everything that happened was a dream, but Gemma is draped over me, sobbing.

"What...?" I try to sit up, but everything in my body aches. "What the hell happened?"

Gemma is in hysterics, her body shuddering. I put a hand on her back, shifting to sit up fully. She sits on her legs and covers her face with her hands. There's a cut along the side of her arm, dried blood caked all around it.

I glance around at the silent crowd; everyone is *staring* at us—Jet, Tilly, Margot, and even Caleb. No one says anything.

"For fuck's sake," I spit out. "Someone fill in the gaps. We were being attacked and... wait, no." My head swims as I try to get everything straight, the memories of Caleb telling us about the test this morning rising to the surface. "It was Henry's illusion..." I trail off when I lock eyes with Dennis, and the uncertainty on his face sends a shiver down my spine. Ice lingers through my chest until it's hard to breathe again. "Where's Nora? Zay?"

"We're fine," Nora chokes out. I twist my neck to see her, her arms wrapped around Zay.

Simone stands behind them, and somehow, she manages to look wholly unphased. Elise pushes through the crowd and holds out a hand, helping me to my feet. Then she punches me in the arm. Hard.

"Ow! What the hell—"

"You died, you fucking idiot," she shouts at me.

"Wha..." I glance down at Gemma, who's curled into herself like she can't face the room.

Elise punches me again. "Don't ever do that again!"

"I didn't mean to," I say out of instinct.

But seriously, what the hell?

Tilly seems to remember herself. "The test is over. Everyone back to your jobs. If you're not working, go find somewhere else to be," she barks. "You." She points at all of us, including Caleb. "War Room. *Now*."

Nora moves to pull Gemma up off the ground, and my heart aches for her, but I'm so damn confused. I need someone to explain this to me like I'm a child.

Dennis finally exhales and pulls me into a hug, crushing me. "You had us scared for a minute there," he breathes.

"I'm sorry?"

When he lets go, it finally starts sinking in that maybe I *was* dead, even though this was only supposed to be a test; no wonder Gemma is barely holding it together. No one said anything about being able to die, so what the fuck?

The events are twisted in my mind, and I can't tell which way is up, but I take her from Nora's arms and hold onto her.

Pieces flash. I saw my dad. *Didn't I?* It's like I have the full story, but I can't put it together yet. Everything is too jumbled and out of focus.

"My god, Theo," Gemma croaks. "I thought I lost you for good."

"I'm right here," I whisper.

Her body trembles within my arms, but Tilly demands we follow. I would rather lie down right now, but I reluctantly let Gemma go, keeping her hand in mine as we all funnel into the room.

"Who wants to tell me what just happened?" Tilly demands after everyone has a seat, her shadows unfurling around her, darkening half the room. When no one immediately answers, she adds, "Caleb, I thought you told *all* of them about this morning's test."

Caleb has the audacity to smirk. "I figured her boyfriend would fill her in."

Almost everyone else glances at me like this is somehow my fault, but Henry's illusion began before Gemma made it to breakfast. Even if he *did* ask me to tell her, which he didn't, I wouldn't have had the chance to. But Tilly seems to be thinking the same thing because she's the only one who doesn't turn away from glaring at Caleb.

"Are you kidding me?" she hisses. "You had direct orders to tell them individually."

He shrugs. "Now we know a little more about our new friends' abilities—especially Gemma's."

Tilly's shadows transform into a tornado as they rage around her, plummeting the room into even more darkness. "This is *not* how we do things around here. Don't think for a moment that I'm done with you, Caleb, but what I'd like to know is how any of this is even possible. What kind of power is that?" She towers above us all, pressing her fingertips into the table, her shadows slowing but still darting back and forth in agitated wrath.

"I think Roberts has an answer for you," Caleb says, offering Gemma up on a platter.

"I..." Gemma's gaze flickers between Tilly and Margot, and Margot barely nods, encouraging her.

"Gem, wait," I growl.

She can't, she can't possibly tell everyone right here, right now. There are too many people.

"Wait for what?" Tilly asks through clenched teeth.

"I..." Gemma begins again. "I haven't been entirely truthful."

I hang my head back against the chair. It's her secret to share, but that doesn't mean I like the idea.

"I'm not a mutant," she continues, hammering a nail. "I was made."

Tilly's shadows pause mid-spin.

Jet leans forward. "How exactly were you *made*?"

"When I was a baby..." Gemma glances around the room. Fucking Caleb is in here, of all people. Now, at least, Esha will get her answers. "My parents stole a piece of someone's ability and injected me with it.

"I don't know how it all works, honestly, but his name was Draven Wilkins, and I have a slice of his power."

The final nail in the coffin.

"The first," Jet whispers, and I close my eyes.

And now we've come full circle.

"The first? What does that me—" Gemma asks, but Tilly interrupts.

"What does this have to do with what happened tonight?"

"I can siphon energy from anything living. I couldn't control it at first, but M—" Her words stop as her gaze darts to Margot, like she's worried about getting her in trouble, too.

Margot sighs, taking off her glasses and rubbing tired eyes. "I helped Gemma. I created a necklace that lets her siphon energy from her crystals rather than risking anything living."

"You knew?" Tilly thunders.

"I did." Margot puts her glasses back on, standing straighter. "And as head of the science department, I felt it crucial we kept it on a need-to-know basis. Gemma wasn't a threat, and there was no reason she needed to spill her secrets to everyone."

I slowly open my eyes, exhaling as Margot takes all the blame. "As the head of this *base*, I should be privy to *everything*."

"You may feel that way, but this was a scientific decision. For Gemma's safety, I deemed it necessary for her to speak her truth when she was ready."

Tilly's jaw twitches, but Jet clears his throat before she can say anything. "So, you can siphon energy, okay... and..."

"Well." Gemma rubs her hands together. "When I saw Theo drop, I... I don't know. I lost it. I didn't realize none of it was real. I thought the base was actually under attack. I thought the Authorities finally found us." She continues her rambling, the words spilling out over each other. "I can't describe it, but I was shot before then, and the pain *was* real." She points to her ruined arm. "*This* is a real wound. So... so, when he crumpled, I knew he was gone. I stopped thinking. I just ran and figured if I could siphon energy out of people, I could pour some back in.

"I gave all my energy to him, to keep him with me, and I..." Tears slide down her cheeks. "I wasn't sure if it was working, but then Amber..."

Amber. My pulse slows. *What did she do? Where is she?*

"I don't know how she did it, but she was right there. She had her hands on Theo's shoulders, closed her eyes, and then he was awake."

"What about that projection we saw leaving your body?" Tilly demands.

"I don't know what you mean since I didn't see any projection, but I pulled him back from the other side," Amber answers, confusion creasing her brow. She stands at the open door with Judy behind her. Her veins are black, stark against her white skin, and her normally blue eyes have lost all color.

I almost throw up on the spot, my head swimming as it hits me how much this cost her. I'm certainly not worth the price.

"Amber," I breathe. "What did you do?"

I've got you.

The memories come into better focus, all aligning.

She was there. She pulled me out.

"I've never pierced the veil before. But when the illusion ended, and I saw Gemma crying over his body, I couldn't accept that he was really gone." She squares her shoulders in defiance as the entire room holds their collective breath. "I've never done more than speak to ghosts. That wasn't a lie. But it was like a curtain appeared before me for the first time when the test ended, and I could pull it back and glimpse the other side. And I saw him there. So, I reached in and pulled."

I close my eyes again.

All of this is too much.

Amber ruined herself for *me*.

"Maybe the projection you saw was Theo being pulled back?" Gemma offers.

Tilly shakes her head and folds her arms. "No. Whatever tran-spired was between you"—she points to me, then roves over to Gemma—"and you. Not to mention, it was purple."

My hand flexes and I refuse to look at anyone, but the words slip out anyway. "So, it's true? I really died?"

Gemma's hand finds mine, and she squeezes. "But you're back now."

As if it's that simple—like I fell asleep briefly. Before anyone can continue, I launch out of my chair and leave it all behind. My mind catches up when I burst onto the roof, gasping down large mouth-fuls of air.

I was dead. I was dead. I was dead. Holy shit. I stopped living.

What does that mean? Did I actually see John? He said it was too soon. Does that mean my mother is dead? And Amber—my stomach clenches. What does this mean for her? Is she marked forever because of me?

I study my arms, the black ink that already exists.

Are her veins black because of *me*? What am I? A freaking zombie now? And Gemma was *shot*? I heave. There's nothing in my stomach to throw up, but that doesn't stop it from lurching over and over as I collapse in the corner.

My blood chills as the gagging ebbs away. Sweat drenches my shirt, and I rub a hand across my forehead, feeling for any marks.

I remember the pain now and how badly my head hurt. Shot in the head. What a wonderful way to go. At least it was quick. I think. And where the hell was I before Amber dragged me back out?

My dad was there, but my mom was, too; was I in heaven or hell?

Chapter Twenty-Six

Gemma

I'VE SUCCESSFULLY MANAGED TO tear Command apart with my statement.

Everyone continues to yell over each other in the War Room, and all I can do is sink further and further into my chair.

I didn't think. I acted.

I wasn't going to sit there and watch Theo die. I poured all my energy into him to keep him tethered to me, and it worked. I would do it again and again if it meant saving him, and they will never make me feel guilty about that.

But should I have told them sooner about Draven?

Margot didn't push me to tell everyone. She understood why I didn't want to shout it from the rooftops. But I couldn't risk Theo dying to keep my secret.

The fact Amber could pull him back to the land of the living, though.... that's... I blow out a puff of air.

Theo ran off after that, and every fiber in me wanted to chase after him. But he needs his space to wrap his mind around what just happened, so I stayed put and listened to everyone argue over me.

I'll find him after this is settled, and hopefully, I won't be shunned by Tilly. Or worse.

If Margot wanted to experiment on me, she would have by now. She would have told Tilly and Jet, and let Esha open me up herself, so at least that's one less thing to worry about.

"What I want to know," Dennis says, finally breaking his silence. He hasn't spoken this entire time, only listening to the explanation of the events that unfolded. "Is how you would ever let potential harm come to those in your test. What happened to this being an illusion?" he barks. "My daughter was shot!"

My eyes fill with tears again, and I have to blink them away.

"And you let that poor boy *die*? What would have happened if Gemma couldn't keep him going until Amber was there? Or if she wasn't even able to do something to bring him back? What then?"

Tilly lets the unbearable silence build before responding. "We allow these tests to be as real as possible because there is always a risk of dying out in the field. They need to understand the danger."

When Dennis slams a fist down on the table, Tilly raises her own hand, her shadows guttering.

"*But...*" She hesitates. "We do take certain measures if there's ever an injury that can't be healed."

"You rewind time," Zay says, clarity dawning. "Singe. You let him rewind time."

Tilly bows her head. "There's a *very* limited window where the twins can alter events. In this case, we would have stopped Theo from being shot, and then Gelid would have fast-forwarded to realign his timeline with ours, but Gemma acted too quickly. It cemented everything into place before Singe could react."

My heart sinks. "So... if I had waited..."

"He would have been fine," she says. "More than fine. It wouldn't have happened at all."

Oh, god.

I put my hands over my face, despair ripping me apart. Now, because of me, not only did Theo die, he has to live with that and whatever effect that will have on him. But I put Amber in harm's way as well.

"Oh, god," I repeat again, this time out loud. "What have I done?"

<hr>

EVENTUALLY, WE'RE ALLOWED TO leave the War Room. We're not banished, thankfully, but Dennis isn't overjoyed with how they handled things.

Command has a point... Theo could just have easily died on a mission. But Dennis is equally right. We shouldn't have to worry about dying during a test. I get they're trying to prepare us for war, but some lines shouldn't be crossed.

The entire thing is a nightmare.

After they finish stitching up my arm in the infirmary, I escape to find Theo. He also needs to go there to be cleared, and Margot wants to look at him afterward to ensure he's... fine.

I check the basement, dining hall, and his room before giving up and checking the roof, where I find him sitting alone, head in his hands.

My heart crushes in a vice. I did this to him. I'm so selfish. Command would have fixed this if I had just waited a second longer, but

I wasn't thinking of any other possibility. I needed to keep him here with *me*.

But it's also their fault for allowing any of this to happen. If Caleb had told me about the test, or if they had told us about Singe and Gelid fixing catastrophic events if the time frame allows—*any-thing*—we might be in a different position.

They might even be more guilty than I am, but it's still my fault he's left with the memories of being dead and causing Amber harm for what she had to sacrifice to bring him back. If I only thought before acting for once.

I slide my back down the wall, sitting next to him.

Do I tell him? It wouldn't change anything. And would admitting my guilt just make *me* feel better? If so, that isn't fair to him. But we also agreed on no more secrets, and hiding how it's my fault that he now has to deal with this would certainly be a dark cloud hanging over us.

Theo says nothing, and it's impossible to begin. How do I make up for all the wrong choices I've made?

I close my eyes, going over the entire meeting. Considering how many people were there, it's going to come out one way or another.

"Theo... I'm so sorry." I thought I was done crying, but more tears escape, and I bury my face in my sleeve.

He lifts his head from his hands, sadness filling his empty gray eyes.

"Hey." He throws his arm around me. "Don't be sorry. I'm alive because of you."

I shake my head, words failing me, as I cry harder into his shirt.

"That's not true. They would have undone everything. Singe—If... If only I'd waited a second longer, they would have fixed everything."

His body stiffens, and I hold my breath, waiting for the other shoe to drop. An eternity passes, and I finally glance up at him, waiting for him to glare at me, to yell at me, to do *something*. But he focuses on part of the wall that's opposite us.

"Theo?"

He blinks a couple of times, glancing down at me. "It's okay," he breathes.

"But—"

"If I had your gift, I'm willing to bet I would have done anything, too, if the roles were reversed." He fingers the white bandage around my arm, glancing away like he's the one who's ashamed.

"But in a weird way... you died *because* of me. Singe would have skipped back a few seconds. It wouldn't have happened at all."

He shrugs. "You didn't know, and I'm okay. I don't know about Amber... but I'm okay."

"Amber," I groan.

The body count of lives I'm ruining is growing. I've already eradicated four, but now I've successfully killed Theo and disfigured Amber. The guilt yawns wider, threatening to swallow me whole.

"Margot signed off on her. She's all right... considering. She doesn't know if her eye color will return to normal or if the black in her veins will disappear, but physically speaking, she's healthy. It didn't do any lasting damage.

"Her best guess is that she overstepped. While her power grew, allowing her to access the veil, there could be some sort of damage for her going *into* the veil and bringing..."

"Me back," he says, defeated.

"She doesn't regret it." I lean into him. "She loves you, too, you know."

"That doesn't make it okay," he whispers. "Both of you risked way too much, especially with not knowing how it would turn out."

"I would risk anything for you."

We lock eyes, and as the steel in his melts back into silver, I can't take it anymore. I climb into his lap and kiss him until I'm a hundred percent sure that he's still here with me. I've almost lost him once, and I'm never letting go.

LATER THAT NIGHT, THEO'S cleared from the infirmary. Margot shakes her head in amazement, but she can't find anything wrong with him.

He escaped death unscathed, and while that should be something to celebrate, the guilt of what he's done to Amber weighs him down.

She's yelled at him multiple times by now that she's fine, and she swears the changes don't bother her, but his shoulders hitch every time someone does a double take to get a better look at her.

I keep reassuring him that all this will pass. Eventually, everyone will get used to it, and if Amber's not bothered by it, he shouldn't be either. But easier said than done. The guilt rolls off him anytime he starts overthinking.

Amber's surprisingly not lying, either. I've sensed nothing from her that indicates she's bothered by this. She saved someone who's like her brother for a price she was willing to pay.

Hopefully, in time, Theo realizes that as well.

None of us eat in the dining hall tonight, though, to avoid everyone's stares after today's events, and Simone is kind enough to deliver sandwiches to our rooms. We all eat in mine, sitting on the beds and using the one available chair.

I'm relieved I haven't encountered Caleb or any of his cronies since the incident. I don't know Tilly's punishment, but I'm pretty sure my anger would take over. Hopefully, it will cool before I see him, or I might hurt someone else.

Amber and Zay are arguing about comics again, Elise and Theo are getting along for once, and Nora and Simone discuss Nora's meditation. Despite all that's happened, we're enjoying a normal evening with each other, and it makes me so emotional that we're all still alive to sit here like this.

If I could pause this moment forever, I would. My throat begins to close again, and I have to force the food down, tossing my half-uneaten sandwich to the side and fighting back tears.

I can't believe I almost lost him. I don't think I could handle losing him *and* Oli. It would be the death of me, too. My hands shake, and he glances at me, but I muster a smile.

Once everyone heads out, I stop Amber and pull her into a bone-crushing hug.

"Thank you," I murmur.

"You don't have to thank me," she starts, but I stop her.

"I do. What you did..." I pull away from her but keep both hands on her shoulders, bending to meet her pale eyes. "*Never* do that again. I don't want something to happen to you either, but seriously... thank you."

She nods, giving me a lopsided grin, then ducks under my arm and heads for her room.

Elise slides off her bed, eying Theo and me. "I'm going to find somewhere else to sleep tonight. Have fun, you two," she says before skipping out of the room.

I don't have much time to ponder how she might feel about all this since it's primarily Caleb's fault and his failure to listen to orders because once it's just the two of us, my shoulders sag.

I don't think I will *ever* stop crying. It's embarrassing. But the weight on my chest is crushing, and it takes everything in me to stay upright.

Theo crosses the room and wraps his arms around me. "I'm right here."

"I know," I hiccup.

"I'm not going anywhere."

"Ever," I demand.

At least he's able to chuckle now.

"Will you stay here with me?"

"Really?" he asks.

"I might turn into a stage five clinger now, but I don't want you leaving tonight. Please."

His lips brush mine, and then I'm deepening the kiss, and I can't get enough of him. The possibility of never touching him again was so real that I now can't stop. I can't let go of feeling his soft lips against mine or gliding my fingertips over his skin.

We stumble backward as I drag him along with me, the hunger intensifying until we're both on the bed, the weight of him on top of me is reassuring—Theo's still here with me.

He was dead. He ceased existing.

I continue grazing my fingers over his face and arms, outlining his features, tracing his tattoos, and running my hands through his soft curls, memorizing every inch I can, but I need *more*.

His lips trail kisses up my neck, and the hunger for him takes over as I peel off his shirt, pulling him closer until he's on top of me again, the heat of his skin sending shivers up my spine. Our bodies intertwine, and I can't tell where I end and he begins, but none of it matters because I can't get enough.

I want all *of him.*

He kisses me fiercely, leaving me panting as his fingers skim under my clothes, leaving goosebumps across my stomach in their wake. I twist, pulling my shirt off, and toss it on the floor next to his, allowing him better access as he leans back, gray eyes following my every movement.

I bite my lip as his gaze meets mine, and I feel like I'm about to implode. His need mixing with mine almost pushes me over the edge, and if I don't do something *now*, I might melt into a puddle right on this bed. I grasp his chin, pulling him down to crash my lips against his, but he peels away after a moment, gasping for air.

"Are you sure?" he asks me through harsh breaths.

"Yes." I nod for good measure to get the message across loud and clear.

I've never wanted anything more in my life.

* * *

THERE ISN'T ROOM FOR both of us to be entangled on the twin bed, but I couldn't be more content. Even though he no longer smells like his signature citrus soap, instead blending in with the rest of the base's standard sandalwood, now mixed with sweat, he's still Theo, and I pull him closer until there's no space between us.

"Was that okay?" he asks. "Are *you* okay?"

I squirm against him, muscles aching, but in the most refreshing sort of way. "That was perfect," I say.

We lay in silence for a while, his fingers playing with mine. But eventually, he speaks, his chest rumbling against my cheek. "I don't want to ruin this moment. I wish we could stay like this forever, but something has been on my mind since I... woke up..."

His words trail off, and his previous contentment turns to worry, even dread.

I lean on my elbow to get a better look at him, scanning his face in hopes it can shed some light on whatever's bothering him. "What's wrong?" I ask when he doesn't continue, entwining my free hand with his.

"Never mind." He shakes his head, trying to downplay the sadness creeping over him as he stares at our joined hands. "Just forget it. I'm okay."

"Theo," I deadpan. "I know you're not. Tell me."

"Are you sure?" He glances up at me with such sadness that I'm almost angry at whatever hurt him. "It might pop this perfect bubble we're in right now."

I give him the most reassuring smile I can. "There will be more bubbles; don't worry."

"Oh, is that so?" His laughter is light, but then it dies off, and my heart aches for him, even though I don't know why yet.

"I think my mother is dead," he finally whispers.

When my fingers jolt and squeeze him, he continues, "I saw something when I was... wherever. My parents were together. And happy. But John told me it wasn't my time."

"So, you think..."

His body shifts, muscles tensing as he focuses on the ceiling. His tone softens even more when he says, "Amber hasn't seen him in a while, so maybe he moved on, like Olivia. And if my mom was there... I don't know. Then everything started to fall apart around me, and that's when I heard Amber's voice."

Okay, so he wasn't wrong; the bubble has definitely popped.

I lay my head back on his chest, wrapping an arm around him to pull him closer. "I'm so sorry."

I search for more words to say, but nothing comes to mind. From what I've learned, she wasn't always a great mother, but that doesn't mean he'd be okay with her being dead.

"Do you want to talk about it? Or about her?"

Silence hangs in the air for a few beats before he answers. "Not really."

I bite my lip, not knowing how to proceed. "Try to get some sleep," I finally say. "Maybe we can find some answers about what happened to her later."

He doesn't respond but mechanically rubs my back, and soon, his breathing shifts. He's asleep, but I'm unable to close my eyes because every time I do, I see his crumpled body on the ground.

Chapter Twenty-Seven

Theo

There's only darkness for a while; dying must take a toll on you, but eventually, my sleep evens out, and I end up restless enough to see Riley.

I should probably tell her Mom's dead—if she'll even let me.

I pick her less-hostile spot and step out onto the beach. Riley's back is to me as she focuses on the waves crashing on the shore.

The wind whips around me, pulling at my clothes, and the sky darkens with incoming rain. I didn't intend to bring bad weather, but the storm is inside me as much as it is outside.

Riley's shoulders hunch the closer I get, like she's already sensing my presence, but I don't give her enough time to attack.

"Mom's dead," I say, my voice carrying with the wind.

At first, she doesn't say anything or even move as if she didn't hear me.

I take a step closer, holding my breath. Will she finally let me in? Is this going to be the moment that bridges the gap? We're both officially orphans now. And while I should ache from knowing I'll never hear my mother's voice again, it somehow doesn't bother me.

She started all this. She wanted a divorce. She reported Riley to the Authorities. After I ran away, her dreams never changed.

I never tried finding her. It's no use chasing a ghost now.

I'm close enough to reach out to Riley, but my hand hesitates in the air when she turns toward me.

"It's just the two of us," I say.

Riley's half-shaved hair has grown out, but it's still short and choppy. The black brings out the hazel in her eyes.

I scan her face, searching for any traces of sadness, pain, or even hate, but it's blank. Devoid of any emotion at all until she bares her teeth at me.

"It's just you now," she sneers.

I open my eyes, back in the base with Gemma, who's wrapped around me, fast asleep. I take a deep breath, slowing my pulse.

My grip tightens on Gemma's arm until I remember the bandage and that she was shot, and I loosen my hold. But the point stands.

It isn't just me now.

It never was.

April

GEMMA'S ARM IS HEALED, and I've shown no side effects from cheating death. But Amber... She's not the same and never will be again.

Her power expanded, allowing her to save me, but it expanded too fast and too soon. She broke a boundary that can never be undone. And now, because of me, she has to live with the consequences. Lifting the curtain opened up the other side to her, and now she sees ghosts as often and as lifelike as the living people around her.

And there's nothing I can do to help her.

The guilt takes its toll on me, and even though enough time has passed that my dying has more or less blown over, I still can't fix what's been done.

Tilly must've forgiven us enough to allow us back into briefings because Gemma and I are called into the War Room. And she doesn't beat around the bush when we get there. As soon as we enter, she informs everyone, "We've gotten word that the Authorities are using their device on civilians. They started in Morrisville."

"Were any mutants found?" Caleb, who's already seated at the table, asks.

"We're not sure if the numbers are up to date and if they've all been processed, but what we received from Jason, they've found three already."

"Three in the whole city?" Gwen asks.

"How are they even doing the testing?" Ivan asks at the same time. "Are they bagging and tagging everyone? It seems impossible to track."

All the televisions in the room change to the same **BREAKING NEWS** alert simultaneously, halting all conversation. Tilly stands ramrod straight when her father appears on the screen, addressing the news stations' cameras. Each shot is a different view of him, allowing every angle possible, showing how many ways he's in utter contrast to his daughter who runs this base. I've never seen pictures of her mother, and the president has never spoken of her—neither has Tilly, for that matter—but it's safe to assume she has more of her mother's genes than his.

His white, balding hair matches his wrinkled and weathered skin, aging him even further. His dark, beady eyes peer through thick-rimmed glasses as he glares at the crowd, some cheering, some booing. His shoulders hunch over the microphone as he waits for the noise to settle.

President Thaddeus Gray—father of a mutant and the head of the Authorities hunting them down.

He raises his hands, quieting the mass, then shuffles through the index cards before him, like he's letting the tension rise with the disquieted silence.

Everyone in the War Room holds their breath, too.

"There's a crisis on the horizon," he begins.

Ivan scoffs, throwing his arms up as he leans back in his chair, uttering profanities.

"To keep our citizens safe, we've developed a blood test to see if you've been exposed to radiation."

"What a crock of shit," Ivan continues, but Gwen shushes him, slapping his arm.

"If your results show a high level of radiation, you'll be provided instructions on which hospital to go to for proper treatment."

President Gray pauses as cameras flash, documenting this moment in history.

"Natural disasters of different variants can cause higher than normal radiation levels, and while we are doing our best to combat their effect, we need to take precautions and treat those who may be vulnerable."

Margot inhales at the same time Tilly's shadows leak out of her. Even Caleb loses it, launching out of his chair to pace on the other side of the room, his fingers entwined behind his head.

"Symptoms can include weakness, fatigue, fainting, confusion, and eventually lead into worsening symptoms that can result in comas, and sometimes death. If you show any signs of radiation sickness, please go to your nearest clinic immediately. We will get through this as a nation, as we always have. There is no room for fear here, so do not be afraid. But you must do your civic duty and comply with our administration and get tested as soon as possible so we can save as many people as we can from this..." He pauses ever so slightly, his jaw working like he's trying not to show disgust before he utters, "... natural disaster."

Mutants... In a way, I guess we are natural disasters to him. My heart hammers at his implication as I try to reign in my emotions over what his speech means—what's starting now that the government has officially declared war on us.

The president continues, "This test will be available in all cities as soon as possible, but if there is no current testing site near you, please go to the government website to find your nearest location. Thank you, and God bless."

The screens switch back to their regular broadcasts, covering other violent atrocities occurring nationwide. One camera pans to footage of people stampeding over one another to get into some event or another because, apparently, we can't form lines anymore. Everyone is quick to anger, lacks patience, and, at this rate, aims to kill.

"Variants," Caleb sneers, pulling my thoughts away from the state of the world. "He outright said *exactly* what he's trying to eradicate, but society doesn't know that means *people* because we're too afraid to come out and show ourselves."

"Son," Jet growls, but Caleb spins on him.

"No, fuck you. You're a part of the problem."

When Jet stands, Asher and Louis usher Caleb out of the room, presumably to get fresh air so he can calm down.

Good fucking riddance.

The rest of the room sits in uneasy stillness as everything soaks in. The tests are happening, and we're officially at the beginning of the end.

"It's a scare tactic," I eventually say. "Despite what he eloquently claimed, they want people to be afraid."

Tilly rubs her temples, a pained expression creasing every line in her face. "Jason told us a little more than what the president is willing to say on live television... The device scans their photo ID, so they instantly have your name, date of birth, and address. You're logged into the system immediately, and when they do a finger prick, the results of whether you're positive or negative for 'radiation poisoning,' aka show a mutated gene, are immediately attached to the file. For those underage, they're attaching a profile to their guardian."

"So they can figure out who doesn't bother getting the treatment," Ivan states.

"Yes, but they can't take someone right off the street. It's too noticeable. Even if people are already affected by the radio waves, they want to scare them, but they don't want a riot on their hands either."

"They'll track down and kill anyone who doesn't comply," Jet adds.

"And who knows what's going on inside those hospitals." Gemma's worried gaze meets mine.

I don't need to read minds to know she's thinking of Nora's visions right now. Is the girl from her vision already in one of them?

"What do we do?" Simone asks.

Margot clears her throat. "We're close to finishing our own device that can essentially do the same thing, but there are too many people in the country. Hell, in the world. And there are too few of us, and we can't create the kind of devices they can. We don't have a mass industry behind us to produce them. So..." She pauses. "If we can't beat them and we can't join them, we need to figure out a way to hide the mutants."

The room stares at her dumbfounded—as if that's somehow an easier feat.

"I'm going to need Griffin."

After lots of debate, it's determined that Griffin wiping the system clean is too obvious, and even if he did, they'd improve their measures to keep him out. So, to beat them at their own game, he's going to try to hack their system and alter the equation.

If the blood tests keep showing up as negative, then no one will be marked for death.

It sounds too easy, but it'll take some time for him to hack the appropriate system and for one of Margot's team members to alter their equation enough for it to work but not be noticeable. Basically, all we can do right now is hope they don't discover too many more during the process.

Tilly dismisses the room but asks Gemma and me to stay put.

"Jet and I have talked it over, and we need you two in the field. War is coming, and we need all hands on deck. But we understand if you have any... reservations... about joining the ranks."

"I'll do it," I say before she finishes the sentence. "I'm in."

Gemma's stare burns a hole in the side of my face, but from the corner of my eye, I see her straighten her shoulders and meet Tilly's gaze. "I'm in, too."

"I think you both know that we can't guarantee your safety. Especially when it's real life and not an illusion. If you'd like to talk about it with your family first—"

"I don't need permission," Gemma cuts her off.

Judy won't like her decision, but it is her choice. And Command doesn't care about age, not really. They try to keep the younger kids out of it, but once you've graduated from their version of school and completed the physical training, you're on your own. I'm surprised Nora hasn't been drafted yet, to be honest.

"Very well, then." Tilly hands each of us a folder. "We're going to start you on easier missions. Supply runs and things of that nature so you can ease into it. Eventually, you'll go on scouting missions to find others. But for right now, we're hitting up a medical warehouse to gather more supplies. You leave tonight."

<hr>

A couple of hours later, I'm strapped into my tactical vest, waiting to depart, when I catch Gemma struggling with her gear across the lobby. My lips twitch as I try not to laugh at her, but she nearly drops the vest Griffin hands her.

She slings it over her head and tries to pull the straps around the side but ends up spinning in circles, trying to cinch it tight enough. I sneak up to put her out of her misery, but she does a double take at my outfit—just plain old cargo pants with a black shirt under my vest—and audibly swallows. And then stumbles.

"Are you all right?" I lift an eyebrow as I pull the straps tight around her stomach.

She nods, blinking rapidly. "Fine."

Once I finish strapping her in, I slide a finger under her shoulder straps to check their fit. In doing so, my hand brushes against her collarbone. She shivers, and I straighten out the crystals on her necklace, rolling the marble shapes across her skin.

Gemma reaches up, brushing the curls out of my eyes. Her violet eyes are so wide open that it's like she's trying to peer into my soul. I capture her hand and kiss her palm.

"If you don't want to do this," I breathe.

"No, it's not th—"

"Roberts!" Gemma jumps when Caleb shouts, ripping us out of the moment.

She groans, but I smirk before kissing her hand once more. "Just ignore him."

"He's the lead." She rolls her eyes. "Somehow. I'm surprised Jet didn't assign it to someone else after his outburst earlier." Her gaze narrows on him as she muses, "His month-long probation must be over for the stunt he pulled, but he has to be on thin ice still."

I shrug, not letting it get to me. Caleb is an idiot, but I've learned to ignore him. He likes getting a reaction, and if I don't give him one, I find myself feeling a lot better when he visibly struggles with my lack of response. I'll behave on the mission, but for this brief moment, he's not in charge of me.

"Gemma?" Judy's standing off to the side, waving her over. Gemma glances at Caleb again, and he animatedly looks up at the ceiling, waving a hand for her to go ahead.

See? I think. *Reactions.*

Caleb wanted to break us apart, and I didn't take the bait. I smile to myself, keeping my distance from Gemma and Judy so I don't intrude. I don't move far enough, though, and end up overhearing their conversation anyway.

"Yes?" Gemma asks.

Judy's hand is wrapped around her throat, a sure-fire sign she's upset, but even I notice the anxiety surrounding her.

"It's going to be okay," Gemma says before Judy gets any words out.

She tucks a piece of hair behind Gemma's ear. "You don't have to do this, you know."

"I know."

"You can just stay here."

"I'm not a kid anymore. And I'm the best chance they have."

She tilts her head at Gemma, her eyes brimming with tears. Judy wants to protect her as much as I do. Nevertheless, I guess I've gotten my answer. Gemma isn't second-guessing herself or her part in this mission.

"That doesn't have to be your concern," she tells Gemma. "They've lasted this long without your help."

I immediately think of Holt but keep my mouth shut. It definitely wouldn't help Judy's case.

Gemma clasps her hand, her knuckles turning white from squeezing it. "I'm going to be just fine, thanks to you and Dennis; I know who I am now. I have control of my powers, and I'm in a good place. I need to do this."

Judy nods, her chin wobbling as she pulls Gemma in for a hug. I turn away. This moment isn't for me, and I shouldn't be intruding. I exhale, rolling my shoulders back, hoping the stiffness will pass, but the night is only beginning.

"Roberts," Caleb shouts again. "Time to go."

I glance at Judy and give her a small salute as Gemma says her goodbyes and follows the team out of the lobby.

Our first mission will take us to a medical warehouse. We've been provided with a list of supplies to look for: bandages, gauze pads, and more intense things for major traumas, including tourniquets, burn supplies, and AEDs.

The mission should be easy enough, and I've been on countless runs myself, let alone with an entire team of mutants. Regardless, as I ride in the back of the truck, my body bouncing from the rough terrain, I hear the echo of Holt's screams and recall images of them dragging his broken body back into the base.

Gemma's fingers find mine; she's probably thinking the same thing. I squeeze her hand and offer a small smile, hoping I can convey that we're going to be fine and that this is going to turn out differently—different from when I died, too, *hopefully*.

I blow out a puff of air, leaning my head against the rocking transport and letting the engine drown out my thoughts. Before I know it, Gemma is nudging me awake.

Her hands tremble, and I would do anything to take away her fear. But as we climb out of the back of the truck and take in the large building leering over us, all traces of doubt are wiped from her face.

Gemma squeezes my arm before heading to her side of the perimeter. Asher takes the furthest point while Caleb stays within range of the truck Ivan drove us in.

Griffin rejoins us, jogging back from the security camera planted outside. "The cameras are all dead, and you'll want to jump us into the back left corner room." He closes one eye, pointing. "That window? Second one in?"

I nod, clutching the straps to my vest.

"Security. We have about a minute until they notice."

"Ready?" I ask him and Simone. Both bob their heads, and then we all wait for Caleb to give the signal.

Seconds pass, and the night is so silent that it doesn't seem real. No animals, insects, or vehicles—it's unnaturally quiet, and I don't like it.

Caleb finally gives the signal, pointing for us to go, and I grab Griffin and Simone, transporting them inside. There are two security officers, but we take them so off guard by randomly appearing in the room that Simone knocks them out before they can make any noise.

Griffin's hand touches one of the computer monitors, and all the screens go black. He flips a couple of switches, enters a password he found somewhere in the system, and turns a lock with the key already poised in it.

"Alarms are off. We're good to go."

I blink out of the room, bouncing from one warehouse aisle to another, scanning the pods.

"Hello," a mechanical voice calls out behind me, nearly giving me a heart attack.

I spin around and find myself face to face with a robot with a nametag—George. He looks like a post office box on wheels, but instead of blue, he's silver, and in the center of his "chest," there's a flashing red scanner.

"Please scan your barcode," he says.

"Uhh... guys? We have a problem." I say out loud, knowing Simone can hear me from wherever she is in the building; I just hope she's still with Griffin.

"What?" she asks, channeling her voice back to me.

"Please scan your barcode," he says again.

Does he sound meaner this time?

"What was that?" Simone asks.

"George."

"Who's George?"

He wheels closer, and I back up a step, bumping into the shelves.

"Please scan your badge number," his synthesized voice grows incessantly.

"The robot who's smart enough to know I shouldn't be here. A little help, Griffin."

"Please scan your badge number."

Okay, the mechanical voice is *definitely* different now. If this thing had eyebrows, they'd be furrowed at me.

"He's getting not nice."

There's a beat before Simone asks, "The robot is being mean to you?" I swear I hear her chuckle.

"Where are you?"

"Section five."

I teleport to them and drag them back to the robot mailbox, which is now spinning in circles, searching for me.

When we appear, I push Simone in front of me, and the voice returns to his monotonous tone: "Please scan your barcode."

"Terrifying," she deadpans.

"He knows me," I argue, shaking my head. *Am I really defending myself over a robot?* I glance at Griffin. "Can you just shut him off?"

Griffin places a hand on George's back and closes his eyes. "He's a mobile robot that retrieves pods when orders are placed. He has an entire database inside him."

"Super."

Simone laughs again. "What's your beef with robots?"

"They're unnatural."

"And we aren't?"

I roll my eyes. "At least we're still living, breathing humans. These AI things"—I wave a hand over George—"aren't right. Goes against nature."

"And we don't?"

I sigh, giving up. "Can we get this over with?"

Griffin finishes extracting all the locations from George and then shuts him down. We're running behind schedule, but as Simone and Griffin gather the supplies in the middle of the floor, I teleport them outside the building so the rest of them can start loading.

My brain switches back to autopilot, and it's like I'm on one of the countless runs I've had before, but this time, for medical supplies instead of food.

Sometimes, I don't know which is better.

Chapter Twenty-Eight

THE PAIN IS UNBEARABLE, but there's no voice to scream. No outlet. It's not real. It's only a memory, like the rain.

The blaze quiets, the goosebumps lower, and the teeth stop chattering.

Inch by inch, blood pumps through. From toes to fingers, feeling expands across every limb. The tingling spreads, pins and needles poking every muscle. But the muscles don't move—not yet. They remain filled with lead, glued to the hard surface.

Stone, or wood, or metal.

A rumbling shakes the foundation, and more words trickle in like the impossible water that never comes.

Thunder.

Thunder, rain, storm.

Another *boom*.

Ice follows the flame and tempers the heat. Shattered bones mend, skin stitching itself together.

The larvae die. The worms leave. The pain increases.

Time passes, and nothing changes.

Chapter Twenty-Nine

THEO
October

"Can we talk?" Elise glances over her shoulder, looking into the hallway before stepping into my room and shutting the door behind her.

"What's up?" I sit on the edge of my bed, scrubbing my wet hair with a towel.

It feels like it's been months, if not longer since we've had a proper conversation. She's around Caleb as often as I try to avoid him.

"I think something is wrong."

My hand stills. "Like what?"

"I don't know. I can't get a read on anyone because, lately, everyone is primarily anxious, and their auras look the same. But"—she licks her lips—"I think someone here can read minds somehow."

I bark out a laugh. "What?"

We've been here for nearly a year. If someone could read minds, they'd need to have a second ability to somehow manage to keep that secret.

"I don't know, but Caleb..."

My teeth clench together. Of course, he'd be involved. "He what?"

Elise sighs, sitting down on Zay's bed. She wouldn't say all this if Caleb weren't on a mission. And suddenly, it's back to being the two of us on the run. Before Nora found us, and all we had were each other—when she was my best friend.

"What'd he do to you?" He's lucky he's not on the base because I would love to punch him in his stupid face. Just give me a single reason.

She eyes me, holding up placating hands. "Whoa, you just went crimson. Calm down. He didn't do *anything* to me. Thanks for caring, though."

My hands slightly unfurl, but I remain quiet so she can continue.

"He knows some things he shouldn't. I think someone is feeding him information. And I don't know how else they'd know if it weren't for a mind reader."

"What does he know?"

"He... well... agrees with me. That..." She squirms, and it takes everything in me not to shake her.

"Just spit it out," I sigh.

"So, he wants Gemma to join his cause, right?"

My back goes rigid again. Anything to do with Elise and Gemma being mentioned in the same conversation is never a good idea.

"Well, one night, he was complaining, and I *thought* there was no way Gemma would ever turn her back on you. You two are clearly a match made from some God above, and he's ridiculous if he thinks she's ever going to disappoint you or her family to join some cause of his to free the mutants."

"And?"

"Well, the next day, he told me I was right."

The silence stretches between us for so long, but the accusation of her hanging us all out to dry must be plainly written on my face.

"Theo." She stands up, crossing the couple of feet to sit on my bed. "I swear on my life, I didn't say those words out loud. I'd never do that." The hurt in her eyes is overwhelming, and I have to glance away for a second. "We were in the dining hall when it happened. I was just thinking while he was rambling. So, someone else must have heard my thoughts and shared them with him."

"But who?" I scoff. "There's no way someone could keep that hidden. They'd slip up. And why wait until now? Why would Caleb show his hand? It doesn't make sense."

"I don't know." From the corner of my eye, I watch her pick at the hem of her jeans, pulling on a string. "All I know is that I'm afraid I did it again—I feel like somehow my thoughts put a target on Gemma like he's going to take more of an interest in her or something to get her away from you. All he did was agree with me, but I don't know," she repeats. "I'm not trying to choose you guys or him. That's not me anymore. I don't want to draw any lines in the sand. But... We want the same thing."

Her eyes drop to her hands when I turn to study her fully.

"I've learned my lesson. I shouldn't have tried to trade Gemma's life for power. I'm an idiot. I can accept that this is all I am." She throws her arms out wide. "But I still can't stand them. I want all the Authorities to pay for what they did to me. To my parents. To *us*." She grits her teeth. "I will do whatever it takes to take down as many as I can, and Caleb is right. Sitting here hiding isn't going to do anything.

"There's more of them than there are of us. The longer we sit here, the more mutants they'll kill. And I can't take it anymore. I might not have enough power to fight them, but I *will* kill them, which will lessen their chances of finding more of us."

I place a hand over hers as her body shudders, but she continues anyway.

"I messed everything up, I know that. I'm not asking for your forgiveness; I don't want you to forget what I did. I'm sorry Draven ever happened. I'm sorry I hurt Nora, but I'm not sorry for wanting revenge on those monsters. I just want to do better this time, so be careful." She swipes underneath her emerald eyes, which seem to glow even though she hasn't shed any tears. "Caleb is all about 'saving his people,' so I don't think he'll do anything dumb, but I wouldn't be able to forgive myself if I kept this quiet. Watch your back and tell Gemma to do the same, okay?"

I swallow the lump lodged in my throat, still clutching her hand. "I will. But Elise..."

"Don't." She pulls her hand away from me.

"You don't have to do this. It's a suicide mission. I don't know what Caleb's plans are, but if you keep heading down this road with him, you're going to get yourself killed."

She stands, smoothing out her black sweatshirt and fixing her disheveled hair. "That's my problem."

I wince. "Come on, you know that's not fair."

Elise walks over and opens the door. She keeps her back to me, uttering, "I know how to take care of myself. I'll be fine, Theo." Then she's gone, closing the door behind her.

I flop back onto my bed and screw my eyes shut to block out the imaginary smoke that's threatening to suffocate me. It's not that I'm losing Elise; she was already semi-gone, like trying to hold a handful of sand. She was within reach—here if we needed her. But now, it feels like the last pieces of her have slipped through my fingers completely.

There's no reprieve because Nora comes barging into my room minutes later.

"I give up!" she yells, throwing herself onto Zay's bed, where Elise was moments ago.

"What's wrong?"

"The hospital girl won't leave me alone, and I can't seem to get any more pieces. I have her name and the hospital room number, but I haven't found the location yet. I can't do anything until we have it!"

"You have her name now?" I sit up, leaning on my elbow. "Did I know that?"

Nora waves a hand. "I don't know. I found it during my last vision with Tilly."

"Well, what is it?" I ask.

"Lina Gibson."

I freeze. "Gibson?" I repeat the last name to make sure I understood it correctly.

Nora frowns at my reaction and sits up, folding her legs beneath her. "Do you know her?"

"No, but I think I know who does."

Jason. I get up so quickly that I'm light-headed and have to pause to get my bearings. His mentor had the same last name. I might've been drinking, but I wasn't drunk enough to forget our conversation. And before, back in the War Room, he seemed lost in his own thoughts when he learned I can jump into anyone's dreams as long as we're both asleep.

Nora stares at me wide-eyed, picking at her lip, waiting for me to provide clarity.

"What if you weren't dreaming about Lina? What if you were dreaming about Jason?"

"Jason?" Her brows furrow. "What's this have to do with him?"

"I don't know," I admit. "Let's find out."

We corner Jason in the small library. I'm a little surprised not to see Gemma since she spends most of her free time here. But I force the thought away, focusing on Jason. He glances up when we come rushing in, peering over the book he's reading in one of the recliners, but otherwise seems unphased.

"What is it?"

"Lina Gibson," I blurt out, trying to catch my breath.

Jason flips the book shut and sits up. "Do you mean Ava?"

"No," Nora answers when I glance at her for confirmation. "The hospital board said *Lina* Gibson."

Jason gestures for Nora to hurry as if he's not the one who asked the question. "What about her?"

"You know her, right? Because of Gerald?" I ask.

"Yeah." His face pales. "What's wrong? Is she okay?"

"I've been having visions of her," Nora says. "I think she's a part of this somehow. Maybe she can help us."

Jason shakes his head, focusing back on the book. "She can't."

"I normally have visions of mutants, and I've been seeing her in that hospital bed for *months* now. It has to mean something."

"She's not a mutant," Jason says with a sigh, leaning back in his chair. "I don't know why you're seeing her, but she's one of the ones we lost."

I glance up at the ceiling, blowing out a puff of air as pieces click together. "She can't wake herself up."

"Nope." Jason scrubs a hand across his forehead when I look back down. "I sit with her when I can, but she's at one of the Authority hospitals. I have to be *working* in order to see her."

"So, I'm not having visions of her. I'm having visions of you." Nora's eyebrows crease. "I never see you, though."

"I'm a tracker and part of being able to track people is knowing how to stay hidden."

Nora crosses her arms. "So, that's it then? She's not important?"

"She's important to me." Jason's tone is a little too sharp. "Sorry. I know this isn't your concern. I don't know why your visions led you to me while I was with her."

"Maybe we need to wake her up." Nora's shoulders sag. "My visions never steer me wrong. At least so far."

"How would we do that?"

"Me," I say. "That's why you were asking those questions before, right?" I shove my hands in my pockets and lean against the book-shelf. "Maybe if I can find a way to get into her dreams, I can help her wake up. There is a problem, though. I've already tried entering to figure out who she was, and I'm blocked. Maybe coma patients dream differently? I don't know, but if we can figure it out, there's a chance."

"It's not the coma," he says. "Well, probably not. But you mentioned before about being blocked from Judy and Dennis, so maybe the Authorities have created something in the hospital, too?"

"So, if I go in person, we can dismantle whatever's blocking me..."

Jason stares at me for a moment before shaking his head. "It's too dangerous. It would be walking straight into the lion's den."

"Good thing I can teleport."

Jason's smile falls flat as he toys with the book in his hands. "Your dad would kill me if he was still around."

"I won't lie. The idea of trespassing on their territory gives me serious pause, but if there's one thing I've learned not to question, it's Nora's visions. So, for whatever reason, we have to at least try."

Plus, I've already died once; what's the worst that can happen? I keep the thought to myself, knowing the joke wouldn't land with these two. Between my near-death... or actual death... experience, Elise's confessions, and her suicide plan of getting revenge, if there's even the slightest chance that doing this will help win the war, then the decision has already been made.

"It is a minor facility," Jason muses. "No one is really stationed there. It's more or less a holding cell for those who've succumbed to the brainwashing but didn't die. I can try to figure out what they have set up there that's blocking you in the meantime."

"Great. You do that, and then we'll be in and out."

Jason opens his mouth as if to refute how easy it'll be, but Griffin's alarms blare, shrouding us all in an ominous red light.

"Is the squad back already?" I shout over the wailing.

"They shouldn't be." Jason drops the book on the table, rushing out of the room. Nora and I are on his heels as we fly down the stairs to find out what's happening.

Zay meets us in the stairway, covering his ears. "What's going on?"

"Not sure yet."

He joins the pack as we go down. When Jason whips open the door to the first floor, everything is in disarray. People I've never seen before are pouring in from outside, and it takes a second for my brain to process what's happening.

But they're not the Authorities.

They're scared and injured individuals being funneled into the base, and even though I breathe a sigh of relief that we're not under direct attack, something major has to have happened. I spot Gemma near the lobby entrance, holding the door open as people are hauled in on makeshift stretchers or dragged in by those able to carry them.

I teleport to the other side to open the second door.

"What happened?" I yell to her.

"Another base was attacked." Her violet eyes shine with fright. "They were raided and got out who they could, but they had nowhere to go, so they came here."

My heart sinks. Were they followed? Did they lead the Authorities straight to us?

Jason shoulders past me, heading outside. "Riggs!"

A man with blond hair and startling green eyes turns around and grimaces at Jason. His light skin is covered with blood and grime, and I'm not entirely sure if it's his or someone else's.

"What the hell happened?" Jason asks.

"They blindsided us," Riggs heaves. "Never saw it coming. The entire hangar is up in flames right now. We had to abandon everything. Ten were dead, and five were missing at my last count. Everyone else is here, but I think the death count is going to climb."

Jason squeezes his shoulder, offering no words, but the man seems to appreciate it all the same. His bloody hand clasps Jason's, and Riggs bows his head, seeming to soak in the comfort.

Mainly everyone is inside now, so I let my door close, leaving Gemma to keep the last one open, and approach the two. Jason does a double-take and then clears his throat.

"Eric, this is Theo. John's son."

Eric raises his head, squinting. "Goodwin's kid?"

"Yeah," I say, my cheeks heating. This man clearly went through a lot tonight, and we're somehow talking about my dad.

"I'm sorry," Eric says.

My shoulders bunch, and all I can force out is, "Me, too."

"We should probably get you inside. Are you hurt?" Jason asks.

Eric shakes his head, his throat bobbing. "No. None of this is mine."

"I should have known." Jason smirks, but all traces of humor are gone. "Come on."

I follow them both inside, and Gemma brushes my arm as we pass, holding the door open for the few stragglers lingering outside.

The alarms cut out, but the volume's intensity doesn't dissipate. There are at least twenty people here I've never met, and the infirmary is so full they're overflowing into the lobby. People are lying on the couches, bleeding; most are crying, and Command is screaming orders at one another to be heard over all the commotion.

"How can I help?" I ask Jason.

He cranes his neck, peering around the catastrophe. But Eric responds first. "Grab towels, blankets, whatever you can find, and get them to the injured. We don't need anyone going into shock." Then he stops himself. "Sorry, old habits. You're not in my platoon."

"No, it's fine." I nod, agreeing with his instructions. "I'm better with a plan."

Time speeds by, and I lose the hours as I get sucked up in the rush of motion. Gemma flies around the lobby as much as I do, and I catch a glimpse of Amber in the infirmary before the door swings shut.

Nora and Zay have rallied the children who came with the other base, giving their parents a reprieve and letting them tend to their own injuries. Ruby stands at the door leading out to the courtyard, waving for the other kids to come outside. The hawk perches on her shoulder, its head ticking in small increments as the children hesitantly go to pet it. Behind her, a jackrabbit stands on its back legs; its nose is pointed up in the air like it's sniffing, or maybe it's waiting for its next command from Ruby. I have no idea, but it can't be a coincidence that it's here.

I even spot Elise at one point, discussing plans for what happens next.

There's enough room to house everyone, but the problem isn't space—it's food. And factoring in the number of injuries, the medical supplies we just got are probably already running low.

It's the middle of the night before everything has quieted. A few of us and Command are the last ones standing. I lean against the lobby wall, not sitting on the couch because there's a good chance I won't get back up. I've never bothered teleporting upstairs before to do something as mundane as sleeping, but after today, the stairs just aren't worth it.

"You did good, kid." Jason leans against the wall next to me, fatigue casting shadows underneath his eyes, his hair messy, with dry bits of blood mixed in. Mine can't be much better.

I revise my plan: shower first, then bed.

"Hey, before I forget..." I flex my blood-crusted hands, unsure if I should be opening this can of worms. But it might help Gemma. The timing is absolutely terrible, but I'll never ask if I don't do it now.

"Yeah?" Jason says when I don't continue.

"Is there any way you can see if the Authorities have any records on Draven Wilkins?"

"Draven?" Jason's forehead creases. "Why?"

"I need to look at something, and Jet told me they don't have a lot of records on him here."

Jason's mouth opens as if he wants to ask more questions, but he simply says, "Yeah, I'll see what I can do."

"Thanks." I scan the hotel lobby, our new reality settling back on my shoulders. "What happens now?"

"We figure it out in the morning."

"That's it?"

Jason shrugs. "We live to fight another day. Go get some rest."

I chew on the inside of my cheek, my blood boiling as he walks away. It seems so simple to brush this all off as if it never happened. How many mutant bases has Jason seen dismantled that his reaction is to *get some rest* instead of wanting to do something about it?

I sigh, trying—and failing—to let go of the pent-up anger. I'm only a little ashamed that I do actually teleport to the second floor before softly knocking on Gemma's door.

"Come in," she says.

I crack the door open. "Hey, sorry, I hope I didn't wake you."

She shakes her head, swiping at her eyes. "You didn't."

I'd ask her what's wrong, but this is the first time I haven't heard someone crying in the past six hours, so I can assume she's juggling everyone else's emotions as much as her own.

"I thought this dumb crystal was supposed to work." She rubs her necklace between her fingers, focusing on the sunstone. "I thought it'd dull some of the negativity."

I'm careful not to sit on the bed since I have a mixture of blood, sweat, snot, and tears covering me, so I kneel in front of her.

"You're still human, Gem." I give her a rueful smile as she looks down at me, a tear sliding down her cheek. "You don't need empathic abilities to feel bad about what we witnessed tonight. You're allowed to feel sad. Angry. Guilty."

For the first time, I take stock of all my emotions. Besides being angry, I didn't stop to realize what this all meant for us. I was too busy handing out towels and attempting to stop bleeding wounds as the injured waited in line for our limited medical staff to tend to them.

This is the world we live in.

Orphans like Ruby have no one to claim them. People like Jason miss loved ones, and he sits and watches someone he cares about fall victim to the government's brainwashing. Strangers fight each other for bus seats for no other reason than being angry. Their fight isn't with each other, but they don't realize that.

We've already lost the battle; everyone is too far gone.

And now, a mutant base was attacked, all because we're a little different. And it's not even our fault. It's because of evolution. But it doesn't matter. Most of us are marked for death anyway because we threaten their system. While not everyone succumbs to the brainwashing, there's just enough unrest to keep the world distracted as the power-hungry stay in charge.

Eric said five people were missing, which means the Authorities probably took them, just like they wanted to take Zay at the pizzeria. Who knows what they're doing to them, but they're probably going to end up like Riley, which means more bad news for us.

I clasp Gemma's hand, struggling to swallow. "I, for one, am pissed off at the injustice of it all. I'm sad for those who lost someone. I'm scared of our future." Gemma's lip quivers as she tries not to cry again. "But it all circles back to anger. And I can't stay angry, Gem. I can't do it. You want to know why?"

She squeezes my hand, nodding and sniffling.

"Because then they'd win. Their radio waves might not work on us, but they still win if we let anger control us. We can plan, and we..."

We live to fight another day.

I drop my head, giving a soft laugh. Now I understand Jason's parting words. We lost this battle, but the war isn't over.

"We keep fighting, yeah?"

Maybe not as direct as Elise's plan, seeing as she wants to go in guns blazing to who knows where. And if living to fight another day means retreating and going back into hiding, even if it's just for a little while, then at least we'll be alive to do it. But one day at a time.

"Yeah," Gemma says, breaking me out of my thoughts. "Go shower and come to bed." She leans back against the headboard, pulling the covers up to her chin. "I'll be here when you get back."

I cling to this, letting Gemma be the anchor that keeps me stable amidst the storm.

Chapter Thirty

GEMMA
November

THE AUTHORITIES HAVE EXPANDED their mutant blood tests, now targeting smaller cities like Crystal Cove, Newford, and Elderport. They've also implemented curfews, citing staying in your home as the ideal way to remain safe and away from any violence—as if mutants are on a rampage, running through the streets murdering people.

But no, that's not the case.

It's actually the civilians turning on each other as crime rates skyrocket.

Society still thinks they're testing for radiation poisoning, and everyone is slowly breaking down.

Fear is a powerful weapon, and the Authorities wield it well.

Thankfully, Griffin altering the equation worked, but not before over a hundred mutants were discovered and, most likely, killed. Jason doesn't even know if he has all the data. It's a shame, and a large, empty hole festers within me; no mutants should have ever been found out this way. The worst part is it didn't even stop the Authorities. They continue to overrun the entire nation, searching city by city, looking for someone else to drag away.

"We need to adapt, find another way to protect ourselves," Caleb demands, sitting at the oval table.

I hate to say I agree with him—probably bad news for me. Blocking their testing is great and all, but it does nothing against the dystopian future we're barreling right into. Once more cities fall and they start targeting bigger metropolises, who knows what the world will look like?

"What if we draw them out?" Esha asks, standing behind Caleb's chair. "They're looking for mutants, so... we give them mutants."

At least she's lost the wicked glint in her eye whenever she looks at me. But something about her still gives me the chills. She's never done anything *to* me, but the vibe she gives off is that she'd be happy to rip someone's throat out, especially mine if that means she can figure out how I was made.

Maybe that's unfair of me to say.

She scares me almost as much as Asher's silent strength. I'll leave it at that.

The muscles in Tilly's cheek ripple as she grinds her teeth.

"I know you don't think we're strong enough, but we can't sit back anymore. The time of hiding is over. If society finds out about us, then so be it. Someone needs to stop them," Caleb pressures her.

"Fine." Her voice grates like it's rubbing against a rock on the way out. "But we do this my way. We plan. We won't half-ass this and rush in so we all end up dead or worse—captured."

Caleb throws his arm against the back of the chair, smiling up at Louis *whooping* beside Esha. "It's about time."

I roll my eyes at all of them.

Caleb's the most complex person I've ever met. This cocky, arrogant side would get us all killed within seconds, but he's actually decent when he's in the field and has to lead a mission. He's two different people stuck in one body, and I really despise one of them.

Caleb catches my eye and winks.

That one.

I follow Theo out of the room, where Nora is already waiting in the hallway. "We need to go wake up Lina."

"Now's probably not the best time to try that," he starts.

"What is she talking about?" I ask.

Theo sighs. "The girl Nora's been seeing is… I don't know, someone to Jason. Nora's been having visions of *him* visiting her, but we got it twisted. She's in a coma because she can't wake herself up."

"But you can," I say. It's not even a question, but he shrugs anyway.

"We started talking about it the night the other base was attacked, so it's been off our radar. But it's at *their* hospital. It was already risky before, but now, after the attack? No way."

"It doesn't change anything," Nora insists. "The Authorities wouldn't think we're dumb enough to risk it. If they're already not guarding the hospital, then they're even less likely to ramp up security with the testing going on right now. If Jason can dismantle whatever they have that blocks you from her dreams, we're golden."

"How do you know about the testing?" he asks.

Nora drills him with a look. "It's not that large of a base. Word spreads."

"I don't know…"

"Don't you see?" When neither of us answers her, she sighs, pulling us to the side of the hallway as others funnel out of the War Room. "Theo, if you can wake one up, you might be able to wake them all up." Nora's eyes drown with hope, and it's the first time in a while that the slippery little feeling blooms in my chest as well.

"So, I just go teleporting around Authority hospitals, *fall asleep*, mind you, and wake all these strangers up? Sounds like a blast."

Nora waves a hand. "We'll figure out the rest later. We just need to try for right now. If you can wake up Lina—"

"What?" Eric interrupts from behind us, making all three of us jump. "You can do that?" He takes a lumbering step toward us, and if I hadn't seen him speaking with Theo and Jason over the past couple of weeks, I'd scram.

"She's been asleep for so long..." he mumbles to himself. Then, blinking rapidly, he focuses back on Theo. "Does Jason know?"

"Uh—" Theo's mouth drops open.

"Do I know what?" Jason joins the group now, and as more people join, the more Theo's shoulders hunch.

"If Theo is able to wake one up, he can probably wake them all!" Nora excitedly announces, which elicits a groan from Theo.

I can't help but chuckle.

Jason and Eric exchange comments on its practicality—Jason didn't find anything in the facility that could potentially block Theo, so they discuss how she's in a coma, which might be making things trickier. I trail off from listening to all the possibilities and how Theo going in person is still their best chance and catch Caleb sitting in the War Room, staring at us.

He rubs his bottom lip absently, focused in on the conversation—*our* conversation. Snapping out of it, his gaze flashes to mine, and he jumps out of his chair, grabs his coat, and leaves through the room's back exit.

Dread coils in my gut, but Theo would never fall for Caleb's antics. He'd never allow Caleb to use his power, so whatever bright ideas Caleb has rolling through his mind right now will have to pass.

"Gem?" Theo asks, and I twist to face him again, shoving Caleb to the back of my mind.

"Everyone's set on the plan, right?" Jason asks again.

Jet reluctantly sanctioned this mission; if Theo wakes up Lina, it could be a game changer. There's a chance we can help save those who've succumbed and are pointlessly locked away, attached to machines to keep them alive.

The details have yet to be worked out, but as Nora said, we need to start with one to see if it's even possible.

Two teams are going, but one is for backup. There shouldn't be any trouble, but if there is, Caleb, Asher, Louis, Simone, and Elise will be there to help. I tried telling Elise she wasn't needed on a mission like this, but she adamantly put her foot down on being left out of any more assignments. She said she was done with being just a cook and wanted to take a stand.

Henry's illusion flashes to my mind, and I try to shake the images away. When that doesn't work, I focus on Elise shooting at the Authorities and how unafraid she was. The test changed all of us, and I'm unsure whether it was for better or worse.

Theo grabs my hand, running a thumb over my knuckles, probably sensing that I'm barreling toward a dark place. I sometimes struggle to pull myself away from the cliff when we're on our way to another mission. Whenever I think I'm doing better, an attack happens, and I'm right back to square one.

Fear, it seems, is a lot like grieving.

None of it is linear, and you never know when it will pull you under or when the water will be tepid enough to keep your head above it.

GRIFFIN, GWEN, IVAN, JASON, and two others from the attacked base I haven't had a chance to meet properly are coming inside the hospital with Theo and me. Nora was the first one in the back of the truck, stating that none of this would be happening if it weren't for her, but Jason won't allow her to come inside. The truck is as far as she goes.

A selfish part of me is glad she's here. Zay and Amber are both too young to join the ranks, and while I'm thankful they won't be in danger, it does seem like there's a chink in our armor—two of our own are not here to make a cohesive unit. But they're safe at the base. That's all that matters.

Everything is fine.

"All right, we're here," Ivan's muffled voice travels through the truck cab. Griffin and Theo get out first, doing what they need to do to shut down the security cameras.

My hands tremble, but I force myself to take deep, steadying breaths to clear my head.

I'm a risk to everyone if I can't keep it together.

I clutch the crystals at the base of my neck, counting to ten. When Theo opens the back door for the rest of us to join, I blow out a breath.

"I can't shut down the cameras because it'd be too noticeable, so I put them on a loop. They're looking at an empty parking lot right now." Griffin beams, proud of his trickery.

The second truck pulls up, carrying the backup team, and Simone pops her head out of the passenger seat window. "There's one man stationed on each floor patrolling and one at reception."

I stretch my arms over my head, pulling at my neck muscles, and twist my torso to release all the tension. Shaking out the tingling sensation in my fingers, I count again for one final zen moment as I stare up at the ten-story hospital.

The parking lot is empty, and the building itself is in disarray. Even though the air is hot and sticky around me, a chill runs through my body.

"In and out," Theo reminds me. His gray eyes are encircled with shadows since he pulled an all-nighter to be tired enough to fall asleep on demand, and each time I look into his eyes, I fall in love with him a little bit more.

I'm not going to lose him, I remind myself, like I do every time we go on a mission.

"In and out," I echo.

While it'd be nice to take Lina with us and try to wake her up at the base, we can't risk it because of all the hospital machines she's hooked up to. If Theo can't wake her up, she'd never survive the drive back, let alone the infirmary, which doesn't have the kind of machines the hospital does to keep her stable. If he can't wake her up, she has to stay here.

"Jason's past the guard," Simone says. "Meet him in 940."

Theo nods to Nora, who makes herself comfortable in our truck's passenger seat, reminding her to stay put before depositing everyone from team one on their respective floors so they can handle the guards, then returns for me and transports us to Lina's room.

There's a heavy silence when we step out of the void, catching Jason standing next to her bed, his hands shoved deep into his pants pockets as he examines her sleeping body. It feels like we're intruding on a private moment even though there's nothing else to do but stand here and let him finish his thoughts.

"I hope this works," he whispers more to himself than us.

Theo glances at me, lifting his brows in a *here goes nothing* gesture, and plops himself into the recliner next to her bed. His eyelids flutter shut, his throat bobbing as he tries to relax, but his shoulders are still rigid.

I cross the room, resting a hand on his shoulder. "It's all right," I say. "I'll be here when you wake up."

He cracks one eye open, peering up at me, and then shimmies in the recliner, getting more comfortable. I continue rubbing his shoulder, my thoughts wandering as my eyes flicker around the dull room, catching on the whiteboard that lists her full name, Avalina Gibson, along with her room number, 940.

My gaze lands on the girl stuck in this bed, and I feel sorry for her. She's pretty, but there's something lifeless about her, like the coma seeped all the energy from her. Her reddish hair is dull, her skin so pale it looks like she's already dead. Her fingernails are short, and the idea of Jason sitting here late at night, keeping her nails trimmed, lodges a stone in my throat, and I have to turn away, blinking back the sudden rush of emotions, wondering what I'd do if I were in his situation.

Theo's breathing evens, his shoulders slumping back down, and this is the moment of truth. If he doesn't wake soon, he's in there with her. I'm not sure what's worse. If he *is* in there with her... who knows what she's dreaming about?

Jason hasn't stopped pacing the room while I sit in the remaining chair, waiting for Theo to wake, hopefully with Lina in tow. It's been long enough, which is probably good—

A shot rings out, and I flinch so severely I almost tumble out of the chair. Jason is already examining the hallway, glancing up and down in both directions.

I race over to Theo, shaking him. "Wake up!" But he doesn't move. I continue to shake him, terror twining around me, squeezing so tightly I can't catch my breath. "Theo! Wake up!"

But he's too far gone—too deep into Lina's dream to hear me.

"Caleb!" Jason barks, waving him down to our room, and my breath loosens a fraction. "What the hell happened?" he asks when Caleb comes jogging up.

"Gwen ran into problems. We were already on our way inside since Simone caught the scuffle. But she discharged her weapon before we got to her."

"What about the others?"

Caleb shakes his head. "We've spread out. Haven't heard anything yet, but we need to move. Any remaining guards would have heard that shot."

Jason exhales, glancing at a sleeping Theo and then back to me. "Go with Caleb and get out of here."

"I can't leave him," I start.

"I'll make sure he gets out. I promise."

I take a step backward. "I can't. I told him I'd be here when he wakes up. I won't leave him."

"We have to go now, Roberts—wait." Caleb cocks his head like he hears something in the now silent hallway.

"What is it?" Jason asks.

"Nora." His eyes grow wide, a pinch of uncertainty creasing his features when his gaze meets mine.

Jason curses as my stomach lurches. I grab Caleb's arm. "What about her?"

"She's inside. She must've followed us in."

"Why would she do that?" I ask, not expecting an actual response, but my heart gallops in worry anyway.

Did she see something?

I stare at Theo, counting the seconds, willing my mind to still again, but it's too frantic. "Take care of him," I say to Jason. "We'll go get Nora."

He nods, shutting the door behind us.

Caleb repeatedly hits the call button on the elevator. But another shot echoes down the hall, and he pushes me toward the opposite staircase. "We gotta move."

I go first, my hands lighting up as I check the stairwell. It's empty. Caleb walks backward, ensuring no one sneaks up behind us. Once we're both in the stairwell, we start spiraling down the steps.

"She's in one of the exam rooms. She must be looking for something," he says, panting. He's out of breath, and his worry makes me rush down the stairs faster.

A door on a lower floor bangs open, and I halt mid-step, trying not to fall as Caleb slams into me. He goes up a landing, wrenching open a door. When I open my mouth to question whether it's one of us, he stops me, holding a finger to his ear, motioning how he can hear them.

So, he already has the answer then. It's not a friend.

I follow him to the fifth floor, ducking into rooms and checking each one to see if Nora is in there. I want to scream for her, but I don't know where the Authorities are, so I keep my lips glued shut, even though the panic is crushing my chest.

"In here," Caleb hisses, pushing open a random door.

It's a small surgical room with a metal table in the middle and various devices on the counters that line the walls. A second door leads to the next room, and I dash over, peering inside.

"Gemma!" Nora screeches. She runs over to me, throwing her arms around my neck. "I'm so glad you're okay—"

"What are you doing here?" I hold her at arm's length. "You were supposed to stay in the truck!"

"Caleb said you... watch out!" she screams as she tries to pull me out of the way.

I whip around, but Caleb is already there, plunging a needle into my neck. I hiss in pain, grabbing my throat, my vision blurring slightly. There's a wicked gleam in Caleb's eye as I stumble back into the window, the curtains flattening behind me as my heartbeat rushes in my eardrums.

"What are you doing?" I try to snarl, my hands sparking to life... but wait... *no*, that's not right.

My heart skips a beat, and I focus on my hands, two blending into four before straightening back into two. But they're not glowing.

My power... it's... it's *gone*.

Fear settles in my bones, and I lock eyes with Nora, who's cowering in the corner. Did Caleb lure her in here? *Was everything he told me a lie?* He was so convincing. But why doesn't Nora run? Why doesn't she get help?

I squint, her blurry body coming back into focus for a brief moment.

Caleb's gun is pointed right at her.

"I will kill you," I growl. I take a step closer, but my legs feel like jelly, or like they're asleep, or I don't know what. But I can't move right. I don't have control. "Simone." My head throbs, and I lean across the table in front of me, bile burning my throat. "Simone," I say again.

Caleb laughs. "She can't hear you." Then he waves the gun at Nora. "You, over here. Strap her down."

Nora's at my side in an instant, wiping my sweat-drenched hair out of my face. "What do we do?" she whispers.

"Just listen to him," I say, too distracted from trying not to heave to do much more than be honest.

Caleb can hear us because of Simone, and she can't hear us because of Louis. And whatever he injected me with is blocking my power. He holds all the cards, and there is absolutely nothing we can do about it.

Someone raps on the door, and Caleb cracks it open an inch to address them. With his back turned, Nora snatches a scalpel from the edge of the table, sliding it behind her back as my vision swims once more.

"Where is he?" a voice asks.

I cradle my face with both hands, and it takes everything in me to focus on the door and who's standing on the other side.

Caleb's muffled voice sounds briefly submerged, coming back up for air at the end. "—upstairs."

"Help," I call out, my voice hoarse, but Nora glances at me, eyes wide, shaking her head.

Caleb tilts his head back, opening the door further, and my stomach plunges. When it does, everything in it comes up. I lean over the edge of the table, vomiting on the floor.

A girl with hazel eyes and black hair grills me, and oh god. I've seen her before, back at the cemetery where Draven tried to trap me in his dollhouse. All the horrible pieces click into place. All the phone calls. Caleb's anger after Holt died. The ambush tonight.

"You son of a—" I gag more, choking down any remaining vomit. Tears spring to my eyes, and Nora pulls me back onto the table to lie down.

"How could you?" I accuse Caleb, but I'm losing to whatever he poisoned me with. The darkness around me creeps in, and I don't know what's going to happen to Nora or Theo—

God, *Theo*.

I struggle to sit up to face them. *Both* of them.

"Don't you dare hurt him," I snarl, baring my teeth.

A second wind fills me for a moment, the darkness fading, and the room stops spinning. The girl's jaw ticks, her gaze darting to Caleb before turning on her black-heeled boot to leave.

"Riley," I yell. She stops but doesn't turn. "*Please.*"

Her back straightens, and she leaves without a second glance. I train my eyes on Caleb, struggling to find the effort to move my legs and get off this table.

"You probably have questions," Caleb declares. "Too bad we don't have time to answer them."

"How could you? Why are you working with them?"

He exhales a drawn-out sigh. "Riley and I want the same thing. Free the mutants! Stop the unnecessary slaughter by the Authorities. So on and so forth." He waves the gun around passionately. When I don't say anything, he elaborates, "Vive la révolution!" His mouth quirks as if he's disappointed we're not joining in on his good spirits.

Nora springs, swiping her scalpel at Caleb's face, but he dodges the blow—almost. She catches his cheek, but he's already twisted her arm, slamming her into the counters. Nora lets out a startled yelp, dropping the blade as he continues twisting her arm behind her back.

"Don't!" I plead, but the second wind is quickly leaving me, and the next round of losing to the drugs begins. "Please. Whatever you do, don't hurt her."

Caleb shoves Nora away, and she trips over her feet, landing hard on the ground. She crawls into the corner, pulling her legs to her chest, and with a startled pang, I see Amber all over again, back in the dress shop a lifetime ago, when she first witnessed me using my power.

"I tried to be nice." Caleb stalks closer to me. I squeeze my eyes shut, blocking out the line of crimson running from his cheekbone. "I did everything right." His voice hitches in anger, and the more he rattles on, the more I lose focus, the spots in my vision returning. "I even rescued your damn parents! But what do I get in return?"

"You can have my powers." I grit my teeth. "Just let Nora go."

"It's not that simple."

I risk opening my eyes, studying him until he stops moving.

"You're not a mutant." When my mouth opens and nothing comes out, he continues, "Permission doesn't work with you, Roberts. That was quite a wrench you threw me that day, rescuing your boy toy. But Riley and I talked it over. Since you took your powers from Draven, that means I can take them from you."

"I didn't!" I try to argue, but I'm failing. "I didn't... I didn't take them."

He ignores me, grabbing different objects and tossing them onto the metal tray next to my head. He glances at Nora every so often as if ensuring she doesn't try to bolt.

Caleb ties a tourniquet around my arm, and I push him away from me, or at least I think I do until I realize my free arm didn't move. I've lost all control of my body, and even the panic begins to trickle away.

He draws my blood as I blink up at the lights above me, the fluorescent bulb swaying in and out of view. All I can hear is my harsh breathing.

That's me breathing, isn't it?

Or did I stop breathing?

Is my heart still beating?

We keep fighting, yeah? Theo's voice blooms in my head, and a surge of energy rushes through my veins. I focus on my crystals, struggling to swallow as a tear escapes. *Fight this. Snap out of it.*

Outlast him.

I grind my teeth together, using all my strength to turn my head. He injects himself with my blood, and my mouth goes dry. My parents injected me to give me Draven's power, but they extracted it from him somehow. It wasn't *blood*. My mother did some ritual, and the power poured right out of his mouth into a bottle that they *then* injected into me.

But how does Riley fit into all this?

"Your turn." Caleb spins on Nora. "Take her memories away."

Nora's eyes fill with tears, and she shakes her head.

"Oh, I'm sorry." He crosses the room in two steps and yanks her to her feet. She cries out, but he grips her arm harder, her skin losing color from the pressure. He tosses her at me like she's a rag doll. "It wasn't a request."

Nora weeps, and he cocks his gun, pointing it at the back of her head. She stands over me, tears streaming down her cheeks.

"I know you can do it. I heard you managed to erase memories of yourself from your entire family. Only that idiot Henry remembers you. So do it. Erase her mind. She can't remember that I took this from her."

Nora whimpers, her body shaking. Or is that mine vibrating? My teeth chatter, my extremities turning cold.

"Shhh," I soothe, but my tongue sticks to the roof of my mouth and feels too large. I run my fingers over her braid before laying my hand on her chest, my fingers aligning with the scar I left behind. "It's okay."

She hiccups back a sob, failing to calm her breathing.

Barely above a whisper, I remind her, "You know what to do." Nora's tears continue to fall, but she nods, her teeth tearing into her lip.

"I'm sorry." Her voice turns into a whine, reminding me how young she is. How young all of us are.

"Let's get on with it," Caleb growls, interrupting our moment, and Nora's face crumples again.

"It's okay," I repeat, louder this time. "It's going to be fine. Tell Th-Theo—" My words slur as the drugs finally pull me under.

A girl screams over and over, her voice fading into nothing.

You have to remember.

Darkness surrounds me. It's suffocating. I can't tell which way is up. Where am I? Where is Olivia? My heart jolts. Olivia. Olivia! The truck. She's hurt. She's—

You have to remember.

... Remember *what*?

Chapter Thirty-One

Nora

A HARROWING *BOOM* RATTLES the building, and the ground shifts beneath our feet. I throw my arms over my head, ducking as the ceiling cracks and plaster drops around us.

I cower in the corner of the room, squeezing myself between two medical fridges, but my focus remains on Gemma, who is passed out on the exam table. Tears stream endlessly down my face, and I want to scream at her to *wake up*.

She can't leave me here with Caleb, the monster who did this to her—the guy working with the enemy, with Theo's sister.

I don't know if it worked, but Gemma has to remember.

She has to.

Whatever exploded must have killed the power, leaving only the emergency lights, which cast the three of us in a sinister red glow. It's fitting, if anything.

My bottom lip begins to bleed as I bite into it when another explosion sounds, this one even closer. Incoherent shouting surrounds us, and I can't determine who's who. Are the Authorities attacking? Where is the backup team?

None of this is right. My breathing goes shallow, and I screw my hands into fists. I didn't see *any* of this coming. What's the point of having visions if they don't warn you? Where's Theo? Elise?

Gemma, please wake up.

I choke back a sob.

Caleb races over to the table, shaking Gemma by the shoulders, but she doesn't wake.

"Come on!" he yells at her unconscious body. "Why aren't you waking up? You're supposed to be awake by now!"

Rapid-fire gunshots spring down the corridor, and I let out an involuntary scream at their proximity.

I can practically see the calculations clogging Caleb's brain; he wasn't expecting it to go this way either. He presses his hands against his head, one still clutched around the gun.

He suddenly spins, aiming the weapon at me. "What did you do?"

I try to scramble backward, my shoes slipping over the slick tiles, but I'm already as close as I can get to the corner. My hands splay out on either side of the fridges.

"Why won't she wake up?" he growls.

"I don't know!" I shout back at him. Tears dry on my cheeks as I pull myself together. I won't let him get away with this. Theo will find us soon; I just have to stall him a little longer. "I did what you asked me to!"

"I don't believe you!" he bellows back at me, pacing in circles as the gun flails in his hand before he starts talking to himself. "This was a trick. They played me all along. Riley, Roberts, Nora. It's all a trap," he mutters to himself, and with each unstable statement, my chest gets tighter and tighter.

Someone bangs on the door; please be Theo. *Please.* He can fix this.

Another thud.

The knob twists but doesn't open.

I screw my eyes shut, chest heaving. Theo would teleport inside if he could.

That isn't him out there.

We're going to die.

It's just a thought, not a true vision. I don't see my own death, but there's a certainty in it. The Authorities will bust down that door at any moment, and they won't need someone like me.

They will kill me.

My eyes slide back open, focusing on Gemma's still body. Caleb also stops, his hands lowering to his sides as he fixates on her as well.

It seems like a decision has been made, his calm demeanor sends goosebumps across my skin.

He turns to face me again, hand gripping the gun, fingers no longer trembling. He aims it straight at me, and somehow, I'm at peace. I won't have to see what's beyond the door if I'm killed by Caleb's hand. I was a fool for thinking I'd ever survive this. He can't risk letting anyone know what he's done.

If Gemma can't remember, and I'm not around to talk...

My body stops shaking, and I lift my gaze to meet his.

If he's going to shoot me, he's going to have to face me when he does it. I think of Amber and her ability, and I almost smile.

I hope I get to haunt him forever.

"No!" Elise screams from the other side of the door.

This fractures my charade, and my hands shake, but only a little. The crack echoes deep within my chest, though, when Elise repeatedly screams my name.

She's here. She cares about me.

Theo, my lost boy, the one I needed to find and save. The one I saved from himself all those years ago.

What is he going to do now?

"I'm sorry, Elise," Caleb murmurs.

His throat bobs as he gives a hard swallow.

The banging increases as Elise slams her body against the door, the metal groaning. "I swear to god, Caleb," she continues to yell. "I will hunt you down if you hurt her."

Caleb and I lock eyes again, and the guilt in his gaze is so fierce that I almost pity the man who's backed himself into such a corner that this is the only way he sees out.

I close my eyes, calmness stilling my trembling fingers, and he—

Chapter Thirty-Two

THEO

I OPEN MY EYES. I'm still in the hospital room, but this time, it's some hellish alternate version of it.

Lina's bed is empty, and Gemma and Jason are no longer gathered around us.

Is she aware of where she is? Is that why she's dreaming of it?

I'm slow to get up, peering at the red emergency lights flashing in circles. There is no noise, which makes the lackluster alarm even more disconcerting.

There's a notebook on her bed, and I pick it up, frowning at the words sketched into it repeatedly: "It's futile to resist."

Well, that's probably not a good sign.

I drop the notebook back onto her bed and walk through the deserted hallways; the entire hospital is abandoned. No Authority members are patrolling the halls in this version, and I suddenly stop. There are no doors or windows that lead outside, either.

Where could she be?

"Lina?" I call out in the deafening silence, but no one responds.

In blood red, painted words appear on the walls: "It's futile to resist," written over and over, just like in her notebook.

Did Lina do this herself? Or was it here first, and she copied it into her notebook?

Is this her nightmare or another tactic from the Authorities?

How far can their brainwashing reach? Do the Authorities have their own sick simulation that will torture people until the end of time?

I wouldn't put it past them. I pick up my pace. Maybe I really can help the others; I just need to wake up Lina first. If there's even a remote chance they're all "living" in this hellish dreamscape, I have to at least give it a shot.

The only sound is my increasing heartbeat as sweat trickles down my neck. I remind myself I'm in her head, so no one else should be present. But that doesn't stop me from looking over my shoulder every few seconds.

Change the scene, I think, but the nightmare persists.

If I can move us to the beach Riley seems to be so fond of, maybe it'll be easier to get through to her if she sees her "reality" change in the blink of an eye. But no matter how hard I try, the dream doesn't alter.

I drift through the unoccupied cafeteria and out through another door leading to a new hallway.

"Lina?" I call again. The sound of something clattering clangs down the hallway, and my heart races into overdrive. "Lina Gibson?"

I round the corner, and Lina, wrapped in an ill-fitting hospital gown, lunges at me, snarling like a wild animal. I teleport at the last second, appearing right behind her, and trap her arms behind her back.

She bucks against me.

"Whoa, whoa, whoa, stop!" I attempt to move with her so I don't accidentally hurt her as she kicks and screams. "Jason sent me!"

Lina loses momentum, and I'm not sure if it's because of what I said or if she tired herself out, but she sinks to the ground, and I sit with her, clutching her arms. Her chest heaves as her stringy hair covers her face. I want to let go, but who knows what she's capable of?

"My name is Theo," I begin. "I'm a mutant. I can get into people's dreams. Jason sent me, hoping I could help you wake up."

She doesn't respond, but the fight leaves her body, and I slowly let go, backing away. I give her a wide berth as she sits in the middle of the hospital floor and then kneel in front of her. My arms rest on my knees as I sit on my haunches, ready to spring back if she lunges for me again.

"Are you..." I rub the back of my neck, words failing me. "Uh... okay?" My cheeks heat, and I feel incredibly stupid for asking. But considering she hasn't done anything but snarl at me, I'm not sure where her mental state is.

Maybe the Authorities did more than trap her here.

"Can you talk?"

Her shoulders rise with her breaths, and she does nothing to move the hair out of her face.

"Do you remember Jason?"

Slowly, hardly even noticeable, she nods.

"Good!" I say, trying to lift her spirits. "That's good! He's been really worried about you."

The silence stretches, and my legs grow numb, so I sit on the ground. She seems docile enough now that it's probably safe—hopefully.

"It's futile to resist." Her voice shatters the quiet, and the hairs on the back of my neck rise. I swallow a few times, dislodging the dread clogging my throat.

"It's not." I lean closer to her to get her attention. *Please look at me and notice I'm real and right in front of you.* "Trust me. You can fight this."

She shakes her head, covering her ears. "It's futile to resist," she mumbles again.

"Ava—" I stop short, reaching over and softly touching her arm when her movements become more frantic. She jerks away and glares at me, peering through her tangled hair. "I'm right here. I'm real."

She blinks a few times, the gold flecks in her green eyes glinting due to the lights flashing above us. Her pupils dilate, and it's not quite recognition that I see because we've never met before, but the familiarity of another person, like she finally understands that I'm not a figment of her imagination.

"I'm here," I say again. "Jason sent me. You have to wake up. None of this is real." I throw my arm around the hallway, indicating the hospital. "This is all happening in your head, but I can *enter* dreams. I'm next to your hospital bed right now in real life. If you wake up, we can talk there."

Her eyes narrow, suspicion filling them to the brim.

"Jason told me about his mentor, Gerald. He's related to you, isn't he?"

Grief spasms across Lina's face; I hope it's a good response, even if it hurts her. I need her to believe me, and recognition helps, no matter how painful.

"Jason told me he's a tracker. He's a cop, too. He used to be partners with my dad, John. I don't know if you ever met John, but he wasn't a mutant." Words tumble out; maybe if she knows my story, she'll be more likely to listen. "We didn't get along very well in the end. And then he died protecting me, and it's too late for me to take back anything I did. I should have trusted him. So many things would be different now if I had."

Lina continues to peer at me, but the suspicion is draining as she listens intently to my ramblings.

"I'm asking you to trust me now, Lina," I plead. "You have no reason to, I know. I'm asking for so much. But just believe me when I say that this *isn't* real. You're in a dream. You need to *wake up*."

I clutch her hands, and she jerks away but then freezes, allowing me to keep my hold.

"Wake up," I demand.

My eyes reluctantly open, zeroing in on the fluorescent lights above me, which remain red. There's no noise, and it's as if I'm still sleeping, and none of this is real. The thick air is unmoving, and the sting of disinfectant lingers. It's so silent that it takes me a second to remember where I am.

The hospital... Lina.

I deeply inhale, shattering the peace around me, and then chaos descends.

Deafening gunshots blare, and I wince with each *bang*. I startle upward, and at the same time, Lina groans from her hospital bed. *She followed me out of the dark.* The victory is short-lived as Jason peers over his shoulder at the noise but focuses back on the doorway, firing another shot.

"What the hell is going on?" My blood turns to ice when I scan the room... *Where did Gem go?*

"We need to move!" Jason shouts.

After his last shot, he steps out into the hallway, craning his neck in all directions before diving back into the room. He rips off a blood pressure cuff, disconnects the IV from Lina's hand with a little more grace, and pulls the oxygen tubes from her nose.

Instinctively, I go to her other side and start peeling off any of the sticky tabs, attached to wires, that I find along her arms and legs.

"What's happening? Where's Gemma?" I ask.

Once she's free, Jason scoops Lina up in his arms. Another noise leaves her, but she's not entirely with it yet.

At least she's awake, though.

I think.

I grab his arm, stopping him from rushing past me. "Where's Gemma?" I repeat, my voice streaked with panic.

"She left with Caleb to find Nora. Now *we* need to go."

Nora? What the hell?

The hallway looks like it was bombed while I was under, even though that's impossible. There's no way we'd be this close to a blast and survive. But there are cracks lining the plaster of the walls, like the building is about to be ripped in half. Parts of the ceiling have caved in, and we have to step over loose rubble and dodge more falling parts. Smoke billows from the end of a passageway, and Jason halts, spinning in circles with Lina in his arms before settling on a direction.

"Follow me!" Jason yells over his shoulder.

But I'm still looking behind me down the corridor we just left. Did the others get out in time? Are they safe? Fear paralyzes my muscles. I can't leave them here. If they didn't get out... I cough through the fumes.

When I turn around, Jason is gone.

I have no idea what direction he took. I just stand there like an idiot, unsure where to go.

Until I see her.

She stalks down the middle of the hallway, fire blazing at her fingertips. And we are certainly not in her dream.

She's so close, yet so far away.

I bolt, heading down the opposite corridor, flinching as a fireball just misses my head. The doors are closed at the end of the hallway, and I run straight into them, but they don't budge.

The ward is locked.

I slam against the handle with all my weight, but it won't move as another flame bursts into life next to me—the plaster cracks from its impact, exploding out of the wall. I squint against the sudden dust, but a piece of wall hits me above the eye. Blood drips down, forcing me to blink it away as I slam into the door again. But there's no use.

Though my pulse rages, I steel myself to turn around to face Riley, who's successfully planted a ring of fire around us. The hallway disappears from view as the smoke shrouds us in darkness.

I try to teleport, but my body doesn't move. I'm blocked. I can't see Louis, but he has to be here somewhere, unless Riley has her own shield. Her flames work just fine, so whoever is blocking me, it's intentional.

It's almost laughable, considering how many times Riley has tried to kill me in her dreams. There's nowhere for me to run, and I'm not able to turn this scene into a beach—I'm so fucked.

The fire blazes around me, the flame reflecting in Riley's eyes. A snarl escapes her throat as she surges forward, effectively trapping me. My heel catches on a loose stone, and I lose my balance. My back cracks against the tile.

She's on top of me in an instant, her hands wrapping around my hoodie, pulling me closer to her as the hate in her steely gaze ignites hotter than the air around us.

I reach for her. I don't know what to do but try to comfort her. Even after all this time, she's my little sister. I curl my hands around hers, noticing how delicate they seem under mine. We're eleven and thirteen again, holding hands and crossing the road. Black ink tries to hide the scars, but they're there.

They're always there.

Riley glances at my hands before her eyes lock back onto mine, and her lip curls in disgust, but I swear I see recognition flicker across her face.

An eternity seems to pass as we stare at one another. Now that we're finally here, finally at the end, neither of us seems sure about what to do. Smoke surrounds us, but only my lungs burn. Riley is as unaffected as always. The fire doesn't bother her.

It never has.

"You left me," she growls.

"I tried—" Her grip on me tightens. "I tried to get you out. I didn't know! I didn't—"

The smoke crawls down my throat, and it hurts to breathe. I'm right back there; the staircase collapsed, fire licking my fingertips.

"You should have tried harder." She shoves me back to the floor, and I raise my hands in surrender. Black spots fill my vision. "You should have come back." Her voice cracks on the last word. "You swore you would protect me."

My heart surges. I'm running out of time, out of air. But that's not the worst part. The worst part is that she's right.

I should have done… I don't know what. But I should have done *more*. I should have at least looked for a body to bury, if nothing else.

Instead, I ran.

And I've been running ever since.

"I'm sorry," I finally choke out, the words dying on my lips. "I'm so sorry."

"Sorry isn't good enough," she spits out, but she's sitting back on her heels, her weight leaving my body. Riley throws a dagger into the smoke, her shrewd eyes never leaving mine, and a body collapses against the tile.

I break her gaze, stretching my neck and squinting through the haze. Louis is lying on the ground, and my mind spins with so many questions, but none of them come out of my mouth. I'm running out of air. I roll onto all fours, gagging as the fire rages, eyes burning with tears.

"Come with me," I plead. "Let me make this right."

Riley stands, still unaffected by the flames blazing around us. She brushes the dirt off her shirt, gazing down at me, cool and collected, even though we're locked in an inferno, and she just killed a kid, someone her own age—another mutant.

"Things will never be right." She leaves me there, hacking on the ground. But she didn't kill me when she easily could have, and that's all the courage I need to stand and keep fighting.

It might be poetic, her leaving me to die in a burning building, just as I did to her.

But I don't think she's that stupid. If she wanted me dead, I'd be dead.

No, she's giving me a chance to escape.

The billowing smoke fogs the red haze, making it even harder to see. I don't know where anyone is until Simone runs up to me, pulling me through the darkness.

She clasps my hand, pulls me to the stairwell, and leads me down.

"Where are the others?" I try to ask, but my throat feels like it's on fire. It's raw, and hardly any words come out.

"We need to hurry!" The heartbreak in her eyes is my undoing. Something is wrong. Very wrong—somehow worse than the hospital being on fire.

"What floor?"

"Fifth."

I take us there, and we stumble out of the void to see Elise slamming her weight against the door. Nails clawing into the metal, her fingertips stained with red.

"No!" she screams. "No!"

"Elise!"

She doesn't stop trying to break her way in. "I can't hear her anymore!"

"Who?" My heart is about to stop, my vision swimming. "Who's in there?"

Elise's body sags against the door, her cries turning into mewls. "It's too late," she croaks.

Panic weaves its way through my entire being, and I leave Elise on the other side as I teleport into the room, worry thrumming through me.

There's a ringing in my ears when I appear on the other side of the door, and the first thing I see is Gemma unconscious on the table. A distant part of me is aware enough to unlock the door for Elise, but I stumble forward, holding my breath.

Is she dead? Is that who Elise can't hear anymore?

I stretch a shaking hand closer to Gemma. Please. *No.* But when I clasp her wrist, a steady pulse beats through my fingertips, and I almost pass out with relief... until Elise's sobs pierce through my fog.

There's someone else in the room.

I turn, and my knees buckle.

Elise pulls Nora's lifeless body into her lap as they both sit in a pool of blood. Elise sobs over her, her tears landing on Nora's still face.

No. No, no, no. No.

This can't be right. This can't be how it ends.

"Who? *How?*" My voice cracks as my chest splits wide open. My ribcage is ripped apart, and my heart is torn from my chest, smashed to pieces, damaged for good, completely irreparable.

I crawl over to them, closing Nora's eyelids. The image of her vacant eyes sears into my brain as a shudder violently seizes my core.

"Caleb," Elise spits. "I'm going to kill him. I'm going to rip him limb from limb."

"Caleb?" I ask, the realization of what he's done not quite registering through the pain.

My hand hovers over Nora's chest as her face already begins to pale. I want to stop the bleeding, but I don't know where it starts. There's so much blood, *too* much blood. I can't save her. But I have to try. I have to... *Amber.*

Amber can fix this. She can bring her back.

Simone is behind me, grabbing my shoulder. "We need to go." She's crying, too, but she shouldn't be. She doesn't even know her.

I shrug out of her grasp.

"Theo, please." Simone spins frantically, like she doesn't know where to start. "I can hear them coming. We need to go."

"Did you know about this?" Elise snarls at Simone. "Did you know he was going to do this?"

"No, I swear. He's been shielding himself from me. I didn't know—"

"Enough." I don't even recognize my own voice, but we need to get Nora back to Amber. She can fix this. Who cares about the Authorities? Who cares about Caleb? We need to act *now*.

Elise's eyes fill with tears again as I scoop Nora into my arms, and she almost slips from my grasp. "I can't." Elise shakes her head. "I can't do this."

"Elise, please. We can't leave her here." A numbness spreads through my limbs, and it's like I'm watching from outside my body. I'm trapped inside, raging, screaming, and crying, but outwardly, I'm calm.

"Amber can fix this."

Elise stills, but Simone sharply inhales. "Theo..."

"She can," I spit out. "We don't have time to argue about this. We need to get her back to the base."

I block out Nora's blood coating my arms as I successfully pick her up, her head lolling against my shoulder.

Elise and Simone grab Gemma from the table. They don't say anything as I bring us all downstairs. Jason comes running back into the building as soon as we exit the void.

"There you are!" His relief is evident, but his steps slow when he fully takes us in. He doesn't bother saying anything more as he takes Gemma into his arms.

He turns to run back outside, and we follow him soundlessly to the truck. The two climb into the back first and help Jason with Gemma. As I stand there and wait, my mind further detaches from the scene. I can't even look down and pretend she's sleeping. There's too much blood for that.

Distant screams echo around me, but the ringing in my ears is too loud to make any sense of it. It might be the other truck loading up to return to the base, but it could also be more of the Authorities rushing in to finish the job.

At this point, it doesn't really matter which one it is.

Jason's movements are jerky as he tries to be quick but respectful, sliding Nora out of my arms and getting her onto the truck's floor. He grabs a blanket from the bench and covers her. When he turns, he locks eyes with me, his lips thinning to a straight line.

"I'm sorry," he says, but I barely register it.

I climb in last, shutting the truck door behind me as Jason takes us away from this place. The three of us don't say anything as the truck jostles us around.

Slowly, ever so slowly, I sink back into my body. The autopilot shuts off, and I face the harsh reality of losing everything.

Chapter Thirty-Three

GEMMA

WHERE AM I?

My limbs are filled with lead, and my mouth is so dry that my tongue sticks to the roof of my mouth. I lick my chapped lips and swallow a few times, struggling to sit up.

I lean up on my elbows, peeking around the empty room. I'm in a hospital or something, but it's too quiet... Hospitals are busy, hospitals are—Olivia! I jolt, sitting upright. The truck with the cracked windshield came around the bend, and I... Oh god. Where is she? Where's Olivia?

Is she here? Was I hit, too?

I swing my legs off the edge of the bed, my strength slowly seeping back in. With the movement, something bounces against my throat. I clasp the necklace and roll the little stones back and forth against my skin.

What...?

I rip it off my neck as my throat continues to close, the unknown stealing any ability to breathe.

The door opens, and it's *him*—the boy from my dreams. His eyes widen, and he turns away, shouting to someone that I'm awake.

He rushes closer, but I hop off the bed on shaky legs, avoiding him, and back against the wall. There's no way this is real. I screw my eyes shut. He doesn't exist. *He doesn't.* But when I open them again, he's still standing there, his eyebrows hiked in confusion.

Olivia. Numbness spreads from my hands to my elbows, and my lips tingle as my lungs stop working; all oxygen leaves my body, and I can't catch a single breath.

Was he the one driving the red truck?

"What'd you do to her?" My fingers shake, and I hide them behind my back so he doesn't see them glow. "Where is she?"

Fear swirls in his gray eyes—so familiar, but not. He's a boy I dreamed about; he can't be real. This isn't happening.

"Who?" he asks tentatively.

"My sister. Where is she?"

His mouth opens and closes, and he takes a step closer.

"Stop!" I scream. "Just tell me where she is!"

He grimaces. "Gemma..."

My name comes out stilted, like he's trying to control his own panic. Sadness pours out of him, but it doesn't make any sense. And how does he know my name? This isn't right. Olivia. She's hurt, and I need to get to her.

"No! You're not real. You did something to me. To *her*. You don't get to act like you know me."

My heartbeat rages inside my chest, and anxiety eats me alive. He's so scared for me. *Of* me. The lights in the room flicker on and off, and he peers up at them, then glances down at the little marbles rolling around the floor from my broken necklace.

"Gem," he warns. "Breathe."

No. I squeeze my eyes shut. This is all *wrong*, and I shouldn't even be here—wherever *here* is. *Where is Olivia? The truck drove by, and I found her on the side of the road...*

He tries to get closer to me, and I hold out a glowing hand, stopping him in his tracks. Although his jaw tenses, he's not startled by it; he seems more scared of the moment, not that I'm different.

I shake my head. "Stop. Just stop!"

He holds up both hands. "Okay, but I need you to calm down."

"Don't tell me what to do. Where is she?" I cry.

The door opens again, and it's Amber. I suck in a breath; *what happened to her?* Her blue eyes are pale, and all her veins are tinged gray. What did they do to her? My hands flare, turning into a fully formed purple flame, my powers picking the absolute worst time to grow.

"Amber!" I screech. She looks at the boy and then back at me, her creepy, pale eyes wide open. "Get away from him!"

"Theo?" She now stares at me like I've grown three heads.

My hand stops burning, and I reach forward, grabbing her arm and pulling her back into the corner with me. Whatever he did, he got to her too. He killed Olivia, and hurt Amber, and...

Amber twists out of my arms. "What is wrong with you?"

The boy she called Theo exhales. "I think Nora..."

"Oh, no." Amber slaps a hand against her forehead.

"Yeah."

What is happening? My hands curl into fists, and the lights above us go out, casting us all in shadows.

"Where's Olivia?" I ask Amber, ignoring the dream boy's gaze.

I don't know how he fits into all this, but I will kill him if he was the one behind the wheel. And why does Amber look like that? I slide down against the wall, my legs losing all strength. For the first time, I take in the jeans and hoodie I'm wearing. What happened to my dress? Who changed my clothes?

Amber's forehead wrinkles. She spins, facing *him*. "Go get Dennis. *Now.*"

Dennis? Dennis is here?

Where even *is* here? And why won't anyone explain what's happening? I cradle my head in my hands while the unknown tears me apart. Dread crawls along my skin as my lungs fight to inhale.

"Please," I beg. "Where's Olivia?"

"Olivia..." Amber sits on her heels across from me. "Olivia died over a year ago... Fourteen months, to be exact."

No. *No, that's not possible.*

My teeth chatter as my body begins to quiver. "You're wrong. We were at homecoming last night."

Amber shakes her head, and I have to divert my gaze from her milky white eyes.

"What day do you think it is?"

I close my eyes, thinking back. We were walking home from the homecoming bonfire, and the truck... A tear slides down my cheek. "September 25. Or maybe the 26, depending on how long I was out." I blink through the tears, glancing around my surroundings. "Where are we?"

Amber sighs. "Nora did a number on you."

"Nora?"

Dennis rushes into the room, and my heart leaps, but it brings more questions. Judy is right behind him, and so is... what did Amber call him? Theo?

"I don't want him here." The words leave my lips before I can think them through, and I turn away from the hurt expression on his face. "Please." I lock eyes with Judy, who glances at Dennis. Dennis doesn't say anything but squints at me like he's questioning my request.

Judy turns to Theo, giving him one of her signature sad smiles when she's feeling awkward about something. "We'll figure this out," she tells him.

He nods, shifting to exit the room, though it's like his body is fighting him every step of the way. He stops once to glance back at me. His gaze locks on mine, and my stomach flips. It's like I know him, but I don't. It's all too confusing.

And Olivia is gone, and Amber is... I don't know what.

And where are we?

And oh my god, my head hurts so bad. A radio on the counter starts flipping through stations, getting louder and louder as my heart pounds. I just need answers, and the boy from my dreams showing up in real life is not helping whatsoever.

I close my eyes, blocking him out. When I open them, he's gone.

❦

HOURS LATER, MY HEAD spins so much I can hardly see straight.

What Amber told me is apparently all true. Dennis, Judy, and Amber have walked me through the past year of my life and even showed me current news stations to prove they weren't lying.

I don't know why they would be, but I can't wrap my head around the fact that I've missed it all. Losing Olivia feels like it happened yesterday—it *was* yesterday—but at the same time, it wasn't. And I don't know how to rationalize that.

I've met members of... Command, I think it was? All of them clearly know me, but I have no memory of ever speaking to them before—not even a hint of familiarity. They say I'm the strongest person in their ranks, and I get lightheaded at the thought.

And who the hell is Draven? I pace the room they have me in, a medical lab outside of their infirmary, and try to keep my breathing even because they've had to replace the lightbulbs multiple times now. But at least I haven't burned down the place, which, according to Amber, I've done before—or, at least, the woods.

Amber moans, leaning back in her chair as if this entire ordeal is exhausting. "You're in love with Theo," she reminds me again.

I shove my fingers through my hair, applying pressure to my scalp. "Just stop!" I yell at her, but she doesn't flinch like I expect her to. New Amber is not like the old Amber. She's so much more confident and seems less like the annoying little sister I remember.

She launches out of her chair. "I'm not going to stop until you remember him." Her eyes narrow, and if she could set *me* on fire with her looks, she would. "I did not pull him back into the land of the living for you to forget him!" She quite literally stomps her foot and storms away.

Okay, so maybe she still has that annoying little sister thing going for her. But... "What does she mean, *pull him back into the land of the living?*"

I glance at Judy and Dennis, who both outwardly gape at me from their respective chairs. All three of them have been by my side as I try to swallow the news, but none of it seems to be sticking.

Judy collects herself first. "We... lost Theo, momentarily... and you..." She glances at Dennis for assistance.

He channels his hands together like he's pouring something invisible out of them. "You... gave him enough energy that he was sort of in this in-between—"

"The veil," Judy interrupts, nodding along and pointing at Dennis's hand motions.

"The veil, yes." He bobs his head at Judy as they riff off each other to jumble some sort of explanation together. Their awkwardness over the entire situation adds weight to my inability to recover my lost memories. None of this makes any sense. "Amber was able to pierce the veil and kind of... pull him back."

I stare at them both, and Judy gives that infuriating smile, clutching her neck. "A lot has happened. But you should be able to get your memories back. You just have to remember."

I scoff, throwing my arms in the air as I stop pacing. "How do I do that? I don't even know what's gone!"

"Nora would have left a clue behind. So, we have to figure out what it is and trigger it."

"Great. Someone I don't know left something I don't remember behind. Why can't we just ask her?"

When neither responds, I cross my arms over my chest. "Well?"

"She didn't make it." Judy's eyes fill with tears, and my heart cracks a little for the girl I can't remember.

I can't explain this feeling inside me. It's not something I've ever experienced before, but my body mourns the loss of someone I can't even picture. How can my heart grieve when my brain can't? I feel like I'm suffocating, and I don't even know why.

"Were we close?" I curl my shoulders in, bracing for the worst.

"You were," Dennis whispers. "But she and Theo were a lot closer... He's really struggling right now."

"And that's my problem?" I ask, but it comes out harsher than I intended. I blink back tears, shoving my tongue against the roof of my mouth to keep them in. I don't know if they're for the girl they call Nora, or because I can't remember who Theo is, or because I'm unable to remember *anything*.

I point at my head. "You're all telling me I'm in love with this boy who has only existed up here."

"Just... take it easy on him, okay? You don't have to do anything you don't want to. But if you cross paths, know he's grieving pretty hard right now. For both of you."

I clench my hands, nails biting into my palms, and turn my back on them as I swipe more tears away. "I think I need to be alone right now... I need some space to think."

"Of course," Judy says, and chairs scrape as they stand, Dennis grunting from the effort.

He's changed, somehow. This past year has transformed him as much as it's altered Amber. And it's not just physical. Although his low-fade haircut has grown out, he's shaved his beard, and there's a new scar near his temple, there's something different about his demeanor. Dark energy that I can't place surrounds him. But then I catch the twinkle in his eye on his way out, the one that was there before everything went wrong, and I take a shuddering breath.

I pace the room when they leave, but it does nothing to piece together the puzzle. Every thirty seconds, I remember Olivia is gone, and I have to fight against the current to realize that she's *been* gone for a long time now. They even showed me her urn.

I miss her so much, but at the same time, it's hard to swallow the fact that she's not about to walk through the door, and the constant whiplash of the two realities tearing at my mind makes me want to scream.

I need air. I need to get out of this place and be alone, and screw Command and them telling me *I'm the strongest in their ranks*. They're all toying with me.

I'm weak and pathetic, and there's no way I am who they say I am. I don't *help* people. I hurt them. I scared Amber at the dress store, and those girls were injured because of *my* broken lights, and Olivia is dead—

I whip open the door, and a boy who's way taller than me, with coiled corkscrew hair and chestnut brown eyes, startles backward away from the entrance. He's close enough for me to spot the few freckles dotting his brown skin just around his cheeks, and my heart tugs with an instinctive need to hug him and console him, but as he stares at me, the feeling leaves.

I don't know him either.

"Gemma?" he asks.

I let go of the door, my palm slapping against my thigh. "Look, I'm sorry. I'm sure we were friends, and it sucks I can't remember that, but I really need my space, okay?" I try to brush past him, but my steps falter when, out of the corner of my eye, I spot him sagging against the wall, covering his face with his hands.

His shoulders hitch, and that tug is back. He's not Theo, but Dennis's words still help me empathize. People around here are grieving, and it's not their fault I'm in this situation.

"Did you know her?" I lean against the wall next to him.

"Her name was Nora." His voice is muffled behind his hands.

"I'm sorry," I say again. "I lost my sister..." I start to say, but then the words trail off. This is different, isn't it? Their wounds are fresh, and while mine seems to be, it's an old scab that only feels like it was recently ripped off.

This kid is already struggling enough. I raise a hand to pat him on the back, but it halts in mid-air, the movement lacking somehow. I can feel his pain, his sorrows mixing with my own. And somewhere, deep down, I know him. But I don't—not really.

I let my hand fall and back away without saying goodbye.

Chapter Thirty-Four

Trapped inside a skeleton that refuses to heal completely. A ghost of somebody—*something*.

The alphabet travels through an empty brain, connecting itself from one vessel to the next, establishing connections that were once there. But they don't arrange themselves into proper thoughts. Not yet. Words continue to form over time, but some remain hidden—out of reach.

Who.

What.

Distant ideas are too confusing to understand, and the pain is too much to bear.

When will the madness end?

Footsteps echo down the hall. Wait. Is that correct? Yes. More words return. The air is chilled, and a door slams.

A room locked tight.

Powers, powers, *powers*.

What is that word? Familiar but strange. Nothing connects to it. Nothing happens. The thought was fleeting.

Yet getting stronger all the same.
Time comes and time goes.
Waiting, waiting, waiting.
Blood pumps quicker.
Bones no longer ache.
Muscles respond.
Thoughts are produced as the brain fully functions.
The air smells like disinfectant, and memories return.
Questions are answered.
Why.
When.
How.
A face comes into view, eyes gleaming. A sinister smile. A warning.

Chapter Thirty-Five

Theo

Jason finds me on the rooftop and wordlessly hands me a beer.

A streak of lightning lights up the sky, the thunder rumbling shortly after. There's no rain, but this is no natural storm. It's been two days of this as Zay tries to process everything.

Jason sits in the lawn chair next to me, staring across the desert's expanse.

"I can't go down there," I say, breaking the silence. "I can't go to her wake and say goodbye. I won't do it."

He takes a long swig of his beer, wiping his mouth with the back of his hand. "That's your right," he says. "But I think you're going to regret it someday."

I pick at the label on mine, peeling the paper off with my thumb. My knuckles are all split open, bruised and cracked, and at times, still bleeding if I make a fist, popping the scabs. I destroyed the training room, even shattering their long mirror, but they let me have at it. No one bothered stopping me until Jason pulled me away once he realized I was punching concrete and not the mat.

"How's Avalina doing?" I ask, wanting to avoid the topic of Nora's wake. I haven't been to see her yet, but she's been in the infirmary—*awake*—since we got back.

I glance at him, holding my breath, waiting for him to respond as he uncomfortably shifts in his chair, clearing his throat. Here's the moment where I can tell him I hate him. I can scream at him; I can even hit him if I want. He'd take it all.

If we'd never been in that dumb hospital, none of this would have happened.

"We don't have to talk about—"

"It's fine," I huff, diverting my gaze to the open stretch of land. "If it was at least worth it..."

"It was," Jason adds quickly. "Ava's doing great, actually. She's a little scared about what happened, naturally, but she's adapting. I know that doesn't help anything, and it seems like a minuscule win in the light of things... but you did it, kid. You were able to wake her up. Thank you. I can't"—he shakes his head as if in disbelief—"what you did... Thank you."

I grind my teeth, clutching the beer bottle so my hands don't shake. "Good, I'm glad she's doing well."

The lightning flashes again, a crack of thunder sizzling above.

"Anything else?" I finally ask after the silence swells around us once more.

"Do you want the bad news or the bad news?"

I bark out a humorless laugh and gulp my drink. At least Jason hasn't tiptoed around me. If I get one more pitiful look, I'll lose it—again.

"Hit me."

"We've put as many pieces together as we can. Elise's power expanded... she can read minds now. She told us she got inside Caleb's head, and she knew he injected himself with Gemma's blood. We have no idea whether that means he has her power or not. But Elise said Caleb seemed especially unhinged at the end since it didn't seem to work.

"It appears he's been working with Riley for quite some time. We don't know when or how those two teamed up, but we're guessing she double-crossed him. She knew we would all be there that day and probably knew about his plan to get Gemma's power. What he wasn't expecting was for her to call in backup.

"That's why he fled. His plan went to shit. Gemma wouldn't wake up, his stolen powers wouldn't work, and Nora was..."

"A loose end." My throat seizes, and I take another swig.

Jason flips his hand over, palm facing up, as he leans closer to me. "I don't know if I'd necessarily put it like that... but if he wanted to cover his tracks..."

"Like we wouldn't put two and two together when Gemma woke up not remembering anyone." I scoff. "Elise already knew he was in the room with them. He had no reason to kill Nora."

"I don't think it was about that. I think he was worried that Nora could somehow undo what she did. He doesn't know what we know since she practiced in Margot's lab."

I finish my beer and smash the bottle against the wall. Jason doesn't say anything as he hands me another from the six-pack he brought with him.

"Was that the bad news or the bad news?"

He smirks, but it's painful and not at all reassuring. "They took Griffin with them."

"The Authorities?"

He nods. "We lost two others—neither from here—both dead. Gwen went back for their bodies. Griffin was the only one they took alive."

"Three." When Jason squints at me, I add, "Louis. Riley killed him in front of me."

Jason shakes his head, running a hand over his face. It doesn't look like he's slept or shaved since we've been back.

"Gwen didn't find his body... we assumed he left with the others."

"Nope." I pull the lighter out of my pocket, flicking it until the flame burns my thumb. "He was all a part of their plan, but Riley killed him to let me go."

"The Authorities must have taken his body. You're sure he was dead?"

I close my eyes, picturing Louis's still form, his wide-open eyes. Not much different than Nora's before I closed her lids. She stared out into a void no one else could see.

"I'm sure."

"Well, that's probably not good news."

"Neither is Griffin being alive."

Jason focuses on his beer, regret written all over his face. It mirrors my own. So much would have been different if we hadn't tried to wake Ava, and as much as I want to put all the blame on Jason, I can't because it's not all his fault. It's mine, too.

I clear my throat. "Poor bastard."

"We're going to try to get him back. It's not over yet."

"Yeah, sure."

"I'm off the force." He lifts the beer to his lips, smiling quickly before he finishes it. "I had a damn good run, but my cover is blown. Also, thanks to Caleb."

"So, there goes our intel, too?"

Jason shrugs. "I have some friends. It might take a while to contact them again, but I wasn't the only one working both sides."

My thoughts drift to John and what he would say about all this.

"Anything else for me?" I huff, leaning back. "Might as well get it all out now."

Jason pauses for a long time before setting down his empty beer bottle, circling back to the previous conversation. "It isn't fair that I get my person back when you lose yours. I'm sorry, Theo. I really am."

I shake my head, unwilling to give up yet. "I'm going to get her back," I say, echoing his own words. "It's not over yet."

Jason nods, bracing himself to stand up. "Think about coming downstairs, okay? Your friends need you right now, and I think you need this, too."

He leaves the remaining three beers and heads to the wake. I take my time finishing them all, and when my head is woozy enough to contemplate heading there myself, the roof door opens.

"Oh, sorry," Gemma says, and my heart stops inside my chest.

I haven't spoken to her since she said she didn't want me there the night she woke up, and even though it goes against every fiber of my being, I gave her space. My pulse ricochets in my veins, but my body doesn't move. I sit there, staring at her like an idiot.

She pulls her hoodie sleeves around her hands, twisting the fabric. "I'll, uh—"

"Wait." My voice cracks, but she stops.

It's too dark to notice how violet her eyes are, but they study me, and it takes everything in me not to beg for her to remember. Remember me. Remember *us*. Because this has been the worst few days of my life, and I need her with me.

I've already lost Nora and can't lose her, too.

"Your favorite color is gray."

"What?"

I close my eyes, blocking out her stare. "Your favorite color is gray, and your favorite drink is sweet iced tea, and your favorite food is French fries. You can't pick a favorite band because it depends on your mood. And you never told me what day you'd want to relive because life flipped everything upside down. But you still owe me that answer."

She shifts her weight, and I finally get out of my chair but not to close the distance, because I can't get too close.

It would *kill* me.

"Not right now," I say. "Not like this. You're going to remember. I'll fix this, and when I do, I want your answer then."

"I'm sorry." Her shoulders hitch. "I wish I could remember."

I lick my lips, stuffing the lighter back into my pocket, clenching it so tightly that my bruised knuckles ache. "Me, too."

I race for the door, not bothering to stop to look behind me because if I do, I'll never leave. And I need to make this right since I couldn't fix Nora. I brought her body back, yet Amber couldn't do anything.

She wasn't in the veil; we had to burn her body on the fake lawn.

I failed her.

Nora is dead, and I'm spiraling. And Zay needs me. And Amber is still around. And Judy and Dennis. And they're all at her wake right now.

Jason is right. I should be there, but how do I say goodbye?

I couldn't save Nora. I couldn't fix what was broken, but I at least owe her this.

I stumble into the dining hall, and everyone turns to look at me. The hush in the room is deafening, and I nearly backtrack, but Elise raises a glass, locking eyes with me. She repeats the passage Tilly gave all those months ago.

"For mutants like us, death is an honor. May we go quickly into the light and find what awaits us next. Here's to you, Nora. You'll be missed."

Chapter Thirty-Six

Gemma

THEO LEAVES ME ALONE on the roof, and all I can do is focus on the shattered glass around me.

Thunder rumbles in the distance, and it's so fitting to see all that's broken that I begin to laugh. But the laughter turns into a sob, and then I'm clutching a hand over my mouth, trying to keep it all at bay.

Much like this beer bottle, my life is shattered around me, and I can't pick up all the pieces. Every time I try, I get cut, and the unbearable pain makes it impossible to put them back together.

I'm still trying to process the fact that Olivia is gone. And the more people tell me about what I've forgotten, the more I want to run away and hide. By now, everyone has told me *something*, and it's all too much to take in.

The necklace I ripped off was from Margot; it allowed me to channel my power so I never had to hurt anyone again. And I broke that, too. Not to mention, I murdered four Authority members the day Judy and Dennis were kidnapped. Oh, that's right—Judy and

Dennis were abducted. Theo died in my arms, but Amber brought him back because, apparently, that's something she can do now.

And that's not even touching the outside world. That's just all that's happened within my family. The government is using radio waves to brainwash civilians into hating each other, and they have blood tests to sniff out mutants, so cities are in lockdown as they try to capture us all because the test is no longer accurate, thanks to Griffin. Who, I guess, is my friend but has been taken and is undergoing who knows what by our enemies.

And I have enemies!

What feels like last week, I was hiding in the gym locker room, scared of the other high schoolers figuring out my secret, but now I'm the most powerful of everyone here because of Draven, the guy my parents murdered to inject me with his powers.

It's all too much.

I can't stay here, and I can't help these people. I don't know what they want from me, but it's too much to ask. My hands light up—thankfully, not a flame this time—but the glow has been happening more and more these past couple of days. I focus on breathing to calm down.

I'm just a kid. I'm not who they think I am. I can't be.

That Gemma, who lived a full life in the past year and more, is gone and locked away somewhere deep in the recesses of my brain. They say I can somehow remember; I just have to figure out how. Discover whatever clue Nora left behind. But do I want to? Do I want to return to a life that's so obviously messed up?

What if I leave? If I do, they can't stop me. Tilly already said what happens next is my choice. I can stay and work on getting my memories back, retrain if I need to, and continue fighting with them. Or I can leave.

Evidently, I've already run away from Judy, Dennis, and Amber once. I don't remember it, but surely, I can do it again. I'm sorry they got sucked up in all this, but they deserve more.

Better than me.

Theo... I sigh.

I lean against the roof's edge, my head spinning with his revelation. He said he would fix this, and I believe him. I don't know why, but I do. It's like I'm spellbound to him, like I was in my dreams.

How we found each other is a bit gray, considering no one who knows that story has told me about it.

Amber filled in some gaps, like how I lived with Theo and the others for a while, which makes me feel even more guilty that I'm not downstairs mourning the girl who lost her life in front of me.

But how do you properly mourn someone you don't remember?

And all that emotion... I don't think I can handle channeling everyone's grief right now.

I blink back tears, facing the storm above me.

What do I do?

Olivia, please. If you're there, somehow give me a sign and point me in the right direction.

How do I face an unknown future with nothing but unanswered questions?

Where do I even begin?

The roof door opens, and I'm afraid to turn around. Because if I do and it's Theo, I might stay. For him—to see where this road leads. I've broken his heart more times than I can count in the past few days. Every time, his feelings pour out of him like a leaking faucet.

He's not lying about us. Even if I don't remember, my body does. Like a magnet, I'm drawn to him, and I don't know if I have the strength to stay away.

But when I turn, I'm taken off guard.

A boy my age with white hair cropped short on the sides, the top longer and smoothed back, stands in an all-black outfit, his hands in his blazer pockets. His pale, hollow cheeks cast shadows in the already moody light, and I squint during a flash of lightning to see if I recognize him, but it's a fool's errand. He stalks closer, the smell of tobacco and vanilla mixing around me, and the hair on the back of my neck stands up on instinct. He's the hunter, and I'm the prey, and I have nowhere to run. I don't know what I did to this guy, but everything in me is telling me to *run*.

He stands inches from me, his ice-blue eyes narrowing as he stares down at me, but then he smirks like it's all a game.

"There you are, little mouse."

Chapter Thirty-Seven

CALEB

THIS WASN'T HOW ANY of this was supposed to go.

It's been a week since Riley screwed me over, and we've been on the run ever since. Esha and Asher caught up to me, meeting at our rendezvous spot on the off chance that something *did* go wrong. But Louis was never supposed to die.

I shake my head, disgusted with the loss.

Riley, that backstabbing bitch.

Esha kicks me. She's lying on the ground, her jacket pulled over her. "Get another log. I'm freezing."

I blink, focusing back on the fire before us.

"Asher, grab some wood."

Asher grunts but gets up anyway, stalking off into the tree line. Seconds later, the cracking of a tree branch, followed by a large thud, trails our way. Asher drags nearly an entire tree over to us, and he yanks off another branch, tossing it in the flames.

No, we should *not* be in the middle of nowhere, essentially homeless, as we figure out our next steps. Word would have spread by now, so it's not like another base would take us in since they must know I killed that girl—one of our own.

I hold my hands in front of me, silhouetted by the flames, but they're not glowing.

I didn't set out to kill a mutant; that's not what we're about. We're supposed to lead our people, not have them fear us. I thought Riley understood that. But I did what I had to do. As Jason so fondly says, I did it *to fight another day*.

I roll my eyes. What an idiot.

It's about time we got away from them all.

There have to be more mutants out there who want to follow our lead. We can't be the only three in existence who are sick of Command's bullshit.

Now is the time to fight. It's us against them, and if they're not on our side, then they're in the way, slowing us down. The time for hiding is over.

We'll take our stand and figure it out along the way.

It's just going to take a little time.

I stare harder at my hands, focusing all my mental energy on them. Seconds pass, but nothing happens. I almost give up, exhaling a harsh breath, until the tingling begins. A tremor starts in my fingers, shooting pins and needles up my arms. And then they crackle blue.

I smile—a large, genuine smile. It feels like a weight has been lifted, and I'm seconds away from running around, hooting and hollering.

"A little time and a little more manpower, but don't you worry," I say to Esha as she greedily eyes my glowing hands. "We're going to be just fine."

Acknowledgements

I made pizza rolls before sitting down to write this, and it's fitting because pizza rolls carried me through the entire first draft of this book. Writing around a full-time job and general life stuff often leads to last-minute meals, so here we are.

Anyway, it's a bit surreal to be writing the acknowledgments for my second novel, and I have so many people to thank for helping me get here.

To my husband—my rock—Chris, thank you for being a constant in this turbulent world. Publishing (and life) have highs and lows, but I know you're always steady. It keeps me stable. Thank you for being you. I couldn't do any of this without you backing me.

To Sarah, my severely underpaid personal assistant, aka my best friend for nearly two decades now. Your support is unwavering. Thank you for coming to all my events, now including festivals out of state, and learning all about the publishing world throughout the process. Maggie, my other dear friend of nearly two decades now, thank you for also coming along for the ride. Your support means everything. I love you both so much, and I can't wait to travel to new places with you.

To Kate and Michelle: Between writing retreats, trading manuscripts, sharing a few drinks, and singing karaoke songs together, I'm grateful for meeting both of you. You make me a better writer and a better person. I'm indebted and in awe of you both daily. Thank you for being in my corner and willing to travel out of state to support me. I love you!

I owe so much to Marissa. You were the first person to read *Strangers in Our Hearts* and then sat with me for hours, going through plot point by plot point to ensure it was the best it could be. I appreciate your input so much. I love brainstorming book ideas and am always excited to learn new things with you. I cherish our friendship.

To Erin, your support means everything. Whether we're taking a night off of writing responsibilities to clean our houses together or bouncing ideas back and forth and swapping manuscripts. You're amazing, and I'm so lucky to call you a friend.

To Mary and Sam, thank you for reading an early version of *Strangers in Our Hearts*. I appreciate your input so much. To Kristin, thank you for always being an early reader for me as well. Your support has carried me through for years now. To ARC readers and everyone on my street team, thank you!! You keep me going when I second-guess myself.

Jennia, my editor, my friend, my same-taste-in-music twin, thank you. Strangers as a whole would not be where it is today without your guidance. Thank you for caring as much as I do about the chaos crew. Your wisdom has helped make this entire series so much better, and I can't wait to work on book three with you.

To Emily from Emily's World of Designs, thank you for, once again, nailing it out of the park with my cover. I get a bit emotional seeing the two side-by-side. I can't wait to work on the third cover with you!

Ashley S., Aileen, and Ashley R., your friendship and support are invaluable. Thank you for all the walks, the texts, and the gushing of books. Sometimes, it's extremely nice to leave the book world entirely, get out of my head, and be reminded that there are other things going on. It's refreshing.

To the Women's Writing Group, I adore our weekly calls. Brainstorming, writing exercises, and more help me grow as a writer, and I appreciate all of your input!

To the family who always shows up, thank you. It means so much. And to those who are no longer with us, I'm thinking of you always.

Lastly, thank you, dear reader. Thank you for taking the time to read my books and let me share a little bit of magic with you. If it weren't for you, none of this would be possible.

I'm sorry if I missed anyone. If I did, please know that I'm entirely overwhelmed by emotions and am dangerously close to gushing. It wasn't on purpose. If you've ever supported me, please know I'll always be grateful.

Go Bills.

Strangers in Our Hearts Playlist

Music plays such a huge role in my life, especially in my writing. So, of course, I have an entire playlist for Strangers # 2 that got me through the months of daydreaming, writing, and editing the final version of the book. Here's the list:

The Hunted – Slipcast
Soldier – Fleurie, Tommee Profitt
Sleepy Baby Sleep – BROODS
Sirens – Fleurie
Deep End – Ruelle
Storm Song – PHILDEL
OUTRUN MYSELF (with Travis Barker) – Jack Kays, Travis Barker
Numb – The Used
Long Way Down – Robert DeLong
Anything's Possible – Foreign Air

I Know You Know Me (With Matt Berninger) – Caroline Spence, Matt Berninger

Afraid – The Neighbourhood

I See You – MISSIO

Fever – Sunsleep

Train – Brick + Mortar

If I'm James Dean, You're Audrey Hepburn – Sleeping With Sirens

Image Of The Invisible – Thrice

Falling – The Civil Wars

Too Far Gone – Sir Sly

Ready to Start – Arcade Fire

The Suburbs – Arcade Fire

Uprising – Muse

Wires – The Neighbourhood

Everybode Wants To Rule The World – Lorde

Neon Rust – Frank Carter & The Rattlesnakes

How Not To Drown – CHVRCHES, Robert Smith

My Tears Are Becoming A Sea – M83

Trouble – Cage the Elephant

Dead Hearts – Stars

Run Boy Run – Woodkid

Anthem for the Broken – MISSIO

Pa Pa Power – Dead Man's Bones

Bottom Of The Deep Blue Sea – MISSIO

Who Are You, Really? – Mikky Ekko

Bury Me Face Down – grandson

Make a Shadow – MEG MYERS

Used to the Darkness – Des Rocs

We Must Be Killers – Mikky Ekko

Twisted – MISSIO
Heavy In Your Arms – Florence + The Machine
Kings – Tribe Society
Thousand Eyes – Of Monsters and Men
Bang – Sir Sly
Numb – MEG MYERS
Come Back for Me – Jaymes Young
Dark in My Imagination – of Verona
Holding Out for a Hero – Nothing But Thieves
Far From Home (The Raven) – Sam Tinnesz
You First – Paramore
Tragic – Tommee Profitt, Fleurie
Do You Realize – Ursine Vulpine
Astronomical – SVRCINA
Slip Away – UNSECRET, Ruelle
Drift – Emily Osment
Let Me Hurt (Acoustic) – Emily Rowed
Scars – Boy Epic
Madness – Ruelle
This is Our Life – Des Rocs
Mercy – Hurts
Flesh and Bone – Black Math
Bitter and Sick – One Two
The Difference Between Medicine and Poison Is In The Dose –
Circa Survive
Quietly – Manchester Orchestra
Losing You – Aquilo
Wonderful – Tones and I
Teacher Has A Gun – Badflower

Photo by Ashley Staley Photography

Bri Eberhart is a contemporary fantasy writer, and her stories are also published in various online magazines. She has a BA in cultural studies with a concentration in creative writing and literature from SUNY Empire State. She's also an editorial assistant for an online marketing website and currently resides near Buffalo, NY, with her husband and two cats.

You can find her on Instagram and Twitter at bri_eberhart or at brieberhart.com.

Other Works